ANDALON ATTACKS

DREAMERS OF ANDALON - BOOK 3

T. B. PHILLIPS

T. B. Phillips

Andalon Attacks
Dreamers of Andalon, Book Three

Published by Andalon Press
Copyright © 2020 by T.B. Phillips.

Cover design by Lynnette Bonner of Indie Cover Design
Map artwork by Cary Beshel
Book interior design by Stewart Design, https://StewartDesign.studio
www.depositphotos.com, File: # 6366506 – water
www.depositphotos.com, File: # 32041633 – cup
www.depositphotos.com, File: # 119701796 – smoke
www.depositphotos.com, File: # 249834530 – smoky background
www.depositphotos.com, File: # 475234022 – smoke
www.depositphotos.com, File: # 267274700 – wolf
www.depositphotos.com, File: # 267274700 – wolf
stock.adobe.com, File: # 111463948 – pearls

ISBN 978-1-7331805-2-8

This is a work of fiction. Names, characters, places, and incidents are a product of the author's imagination. Locales and public names are sometimes used for atmospheric purposes. Any resemblance to actual people, living or dead, or to businesses, companies, events, institutions, or locales is completely coincidental.

Books by T. B. Phillips

ANDALON SAGA

Andalon Origins
Andalon Project (April 2022)
Andalon Paradox (April 2023)
Andalon Prophecies (expected Winter 2023)

Dreamers of Andalon
Andalon Awakens (June 2019)
Andalon Arises (July 2020)
Andalon Attacks (December 2020)

Children of Andalon
Andalon Legacy (September 2022)

CHILLING TALES

Ferryman (October 2022)

CORRUPTED REALMS

Knight of Shadow (Expected Fall 2023)
Wailing Tempest (April 2021)
Howling Shadow (September 2021)

Ashen Tundra
Fjörk
Ataraxia
Eston Diaph
Logan
Estowen's Landing
Norton
ANDALON
Caldera of Cinder
Steppes of Cinder
Middleton
Forbidden Wastes
Weston
Ashen Waste
Eskerra
Saston
Islands of Deception
N
W
E
S

Southern Continent
Cargia
Metzi
Tlaloc
Nazcla
KEY
- Hacienda
- Puebla Aztecá
- City

N
Winter Oracle
Oslot
Autumn Oracle
Bergin
Spring Oracle
Summer Oracle
ASTIA

Part I

Aftermath

Only the son of Esterling can slay him in time.

- Marcus Esterling, 806th year of order

Prologue

Smoke of war lingered in the air, an offensive aroma that hinted of death and fear. The Battle of Estowen's Landing just barely resolved, Samani Kernigan acted quickly before the enemy launched another attack. With a casual stride and furtive eyes he led Kali toward his ship. His eyes scanned the passing soldiers as the two walked, quickly overwhelmed by the weariness and fatigue on every face. Even in victory, they bore gloom and sadness. As depressing a sight as they seemed, they were certainly not the worst visage he had witnessed after the fighting. He averted his gaze and focused instead on the empty husk blindly following the girl at his side.

She was a wretched shadow with barely a trace of her former self. He tried to turn away from her as well, but regret over his future actions held him tightly. Despite the vow, Beth would never be the same as before death. Her glazed eyes stared unblinkingly forward, devoid of natural life and the product of inexperienced restoration. He had promised Kali that he would help her fix her friend. He had also told her that he required her help with a friend of his own. But Samani Kernigan, also known as Samani Nakala, was a liar.

This spring emotant named Kali was strong. He had recognized her strength the moment he witnessed her power during the battle. She rivaled the legendary emotants from the time of Andalon's namesake, and he felt she may even prove stronger than Eusari. She would help him end Astian rule, and his remorse lay in her lack of choice in the role.

He asked her several questions as they walked, genuinely interested in the process she had used during the restoration. She answered willingly, proud of her gift.

"So you see," Kali said with only a hint of boasting, "her owl Aliki had stored enough lifeforce during their bonding, so even though she was completely gone I was able to restore her. I pulled it inside of me and then placed it in her."

He fought the urge to shake his head and tentatively held his fatherly gaze and proud smile. *That had been her mistake,* he thought. *She conveyed the lifeforce, mixing it through her own, instead of placing it directly into her friend.* In a kind voice he said, "That must have been difficult," he said, "to watch your friend die."

Her head bobbed as she talked, "You bet it was! I've never had friends growing up. She and Johan are the first I've ever allowed to get close."

"What's he like? I can't wait to meet him."

She lit up at the chance to describe the boy, betraying her obvious attraction for him. "He's so sweet and wonderful," she said. "Kind of shy, but not in a bad way. He's also brave. He fought six Falconers alone, even before he knew that I had powers to help."

"Tell me about that fight," Samani said as they approached the pier.

"We brought down an entire bridge on top of their heads."

"Was this in Eston?"

"Yes!" She beamed ear to ear, eager to retell the story. She filled him in on every detail. With exuberance she described the way she tangled the vines into the crevices of the stones, wriggling them deep enough that the giant blocks toppled onto their attackers.

"That's even more impressive," he told her.

"What is?"

"It seems at times you worked the winter emotancy into your bond with the plants."

"I did?" She appeared confused.

"You are a spring emotant and Johan favors winter. Through your connection you fed the stalks the water they needed. You also gave them the air they needed to grow. You took that from the Falconers, didn't you?"

She nodded. After a moment she asked a question, "Is it common to work three types of magic?"

"Emotancy," he corrected, "it's science, not magic. Your abilities were encoded in the fabric of your ancestor's cells more than one thousand years ago. Furthermore, you didn't work three. You worked one and are sensitive to the others. If you were to consume an Astian Pearl from a different season, then someone like you would find some success. But no," he answered her question, "even multi-sensitivity is very rare. I once attempted to feed Braen Braston a pearl and his body rejected the foreign essence. And he is one of the strongest emotants I know. He'll never have shared sensitivities."

Kali paused, turning to help her friend when Beth stumbled over coiled mooring lines. She caught her arm as the husk nearly fell into the harbor. "That's what I've got to fix," she explained, pulling her onto the path. "She isn't herself anymore." After a thought she added, "I don't think I did it right."

"From what I understand about the process, you executed it perfectly," he encouraged, "and you were right about Akili holding onto her lifeforce. You see," he explained, "during restoration you have two choices. You can control them as shadows or revive them as pets who are entirely unaware of your control except when you choose. To accomplish the latter you must be careful. When you pour your own into the husk, you must leave enough of them to retain their identity. If done right, they won't even know they've died."

"So," she mused, "if they've been dead too long or have only a glimmer of lifeforce, you can put in too much of yourself and this is the result." Suddenly crestfallen, reality struck that she had fully lost her friend. She fell silent for a long moment, then added, "That's not what I wanted."

"No," he said reassuringly, "I suppose it isn't. But this was your first restoration so you understandably couldn't control yourself."

She turned back to her friend, "So she's a shadow now?"

"In a sense, yes. She'll obey you no matter the command. She will even kill for you if that's what you desire. But yes, in this state, she's nothing more than your shade."

"I don't want that."

"There is hope," he promised. "If we stop her heart and attempt another restoration, you could reassemble her thoughts to appear more lifelike. With enough skill you could even teach her to act like her former self."

"Is that what you want me to do with your friend?"

"In a way, yes."

They reached the brow of his ship where Delilah waited expectantly. She smiled down. "Is this the girl?"

"Kali," Samani said, "meet Delilah." To his longtime friend and lover he said, "This young lady is quite remarkable. I believe she'll be able to help us in every way we need."

Delilah clapped her hands. "That's wonderful!"

"Yes," he agreed, "wonderful news indeed."

They crossed over and stepped onto the hardwood decking. Kali asked Samani, "What's her name? Your friend who needs my help."

"She's my sister, actually."

"I'm sorry. Is she…?"

"Yes, quite dead."

"How did she die?"

"She gave her life for something she believed," he answered. "Suffice to say that she has been restored by another."

"Is she a pet or a shadow?"

"A little of both, I fear." He led the woman and girl below decks and opened a door. Inside Gretchen stood guard beside a bound Ashima.

"What is it you want me to do exactly?"

"I want you to find the bond that holds her and sever it cleanly, leave no remnant behind. Then I want you to connect her to me so that I can protect her and us from those who intend harm." He closed the door as they entered.

"I don't know how to do that."

"It's easy," he said as he drew a blade. Kali eyed it suspiciously, suddenly questioning his trustworthiness. "Relax," he said. "Remember that I must stop her heart." Her posture softened and he pointed at Ashima. "Look upon her closely."

Kali did. The woman's eyes were cold and vacant, even more so than Beth's. Her head was completely bald, without even an eyelash on her lids. "Reach out," he suggested.

The young girl did, but recoiled immediately. Abruptly Ashima thrashed about, biting the air and laughing hysterically.

"You see? Her captors still hold her. Can you sense them?"

"Yes," she nodded vigorously. "I felt their bonds. She's connected to every Falconer." After a brief thought she asked, "Is she one of them?"

"Yes," he answered, "and that is why I must do this." He thrust the blade between the third and fourth ribs, puncturing his sister's heart and lung, and killing her instantly. She slumped in her seat. "Now, Kali. You must help her by connecting us."

Suddenly terrified she stammered, "I don't know how!"

"Follow your instincts," he told her.

She stood over Ashima, frantically searching for lifeforce and, finding none, she poured out her own.

"Not yours," he cautioned. "Use mine because it more closely resembles hers."

She reached out to Samani, "I can't feel yours."

"Try harder," he encouraged.

After a while Ashima's eyes shot open, but Beth collapsed on the floor. Kali turned exhausted eyes toward her lifeless friend. "I lost her," she said.

"Yes," he agreed, "I expected that." He plunged the knife under Kali's sternum, staring sadly into her wide eyes full of surprise. With his free hand he carefully shut them as she collapsed on the floor. "But you separated my sister from the collective," he said, "and for that I am grateful." As soon as the girl's lifeforce had completely drained, Ashima slumped where she sat.

Delilah asked, "Do you have enough for all three?"

"No. I can only raise two," he said as he drew a white bead from his pocket. He immediately popped it into his mouth. "I want her," he pointed at his sister. "And I need her," he said about Kali.

"Then that one remains dead," Delilah said, pointing toward Beth. "Gretchen, dispose of the body discreetly."

Fatwana Nakala watched as the girl named Kali disembarked from the ship. She could only imagine what lies her brother had told the girl, cringing at how the child fit into his schemes. The lead sister drew deep breaths to steady her nerves then started forward. Several sailors moved to block her access, with one demanding she request permission to board.

"I did not and will not ask permission, but here I am, already aboard your vessel. Tell Samani Nakala that his sister has arrived." While the sailors exchanged stares of confusion, she shouted for her brother. A short time later he and a dozen armed sailors emerged.

"What's this ruckus," he demanded. When he recognized Fatwana, he smiled ear to ear and rushed over to greet her. "Stand down, crew. She's with me," he said.

"You're not surprised?" Narrowing her eyes she added, "That means you were behind my coming," she accused.

"Yes, my sister. The decision to bring you here was mine, but I hope you were treated well and weren't too inconvenienced."

She suddenly stiffened, filled with decades of emotion, then stepped forward to ram a hard finger into his chest. She pushed him as she spoke. "We thought you dead, Samani!" He backed away as she pursued. "You never even gave a single clue that you lived. And then," she yelled in his face, "you do it through a Ka'ash'mael? You are the most selfish person I know. I should drag you by the ear to the Council and watch as they judge your treason!"

"Fatwana…"

"No. You don't get to talk, Samani Nakala." She glanced at the sailors still wearing confusion on their faces. "Or whatever you call yourself nowadays! You're behind all of this, aren't you? You'd rather watch our world crumble while you play god with these people's lives!"

"Well," he said when he finally got a word in. "At the very least come see Ashima."

Fatwana abruptly stopped yelling.

Samani smiled back with his smug coyness. "Yes, that's right. I had a reason for bringing you here. Oh," he added, "and it's nice to see you too."

Bringing all three siblings together seemed to calm the situation. *He always was a master manipulator,* she thought. But seeing an animated Ashima brought out her tenderness. "Do you think she's still in there?"

"I do," he responded. "Ashima, do you remember the summer we snuck away to the lake?"

"Yes," she responded coolly and devoid of emotion. "Mother nearly whipped us when she finally found us."

"What color was my bathing suit," Fatwana asked.

"Pink."

"But that color is forbidden by the collective. Why would I, a consummate rule follower, violate the wishes of our parents and pursue wanton pleasure? Why would I have broken the law?"

"Because you found the suit in a trunk of mother's old things," Ashima answered dryly. "You told me that if we were caught, the sight of the suit would silence her argument against our childish rebellion."

"Word for word," she remarked. Turning to Samani she said, "That was a conversation only between her and I."

"Are you convinced?"

"Perhaps…" Whatever she was about to say was cut off by a woman rushing into the stateroom.

"Samani!"

He abruptly stood, hand touching the archaic pistol on his belt. *Even you've accepted the abominations, brother.* Fatwana shook her head in mild disgust.

"What is it, Delilah?"

"News from Eusari."

"It's about time! Have they taken Middleton? Is Skander Braston dead?"

"Yes," Delilah said with eyes fixed on the deck and with a tear on her cheek. "But so is Braen."

Samani slumped into his chair, his jovial demeanor suddenly deflated. "Do you mean that Eusari didn't…"

"No. When the time came, she let him slip away."

"That wasn't what we interpreted." He shook his head in disbelief. "But their love! She was supposed to raise him so that he can fulfill the prophecy. Only he can defeat Skander!"

Fatwana interrupted, "Didn't she just tell you that Skander was also dead? It sounds to me like whoever he is, he's already defeated."

"Oh sister," he replied. "There are forces at work much greater than you know."

Chapter One

The Battle of Middleton had proven disastrous for the rebellion, thrusting Andalon deeper into chaos. Pirate's Cove, the once shining star of freedom, had immediately fallen to Stefan Nevra and his henchman Adamas Creech. Their attack was swift and erased all progress made by Braen Braston and the others. The pirate king's private thugs lurked in the shadows and harassed any supporters of the elected council. They targeted anyone known to have been a friend or backer of the Kraken King.

News of Lord Nevra's seizure of The Cove traveled quickly through the Empire and southern continent. The fanciful dream of free elections and independent wealth had died with Braen and his revolution ended before it had begun. His followers were scattered to the corners of the continent, helpless except to watch the Esterling controlled cities fall to Fjorik raiders.

In the north, several months had passed since the first attack on Estowen's Landing, and subsequent battles were a recurring problem for Shon Wembley. His fighting force had also diminished, as well as his small cadre of emotants. He was needed elsewhere, but had so far ignored calls to join the unified resistance behind King Robert.

Meanwhile, Robert Esterling sat upon an impotent throne in Eskera. The deadly trap sprung by the Jaguars had resurrected and taken control of more soldiers than he could afford to lose. They had cut his force by half. His lingering caused his allies to worry, since their plan had been to depart the city a full month before. But the refugees of Weston streamed in daily, providing him with a fresh source of manpower and giving them hope for a final assault on Eston.

Chief among his allies was Eusari Thorinson, the mistress of Braen Braston, currently deep in her mourning and forcing her body to stay active despite a yearning to lie down and just weep. She remained vigilant of and constantly fought against the melancholy that lurked in the shadows. In the past she would have chosen to brood alone in her stateroom aboard *She Wolf,* but she had grown much since befriending the Kraken King. Somehow, along the way, she had discovered friendship.

On this day she sat across from her first mate, Peter Longshanks. They were joined at the table by Sippen Yurik, Amash Horslei, and Gunnery Sergeant Krill. In the center of the table was a single bottle of wine. The label read "754," and this was the last of their stash. In a kinder world the day would have been Braen's birthday.

Sippen raised the first toast and said with a slight stutter, "Tuh... to Bruh... Braen. Our buh... best friend."

"To Braen," they all agreed.

Pete pointed to the glass in Eusari's hand. "Should you be drinking that, dearie? In your condition it could ..."

She shot a look that silenced him immediately. It would have terrified anyone who wasn't as closely bonded as he to her. He had grown to become her most trusted friend and advisor over the past year, a man who could almost replace her late father, Franque Thorinson. He nodded and offered a silent apology.

But it was too late, Sippen picked up on the exchange. "Yuh... you're with child?" He beamed behind his spectacles. "Thuh... that's wuh... wonderful!"

Krill, always the loudest in every crowd, stood from the table and raised a glass in the air. He opened his mouth to celebrate the news and proclaim it loud enough that the entire ship and dockworkers would overhear. His glass shattered in his hand, cutting him off before he could reveal her secret. When he turned around, one of Eusari's many blades had somehow buried itself in the wall behind him.

"There's another for your stupid eyepatch if you say a blasted word," she snarled.

The pirate took the hint and returned to his seat. "Muh eyepatch isn't stupid," he muttered just loud enough that she could hear. Under the table he held up two invisible fingers, both of which had been sheared off in the Battle of the Southern Ocean.

"It will be when you're wearing two, Cedric," she threatened.

Irritated by the use of his given name, he merely nodded and agreed. Then he sat in silence, seemingly forming another weird idea in that strange mind of his. Eusari's father would have called him "touched," had he still lived.

But she would never do him or any of the others harm. They had each become a daily part of her life and Braston's friends clung to her after their leader's death. They shared mutual love for the man the only way they knew, with loyalty just as he had taught them.

"How long will you keep it a secret," Amash asked in a soft voice.

"As long as my body will let me," she answered truthfully. "I'm different than *her*. I don't have to parade around in maternity gowns that accentuate my state." Everyone at the table nodded, they knew the *her* of whom she spoke.

His second question was more pointed. "Will you keep fighting?"

"Do I have a choice?" She looked up from the drink after only two sips, then sighed and pushed the rest toward Krill. He took it with a grin. "I'll keep going as long as he or she will let me," she said, "I need to keep an eye on the children."

The children were, of course, the spring emotants everyone had taken to calling, "Dreamers." She refused to use that term, constantly warning the men they absorbed the violence around them. She wished she could take the children all far away from the war, and their use had been hers and Braen's first disagreement.

A soft knock on the door revealed a visitor and Eusari answered, "Come in," before she even thought about who would be calling. *I really am distracted,* she thought. To her chagrin the caller was Lady Hester Braston, also known as *her*. She was clad in regally arranged maternity attire that was both gawdy and arrogant. Eusari couldn't help but notice Braen's sigil emblazoned on the shawl. "By Cinder's Crack," she muttered under her breath. *She wears his variation and not her husband's.*

"Today would have been his birthday," the former queen declared. "Why has King Robert not declared a day of mourning?"

"Because the crown doesn't mourn outlaws," answered Amash.

She scoffed. "He was the true King of Fjorik."

"He was an elected official of Pirate's Cove," Eusari argued.

"And Eskera despises pirates," explained Amash.

Krill added, "Jealous of 'em, more likely!"

Hester ignored their explanations. "I wish to speak to the king about this at once. Lord Horslei, you have his direct ear, I expect you to gain me an audience."

"Not a lord," Amash replied, "and barely a Horslei."

She ignored that remark as well, but everyone at the table recognized the quote and tipped their glasses in toast to Braen.

Except for Eusari. She fumed at the woman's presence and decided to press. "What's your real quarry? Tell me what you really want from King Robert and I'll get it from him. I'll do it just to be rid of you!"

Hester stared her down. "As if you could. You're nothing more than a pirate yourself. But if you must know, I demand a ship on which to sail to Fjorik. I must serve as regent until Braen's heir is of age." She also added, "Again, tell me how you would be able to assist with *that.*"

"I have my charms," Eusari responded, meaning it as a quip but hitting a nerve in the queen.

Hester narrowed her eyes and squared her feet. "Oh, I'm sorry," she said with a condescending tone. "I forget your ability to slide into the beds of kings and sway them away from worthwhile endeavors."

Everyone at the table pushed back their chairs, waiting for Eusari to react. Krill's eyes twitched to the blade stuck in the wall and the broken glass on the floor.

When she spoke, Eusari's response was quiet and her composure collected. "Braen's endeavor to change our world was as worthwhile as they get. More so when you consider you whored with that beastly brother of his."

Hester's hand struck quicker than anyone anticipated, meeting Eusari's skin across her cheek.

"Do it again," Eusari demanded.

"What?"

"Do it again," she warned. "Lay another finger on me and I'll do far worse than carve my insanity into your back." She raised her head with eyes full of rage. Eusari stood from her chair and drew a long dagger from her boot. "I'll carve that child from your womb and lay it on a stone for the wolves." She slowly stepped toward Hester, forcing the queen to retreat. With the tip of her stiletto blade making a soft dip in the woman's dress, she leaned in close. "And then I'll bond with each as they devour your spawn."

At first Hester appeared terrified, but her regal bearing returned, and she called Eusari's bluff. "If this were anyone's child but his, I would believe you. But you wouldn't harm the only child of Braen Braston."

Eusari smiled a devilish grin and whispered, "I would, if I knew there were another." With her free hand she touched her own belly. "How far along are you, Hester? Two months and a couple of weeks? How would Fjorik like to know that Braen's heir resides within another? And that he wasn't conceived with a married woman at the time?"

Hester's eyes went round, suddenly noticing Eusari's tightly fitting leathers and the way her jerkin compressed two swollen breasts. She also recognized the slight bulge around the midsection.

"That's right," she snarled with satisfaction. "I carry his heir as well."

"Well then," Hester said as she wheeled around to leave. "I guess it's a race. The first to birth wins the prize." She stormed from the room.

Krill broke the awkward silence that followed, "Well then, I guess the secret's out, and I didn't spill the beans." Since no one else was drinking, he picked up the bottle and drank deeply.

Eusari slumped into her seat. "It doesn't matter. I needed maternity leathers soon anyways."

Amash spoke the words she had hoped to avoid. "It really will come down to the order of birth. If both are boys, she won't stop until yours is hunted down and killed. There can never be question of succession when two possible heirs exist."

"When this war is over, I just want to be left alone," she replied. "But I'll defend my child no matter who hunts him."

Amash nodded and signaled the others it was time to leave. She appreciated his gesture and for the brief time to mourn alone.

Chapter Two

Nighttime in Pirate's Cove was a dangerous place for children, as young Charleigh was well aware. She waited until her parents had fallen asleep before opening her bedroom door, counted to ten, and, when no one stirred in the master bedroom, inched down the stairs to the empty store below. It was dark but she dared not light a flame. If they awakened, she would certainly be punished.

I'm not acting silly, she assured herself. But her nerves couldn't calm. *You've been through worse,* her mind suggested, *when you were trapped in the mudslide and nearly died.* But that had been months ago, and she had a good reason to venture into the night. Eusari had given it to her.

She crept to the front door and slowly untied the bell hanging from the handle. Even the slightest noise would awaken her lightly sleeping parents. With a held breath, she unlocked the latch. No bogeyman pushed it open, so she pulled just enough to slip through. The darkness outside was different against the flickering lamplight. She imagined ghosts and bad men lurking in every shadow, but even those did not dissuade her from finding what she had forgotten.

She found the toy where she left it, tiptoeing forward to retrieve it from the deck. She held it in her hands just as delicately as she had on that special day, running fingertips along the carved grooves of the wolf's wooden fur.

"Peter Longshanks carved it," Eusari had told her, "and made it to look exactly like Gelert." She hadn't been wrong. It matched her wolf perfectly.

She turned to run inside but voices froze her feet. No matter how badly she wanted to move she couldn't. The soldiers came closer, their cruel words audible.

One asked the other, "What was his name again?"

"Ralphe Station," replied the other.

That's my father, she thought as she looked for a place to hide.

"What is he wanted for? One merchant seems like the least of Lord Nevra's worries."

"This one is special to our lord," was the response from a newcomer.

They both turned and saw a tall man magnificently dressed. Charleigh remembered his voice from the election speeches a few months before.

"Admiral Creech," the men said in unison as they snapped to attention.

"This man and his family made a public display of support for Braston, and stood beside him during the christening of *Malfeasance*," Creech explained. "Do the job and report back."

The men saluted as their admiral departed.

Charleigh finally moved her feet, but instead of running into the store, she ducked quickly behind a wood pile. She viewed the two men clearly as they passed beneath a gas lamp. One appeared normal; rugged but healthy. His auburn hair was rustled as if he had just awakened and jumped out of bed. The second man appeared ghastly. The scar on his neck revealed a wound that should have ended his life.

They approached the storefront, and the healthy man tried the handle. "Look at that, the fool made it easy for us." They stepped inside. A few moments later two loud sounds came from within.

Charleigh froze. By now the sound of gunfire was more common, but every time she heard it, she remembered the 'Day of the Kraken,' as the people of The Cove called the day Braen Braston destroyed the entire town. With a hand to her mouth she stifled a scream, suddenly aware of her parent's fate. The door opened and fear gripped her once again. Two men strolled casually from the store, uncaring that they had taken two lives. One of the men had pilfered a paint can and brush from the store. In broad strokes he painted the windows, then tossed the can aside. After he was finished, the three men left the way they had come.

Charleigh crept from her hiding place and read the words painted in all caps, *KRAKEN LOVERS*. She gripped the wooden Gelert tightly and went inside to be with her parents.

Adamas Creech stood before Lord Nevra, basking in the king's splendor and thankful for his benevolence. As soon as they departed Middleton several months before, Creech had assumed complete control over the triumvirate. He had returned to The Cove immediately to profess the death of Braston, adding in a bit about Eusari who had fled to serve Robert Esterling. A few days later he'd dissolved the council and abdicated to the rightful ruler, Stefan Nevra. Adamas was much happier with his appointment as Admiral of the Navy. That carried the responsibility of acting as Stefan's second in command.

"We purged The Cove of his most vocal or prominent supporters," he presently informed his king, "just as you required."

"Good," Nevra replied, "with Braston dead we must not allow them to make him into a martyr."

"No chance of that," Creech replied. "What will you have me do next, my lord? With the Esterling fleet tied up in the north, shall we raid further south?"

"Excellent idea, Adamas." He placed a hand on the shoulder of his stalwart admiral.

"Harangue the port of Cargia, but also send marauders to Metzi, Tlaloc, and Nazcla. Introduce the citizens to my reach of power."

A maniacal smile filled Admiral Creech's face at the thought. "I will, my lord."

Nevra called for his personal guard. "Take our special warriors," he said as four men entered the room. Lord Nevra stood to greet his pet. "Ah! Captain Dominique!"

"My lord." Adolphus Dominique stepped forward. He appeared much as he did before he had died in the gibbet, but had deeper set eyes and his cheeks were gaunter. His hair had fallen out in large patches, but Nevra figured that was due to how long he had been deceased before his restoration.

"We have some more business in the southern continent. While Creech raids, I want you to pay a visit to my childhood friend." He licked his lips at the thought of Charro. "Make him an offer," Stefan said. "Tell him I'm ready to make him King of Cargia."

After they had left, the pox-faced man leaned back in his chair and cackled incessantly. He picked up his log and scribbled furiously as he laughed. His pets patrolled every inch of The Cove, and he had so many that he had difficulty keeping track. They reached all reaches of the kingdom, with some even watching King Robert. *So many eyes,* he thought, *so many wonderful sets of eyes with which to see.* He carefully recorded the name of each in his ledger.

He paused as he scribbled the name Braston, calling the man with his mind. *Skander,* he thought. *Where are you, my kraken?*

I'm nearby, my lord.

Good, Nevra thought. *We have so much more work to do. I'm ready to begin.*

Chapter Three

Fluffy clouds hovered against a perfectly blue sky. They moved slowly, so much so that anyone watching would have described them as lazy. Each changed shape as they drifted, transforming from intricate sailing ships and unicorns into fierce dragons and then back again. Off in the distance, several rainbows painted the horizon.

Beneath the perfect sky, on rolling green hills waved flowers of every color in the slight breeze. Atop the hills, magnificent trees reached high toward the heavens, each bearing a bouquet of fruits and desserts. In the valleys, tranquil ponds dotted the landscape and calm rivers transformed into torrid waterfalls as they cascaded from tall cliffs into the blue sea below.

High upon one prominent hill rested a fairytale castle adorned in splendorous banners. Green ivy climbed the walls, and a wide moat encircled its base. Several large sharks swam in the crystal-clear water, as did a whale, a few dolphins, a large squid, and an oversized crayfish. Atop each sea creature rested a small child or a teen, each sunning themselves and drifting along the lazy current.

"This is fun, but I'm tired of only going in a circle," said Cuyler, the eldest of the Dreamers with his sixteen summers. The others had looked to him as their unofficial leader following the death and reanimation of Beth. Her sudden disappearance had upset them all, and his assumption of the leadership role made sense.

Caroline sat up on her whale and peered into the distance. "You're right," she said and closed her eyes. Soon a new vein broke off from the moat, reaching out into the distance. The Dreamers steered their creatures along the new channel. She asked, "Better?"

"Not yet," replied Jasper, the young boy who had brought Kernigan and his party to Estowen's Landing. The boy stood on the back of his crayfish and waved his hands like a conductor before an orchestra. As he did, branches emerged from both sides of the riverbank, twisting and unfurling leaves as they grew into giant cherry trees, complete with white blossoms that snowed down upon the shoreline.

"I have an idea," shouted one of the girls. She sat up from her shark and pointed her fingers like she was shooting pistols. Fairies emerged from the trees ahead and darted about, squirting water at the children with tiny rifles.

As they threw their hands up to block the spray, the others shouted in unison, "Bad idea!"

"Sorry," she said. "I was trying to help." She snapped her fingers and the water guns transformed into ice-cream cones which the fairies offered to the passersby.

Cuyler took one of the frozen treats and handed it to a chubby young boy named Bearnard. "Any luck getting Sebastian to come along?"

"Not a chance," the boy replied. "He refuses to step foot in this place. He hasn't been the same since Suzette and Nico died."

Cuyler nodded, suddenly feeling crestfallen at their rapidly diminishing numbers. So much had happened between their rescue in Diaph and this lazy day in their dream world. He noticed that his sadness was affecting the others and spoke up, trying to boost their morale.

"We've lost so many from the original crew that I don't blame him for being sad," he said. "But we've come so far. Soon this war will be over, and we can decide how we fit into the new world." He closed his eyes and focused a portion of his mind toward Sebastian. *Get here now,* he ordered. *We're all gathered.*

"I asked Eusari to open a school," said Caroline.

Cuyler raised an eyebrow and asked excitedly, "What did she say?"

"That she'd think about it." Caroline shifted her weight atop the dolphin and added, "She said she wants us to quit fighting, that too many of us have died."

"Well," said Cuyler, "she doesn't get to choose for us. Samani said that this world will be ours someday, but we have to stand up for ourselves. He said more and more will be born in the future and we'll no longer be the minority."

"Eusari doesn't trust him," Caroline pointed out.

"Eusari doesn't trust anybody," Cuyler argued. "Shon said she doesn't even trust him, and he's her family."

"She has good reason not to trust Shon," Caroline retorted. She was the only of the Dreamers in whom Eusari confided her full story.

"She trusted Braen," came a voice from the riverbank. No one noticed that Sebastian had appeared. He shot Cuyler an irritated look as he rode atop his giant salamander, obviously displeased by his summons. "But now he's gone too. Everyone's dying."

Another voice from above cut in, "Not everyone!" The Dreamers looked up to see Marita floating above them, laying on her side with her head rested casually on her hand.

Cuyler couldn't believe his eyes. "How are you doing that?"

"I fly now! Both here *and* in real life!" She smiled back at him with her silly grin and two thumbs pointed up at the sky. Then she swam a backstroke to keep pace with their sea creatures. The others rolled their eyes the moment she turned her head.

One of the younger girls stood and jumped from her shark, waving her arms in the air and trying to join Marita. She immediately fell into the water with a splash. Her shark, suddenly free of its rider, turned and swam off to patrol the moat. The others laughed. She crossed her arms and disappeared, seemingly done playing in the dream world and returning to The Cove.

Ignoring Marita, Caroline smiled at Sebastian. "I'm glad you came," she told him with a wink. Their friendship had grown stronger while working closely with Braen and Eusari.

He shrugged. "I had to try again eventually. Besides," he said, "the bad woman's gone."

"She's not really gone," said Cuyler. "Samani found a way to wipe her mind and remove her from the collective. She's back to being his sister again."

Sebastian shuddered, his face stricken and full of fear. "She's alive?"

"Sort of," the older boy said, "Sam says that she died a long time ago and they brought her back to be a Falconer. He swears that she's fixed now, but still dead." He thought for a moment then added, "Walking around but still dead." He shivered despite the warm temperature of the water.

"It was my idea to keep her alive," said Marita. "I could have killed her, but I didn't. Samani needed her."

Leana, almost the same age as Cuyler, gave an audible sigh. "Oh shut up, Marita! You're always making things up. '*I can fly,*' she said. '*I let the Falconer live on purpose.*' For Cinder's sake quit it! You're always acting weird," she said.

Marita did a backflip in the air and then gave the girl a rude gesture she had learned on the ship. "Well who cares what you think. Alec Pogue is my daddy now, and he's a duke!"

"See!" Leana shouted, "Like that! He's nothing but a captain of the guard, not a duke. You're always making things up." She looked to the others for support. They all nodded their agreement.

"It really isn't good when you make up stories," said Cuyler. "We all get tired of hearing them."

"Well," said Marita with her arms crossed and hanging upside down in the air, "I *am* the daughter of a duke and she," she pointed at Leana, "ain't nothin' but a dirty tavern turner." In the blink of an eye she was gone.

"What even does that mean?" asked Leana. None of the children knew.

As they rounded the bend, Cuyler waved his hand and rapids appeared up ahead. The children screamed with delight as they rushed forward with the suddenly tumultuous current. It was just enough, the boy calculated, to add adventure to an otherwise boring day.

Caroline disagreed and yelled, "Stop it! You'll get someone hurt!"

"Whatever," he said, "nothing can harm us here. It's our world and we can do as we please. Why not have some fun?"

"Eusari says that we have to be careful with our powers. She said that..."

"Can you shut up about Eusari?" The interruption came from Bearnard. "Cuyler is the oldest and he's in charge. Captain Thorinson isn't a Dreamer."

"No," Caroline argued, "but she's the only one who gives a demon's ass that we're losing Dreamers. This isn't our war, she says, and the grownups need to fight it without us."

"Not a chance," replied Cuyler. "Samani and Shon insist the war is bigger than the Esterling spat, and everyone's help is needed if we're to rid the world of Falconers."

"Don't forget the Jaguars," Sebastian added.

"And those," Cuyler agreed.

"Well," Leana added, "can we at least agree that Marita's a liar? She doesn't have to help since she lives down south, right?"

"No," Cuyler insisted. "We need everyone, including her. So quit arguing and getting her riled up every time she's here." As soon as he turned his head, Leanna stuck out her tongue and shot him a raspberry. With a wave of his hand, a rock appeared ahead of her turtle. It flipped over and she was tossed into the current. She gave him the same gesture that Marita had given to her and then also disappeared.

Caroline gave him a look of deep disapproval. "That was mean," she said.

"She needed a lesson," he said without remorse. He paused a moment then apologized, not wanting to upset Caroline. He liked her and didn't want to burn a bridge between them. Instead he changed the subject, returning conversation to their plight. "But Samani is right," he insisted. "There's a much bigger threat to our world than those stupid Falconers. As soon as King Robert defeats his brother, some of us will need to help Kernigan against the Astian Council. That's the real war."

"Like I said," Caroline argued. "Eusari doesn't trust him and neither do I. If you want to get yourself killed following him then go ahead." She snapped her fingers and was gone.

"She's right, Cuyler." Sebastian's salamander had to run to keep up with the faster current and his voice vibrated as he bounced on its back. "With Braen dead, there's no more Destroyer. Samani can't fight the council without him."

The older boy didn't answer. He just frowned at the jagged mountains lining the horizon. *Then it will be one of us who destroys them,* he thought. *And I hope it's me.*

Chapter Four

Estowen's Landing, found abandoned and repopulated by pirates and outlaws, no longer promised safety as their seaside port. Instead the town resembled an ancient ruin with collapsed buildings and weakened walls. Their fortifications held, but just barely. Shon Wembley hung his head in dismay, exhausted and spread thin like his troops following the harrowing assaults by Esterling's forces. He turned to Marque for the latest status report.

The lead scout began, "Defensive barricades are somewhat effective at holding them back, but I don't know for how long," he said. "Boss, we're pouring resources into those when we should be building weapons for the assault on Eston."

"I know, my friend. But what else would you have me do?"

Marque told him truthfully, "I never thought that Marque Garett would recommend this course to the great Shon Wembley, but we should cut our losses and retreat. Load up every ship and take us around the continent to join forces with Robert Esterling and Eusari."

Madelyn stood closely beside Marque. The two had somehow found a way to form a relationship despite the ongoing war. *Despite? Perhaps because of the war.* The two shared so many similarities that they seemed cut from the same cloth.

Shon turned to her, "What do you think, Madelyn? This isn't even your fight."

"No," she replied, "it wasn't at first, but it has become mine." She stole a glance at Marque and betrayed a slight blush at his adoring smile. "Since the death of Pearl, I'm fully entrenched in your camp. But we're useless here."

"What is your advice?"

"Evacuate the Landing. There's a reason Charles Esterling abandoned this position; it's indefensible by land."

"We're holding well now, wouldn't you say?" Marque glanced out the window as he spoke, scanning the tree line for activity. Old habits die hard.

"For now," she replied. "But have you noticed that the summer has been unusually wet?"

"Aye," replied Wembley. "But that only works in our favor by further slowing their ground attack."

"Who's watching the river?" She put her finger on a map, directly east of Eston. Certainly they've freed their ships by now. If not, raising the water level will allow them to navigate south of the city and make their way to the coast."

"Cinder's Crack," exclaimed Marque, "She's right! If those ships get around, we're trapped."

"I agree," Shon replied. "It's time we evacuate the Landing." He put his hand on Marque's shoulder and ordered, "Assemble the Dreamers. We need to get word to Eusari and inform her of our decision."

His lieutenant scurried from the room, leaving Wembley alone with Madelyn. "I know losing her was hard. I didn't know her long or well, but I respected the hells out of that woman."

"There were no *hells* in Pearl, Shon. That woman was the last pious member of the Society. Especially compared to Samani."

"Kernigan?" He disliked the man, even trusted him less than the late Braen Braston. And that was saying much given the northerner had murdered Shon's brother-in-law and best friend, Franque Thorinson. "What about him?"

"Pearl confided in me before her death. She had always feared that he had moved from observation to a more intrusive role in Andalon. I think she's right."

"I don't know," he said. "That's a steep allegation and there's no proof." As soon as his words came out, he realized how he sounded.

Ever the lawman, eh Constable Wembley? Former constable. He had thrown that career over the bridge when he chose this new life. "I'll bear that in mind, Madelyn. Thank you."

The woman nodded and turned to leave but the outlaw stopped her.

"Please pass a message to the harbor master. Let him know to make his preparations for withdrawal." He paused, suddenly remembering the spying eyes in the trees and clouds. "Tell him to load the ships under cover and as discreetly as possible."

"Aye." She turned and walked from the room.

Shon couldn't help but notice that she and Marque shared a similar posture and gait, as if they were always walking undetected in the forest. He chuckled at the perfection of their match. Then the smile dropped as he remembered the dire situation his soldiers faced.

Marque found the Dreamers taking their midday meal together in the tavern. But they were not alone. Samani Kernigan laughed and joked with all of them, obviously a great friend to each. His sisters sat next to him, one gazing off into the nether and the other staring coldly at her brother. Marque cringed at the presence of the former Falconer.

"Does she have to be near the Dreamers," he asked gruffly.

"I don't see what it hurts since she's been severed from their collective."

"So you say, Kernigan."

Marque recognized the lead Dreamer Cuyler sitting at the table. The boy was a born leader and perfect choice after the sudden disappearance of Beth. No one knew where the girl had gone in the spring, but whispers suggested she had joined the Falconers hiding in the forest.

"Cuyler, Shon needs you to pass a message to Eusari. Can you do that?"

"Aye, Marque," the boy answered. His voice was steady and gave him a more mature appearance than his actual years. "What's the message?"

"Inform her that we're leaving Estowen's Landing tonight, bound to rejoin her and aid Robert Esterling in their western assault on Eston."

"No," Samani protested. His voice trailed off as he added, "That's not right at all." Suddenly perking up he added, "We must remain here and then meet you in Eston."

His sister, the alive one, asked, "Why here and not with the rest of your revolutionaries?"

"Because deliverance from Astian tyranny starts here, just as it did twelve hundred years ago."

She looked around. Standing, she strode to a window and looked out at the harbor. "Is this the spot of the original landing?"

"Yes. Estowen's Landing was built atop the soil walked upon by Dr. David Andalon."

"Then his original prophecy..."

He nodded and finished her statement, "Must begin here before it can end in Eston."

Marque interrupted the moment. "Feel free to stay, but we're leaving." He nodded to Cuyler who stood, gesturing to the four remaining autumn emotants.

He called out to them, "Galayn and Jasper. Come with me. Leeyah and Daryn, you will form the boundary to keep the connection secure," he stole a glance at Ashima as he said, "from prying eyes of Falconers." They followed Marque from the room.

After the others had left, Samani closed and locked the door to the tavern. He returned to the table and sat.

Johan, the boy who had traveled from Logan with Kali, watched him latch the lock. "What was that for?"

Kernigan responded, "Because we need privacy when we discuss a course of action."

"That's simple," the boy said. "Kali and I are going with them. We have a war to fight to free Andalon."

Sam sighed. "Oh son, you must expand your mind. The war for Astia is much bigger and includes all of Andalon. If we fail across the sea, they will reset this entire continent and kill you and your family and friends. Then, after they've enslaved those they consider 'seeds' for a new experiment, they will raze the castles and cities to the dirt. They will build new towns and force you to live as subjects to a new monarch of their choosing. Then they will send Falconers and Jaguars in to cull and cultivate the harvest that feeds our oracles."

Fatwana spoke up, "You were brought here for a reason. What is your plan, Samani?"

"Before I answer, I need to know if you two," he indicated Johan and Kali, "are going with us to fight the real war."

"No," answered Johan.

"Yes," replied Kali.

The boy turned and stared with mouth agape. "But you said months ago that we would be loyal to Shon."

"Things changed," she said. "Pearl gave her life for the Society. Why would anyone do that if it weren't a true cause?" She reached out a hand, touching his. The boy blushed, yearning months for her touch and now unsure how to respond.

Good, ordered Samani, *now lean in and repeat these words.*

Kali said, "Johan, I like you a lot. I have since we wandered in the forest. But I cannot go with you. If you choose to leave, then you do so without me. Samani knows more about who we are and what we are capable than anyone we've ever met." She leaned in closer with pleading eyes. "Are you with us?" The boy trembled with nerves and expectation.

Samani almost smiled. *Tell him that you love him and want him to stay with you.*

"Stay with me, Johan. We are a team and I... I love you." Then she reached up and kissed him gently on the cheek. The boy blushed a deep shade of red.

"Well, Johan," Samani said, "it seems you have at least one reason to stay."

"Okay," the boy answered with eyes locked on Kali's and yearning to lock lips. "I go where Kali goes."

"Good answer. Now, Fatwana, have you noticed that Cassidy has not returned from her scouting mission?"

"Yes. I've not seen her for several weeks."

"That is because she's on Society business," he cleared his throat, "of which you are all sworn to secrecy."

His sister stammered, "Sam, I..."

He cut her off harshly. "You made your choice when you handed over the prophecies to the Dragon." More tenderly he added, "Whether you like it or not you are committed to the outcome."

She said nothing and watched, listening close to his next words.

He shocked them all when he reported, "Chancellor Jakata ordered the reset two months ago."

Fatwana gasped.

"His order cannot be rescinded, not by the council. They will have to elect a new chancellor to counter the order, but in the meantime the Astian Council's secret army is on their way here. They will arrive within the week," he estimated.

"I don't understand," Fatwana said. "Why would they need to elect a new chancellor? What is wrong with Jakata?"

"Except for the fact that he overdosed on Astian Pearls, one of each color I might add, he is very much the same. Only without a pulse or lifeforce."

Fatwana placed her hand to her chest and paled several shades. Samani feared she may even pass out. She tried several times to ask another question, but fell silent each time.

Kali broke the silence. "What will they do? What are we facing?"

"Excellent question, young lady. I couldn't have phrased it better myself," he said with a wink. "They have weapons, the likes of which you have never seen. They are similar to our rifles, but can fire between thirty and one hundred projectiles faster and without reloading. They also have explosives, poisonous gas, and armor plating."

Johan gasped. Kali did too, a moment later. Both looked toward Fatwana for confirmation. He asked, "Is this true?"

"I'm afraid so."

"Won't we see their ships?" The boy's mind pondered all the ways he could manipulate the water. "Can't I sink them before they arrive?"

"Alas," Samani said, "that would be easier, but no." He sighed. "Their boats, much like the one that carried over Cassidy and Fatwana, sail underwater."

Kali gasped, "That's impossible! How do they breathe?"

"Another great question, Kali, but one that I don't have time to answer. Suffice to say they can, and they do. What they don't know is that the Society has already placed agents on the beach. Cassidy is meeting with them now and organizing an ambush."

Fatwana gasped. "The weapons the Dragon was loading into crates?"

"Yes. You weren't supposed to see those, and trust me, those responsible for indiscretion were dealt with." He continued, "He organized the attack and slipped submersibles past Astian patrols the moment the order was given."

"Sam," she said. She only called him Sam when she was ashamed of him or he had done wrong. "How do you know all of this? Do you work directly for the Dragon?"

"Let's just say that he and I are very close." He winked. "I used to be part of his *Inner Sanctum,*" he said. "But here we called him, Artema Horn."

Fatwana did not recognize the name at first, but then shock filled her eyes and she gasped. "Jakata Horn's youngest son?"

"The same." He replied. "Now, since you are all on board, we need to move to safety, or we will cease to be anything once those troops storm the beach. Cassidy said that they will arrive any day."

Chapter Five

Robert Esterling stood atop the main gate of Eskera, discussing his next move with his newly appointed general, Frederique Titus. The attack two months previous had done a number on the city. The repairs to the wall moved slowly, but the worst sections had been fortified and it appeared defensible. Truthfully, the exiled king had no interest in defending the position and desired to march northward with haste.

His original plan would have put him and his army in Loganshire by now, but for the continued arrival of Weston refugees. Their reports had astonished both him and General Titus and he had flown in the mind of his eagle Arne, taking him north to verify the outrageous claim. The reports were true. The city had disappeared, reduced to a crater. Lake Weston, as the people called it, was all that remained.

Sarai's voice caused him and Titus to turn. "You're not really up here to check out the fortifications, are you?"

He faced his wife. "What else would warrant my attention?"

She didn't have to point. He knew immediately what she had meant. "They've camped there a month and haven't made any attempt to move closer."

Robert nodded. "Taros fears me after our last encounter."

"No," she said, "he's mastered his powers. If the reports are correct, he single-handedly leveled that city and every Falconer within." She wrapped her arm in her husband's. "Don't underestimate him. Also, remember that beneath his anger, he's a sweet boy with a good heart." Despite her words she absent-mindedly touched her scars as she spoke.

He had almost killed the boy for those. Taros had fallen for Sarai and did not take her rejection well. He lashed out, unable to control his rage as his wild flames burned much of her body. Robert touched her beautifully scarred face. Her sapphire eyes stared up, less bright during the pregnancy and sunken from stress. She had recently taken to wearing a headscarf and claimed that she was embarrassed by the scars on her head, but he knew the truth. The hair in the drain of the tub was excessive, and she lost more and more each week.

He placed his hand on her stomach, round and full of their baby safe within her womb. "How's my heir," he asked with a smile.

"Kicking at the moment." She laughed.

"I can feel." Robert turned his eyes back to the Pescari camp. "I will ride out there today and dispense with this game. If he has something to say, then he needs to get it off his chest."

"I will go with you," Sarai responded.

He protested, "No. Not in your condition."

"It will help if he can look upon me and see how close I came to death," she insisted.

That idea gave him pause. "Perhaps," he mused, "but seeing you with child may remind him that you refused his love. It could push him to anger."

"Then my husband had better defend me," she said, pulling away and leaving the way she had come. "I'll leave you boys to your scheming," she called over her shoulder.

Robert turned back toward Titus. He looked sickly as well. His eyes were as dreary and sunken as Sarai's. "When was the last time you slept, General?"

"Honestly?" The military man let out a chuckle, "not since you promoted me two months ago."

Robert flinched at the words. The battlefield promotion had been a necessity, having lost both Maximus Reeves and Merrimac

Lourdes in the same fight. *The way the Jaguars had laid the trap,* he mused, *had nearly worked.* Esterling and his allies learned early on that the beast-like creatures could perform necromancy, reanimating the dead with their collective chanting and mental connection. But they hadn't expected that they commanded an entire army, or that they had slipped their puppets close to the king. Had Max not stepped between Robert and the blade, this entire war would have ended with a single stroke.

The king's eyes flicked to Titus' belt at the thought of the blade. The general had taken to wearing it since the attack, as homage to both its previous owner Merrimac Lourdes and also for Maximus Reeves, his mentor, whom it had slain.

Robert pointed at the weapon. "That sword has a history, you know."

"Yes, I understand it belonged to Charles Esterling. Lourdes once told me that he wore it through the entire campaign against the Pescari, passing it on to him following their defeat just across the river from Weston." The general paused, then considered. "Would you like to carry it, my liege?"

"Not at all," Robert replied. He indicated Reeve's sword on his own belt. "I'm well-armed with the sword of my father on *my* hip."

Thinking about the death of Max also made him consider how closely he came to losing Sarai. Lourdes' bullet had taken her in the chest, nearly killing her on that day. Had Amash not been there for his sister so quickly, the king would have lost both his wife and child in that same fight. Nothing would ever recreate the joy he felt when he saw that she had survived. He broke his thoughts away from that fateful day and turned back to his general.

"I want to ride out in an hour. 'Better to get the unpleasant business over quickly,' Max always said." After a brief pause, he added, "Ready a carriage for Sarai. She'll join us."

"Aye, sir." Titus saluted and departed.

A few minutes later, Robert heard the soft rumble of a clearing throat. He turned to find Amash Horslei and Eusari Thorinson.

This woman intrigued him. When she had arrived, she and her wolf had barged into his palace and demanded his immediate attention, injuring several guards in the affair. Had Amash not been nearby to vouch for her, Robert would have had her carted away. But she had dire news to share and her urgency was warranted.

At least when Braen Braston lost his life, Robert had gained what was left of his armada and his army. *Allegedly died,* he thought. One of Krist Braston's sons lived. Sarai was certain that it was Skander who had perished, and urged caution upon her husband. *That would explain Middleton,* he mused, *and why Braen rushed off on his own if not to hide his own rise to power.* Regardless of which brother was responsible, recent attacks along the east coast boasted the name of Skander. In each event the attacker used winter powers.

Despite his worries, he smiled welcomely at the woman standing next to his brother-in-law. "What can I do for you, Captain Eusari?"

"Shon Wembley departed Estowen's Landing last night," she reported. "He has several thousand troops, each armed and trained with rifles. They'll arrive in a few weeks."

"A few weeks," Robert asked, "why not sooner?"

"He has lost several of his spring emotants. He won't be able to adjust the wind for such a big convoy."

The king nodded his understanding. "Inform him to meet us at Lake Weston. We'll set up camp on a hill overlooking the Misting River. He can moor his ships there."

Eusari nodded but continued. "That's not all, your highness."

Robert raised an eyebrow, eagerly awaiting the news that brought the pregnant woman up the parapet. Yes, he could tell. Even through her leather armor she was beginning to show. She was keeping it a secret, but the child would ensure that news would get out soon. "What other tidings do you bring, Captain Thorinson?"

"Lady Hester is demanding a ship and her swift return to Fjorik. With Skander dead, she intends to claim regency over the throne until..." Her voice cracked, suddenly choked up by her next words. "...until Braen's child is old enough to sit upon it."

Robert could only imagine how hard it must be for this woman, so truly in love with Braston who not only sired a child upon her, but also with his brother's wife. *I never did like him,* Robert thought. *His arrogance was his downfall, thinking he could do and take whatever he pleased.* At least he was out of the way and would never live out his true ambitions.

"She'll have to wait until after the war is over," Esterling responded. "We need every boat in our fleet. Especially," he added, "after Braen lost *Malfeasance* and his entire armada to Skander." He pulled a dispatch out of his pocket and handed it to Eusari. The next part he said deliberately, watching her face for change of expression. *If Braen lives, she will betray her knowledge.* "Besides, she has no claim over that throne, not while Skander Braston lives."

Both Eusari and Amash paled, filled with shock at the news. "That's impossible," she replied. "I saw him. The bullet pierced his brain. Skander Braston is dead." Her eyes scanned the parchment several times.

Robert watched the anger seething within the woman. *Understandable if he truly killed her lover,* he thought. After a moment he responded, "If that's true and he did perish, then it's worse than we feared. The Jaguars must have resurrected him as well. In that case, we can expect him to join forces with Marcus and fight us alongside him. Or," he flinched as he finished, "flank us up the Misting River. Inform Shon Wembley that's a possibility he must be prepared for."

Eusari and Amash nodded, still reeling from the news. After they left him alone atop the wall, he scanned the Pescari encampment. He imagined he could hear Max's voice whispering caution, *I don't like the looks of it, boy. But the fight is all yours now. You're both a king and a general and you'll have to do it all alone.* The advice was exactly what he'd hoped to hear from his mentor someday, and his eyes briefly misted at the knowledge he would never see his father again.

Another throat cleared behind him. *Good gods,* he thought, *should I move my throne room to this parapet?* He turned and found himself face to face with an unimposing man with spectacles and ink-stained fingers. He recognized the man from Weston. Percy Roan was a well-known crony to Cassus Eachann.

"My liege," the bookkeeper began, "If I may interrupt..."

Robert cut him off, "You absolutely may not. How did you gain access to me?"

"You sent away the general, and the guards below the wall are not very reliable. I simply walked up the steps."

So goes the theme for the day, he thought. "Mr. Roan, I have no desire to do business with you. I know your background and closeness to Eachann. I won't have your presence cluttering my court."

"I don't blame you at all, your highness. But before you send me away, I'd like you to know what really happened in Weston."

Robert pointed over his shoulder at the Pescari camp. "You mean when the fire-flinging, tantrum-thrower destroyed it?"

"Well," the clerk replied, "that's one way to put it, but not entirely accurate. Let me begin with the day you escaped Eachann and fled to Eskera."

With nowhere else to go, Robert listened.

Frederique Titus kept his horse at a trot slightly behind his king and queen. Ten guards flanked the royal couple with five on each side. Slightly ahead rode Eusari Thorinson and Amash Horslei. Once the black-cloaked woman heard of the meeting with the Pescari, no one could keep her away. Amash insisted that she could be an asset and agreed to be her chaperone. The talk of the military formation, though, was her wolf running alongside.

"I heard it bit old Dodger," one of the men whispered.

"No," another soldier said, "she bit him, the wolf bit Private Smithson."

Regardless of who or what bit whom, Titus was tired of the rumors surrounding the mysteriously hooded woman. Her hands were what captivated his attention. Her bare hands held the reins of her horse with more scars than Frederique had ever seen on a single person. They were as countless as the stars above. No, he didn't care about the rumors, he wanted to know her story and what horrors she had experienced.

He scratched his head, pulling away another tuft of hair. That had been happening more often, and worried he contracted some kind of disease while floating in the sewer a few months back. He had been cropping it short, but would have to shave it clean when he returned to the barracks.

The street fighting on that fateful night in Eskera had changed Titus, and he hadn't been himself since. He constantly felt sick to the stomach and found that he ate less and less as the weeks went by. He also couldn't shake the ringing in his ears. It almost sounded like a humming.

He worried. He had been on the stage when General Lourdes attacked King Robert, and instantly realized that the man had died and been resurrected by the Jaguars. He was their agent placed in the city to assassinate the boy and end the civil war. Titus prayed to the gods that the general was their only spy.

Shouting on the road ahead spurred him to a gallop. He quickly caught up to Horslei. "What is it?"

The man pointed, "Riders. It seems that their scouts want to parlay."

"Let's hope that's all," the general replied. He turned his horse around and informed his sovereign that they were about to have company.

Eusari heard the whispers of the men riding behind her. *Let them talk,* she thought, *it's always fun to leave a legend in my wake.* The saddle was uncomfortable. The pressure on her bladder increased her urgency to pee. She would need to stop as soon as she could. She was about to dismount and squat on the side of the road when the riders appeared. *Damn my luck,* she cursed, *I swear this child*

wants me to wet myself every moment of every day! Because of that she fought back the urge to gallop ahead to converse with the scouts. Galloping would have finished the job Braen's heir had started.

Fifteen riders quickly formed a circle around the king's entourage. Amash shouted something in their language and they responded.

"Well," she asked. "What did they say."

"They said to stay mounted and they will escort us to their shappan."

"What in the hells is a shappan," she asked.

"It means father," he explained, "their title for chieftain."

Eusari stared down the men, each with a brand on their faces the shape of a human hand. *How interesting,* she thought. *What kind of ruthless ruler would mark his followers that way?* She shuddered and said, "Tell me about this shappan."

By now King Robert had pulled up alongside and answered for Amash. "He's only a boy," he explained, "probably around sixteen or seventeen summers."

"Not much of a *father*," Eusari quipped. She looked around. She had to find a place to pee soon.

"He won the position by defeating his former chieftain." Robert paused and then added, "He burned him alive."

"How did he do that," Horslei asked.

"He's an emotant like us," Robert told Eusari, "but his affinity is fire."

This got her attention. She spun around, suddenly forgetting about her bladder. "Fire? How big are we talking?"

"This boy destroyed the entire city of Weston. Single-handedly."

Eusari spotted a bush just off the road. "I'd like to hear that story. Fill me in the moment I get back."

The Pescari scouts tried to stop her but moved aside when Gelert's growl spooked their horses. Two of them tried to follow, but quickly turned around when she dropped her trousers to do her business. They quickly blushed and turned their horses. *That's right, boys,* she thought, *don't get in the way of a pregnant woman.*

Chapter Six

Charleigh waited until darkness enveloped the Cove before venturing out. When she was little, she was terrified of the night. Now that she had seen the real monsters, she feared the day. If the neighbors found her, they would remove her just as they did her parents. She ran her hand along the empty shelves of the store. They had taken the food as well. She wouldn't let them take her.

The front door and windows had been boarded shut from the outside, so she didn't use them to exit. She proceeded down the narrow stairs to the cellar where her mother kept the cold stores. Those were gone too. But the neighbors didn't know about her father's secret room, so that's where she had hidden when they came.

She pushed her body against the secret catch and the panel swung away. The cubby was small, but not so tiny that her father couldn't have fit. Squeezing past to the fifty or so barrels was a different story. The first time she had caught a whiff of them she had pinched her nose at the charcoal smell. By now she was used to their odor. At the end of the row she found another loose plank. This was her secret exit and way out of the store.

Her tiny frame was an advantage and she slid in easily, dropping to a tunnel that ran underneath the city. At first, she had been afraid to enter out of fear of rats and spiders. Careful exploration had dispelled those fears, with those washed away on the Kraken King's tidal wave. Now she walked with confidence in the dark.

She had made the trip so many times that she knew it by the number of steps, rather than landmarks. She turned right and then left. There was a raised bit of a ledge here which she used to climb higher.

She pushed aside a plank and entered the palace pantry. It was full of cakes and sweets, but her interest was in the salted meats hanging from the rafters. She could steal one every few days without detection, and they filled her up better than the sugary snacks ever could.

Charleigh snatched one of the hams and a waterskin and turned to leave, her feet suddenly frozen in place. Two sets of eyes blinked back at her in the dark. Her heart raced until the boy, younger than she, whispered, "Please help us." They were twins, a boy and a girl, huddled together and terrified.

"I don't know if I can," she told him truthfully.

"Please," he begged. "They'll kill us."

"Come," Charleigh ordered, and they obeyed.

She pushed aside the plank and led them through the darkness. None of the children spoke until they were safely inside her father's store. Even then they waited until she had pulled out her knife and carved off pieces of the meat. She served the younger children and poured them water to drink. "Eat this," she said.

"I'm not hungry," the little girl whispered.

"It doesn't matter," Charleigh said, "my mother always said that you have to eat if you want strength." With finality she said, "you need to eat."

Both of the tiny children suddenly forgot their fear and eagerly devoured their dinner. After they had finished, the older girl asked, "Why were you hiding?" They didn't respond. They looked to each other in silence as if daring the other to speak first. She finally began the introductions for them. "My name's Charleigh," she tried.

In a timid voice the boy responded. "I'm Neill," he said.

"My name's Nathaira," the girl said, "but I go by *Nat*."

"How old are you, Neill?" When he didn't answer she gave her own age, "I'm eight summers."

"We're both five," he replied.

She asked, "Are you twins?" She rewrapped the meat and wiped her knife on a cloth. She stowed them both away before adding, "I've only met twins one time."

Nat answered for them both. "We are."

"Where are your parents?"

"Dead," they both answered at the same time.

"I'm sorry," Charleigh said. "Mine are too. The bad men came one night and shot them in their beds."

"Ours were killed by Northmen when they raided our village."

"How did you get to the palace?"

"Captain Eusari rescued us and brought us here," Neill said. "She promised we'd be safe."

"But then she left," Nat added, "and so did Captain Braston."

"I know them," Charleigh said. "Eusari gave me this." She pulled out the wood carving.

The children lit up, suddenly filled with excitement. "That's Gelert!" They suddenly forgot their fear and scrambled to touch the wooden wolf.

Charleigh asked again, "Neill, what happened?"

She could sense his lingering hesitation to speak, but his sister coaxed him to tell their tale.

"Everything was fine until Captain Creech came home," he began.

Neill and Nathaira played on the floor while the others trained. These were the youngest of the Dreamers, and Eusari had insisted that they not get involved in the revolution. Magnus, the eldest of the group, had only seen nine summers, whereas Olafur had eight and Kadlin had seven. Hallbera was the teacher of the group, a kind teen of fifteen. She led the older children in their exercises.

"Close your eyes and focus," she told them, "find the shimmer in the air and try to touch it with your mind."

"It tickles," Kadlin giggled. She was the most gifted of the three older children, and often grasped concepts quicker.

"Good, Kadlin," Hallbera praised, "Now, loop it quickly and pull it into your body. Once you have it secure, send it like a lasso and wrap it around the training dummy." All were successful except Magnus. He kicked the ground in defeat.

Neill giggled and whispered something in Nat's ear. She broke out laughing.

Hallbera scolded them immediately. "Everyone struggles at first. You will too when allowed to train." She placed a nurturing hand on Magnus' shoulder and whispered, "It's okay if this isn't your skill. You're our strongest in the dream world." He smiled at her words and tried again, this time successfully forming a very thin strand of air. "That's better," she praised.

A message boy knocked and entered the hall. He approached the oldest Dreamer and said, "Captain Creech has returned from Middleton and requires your immediate audience."

"Mine?" Hallbera was shocked. Her communication had always been with Samani Kernigan or Captain Eusari. Creech had never even spoken to her.

"Well," she said, "I'm almost finished here."

"He said *now* if it does or doesn't please you, ma'am."

"Then I'd better hurry," she whispered quietly. To the children she said, "Take a few minutes of rest and then practice the lassos. When I return, I will show you how to build a net using each other's wisps."

Magnus pulled on her sleeve and said, "Be careful, Hallbera. Remember that Caroline said that Captain Braston died in the battle. Didn't she say that Captain Creech died also?"

"Don't be silly," she replied. "She could have been mistaken. Besides, he's one of the elected leaders. Since Eusari and Caroline are with King Robert, it makes sense that he'd want to talk to me. Now if you'll excuse me, I have to go. Practice your nets."

As soon as she had departed, the older children gathered around Nat and Neill. Magnus leaned in toward the boy, ready to make the younger boy pay for laughing at him earlier. "Let's see you do better."

"I'm not allowed," Neill replied, "Captain Eusari forbade it."

"This isn't training," the older boy insisted. "This is you proving you can do it or shutting your mouth."

A dozen wisps of air suddenly shot into the air around Neill, weaving and wrapping into a single net which he tossed at Magnus with a flip of his wrist. The boy wriggled and struggled against the bonds, but they only grew tighter.

"Release him," Olafur demanded. "We're on the same team."

"Yeah," Kadlin insisted. "We aren't supposed to turn it against each other."

"Fine." Neill flipped his wrist again and the web fell away.

As Magnus scrambled to his feet, Nat grabbed her brother's hand and led him away, giggling and starting a game of hide and seek. The others turned and closed their eyes, counting to ten. As soon as she and Neill were under a table, she weaved the air, forming a shimmering barrier that bent the light around them. They disappeared instantly.

Magnus, despite being the weakest in manipulating the element, was the strongest finder. He meticulously sent pulses through sections of the room, feeling for traces of her magic. Abruptly the door to the hall burst open, ending their game.

Hallbera led six men inside. The children recognized Captain Creech by his elaborate dress and stared in awe. The man spoke to Hallbera. "Have them gather before us."

"Children," she told them, "Captain Creech would like a demonstration of your powers."

"Is this all of them?"

The man smiled but Neill could tell that he wasn't a trustworthy man. Treachery hid behind his kindness. He held his sister's hand and placed a finger to his lips. As long as she kept the camouflage around them, they would remain safe. She nodded her understanding.

Hallbera counted then said, "Two are missing, Captain." To the others she asked, "Where are the twins?"

"They ran off," Kadlin said before the others could answer truthfully.

"No bother," Creech told Hallbera. "We can speak with them later." He gestured to the training dummies. "Go on, have them give me a demonstration."

She arranged the children, turning their backs to the Captain and his crew. "Let's make the web," she said. "Each of you form a strand, and focus on weaving a second over and under those made by the others."

The children obeyed and poured all of their attention into showing off for the Captain. They were so focused that they failed to hear the swords slide from scabbards. A hand gripped each child as the tip of a sword pierced each ribcage. The net vaporized as the empty husks that once were children collapsed on the floor.

Nat and Neill gasped, too terrified to scream. They watched in horror as Hallbera carefully laid the children out in rows.

"Good," the Captain praised his men. "Lord Nevra will be pleased with the cleanliness of the kills."

"I'll be the judge of that, Adamas." All eyes turned to the pox-scarred man who entered the room. Neill had never seen the former king, but recognized him from the stories whispered around the palace. A large rat sat upon his shoulder. It was a hideous creature, with large patches of baldness randomly revealing crusty brown skin. "Yes, I am very pleased indeed," he said, wringing his bony hands. He leaned over the bodies and one by one breathed life.

The sight of Magnus rising from the floor sent fear coursing through Neill. Somehow, he understood that his friend was gone and an obedient subject to Nevra had taken his place. He pulled at his sister's arm and pointed to the rear entrance. She nodded. She held the cloak of air in place as they sprinted toward the door, slipping out and letting it slam shut behind them. Sounds of pursuit echoed behind them.

"And so we hid," Neill told Charleigh. "And that's when you found us in the pantry."

The older girl nodded knowingly, then wrapped her tiny arms around the twins. She hugged them and told them that they were safe now. That she would take care of them until Captain Eusari returned.

Nathaira pulled back and shook her head violently. "No," she argued. "Captain Braston is coming, not Eusari."

Chapter Seven

The body of the lifeless Kraken drifted with the current, tossed by the seas for hundreds of miles until it finally washed upon the beach. Just off shore its belly had been ripped to shreds by the sharp shoals and rocks. As it lay upon the sugary sand, these cuts bled out, painting what was once white with a pale pink. Crabs immediately picked at the carcass, some nibbling the tender organs while others worked on the stomach, trying to reach the fish within. One crab in particular scrambled over the others, finding a narrow cut made from the inside out.

It wriggled into the tiny hole, just as a hand grabbed ahold, pulling it the rest of the way inside. The man, having gone far too long without food, immediately cracked the shell of the crustacean, sucking out the raw meat within. Feeling stronger by the knowledge that he had eaten, he went back to work with his axe, sawing at the hole and making it bigger. He was still too weak to rip it apart.

If he had any of his other weapons, especially his knife, he believed the process would have gone quicker. But, when he awakened, he found they had been removed except for this single axe. He worked until he could fit his arm and shoulder through the slit. Finally his head emerged, blinking away the brightness of the sun. From its position directly overhead he knew that he had somehow landed on the southern continent.

His long blonde hair and shaggy beard were soaked and smelled as foul as the innards of the Kraken that had served as his raft. Sustained only by the oils and salty meat of the fish he found within, it was a miracle that he had survived. When it had rained, much of it found its way into his compartment and he drank as it poured in through his air hole. On the days it didn't, the same water had mixed with the salt. He was still ill from the first time he drank the mixture of bile and brackish fluids from the belly of the beast.

Weakened by his recent efforts he collapsed, naked, on the sand. He did not know how he came about being undressed, but the strips of cloth remaining in the giant squid resembled a burial shroud. They were useless to him now. Here he lay for several moments, catching his breath and waiting for the dizziness to pass. Finally, after what felt like an eternity, he clamored to his knees. His muscles trembled from atrophy and he retched up his recent meal. He passed out.

Several hours later he awakened to tidewater swirling around him. He scrambled up the shore, trying to reach higher ground before succumbing to the ocean he had just narrowly survived. He tried to reach out with his abilities, but the water would not obey. Somehow, he knew in that moment that he would never command the seas again. He passed out a second time.

When he came to, it was with a gentle rain falling on his face. He opened his mouth and let it fall in, drinking and laughing at his fortune. Then the large man rolled over and found strength to move under a nearby tree. He felt the ground in the darkness until he found a large leaf which he curled to catch the water. With one corner in his mouth he drank the steady flow of life saving fresh water.

Braen Braston remembered nothing after his fight with Skander and before awakening inside the Kraken. Despite dehydration and severe abdominal pain, probably from the rancid water he drank inside the beast, he managed a smile. *If only Artema could have seen this,* he thought. *The Kraken King swallowed and birthed by his own brethren.* He wished he could find that dastardly son of a bitch and tell him face to face, right after he punched that face of course.

Naked and afraid he moved at night, mostly up steep hills that challenged his weakened and rubbery legs. After a few hours, he chanced upon a manor house, most likely the property of a wealthy southern lord. He immediately crept toward the servant's quarters where he spotted clothing drying in the night air. He pulled shirt and trousers from a line and pulled them on, finally feeling civilized. Pushing his luck, he crept toward the small building. Peering in a window he found it empty.

Braen tried the handle and it opened easily. Once inside he searched through the meager belongings, quickly finding a razor and small looking glass the size of his palm. He stole these, tossing them into a sack before hurrying outside. Returning to a small stream he had passed on the way up, he knelt to shave.

It took him several minutes to remove his recognizable beard and most of his golden locks. The face that stared back was most certainly a stranger, and he prayed to the gods of Fjorik that his transformation would confound his enemies and any who sought him for bounty. He was a fugitive. Worse, he was a fugitive without power over water or the beasts within.

A sword suddenly appeared at this neck. "Thieving's a crime in Cargia, mate."

Braen froze, not looking for a fight with the newcomer. He said, "I had planned to return it."

"Likely story. There'll be a fine that you'll owe to the lord of the manor."

"I have no money," Braen replied.

"Nor clothes, for that matter. We'll be takin' those back too."

The large man from the north stood, allowing his captor to lead him peacefully toward a magnificent house overlooking what he now knew was the Gulf of Cargia.

Lord Alec Pogue, Duke of Southern Cargia, grunted as he pulled on a robe. His guards had roused him from his slumber, apparently concerned over a thieving vagrant they had found on the property. He fussed with the robe, unable to work the tassels. Finally his wife Mattie rose from bed to help.

"There's too many workings to this thing. I don't like it," he told her.

"Well you're a duke now, so get used to it. Imagine if you were a king," she replied.

"Gods help me if I were. I couldn't bear allowing other people to dress me." He smiled at her playfully and pinched at her beautiful bottom. "Unless it's you who's dressing me, Duchess Pogue!"

She pointed to the door. "I'll stick to the *undressing* if it's alright with you. Now go. Be a duke and return to me my lover."

He kissed her lips briefly but with deep affection. "Always."

When he arrived at the receiving room, Marita met him at the door. She insisted, "Please let me watch this time!"

"No. Go back to bed," he responded.

"Are you telling me that as my duke, my captain, or my father?"

"All three," he replied. "Now go!"

She put on a fake pout and stormed off, muttering sarcastically, "Yes, your dukey- captain-fatherness!"

"And none of that backtalk," he warned. He smiled when she whirled around and stuck out her tongue. *I love that kid,* he thought. The adoption meant so much to both of them, filling a void for her and adding one more member of his family to love.

He had taken her for granted when they first met and she tagged along on missions. He should have remembered at the time what children needed from a role model: patience, virtue, and compassion. But he had forsaken everything in his search for Mattie and the girls. She learned only killing and violence on their journey. And he, blinded by their kidnappings at the hands of Adolphus Dominique, had forgotten how to father.

It was his fault she dragged blades across a man's throat, both the first and the second times. He claimed full responsibility, for she first completed that task with the same precision he had demonstrated, down to the absence of emotion or remorse. At some point during the journey, he felt compelled to put things right and vowed to take her far away from the killing and pirating. Only, it turned out, he brought her to a place where she was forced to send a second man down the river.

Unbeknownst to him, she had been watching him and his friend Amash practice at their swords. She was bright, picking up every move and dancing through difficult katas like a ballerina armed with blades. In the end, she had rescued Mattie and the girls with the skills she had picked up. *Yes, it was her and not me. I was hamstrung at the time.* She had also rescued him on that fateful day, securing their bond forever as father and daughter. He loved her and so did Mattie, Alexa, and Liza. They welcomed her immediately as a Pogue.

Unable to erase her knowledge or unlearn the moves she knew so fluidly, he had since chosen to train her properly. He hoped that she would also develop a conscience and wherewithal for judgement to accompany her deadly precision. She renewed his morality and reminded him daily that a man's duty was to demonstrate compassion and love over revenge and hatred. With these virtues as a compass, he hoped to guide her future as a benevolent and discerning killer.

He pushed open the door and went inside. Captain Tallman stood over a shackled prisoner, broad of shoulder and blonde of hair cropped short against his head. His face was clean shaven, but he was greatly in need of a bath. Alec could smell his fish stench as soon as he entered.

Alec sat in the thronelike chair directly in front of the captive. *By Cinder's Crack I hate this chair,* he thought. But local custom dictated that the lord of the house have one in which to preside over matters. Unsettled, he asked, "What have we got here, Captain?"

Both men spoke at once, causing Tallman to slap the thief with an open hand. The part of his face that turned toward Alec appeared familiar. *Most Norsemen look alike,* he mused, shrugging off the feeling of familiarity.

"He trespassed and broke into my cottage, Lord."

"What did he take?"

"One of my weapons."

"That's a lie," snarled the man. "It was a mirror and a razor."

Alec's ears perked up. Even in the deep northern accent he again detected familiarity. "A razor and a mirror, you say?"

"Aye," Braen responded.

"To shave off the fact that you are a survivor of the raid on Lord Valencia's manor more than two months ago?" Alec Pogue had always been a keen detective. His former job, before he had purchased the manor and surrounding land, had been to serve as Captain of the Guard in Pirate's Cove. "Why else would a man disguise his identity? Why else would a raider from Fjorik try to blend in, unless they were left behind when their brethren retreated?"

The man said nothing.

Alec gave in to his anger. The night his wife and daughters had nearly lost their lives and virtue burned strong in his mind. *Had Marita not intervened when she did*, he thought, *I would have been too late*. He screamed at the prisoner. "Answer me!"

When the man spoke, his quiet voice abstained from emotion. Except, maybe, for a hint of despair. "Has shaving my beard and cutting my hair caused you, my friend, to forget my face completely? Do you truly not know me, Captain Pogue? Open your eyes and look upon me, Alec."

Captain Tallman raised his hand to strike once more but Alec held up his own. "Stop," he ordered. He stood from the throne and walked forward, leaning in as close as the fish smell would allow. "No," he whispered, "you're dead. Captain Thorinson sent word that you had been buried at sea."

"Yet, I walk among you, Alec. How do you explain that?"

Abruptly the door swung open and Marita rushed in. "Captain Braston!" She rushed forward and hugged him tightly. After she had finished, she stepped back and picked the locks to the shackles with tiny wisps of air, sending them crashing to the floor with a rattle. Then she stepped back and smiled her silly grin with thumbs stuck up in the air.

"Marita," Braen exclaimed, "so nice to see you again." He rubbed his hands where they had been pinched by the shackles. He inclined his head to Pogue. "How's your father treating you? Do I need to rescind the adoption papers I signed?"

"Absolutely not," she declared with an air of authority. "He's the best damned father you could have given me!"

"Marita," Alec cautioned, "watch your language!"

"What?" She spun around with a look of confusion on her face. "It's not like I said…"

"Marita Arvid Pogue!" A woman's voice boomed from the door. Everyone in the room turned to see Mattie standing in the doorway. "What have we told you about speaking like a pirate?"

"I can only do it when I'm pirating," she said with an air of remorse.

"That's correct, and *are* you pirating at this moment?"

"No," she responded. But then her face lit up with a ludicrous smile. "But he is! He's the Kraken King! Around him I should be able to say whatever I …"

"Marita!" Pogue's voice was louder than he had intended, but it drowned out the word just the same.

"… please," she finished. She shot her father a smile and he realized she teased her parents. She then turned to Braen. "Are you staying here?" Without waiting for an answer she abruptly squealed with joy at a sudden thought. "I need to tell the others!" In a deep and theatrical voice she added, "Even death could not bind the Kraken!"

Laughing at his daughter Alec offered, "You are welcome to stay, Braen. We can patch you up…"

"And draw you a bath," interrupted Mattie.

"… and get you off to wherever you need to go," finished Pogue.

"I think I would like to stay for a while," Braen replied. "I'm in no hurry to leave."

"Excellent," Alec exclaimed. "Then we'll put you in the honorific guest quarters."

"No," Braen pleaded. "I'll stay, but not as anything but a hired hand if it pleases you. I only ask that you not tell anyone that I am here." He spoke the next words with a lump in his throat. "Whatever you do, please do not let Eusari know that I live."

Alec turned somber. He had heard about Braen's betrayal before the fight. His reunion with Queen Hester of Fjorik had been a point of gossip that traveled as far south as the southern continent. "I'm deeply sorry. I know that you loved her."

"I did and I do. I made a mistake that I can never take back."

"Will it make it worse to know that the queen bears your child? She made the proclamation a few weeks ago."

Braen flinched when he heard the news. "At this point nothing can make the situation better, Alec."

"Hired hand," Lord Pogue mused aloud, changing the subject. "What does a title like that look like to the man once renowned as the Kraken King?"

"Well," Braen smiled wearily, "I saw young grapevines when I came up the hill. I'm assuming that you're in need of a vintner if you are to surpass the finest vintage ever made."

"In that case," Alec agreed, "then I'd better hire the man whose consumed more of that vintage than any other man in Andalon." He reached out to embrace his friend but recoiled. "Can we hug after your bath?"

Chapter Eight

Robert approached the ceremonial tent. The last time he had entered, Max stood by his side. During that visit he was cautioned to let Reeves do the talking, but he would handle this negotiation on his own. The Pescari kept Robert's soldiers outside, but allowed Sarai, Amash and Eusari. They did not try and stop the wolf.

Upon entering, he knew immediately the situation had changed. Previously he was forced to sit along the edge of the long ceremonial flame, while Taros rested at the head. This time the seat of honor was vacant, carefully planned with space for all four Andalonians. As his eyes adjusted to the dark, he recognized the shappan and his uncle seated where Robert and Max had sat before. Esterling did not hesitate to choose Taros' previous spot. The others filled in around him.

Each of the Pescari elders were in attendance but none spoke. They stared at Robert expectantly. Then it dawned on him. *I bested their leader,* he thought. *Could that be interpreted as Shapalote?*

He remembered his and the boy's last conversation. During their fight, Robert had told him, "You can't fight me, Taros, because I'm as powerful as you. Stop now and go back to your people."

The infuriated shappan had answered, "I am a god, Andalonian. You are but a man."

Robert's reply had been fierce and direct, if not prophetic. "You're not a god, Taros of the Pescari. You are a sniveling child who lives because I allow it. I own your life."

He leaned toward Amash and whispered instructions. Horslei stared back with surprise but complied. Turning to the shappan he said, "I present to you King Robert Esterling, supreme ruler of Eston and his wife the Lady Sarai. What petition do you lay before the Emperor of the Esterling Empire?"

Teot began to speak but Taros raised a hand to silence his uncle. Without hesitation he responded, "I have many requests of my king and emperor. The first is that he allows me to apologize to the Lady Sarai."

Robert replied, "Proceed."

"My lady," Taros said in perfect Andalonian, "you were injured in my rage and I apologize for my actions. I have wronged you and shall make reparations in the Pescari way."

Sarai did not smile. Her warmness toward the boy had waned long ago. She waved her hand dismissively and said, "You are forgiven, Taros of the Pescari."

Her irritation with the boy caught Robert off guard. Normally she would have answered tenderly no matter her true feelings. He eyed his wife when he asked, "What do you feel is fair recompence?"

"I offer you my protection, my allegiance, and my lifelong devotion. I will die before allowing you to fall prey to enemies or happenstance."

Sarai appeared shocked, repulsed even, but responded with grace. "I accept your vow."

Robert was equally surprised and asked of the shappan, "What are your other requests?"

"When we last spoke, I falsely claimed the status of a god. I know now that I am merely an agent of Felicima's power. I will always bow to her first, but my second allegiance shall be to my shappan."

Robert suddenly understood. "So you've stepped down? You abdicated your seat of power? Introduce to me your true shappan so that I may deal directly with him."

"To do that," Taros said, "you must speak to yourself. I pledge the same protection to you that I have offered the Lady Sarai."

Robert could not believe his ears. It took everything he had not to lose his regal bearing. All he could do was say, "I accept your protection and allegiance. You shall remain shappan of your gathered people, and I accept you as a vassal and a bannerman."

But Taros was not finished. "I also beg of my shappan... my king... to protect the Pescari. Because of me they are a dwindling people, small in number and tired from the journey. Settle them wherever you please, as long as they are cared for with the same love you show Andalonians."

Amash leaned in and whispered to Robert. He nodded and spoke, "It seems that the land alongside a newly formed lake is both fertile and available. I decree that a new city be constructed in Pescari fashion, to be ruled by tribal law and adherent of the will of your Goddess Felicima.

He felt Sarai grab his hand. She squeezed it so hard that he flinched, looking up to meet hard eyes staring back. *She is not pleased,* he thought. *He has harmed her so badly that she cannot truly forgive.* He cleared his throat and continued, "I am fighting a war against my brother. Taros, will you and your best warriors join me in my fight?"

"Yes, shappan. We shall help you win your war."

"Good," Robert stood as if to conclude the meeting. "We march in three days. Let us prepare our people." He strode from the tent and his entourage followed, leaving the Pescari alone without further discussion.

Once they were out of earshot, Amash Horslei commented, "Well now, that was certainly historic."

Robert let out a breath and dropped his regality. Smiling ear to ear he remarked, "Not even King Charles could force the Pescari to recognize his authority. Today is *truly* historic indeed."

"Well done, my love," ventured Sarai. She shouldered past as if in a hurry, and her voice carried the same irritation as before.

"You're not happy, my love?"

She wheeled on him immediately. "Weston should have gone to Amash. It should have been rebuilt and promised to a Horslei, not given to abominations."

"It's okay," her brother said, "Actually, I don't want it. Besides, control over their own city would help integrate them better into the empire."

"No," she said as they approached her carriage. Robert offered his hand which she ignored, choosing instead to grab the frame for balance. "Humanitarianism died with Cassus Eachann. And that man," she pointed toward Taros standing idly by and watching, "will be the downfall of the empire."

"She is angry, husband." Flaya watched the yellow-haired woman mount the carriage as she took her place beside Taros.

"She has every right," the shappan defended. "I wronged her badly."

"She teased you, flirting and leading on your inexperienced heart. She saw herself a queen even then, and queens do not serve, they rule. She never respected you, merely desired your worship."

Taros turned to his wife, placing a gentle hand against her swollen belly. Changing the subject he asked, "Does my son yearn to hunt tonight? He is kicking as if he runs."

She smiled warmly, hiding a private concern behind her eyes. "He knows that Felicima sleeps and so he yearns to learn the ways of the Pescari." She turned again to watch the Andalonians ride away. "He also knows that his father is a wise shappan, who just secured a future for his people."

"Yes," Taros agreed, "the fertile fields of Weston are ours, as promised long ago to our ancestors. Never again shall the Andalonians drive us across the Forbidden Waste." He gently took her hand and she allowed him to lead her away.

As they walked, she felt her belly once more. Her thoughts turned to the night their child was conceived, and of the love they had shared beneath the windmill. With sadness she also remembered the guard and how he had pushed his way upon her, and of her grandfather who forced her to drink the potion of fertility without knowing she had been with two men. *No matter which his father turns out to be,* she thought, *I must ensure that he grows to become a shappan of his people.*

Eusari had remained silent during the parlay with the Pescari, choosing to watch and listen to the strange ceremony. She knew nothing of their ways, finding them interestingly mystical. *They are such a proud and noble people,* she thought. She watched both leaders after the meeting, both Taros with his quiet wisdom and Robert with his regal calm.

During the return procession to Eskera, she mused whether or not to remain allied with Robert. She had yet to form her opinion of Esterling and was impressed by how much he had grown as a king. Braen's retellings of their first meetings painted the boy as intelligent and wise but hurried, focused on one goal and not open-minded to council. Braston had liked the boy, but worried over his lack of maturity and experience. His only weakness, she could tell, was his wife's influence. That woman could prove dangerous now that Braen was no longer a threat to her husband's rule.

Thinking of Braen darkened her mood. She regretted letting him die upon the deck of *She Wolf* despite her confidence that she could have restored him to the living. She had worried over how he would have emerged if she had. *The act would have been selfish,* she knew, *to restore his life in hopes that he would remain my Braen.*

After hearing how the Jaguars had controlled General Lourdes, she was certain she had made the right choice. *All of their subjects lack free will. Wasn't I correct to assume he would have become my slave?* She missed him so much and yearned for his strong arms around her.

She touched her belly mournfully, but then felt awash with contentment. She would move on from her loss in time, but felt satisfied to carry a piece of him inside her womb. A womb that grew daily, she reminded herself. At this rate of expansion, she would soon outgrow her gear. She decided that she would visit a leathersmith in the morning and adapt her armor to accommodate the future growth of the child.

As they entered the city and approached the palace, she spied Hester waiting impatiently for her return. Eusari groaned. Avoiding conversation with her had become the pirate's every goal. The annoying woman started in before she had even removed boot from stirrup.

"Well? Tell me what he said," Hester demanded. "Will he convey me to Fjorik?"

Always concerned only for herself, Eusari thought as she swung her leg over the beast. She stepped down, handing the reins to a stable boy. "He said no."

"That's it?" Her eyes betrayed panic and darted around the yard for sight of the king. "I'll go talk to him myself."

"It won't help." Eusari cautioned, "He can't spare the ships and we're moving out in a couple of days."

"Well, I'm certainly not *moving out,*" Hester yelled. "I'll stay right here until I find a merchant to take me."

"That's fine if you do, but I wouldn't if I were you."

"And why not," she demanded.

"Because Skander is alive and destroying cities. He's probably on his way to Eskera as we speak." Admittedly, Eusari enjoyed the abrupt paling of the northern queen's face, taking enjoyment in the ability to bring her down off that haughty throne. "So, if you'll excuse me," she added, "I must prepare to move out."

Chapter Nine

Skander Braston casually approached the huddled family. After he was close enough to smell their fear, he knelt as a kind father about to correct a toddler. They shrank with revulsion, staring at the gaping hole that once contained his right eye. Their reaction fueled his excitement, precisely why he had chosen not to don a patch.

He felt absolutely giddy during and after the invasion of Soston, and the promise of spoils only heightened his mood. He reached out a cold finger and stroked the cheek of the youngest daughter, caressing her flawless skin. *So milky white*, he marveled. "Yes," he muttered under his breath, "this will do nicely."

"Please let her go," pleaded the father, a merchant found barricaded in his shop. Behind him, Fjorik soldiers ransacked his wares. "She's young and has so much yet to experience."

"Oh," agreed Skander, "I agree completely." He slowly took her hands in his and helped the girl rise. "Artur," he commanded his first mate, "take this vixen to my cabin and ensure she bathes." He licked his lips lecherously as if tasting her flesh. "Add the herbs we plundered from Middleton. They soften the skin so perfectly." He did not watch as his trusted man led her away, he was too busy relishing in her desperate sobs.

"Please," the mother pleaded, "take..."

Skander abruptly shoved his face in hers, cutting off her words. "And do what," he asked, "take you instead?" He laughed in her face as she flinched away, unable to wipe the spittle with her tightly bound hands. "No," he said, "your skin is not suitable for my games.

I would dull my blade carving your leathery creases." He reached down and fondled her breasts. "Alas," he chided, "these would snag even a headsman's axe." He raised his foot and brought it down hard against her chest, slamming the woman to the ground.

He laughed hysterically as she flopped like a fish attempting to breathe on dry land. Her husband moved to protect his wife, slipping from his bonds. He leapt to his feet and pulled a sword from the belt of a shocked soldier. He drew it across the man's neck, but didn't wait for him to fall. Fury drove him toward Skander, still laughing at the gasping woman. The sword came down.

Skander Braston caught the blade with an outstretched hand and drew a knife with his other. The merchant tried to wrestle the sword free, but the northern king gripped it tightly, ignoring the trail of blood cascading down his wrist and forearm. Taking advantage of the man's fear, he moved in closer and whispered, "Such a pity, I was going to let you watch while my soldiers buggered your bride."

The shop owner said nothing as he fell to his knees, clutching at the knife shoved deep into his heart.

"She's all yours, boys," Skander said with a snap of his fingers. Then he walked away, emboldened by her screams as his men had their fun. He smiled at her torment, invigorated by the day.

His pace slowed as he approached the Rookery. His gait changed not out of hesitation, but from a deep desire to savor the coming moment. The addition of Saber Cats had grown into his favorite pastime and was the process that built his army stronger. The first time, in Diaph, he had allowed Artur to awaken the children. But the second time, when the new voice led him to the Middleton Rookery, he gently roused each of the sleeping emotants himself. *Learn their names,* the voice had instructed, *and if they have none, bestow one graciously as their father.*

He found the doors barred from the inside and tensed. Movement within alerted that Falconers remained inside. *Cowards,* he mused, *hiding from my children and me.*

Several Saber Cats stood nearby, magnificently clad in their hooded white cloaks. *So much more regal,* he thought, *than father's Berserkers.* He had all but destroyed that clan, hated by him as relics of the past. Those he hadn't extinguished would be sacrificed soon. *Emotion is their weakness,* he reasoned, *just as it weakened Braen.* He paused and considered another truth, *just as it weakened mother.*

His children moved quickly when he arrived, one of them testing the door with a razor thin tendril of air. After a few moments, he found the lock and tripped the mechanism. Skander motioned for his Saber Cats to enter first. The door swung open and a gust of wind erupted from within.

The blast would have sent them all reeling, but they stood ready with a shield of their own. It absorbed the shockwave, amplified the power, and then directed it back the way it had come. The Falconers within were nearly ripped apart by the powerful explosion. They were quickly bound by Skander's children.

The king of Fjorik strolled into the Rookery as a true conqueror, barely glancing at the bound specters as he headed toward his quarry. So far, the layout had always been the same. The next door would lead to a laboratory and a storage closet where he would find the black beads. He pushed through and, finding that he was correct, laughed at the predictability of the Falconers. The room beyond the laboratory would lead him to more additions to his cadre. He opened the final door and found it starkly empty.

Skander bellowed his rage. *Calm down, Kraken,* the new voice cautioned. *This may be a trick.* He obeyed. *Good,* the voice said, *now check the walls. They are here, I'm sure of it.* He felt along the smooth stone for any kind of break or crevice that would indicate another door. The search took a long time but eventually paid off. Finding a tiny ledge where it should have been smooth, he pressed. Nothing happened.

He called for one of his children, an old woman he had named Ferra. She hurried in and awaited his command. "Feel this ledge with your power, see if you can find a mechanism like the locks on the door."

She did as he ordered, testing it with air. All at once the lights overhead winked out.

"No!" He roared with all of his might, screaming into the darkness. "Make them light up again." Ferra felt around once more and the lights returned. Suddenly, he had a thought. He turned on his heel and hurried into the foyer where the Falconers lay bound.

"Let's play a game," he told them. "One of you is in my mind and I get to guess who." They stared back blankly, unfazed or uncaring what he would do. The voice immediately understood the rules of the game, and cackled along as he began to play. *Have your fun, Skander. They are expendable.* He liked this voice. He had since it first arrived.

He heaved his axe and stepped before the first Falconer. He lifted the weapon over his head and brought it down quickly, severing the neck cleanly. Then he ran from the room joyfully, checking to see if his children had appeared. They had not.

He rushed back into the foyer and severed the head from the next Falconer. One by one he decapitated them and rushed into the room laughing hysterically, hoping to find his missing children. The game provided a rush of adrenaline as he sprayed blood over the white coats of the watching Saber Cats. After he had killed the final specter, he ran in one more time. His children were still hidden from his view.

His anger rose once more. *Skander, that was enjoyable, wasn't it?* He nodded. *There's probably one still hiding in the Rookery. Seek him out, Kraken.*

He returned to the laboratory and raised the axe above his head, wildly cutting the scores of tubing in the ceiling. Clear fluid poured onto the floor, quickly coating the slick surface. Pleased, he strolled toward the closet just inside the lab. As he pulled on the door, a gust of wind sent him sprawling backward. As he crashed into the opposite wall he laughed.

Thank you, voice, he said in his mind.

You're welcome, Kraken, the voice responded.

Skander rose from the ground, grinning wildly at the advancing Falconer. He watched as his opponent gathered the air around him, weaving it into an elaborate net. The northern king quickly made a weave of his own, gathering the fluid now several inches deep on the floor, and spun a tight rope. With force he sent it flying, up and under the surprised specter's hood. While the enemy gasped, Braston shoved the fluid deeper into the mouth and nose of the beastlike man. It took a satisfyingly long time for the Falconer to drown, but, when he finally did, the veil in Skander's mind lifted and revealed to him his children.

There were hundreds in all, with each stone slab occupied by a sleeping subject. The northern king tried to make calculations, but paused in his counting and waited. The voice was much better at these tasks. *Two hundred and ten, Skander. These plus the ninety in Middleton and the fifty in Diaph bring your Saber Cat army to three hundred and fifty.* There was an audible pause and then the voice added, *minus the four you've culled and the twelve the pirates killed in Middleton.* Those, of course, belonged directly to the voice as agreed when he restored their lives.

The voice added, *Go, Kraken, get to know your children and bring them into our fold.*

Chapter Ten

Marcus Esterling knelt before the hearth, staring intently at the fire raging within. Every now and then he would stab the iron poker into the coals, mesmerized by the suddenness by which the glowing sparks turned into ash. The inferno before him was hot enough to redden the skin of his arm, but he refused to back away. The answer he sought, he somehow knew, lay in the flame.

A strong hand shoved him aside and sent the puppet king sprawling onto the stone floor. With seething anger, he watched as Matteas Brohn doused the flame with a piss pot. "For Cinder's sake, boy, it's hotter than a fumarole in here!" To emphasize his anger, the Captain General hurled the empty urinal at Marcus. "Who lights a fire in the summer months?"

"I was testing a theory," the boy-king replied.

"Well test it in your own quarters, there's no reason for you to be here."

Across the room Lord Campton Shol let out an audible sigh of disgust. "Can we get back to business, General?"

"I never stopped," the man snarled as he sipped from his glass.

"Then tell me," the Chancellor continued, "what is your plan for the defense of Eston?"

"I'm not defending it," the military leader responded. He took another sip from his wine and explained, "Prince Robert is moving north. With Weston destroyed he has nowhere to go but Logan. I've moved my army into position there."

"No," Shol disagreed, "He won't choose Logan. That city isn't defensible. There's no wall or armaments to protect him from our attack. If he had any sense, he would attack Norton."

"You know nothing about the boy," Brohn explained. "He was trained in tactics by Lourdes and Reeves. They were notorious for over caution and habitually slow to attack. That cowardice surely passed on to the boy. No," Matteas explained, "he'll camp outside and try to recruit rebels into his army."

"And you'll attack him there?"

"Absolutely not. I'll wait until he tries to load his army onto ships to circumvent Norton. Then I'll flank him and cut off his retreat at the same time."

The plan sounded viable to Marcus and, if Robert did march toward Norton, they were only a two-day's sail from a flanking maneuver there. Faster with Falconer wind.

Shol nodded his acceptance. "When will our fleet be seaworthy?"

"They already are," Brohn revealed, "and the western approach is nearly cleared."

Marcus listened as the older men discussed strategy. He could tell that Shol wasn't convinced, and would probably hatch up a tertiary strategy involving his spies and assassins. But his Falconers had been defeated every time they had clashed with the rebels, and even the Jaguars had proved useless in Eskera. His latest scheme to assassinate Robert had been interrupted, despite using one of his generals against him. *Shol's arrogance will be his downfall,* the king thought, *and his desperation has drawn out impatience as well.*

"He's joined forces with the Pescari abomination by now," the chancellor explained. "He now has three elements at his disposal and your troops won't stand a chance on open field."

Brohn nodded. "Then I'll change it up and try something new."

"I still have a few surprises of my own, with agents planted close to Prince Robert."

There it is, thought Marcus. *The planted agent strategy.*

"My Jaguars must only influence the assassin and this war is won." Shol seemed to relish the surprise on Brohn's face.

The general asked, "And if it isn't?"

"My troops are returning with the Falconers and Jaguars in the east, their job completed against the outlaws in Estowen's Landing."

Matteas slurred his words when he replied, "You mean my troops?"

"Your troops ceased to serve you when they gave their lives. No, this army is mine and it marches west with haste. I will use it to defend the city while yours are in Loganshire. The Falconers and Jaguars I will send further west."

"Get them into the city and my men will aid." Matteas thought for a moment and then added, "Just find me a way to kill the other emotants."

Marcus sat up at that. He had been waiting for his chance to contribute and show his worth as a king, and this was it. "I have an idea on that," he said. "I've been thinking about both the woman pirate and the Pescari boy."

General Brohn whirled around. He was so drunk that he didn't notice when he spilled his wine on the floor. He growled, "You're still here? Why don't you go play and let the adults plan this war!"

Marcus stood and made a show of dusting off his tunic before exiting to the hall. Looking around he realized that he was finally without his Falconer escort. Matteas, in his drunkenness, sent him away without nursemaids. The king couldn't believe his luck, but would only enjoy an hour or so of freedom before Shol figured out the general's mistake.

He hurried to his quarters and pushed open the door with caution, looking around to ensure that no Falconer lurked in the corners. Satisfied, he rushed to the fireplace and felt beneath the mantle. Once he found the ridge, he pressed, releasing a catch that held a certain brick in place. He ripped it free and reached into his hidden cache.

Marcus drew out a leather pouch containing several black beads. He stared at them longingly, yearning to taste their omniscience. It had been too long since the last time and he half feared that another would prove toxic. Worse, he feared it would be fatal. Despite the risk, his body reached out for the euphoric experience.

The general's words echoed in his mind. "Why don't you go play," he had commanded.

The king grinned. "I'll show you play, father," he said sarcastically. "I'll find a way to rid myself of both you and that cursed Shol." He tossed the bead into his mouth and swallowed hard, forcing it down and instantly feeling the effects.

Aware that he was fading, he quickly returned the pouch and pressed the brick in place. His vision swam away, ripped into a current of space and time that swirled like a vortex. He swayed and swooned as he fumbled around the floor, searching for the edge of his bed. His hand grabbed the bedpost and his heart lurched.

Marcus was suddenly in two places at once. He could see the bed in front of him, but his stomach dropped as part of him soared high into the sky. His feet climbed onto the feather mattress and he stood with hands outstretched as his mind flew. Like an eagle, he drifted on the breeze. Eventually he allowed his body to fall flat, head hitting the down pillow and his consciousness given over to the ether.

Far beneath him was a river. *Diaph,* his rational mind informed him. It snaked between tall trees as it flowed eastward. Along its banks marched the army described by Shol. What once were men flanked twenty Falconers riding in pairs atop covered wagons. The hum of the Jaguars within matched the marching feet of the dead. Shol had been correct that not a single fighting man had survived, and they were all within his power. Behind them Estowen's landing once again lay in ruins. He circled several times, breathing in victory as it burned.

Abruptly, a familiar voice drifted along the ocean breeze. He immediately recognized the carefree attitude and debonair demeanor as it traveled across the ocean. The water below became a blur as he raced toward the conversation, quickly making time as he crossed. Soon the horizon ahead became land.

The landscape beneath him transformed and everything on the new continent appeared alien to Marcus. He slowed his momentum to take in the sights. The land was a series of peninsulas with crystal clear water embracing tens of thousands of miles of coastline. Each time the water hit land it was a different formation with chalky cliffs on the islands to the north and rugged limestone in the south. Sandy beaches encircled the southern coast while the north was rockier and more treacherous.

The interior of this new land was strange to him as well. Tall mountains, higher than any in Andalon, stretched high until they licked the sky. Fuming volcanos dotted the countryside, each actively belching fire. The most aggressive, Marcus witnessed, lay upon an island north of the body of land. The scalding smoke and ash bellowed into the sky, forcing him to turn south and drop altitude.

Instead of villages, his eyes found perfectly symmetrical stone buildings. Each were laid out in rows around a central facility, most likely the common living area. Farms thrived on rich soil, and water sprang into the air as if forced from the ground. It rained down upon the lush crops as if the fountains would flow forever.

Windmills rose up just beyond the edges of these communities, with hundreds spinning in time with the breeze. He marveled at the engineering, pondering if each contained mills or pumped the water for the irrigation of crops. He circled several times until the call of voices drew him deeper into the interior.

The city he sought loomed in the distance. Tall structures rose everywhere along streets paved with the smooth stone of the buildings. Horseless carriages drove up and down the arteries, transporting the residents and depositing them in large squares filled with hundreds of people. The sameness of their dress caused uneasiness in the boy.

Each was clad in uniforms of single stitching. Men and women alike wore the pantsuits that stretched from their legs and over their backs. They fastened in the front with buttons and were of five distinct colors: red, blue, white, orange, and yellow. Marcus noticed that they grouped themselves according to their adornment, avoiding those clad differently.

The voices he followed suddenly became clear and his attention snapped to a building at the center of the city. The round structure resembled a rotunda very similar to the legislative house of his own council. He made for the entrance and marveled at the smoothness of the stone. He ran his hand along the seamless wall as he followed the voice of Artema Horn.

Artema Horn stood before a council. These men and women of luxury were clad starkly different than the common people in the streets, adorned with flowing robes stitched with silver and gold. They exhumed an air of wealth and privilege not seen elsewhere on this continent. Horn tired of their questions, but answered with facts. He kept his personal views private and cloaked himself in an air of dignity. Meaning, he was on his best behavior.

He explained that he had been on a twenty-year mission to Andalon. He oversaw the Pirate Guild, watching closely the otherwise unmonitored. He observed and nothing more. His brother, on the other hand, would have much more explaining if he lived.

"Why did you choose now to return?" The question came from Councilor Praedor.

"It was my father's wish. He ordered me to return the moment our system was compromised." Looking around, he added, "Why isn't my father here? Surely you wouldn't convene an inquiry without the Chancellor present?"

"And what precisely was that moment," she asked, ignoring his question, "when you were compromised?"

"When I realized that Campton had assassinated his mentor..."

Praedor interrupted, "Agent Gedon?"

"Yes," Artema replied, "Agent Gedon. When I realized that he had removed Gedon and promoted himself to Chancellor, it all made sense."

"What made sense, Mr. Horn?"

"Why Campton assassinated the Queen Regent Crestal Esterling."

The council members gasped audibly, and several began chattering among themselves. Praedor slammed a gavel and called for order.

Councilor Merek shouted, "That goes against his report!" He held a lengthy dispatch in his hand, waving it over his head. "This says you were present when she was killed, and that you had a hand in the act!"

Artema's features suddenly turned dark, his voice more serious than before. "I was there, Councilor. I watched as Matteas Brohn drew his sword and removed the woman's head." He placed both hands on the banister and leaned forward. "I wore her blood as he wiped his blade."

"How did the boy respond to her death," Praedor asked. "Campton reported that it had been the boy's idea."

"He was truly and utterly shocked."

"Is that when you 'escaped' and went into hiding, Mr. Horn?" The question came from Councilor Wilman. The emphasis on 'escaped' carried a sarcastic tone.

"I left their company the moment we reached the city. My brother had guardsmen posted to arrest me, but I outsmarted them. I made my way back here immediately."

"How did you make it through our security convoys?" Praedor pressed the question, forcing him to either admit that he had ridden a Society submersible, or concocted a laughable story.

"With this." He held up a device from another time and age.

"What," Praedor asked, "is that?"

Artema tossed it over and she caught it. "This jammed the patrolling radars. I had nothing, no identification and certainly no official orders. I spent twenty years as a successful pirate, Councilor. I assure you I had the means to escape. I stole a sailboat and used celestial navigation to make it to the Astian coast. Then I made it overland to Bergin."

"Where did you obtain such a relic from the lost times?" Wilman appeared almost convinced.

"Again," Artema explained, "my father ensured that I had the means. Search his apartments and his home and I am sure you will find several artifacts that should have been seized by the Council Army ages ago."

"Yes, Praedor agreed, "we are aware of his collection. It has been a sore spot for us over many years."

"When can I see him," Artema asked. "When I was arrested, I was trying to contact him."

"You were never under arrest, Mr. Horn." Praedor explained, "We detained you while we investigated."

"Investigated what," he demanded, "my escape from a failed experiment?" He pressed further and added, "My father should have ordered a reset six months ago when I suggested that the Destroyer had awakened! But he ignored my reports and instead ordered my brother and me to handle it." Artema collapsed on the bannister, feigning defeat, and added, "and I tried to handle it by delivering Braen Braston to the Queen Regent. You should be questioning my brother over why he murdered the ruler chosen by this Council."

"We will, Mr. Horn." Praedor looked to the others who nodded. "Rest assured that your father did order a reset and we expect it to commence very soon. You made it out at a good time. With this new information we shall detain your brother and force him to stand trial."

"Then why," Artema demanded, "am I under investigation?"

"You were never under investigation and will not be, unless your brother provides new evidence."

"Then why was I detained?"

"Your sudden appearance coincided with a high-profile death, and we were investigating the details."

"Of whom was I a suspect of murder."

"We've ruled out murder, Mr. Horn, but your father suffered a severe overdose and passed away several days ago."

Artema feigned shock and grief. "My father? He's dead?"

"We are afraid so."

"How?" He let himself appear outwardly agitated, temper welling and voice raising to inappropriate levels. "How do you know it was an overdose? Why did you rule out foul play?"

"Jakata had unfortunate addictions, Mr. Horn. Among those were different types of Astian Pearls. He consumed one of every color, the combination creating a lethal dose."

"My family has served this council for more than twelve centuries! As a loyal member of the most notable house in the Collective, who will you appoint in his place? Campton or me?"

Praedor turned to the others and scanned their faces. When her eyes returned to his, she said, "Oh, that we wish it were neither. But until he is convicted or cleared you are considered as interim councilor. All in favor?" All hands went up into the air. She asked, "None opposed?" When no one did she told him, "Congratulations, Councilor Horn."

Marcus sat up in bed, dizzy from the trance and unfocused. *Artema Horn served me well with his deal,* he decided. *He kept his promise and vowed to back my rule.* He pondered the words spoken of Campton Shol. *Although he never mentioned, he and the Chancellor are brothers and the animosity between them is clear. I cannot trust Shol,* he decided.

He reclined once more and allowed the bead to reclaim effect over his mind. He fought hard to keep his ethereal vision within the walls of the Rose Palace, and searched the usual places for Lord Shol. He found him, just as suspected, speaking with his confidant and lead Falconer.

"Kestrel," he said, "Matteas Brohn has acted just as I'd hoped. He would leave the walls of this securely defensible city and march his army overland to meet both that of Esterling and Skander Braston."

The Falconer was surprised. "Braston? You believe the abomination will sail to assault Eston?"

"I do," Campton replied. "He was risen after the Battle for Middleton, but not by one of our Jaguars. I want to know who had that power if it was not Braen Braston's lover Eusari."

The specter agreed. "What of the forces attacking Estowen's Landing."

"They're securely ours, now that they've been risen, as are those who retreated from Eskera. They no longer owe allegiance to the boy."

"What is your plan with him?"

"Once the drunken general marches the army westward, we'll seize the city with our loyal troops and Falconers. We'll silence the child-king and defend against any attackers left to challenge the walls."

"What of the reset? If your father has indeed ordered it as you suspect, then Astian forces will raze the city to the ground."

"I've taken care of that," Shol boasted, holding a dispatch aloft. "Councilwoman Praedor alerted me to my father's decision, but also to a plan by the Society to ambush his forces on the beach. She intercepted Jakata's requisition for nuclear devices, and replaced it with one of her own design. Rest assured that any landing forces who survive the assault will not have the firepower to defeat our armies."

Kestrel nodded and turned to leave, pausing briefly as he passed the ethereal Marcus.

The king panicked, fear quickening his pulse and dropping his stomach lower in his gut. *Surely, he cannot see me,* he thought. But, as the Falconer turned again, he appeared not to have noticed anything out of sorts.

"I requested a contingent of my other friends," he said. "It will take them several weeks to cross the sea, but they are in route."

"Good," Campton Shol approved. "Alert me when they arrive."

More was said but Marcus was unable to hear the rest. He awoke in his room, staring at the ceiling and finally clear on the course he must take in securing control of the empire. *I must rid myself of Shol.*

Chapter Eleven

Bachir Dilek despised the ocean. Thankfully, he rode in a submersible and not atop the sickening waves. This was his first deployment, the one he had dreamed of since elevation to the Council's Army. They would arrive at their destination in a little over a day. Nervous, he felt compelled to check his gear one more time.

He laid his satchel on his rack and emptied the contents one by one, careful to organize by groupings. Field medicine, compresses, and tourniquets stayed together, as did water purification and rations. He laid the ammunition beside his side arm. His rifle would be issued by the armory just before deployment.

"What's wrong, rookie?" Simcor Bralog stretched on the rack behind him. "Worried you'll forget something?"

"Just making sure everything is ready." He felt the blade of his knife. It would need a few more strokes across the whetstone. "I would hate to get out there and be unprepared."

"Don't worry about anything," his buddy said. "This is a reset."

"Yes, but the last time was seventy years ago." He calculated then added, "And almost nine hundred since *this* continent was reset."

"Did you read over the narrative?"

"Yes. We land at the old port of Boston and then split into teams. You and I move up the river to the capital city of Eston with units Alpha and Bravo. Charlie and Delta will move south to the old Chesapeake Bay and take out the city called Middleton. Then Alpha and Bravo move further up river to take out Norton and Loganshire. Charlie and Delta then move toward Eskera. All teams rejoin in one month in Weston."

Simcor asked, "What about the villages?"

"We leave the villages and the northern kingdom for the reformation crews to reorganize."

"And how do they do that?"

Bachir thought for a long while, then said truthfully, "I don't know."

"They plant new 'warlords' that are actually members of Echo team. They get to stay behind for twenty years and get things up and running again."

"Why would anyone want to stay in this place for twenty years?"

Simcor shrugged and answered truthfully, "I applied."

"You did?" Bachir was shocked. He thought he knew his friend better.

"Yeah, but it doesn't matter. I wasn't chosen."

"Tell me. Why did you want to stay?"

Simcor sat up and leaned in. In a soft voice he whispered, "I can't stand how we live back home, and I want a change of scenery."

Bachir recoiled, shock taking over his face. "Sim! The collective is everything! It's been our way of life for over a thousand years." He looked around, hoping no one had overheard. Treasonous talk on deployment could end with firing squad.

"Don't worry," Simcor said, "it isn't like I'm a member of the Society or anything like that."

"Good," Bachir responded, "because individualism is evil and led directly to the Great Destruction."

"Of course it is." Sim sat in silence for a few breaths then shrugged and rolled over. "I know that."

After he had restowed his gear, Bachir climbed into his rack and opened the mission briefing. He read a few lines and then put it down. "Sim," he said, "some of them have guns this time."

"Only muskets and single shot pistols. They shoot lead balls, and their accuracy isn't worth shit. Now go to sleep."

Simcor waited until Bachir was asleep, then slipped from his bunk. He reached into a space in his mattress and pulled out a device. Making sure no one had noticed, he slipped it into his pocket. Then he pulled on his shoes and made his way to the mess decks. This late past taps, he found them deserted.

He stepped onto a table and placed the device in the overhead, pressing it deep into the insulative lagging and pressing a series of buttons. It beeped once as it armed. Satisfied, he loosened the starter ballast in the nearest light and turned one of the fluorescents a quarter turn. *That should hide the electronic signature for one day or two,* he thought. If anyone detected the beacon, they would chalk it up to an energy fluctuation from the malfunctioning fixture. Once they repaired it and the pulses still continued, they'd find the device and realize that a Society agent had infiltrated the vessel.

He made sure to pick some fruit from a bowl on the feeding line. He wasn't a fan of apples, but needed an alibi for his stroll. It turned out that no one cared that he was out after taps. He ate it anyway to calm his nerves. He returned to his rack and settled down to sleep, practicing the codewords he would need on the beach.

Cassidy stared out at the water, skipping rocks and listening intently to her radio. The device in her hands was archaic. It had been around since before the Great Destruction but was more of a marvel than anything currently in Astia. The Dragon had promised that it would detect a pulse of energy broadcast from a similar device planted on the submersible. Unfortunately, he could not guarantee her a working range, not with the chaotic atmosphere that wrapped the world. Without it, they would have no prior warning of the amphibious assault.

So far, all she had heard was static for an entire week. Interference was worse on Andalon, though not as bad on the east coast as it would be closer to the caldera. Worse, her power cells had expired earlier that morning. Thankfully one of the Society soldiers had brought her spares. She hoped that these would have enough power to detect the beacon.

Something in the static crackled and she abruptly came alert. She strained her ears to hear, but nothing came. She settled back down and picked up another rock to skip. She was mid-throw when she heard the beep. First one came, and then another. They were perfectly spaced five seconds apart, just as described by the Dragon. She hurried off to ready the others.

Chapter Twelve

Braen enjoyed working with the vines. It took his mind off the world's troubles and kept his hands from idleness. *Idle hands crave axes*, his father used to say. He never understood the expression until now. Of course, things had changed when he died, and the only axe he carried was the one he had been given for the afterlife. It was stowed quietly in a trunk under his bed. His new weapons of choice were now twine and patience.

Alec's vineyard sprawled across the rocky mountainside overlooking the southern slope into the southern gulf. The situation was perfect for growing grapes, and the green house was brimming with seedlings ready to plant. Before they could, he would need to finish tying off the trellises.

He had just finished wrapping a top section when a carriage ambled up the road. It traveled at breakneck speeds, nearly careening around a curve. Braen watched it approach, panicking when the passenger made eye-contact. The northerner looked away, afraid to be recognized even here. He picked up the spool and moved to the next post.

Alec was surprised when Mattie told him that Charro Valencia had arrived. "He's here now? Whatever could he want?"

"Well, he joked about wanting a piece of your northern gardener, but then said it's urgent. He's waiting in the atrium," she replied.

The duke set his ledgers aside and hurried to the open-air space. He found Lord Valencia reclining and eating a piece of fruit. "My lord," said Pogue, "how may I be of assistance?"

"We have a problem, it seems. Have you been receiving dispatches?"

"No," Alec replied. "Our post service has been lacking."

"Hmm," the flamboyant duke trailed off. "I'll see about fixing that," he said. "Well, that's why I'm here. It seems that Pirate's Cove has been attacking the south."

"Charro," Alec said, "they attack southern ships all the time, what's the problem? You get your cut of the taxes as well as the insurance monies you claim."

"Cities, Alec. They're attacking cities."

Pogue paced the floor. "No," he said, "Eusari wouldn't allow that. And I know Creech. He wouldn't either."

"Oh, my dear man." Charro looked upon Alec with sad eyes and said, "I'm sorry that you've been so underinformed." He pulled a dispatch from his breast pocket and handed it over.

Alec read it twice and then collapsed into a nearby chair. "It can't be true," he said. "How is any of this possible?"

"I believe I know how," Valencia replied, "and it's a good thing that you're sitting down."

After Charro's carriage had departed, Alec sent for Braen. He came in sweaty and slightly burned from laboring under the sun. Pogue handed him a southern drink called "lemonade," and urged him to sit. He chose the seat directly across.

"Do you treat all your farmhands this good, Alec? No wonder you don't have to engage in slaving like the other lords."

"I do that on principal, my friend." He took a sip of his own drink, something stronger from the islands called "rum." This particular bottle had a drawing of a Kraken on the label which had convinced Alec to try it. After knowing Braen Braston, he would trust anything with the name or logo.

Braston got straight to the point, "Well, you called me here for something, what is it?"

"Several things, actually. First off, Nevra has control of The Cove."

Braen raised an eyebrow, suddenly curious. "How."

"That snake Creech assumed sole control after you died and Eusari chose to lend aid to King Robert. Apparently, Adamas returned to Pirate's Cove and abdicated to Nevra."

"He can't stand him any more than we. That makes no sense."

"No," Alec agreed, "not to us. But it did to Charro."

"How does Charro know Nevra, besides that he's from the southern continent," Braen asked.

A voice from the doorway answered, "We were friends and at one time even lovers."

Braen looked up to see a flawless man with dark skin and brilliantly colored clothing. "You're Charro Valencia?"

Charro nodded, "And you're Braen Braston." He stepped forward but did not offer to shake hands. Neither did Braen. "Your reputation precedes you, Lord Braston."

"Not a lord, barely a Braston."

Valencia let out a chuckle. "Well you certainly don't dress like one." His face again turned serious and he added, "But you most certainly act like one. Thank you for the wine, by the way. Your friend put it to good use," he said and gestured at the property.

Braen nodded and tipped his glass. The contents had already been drained by his thirst. He had enjoyed it, but found the beverage too sweet for his tastes. "This was good, Alec, but I'd like something stronger."

Alec took the glass and set it aside. With a smile he said, "The only wine I have left is piss or vinegar thanks to a certain pirate. You'll have to make do with this." He poured a glass of the Kraken rum.

Braen's eyebrow raised when he caught a glimpse of the bottle. "Really, Alec?" His friend shrugged and he took a sip. *Much stronger,* he thought. He asked Charro, "What's the problem?"

"I believe that Nevra has a bid to take over the empire."

"Doesn't surprise me, but how is he a threat?"

"He owns the industrialized and incorporated sectors of Cargia and now The Cove. And just this week pirates have raided Nazcla and T'laloc."

Braen considered the possible power moves Stefan could make with so many territories. "You don't have to own a monopoly to have power," he said, "only the key parts of one. He has plenty, but lacks any territory in Andalon besides The Cove. He also doesn't have Fjorik, which he would certainly need."

"Actually," said Lord Pogue, "we think he does."

Braen sat up straighter. "What aren't you telling me, Alec?"

The former Captain of the Guard handed over a dispatch. Braen read it several times and then handed it back. "Skander. He's alive as well?"

"Unnaturally so," agreed Charro.

"Isn't all life natural?"

"Not when the power is derived from Jaguars or other unnatural means."

"I've seen Jaguars in action. You think one of them revived my brother?" Braen paused and considered, "How about me, for that matter? How am I here?"

Both men stared at Valencia who poured himself a drink. "Yours was a natural revival from what Alec has told me. You were bonded with the creature which carried you across the sea. As it did, you were restored with your original lifeforce."

The idea calmed Braen a bit.

"Revival is always a strange thing, even when it occurs naturally. But the process becomes very corrupt when the power is stolen. Thankfully, like all science, laws govern the phenomenon." He noticed that both men lacked understanding so he added, "There are rules to tapping into and restoring lifeforce. First, you cannot remove it completely from a living body."

Braen remembered the trick Marita had worked out in Eskera when she removed air from the lungs of Falconers. "But if they're dead you may remove it?"

"Yes and no. Please don't interrupt further because this is a very complex subject." Valencia walked toward the large panoramic window and looked out. "If I'm to tell you this, then I must start at the beginning."

"The southern continent was reset by Astia approximately seventy years ago. My father was part of the reformation team, but chose to stay on past the normal timeframe. He had fallen in love with my mother, a young lady from a village that once stood right over there." He pointed to a valley across the bay.

"He hid her from the Jaguars and kept their marriage secret by disguising her as a house servant. Since he was the overseer put in place by the Astian Council, no one expected that he would harbor an emotant." He looked over his shoulder and said, "An autumn emotant like me."

Braen turned to Alec who shrugged. "That's what he told me earlier."

"My powers are limited, making me difficult to detect. The Jaguars have never suspected, and that's why they allowed me to live and act as the overseer after his death."

"Your father kept you both safe?"

"No. Since he disguised her as a servant, she was picked up one market morning in Cargia and hauled to one of their accursed dens. She's still there, for all I know." Valencia returned to the beverages and poured another. "Father never looked for her because he knew that she was gone forever. Then the pox destroyed the village and a woman brought her son to the manor. She carried him right up to the doorstep. He was a wretched sight, covered in blisters and spiking a very high fever. He was delirious and died right there in her arms."

Braen couldn't believe his ears. He asked, "Who was the boy?" But he already knew the answer.

"You know him as Stefan Nevra, but his name then was Nevriti and his mother Stefanita. Hence the name he's chosen to use in Andalon." Tears filled Charro's eyes as he recounted his story.

"I revived him and lied to my father, told him that the boy had recovered from the pox and that he and his mother were survivors in need of work. He took them on, of course. Labor was even harder to come by forty years ago."

Braen couldn't hide his shock at this news. "You resurrected Stefan Nevra?"

"Yes, Lord Kraken, I did."

"Can a person control a mind once it's been revived?" The possibilities danced in Braen's head.

"Yes, but the hold is stronger if he is unsuspecting of the bond; which Nevriti certainly is not. I made no show of hiding it from him when we were younger." The duke suddenly became very quiet when he said, "I made him love me, don't you see?"

Braen's mind raced as he absorbed the new information. "What is the range of the mind control? Does it work from long distances?"

"That depends on many factors, but the control normally relies on proximity. You can leave suggestions that the host will carry with them, constantly reminding and nudging them like a voice of a distant memory. But even those diminish over time and the host forgets it's a host.

"So you control him now? Isn't that how it works?"

"I could, but only if he and I are in certain range. Normally, I could reach him as far north as Eston, but his mind broke after a..." he paused, swallowing back the memory they shared. After a moment he added, "Unfortunately our bond broke with his mind and I can't send him suggestions like I once could."

Alec asked, "What happened to Nevra? How did his mind break?"

"As lovers we were caught. My father walked in on us when we were sixteen. He chose to punish the son by making a show of beating Stefanita to death in front of my sweet Nevriti. That's when he cracked. Eventually my father sent him away, but I helped him amass his fortune. I gave him simple nudges here and there until he finally blocked me from his broken mind."

Alec finally understood. "That's why you don't challenge his holdings or he yours?"

"Yes, Lord Pogue. Our love has protected each of us over the decades." He finished his drink and added, "Until now." He waived a missive in the air. "He wants me to serve as his puppet over this entire continent. His first step was to send the Berserkers that Alec met on his first day in Cargia. He hired them to weaken the noble class while strengthening my position. Now he's come calling the debt."

"He knows that he can't come near you, or you will control him. But he's counting on your love for him to save what's left of the southern continent."

"Precisely."

One detail troubled Braen. "What are the other rules that you haven't told us? For instance, why does he appear so alive when the other resurrected I've met are decaying as they walk?"

"The second rule is what was once dead cannot fully revive another. We call those revivals 'vagrants.' They are only halfway living, animated husks if you will, with no free will except the narrative their reviver wishes them to believe."

Braen understood. "Nevra revived Skander, but, since he was formerly dead himself, Skander is a vagrant?"

"Like I said before, alive but unnaturally so."

Alec appeared confused. "How does he have the power to revive?"

"Apparently he always did. He is like me, an autumn emotant with limited power."

Braston was eager for more, swallowing the lesson as quickly as his rum. He refilled his glass and asked, "What is the third rule of revival?"

"Simple, Lord Kraken. Whatever revives itself loses power until killed again and revived unnaturally."

Braen tried to swirl the dark liquid in his glass, using only his mind. Just as the past dozen attempts, this failed as well. "You mean me," he whispered. His powers were truly gone forever.

"Yes, Lord Braston. I mean you."

Braen swallowed down the dark liquid in a single gulp. *Then no one should fear me any longer. Without my powers, I am once again but a man.* Before his powers had emerged, he was a warrior in his own right. He shrugged and reconsidered the need for magic. Although useful, it had proven unpredictable at best, manifesting sporadically depending on his emotional state at the time. *I won't need powers to defeat Nevra, but I will need them against my brother.* He cleared his throat and asked, "Lord Valencia? Will you help us defeat Nevra and save Andalon?"

"I have no choice, but first we must save Cargia from impending attack. Nevra demands my answer to his proposal by midnight tonight." To Alec he said, "If I do not respond, his forces will attack and destroy both of our villas."

"Then we fight."

"Yes!" A shout entered the room from the hall. The door flew open and Marita literally flew in on the breeze with her feet hovering inches off the ground. "Who do we get to fight?"

"No one," answered Alec, who quickly tried to usher his daughter from the room.

Turning to Lord Valencia, Braen said, "Tell the poxy bastard that you're in and you'll rule the southern continent. Hopefully he's here in person so that you can retake control and we can end his charade."

"And if not, Lord Kraken?"

"Then we'll track him down. I've taken The Cove once and I'll do it again."

Chapter Thirteen

Eusari had enough of horseback. She had spent far too many years at sea to continue this charade for Esterling. His army moved too slowly for her liking and the boy showed no urgency whatsoever. There had to be a better way. She spurred the horse to a gallop and rode toward Amash. She instantly regretted the new pace, as she bounced awkwardly atop the beast. She pulled reins and made do with a trot until she joined up with Braen's friend.

Unlike her, the man appeared at home upon a steed. His overly relaxed posture grated against her mood. She pulled alongside, pointed to her ship downriver and admitted, "I regret not riding aboard *She Wolf*." Indicating her mare she added, "The waves are much more predictable than an animal with a mind of its own."

"I beg to differ. It seems we have different problems with the same outcome," Horslei mentioned with a grin. "I can't stand ships but I'm at home upon a horse."

"Aye," she replied, "that's your upbringing. You're a Horslei through and through."

"During our journey together, Alec had a wonderful time at my expense. He teased me for my weakened stomach and shaky sea legs, but I promise to go easier on you." With tender understanding he added, "But you mustn't worry, we'll reach Weston very soon and you can return to your ship."

"How much further?"

"Honestly, we should be able to see it by now."

"Surely it can't be as King Robert described?"

A voice from behind turned both their heads. "Oh, but there's nothing left, you see?" The man who approached was on foot, one of the camp followers who tagged along from Eskera. He was balding with long combed-over strands atop his head. He walked slightly hunched and was inauspicious, yet somehow managing to carry himself with regal dignity.

Horslei narrowed his eyes at the man, either sizing him up or trying to place where they had met. Eusari jumped, suddenly startled when Amash swung down from his horse and wrapped the man in a tight embrace.

"Philip!"

The man was pleased to be recognized and said, "Hello, Amash. I had hoped you would remember me."

"I could never forget you!" Turning to Eusari Amash explained, "This man raised me! He was my tutor and my mentor growing up. Eusari, meet Philip, house steward to the Horslei family!"

"It's my pleasure," managed Eusari. She nodded rather than shift her weight to grasp forearms. Her bladder couldn't take another change of position.

Amash couldn't contain his excitement. "You made it out and followed us? Why would you walk all this way?"

"When Weston was destroyed, I had nothing, not even memories. All that changed when I saw you and your sister in Eskera. Although I couldn't get close enough to speak to either of you, I chose to keep my promise to your father. I followed along in hopes that we would meet."

Mention of his mother perked Amash's mood. "What promise did you make?"

"Oh, several. Too many to speak aloud all at once I'm afraid."

"Take my horse," Horslei insisted.

"I couldn't..."

"Yes, you can, and you will. He half lifted the man into the saddle and led him away. "Let's catch up to Sarai! You have to see her!"

Eusari watched them depart, the older man laughing and nodding as Amash gushed about past memories. A voice from behind turned her head.

"Why don't you get yourself a wagon," the northern queen asked.

"Don't need one." Eusari spurred her horse to quicken its step.

Hester signaled the driver who picked up pace to match. "Oh please, it's obvious that you're in pain atop that thing. I'm surprised you haven't wet yourself."

Well shit, thought Eusari, who had very nearly done just that when she galloped. *Now I can't get a wagon no matter what I decide. She'll think I heeded her advice, and that will empower her further.* She pulled reigns forcing the driver to do the same. She then turned the nose of the beast, facing the woman squarely. "What do you want?"

"Conversation is all."

"I doubt that," Eusari muttered. "You hate me, and I resent you." She asked, "What could we possibly have in common that would make enjoyable conversation?"

"That may very well be true, but I'd say we have a lot in common." She placed one hand on her swollen belly and pointed the other toward a wagon further ahead carrying Sarai. "She does as well, but she's making a point of snubbing us both."

"Not all women welcome gossip as a pastime."

Hester laughed with sincerity for the first time since arriving south. "It isn't that. Haven't you noticed that she avoids everyone? She hides in that wagon more and more each time we camp."

"I'm sure she's tired. She's further along than us."

"She's a snob and she's snubs both of us despite our station. She does this as a political statement." Hester sighed then added, "I don't expect *you* to know this, and this isn't a slight so don't get your knickers in a wad, but wealthy and regal born women have a duty to entertain court. She avoids it like she doesn't know it's expected."

Eusari spurred her horse to a trot and the driver kept pace. "I did notice now that you mention. She doesn't even have ladies in waiting."

Hester laughed, "Nor do I at the moment." She let her guard down for a brief moment, letting out a bit of her true personality.

"The best I've been able to muster was Cedric bringing me a wet towel for my neck."

Eusari tried not to giggle at the conjured image, but failed miserably. She actually smiled. *Crap, now she'll think we're friends,* she mused. "Tell me about Cedric. That man annoys the hells out of me. Has he always been touched in the head?"

Hester fell quiet for a moment as she pondered a distant memory. "There's nothing wrong with his mind." She paused then reconsidered, "Well, nothing physically. He was the odd child when we were younger, but certainly not *touched* as you called him." She shifted her weight in the wagon, moving to a more upright position and continued, "He's a nobleman like Braen." Her voice choked when she mentioned their former lover. "In Fjorik fighting is everything, and boys train on weapons as soon as they can lift a wooden sword. Except Cedric. None of the noble children liked him. He was obsessed with the sea and hung out around the docks all day, chatting with sailors and fishermen. One day Braen followed, curious to learn what he did instead of training in weapons."

"They weren't friends at the time?"

"No. Braen also picked on him at first. Whatever happened that day changed Braen and bonded the two permanently. They were inseparable and Cedric became off-limits to the other boys. Even Skander left him alone out of fear of his older brother. Everyone just accepted his pirate persona after that."

"What about Sippen?" Eusari spied the little man, riding in a wagon and scribbling furiously on his slate. "How did they meet?"

"That's a story you'll have to ask Sippen, but it was pretty much the same. One day Braen brought him to the castle and decreed that he would have access to the library. He also made it quite clear that no one may touch a hair on his head or whisper an ill omen toward him. They've been best friends ever since."

Eusari asked the question that she had avoided for so long. "Did you really love him, Hester?"

The woman turned her blue eyes toward Eusari, each glistening with moisture. "Didn't you?" She sighed and wiped the tears. "But that doesn't matter now. He's gone and Skander lives. The gods are cruel to curse us so."

"I could have brought him back." She uttered the words aloud for the first time since Middleton.

"I know. Sippen explained it to me." The northern queen moved closer and reached from the wagon, gently touching Eusari on her scarred hand. "You made a difficult choice, and no one blames you. He would walk and talk like our Braen, but he wouldn't be him."

Eusari turned slowly and their eyes met for the first time in solidarity. "You really mean that?"

"I do," Hester replied honestly. "No matter which of his children is born first. It is inconsequential compared to one fact – a part of Braen will live on in this world."

Eusari nodded but could no longer continue the conversation. *Gods forbid we become friends,* she thought. Without another word she spurred to a gallop, riding hard to catch up to Amash.

Sarai watched the world pass by her wagon. The scenery reminded her that she was home, and that Weston would emerge on the horizon at any hour. Except it wouldn't. The city of her childhood was gone forever, replaced by a lake of shimmering despair filled by the tears of what remained of her people.

Footsteps announced a rider approaching. The old man was escorted by her brother who led the horse by the reins. Amash lit up when he saw his sister watching. He waved wildly, unable to contain some private excitement. She did not return the wave. She pulled the curtain across the opening to the wagon and shut out the world.

Most of her luxuries were gone, buried at the bottom of Lake Weston or left behind in Eskera. What she did have was a hand-held mirror that she resented more than any other possession in the wagon. She gazed into it, taking in her hideous reflection. *He burned away your beauty,* her voice reminded. *He took it away forever and now he rides with you as Robert's ally.* She ran a timid finger along the scars, nothing more than raised reminders that misgiven kindness is returned as pain.

A rapping on the wagon startled Sarai and she nearly dropped the looking glass. She pushed the curtain aside to see that Amash had closed the distance.

"Look who I found," he said.

She peered closer at the balding man atop her brother's horse. *Your house steward,* she reminded herself. "Aw, Philip," she said, surprised the man had made both journeys from and to Weston, "I'm so happy you survived!"

"Yes, my lady," he replied, "I narrowly escaped the city when it burned."

"Well," she said, "I'm glad you're here. I'll make certain that you're restored to our household. Although," she wondered, "I'm sure that the Rose Palace already has a steward so I can't guarantee you that role."

"It's no matter, your highness. I will be happy to continue serving your family no matter the capacity."

Horns blew in the distance, alerting the column they had reached their destination. "Thank the gods," she said. "I thought we'd never make it. I've ridden enough and wish to walk." She held a hand out for her brother, and he helped her step down from the wagon. Looking around she asked. "Where is my husband?"

"He's there, Sarai." Amash pointed toward the edge of a shimmering lake. Robert sat atop his destrier with head down and conversing with General Titus.

"If you will both excuse me, he and I have much to discuss." She parted ways with the pair and approached her love.

Seeing her approach, Robert swung from the saddle and handed the reins to his military commander. He took her into his arms and hugged her tightly. "I'm so sorry, Sarai," he said with true compassion in his voice. "I know this was your home."

"It no longer matters," she said dismissively. With a tender smile she added, "My home is wherever you take me. I will never leave your side, my dear." He wrapped the embrace tighter and kissed her deeply. After a few seconds she pulled away playfully and whispered, "Kings and queens don't make out in front of their kingdom, silly."

"I'm king," he explained, "and I'll kiss you whenever and wherever I choose."

"And I'll let you," she replied. "I hate to change the subject, but we need to talk. I've been doing a lot of thinking."

His face darkened with concern as he asked, "What's wrong? Are you and the child well?"

"We're fine," she promised, "but I don't like those pirates hanging around. You need to send them away on a mission. Give them something to keep them busy elsewhere."

"But Amash trusts them," Robert protested.

"My brother is too close to them. He doesn't know what they're capable of like you and me. He even doubts the loyalty of Percy Roan, and I like him."

"I mistrust him as well."

"You shouldn't. Pull him close and heed his council. He was brilliant and helped Cassus Eachann rise. Get rid of the pirates," she insisted, "before Braen Braston arrives."

"But what if it truly is Skander? He has the same power as his brother, and dispatches report he's looted every city along the coast."

"Don't be foolish," Sarai warned. "Skander Braston doesn't have the power of his brother. If one of them died in Middleton it surely wasn't the *Kraken King.*"

"I don't understand how you can be so confident," Robert protested.

"Think about it. He abandoned you to chase after Eusari, then mysteriously died at the hands of his ally Adamas Creech. No, husband. She and that damnable Hester are in cahoots. Everyone reported that they were the only witnesses to the death. Then the pair dumped his brother's body over the side. Isn't it odd that they both bear Braen's children? They're both his concubines and will betray you to him."

Robert's features darkened, "You really think it is Braen attacking the cities?"

"Yes," she agreed. "Only *he* wields power over water and has an army of autumn emotants. He is your enemy now as always."

"You may be right." Robert shook his head, trying to clear the fog. "I'll send them to Logan before we change course to Norton. Then I'll camp deeper inland on the prairie so that he can't wield water against me." He hugged her close and then released, darting a glance to a hastily erected tent. "I've got to go. I'm meeting with my council."

"Just remember," she said, "don't trust the pirates."

Eusari observed the queen walking away from her brother and steward. Only after Sarai had departed did the captain approach. She listened to Amash apologize to the man as she rode up.

"I'm sorry," he said. "I thought she'd be as excited as me. It must be the pregnancy," he explained, "or stress over Weston's destruction."

"It's quite alright," Philip replied with a smile. Despite the reassurance, his eyes betrayed his hurt.

"Amash," she pointed at the king and queen engaged in a tense conversation at the water's edge, "I know she's your sister, but she has too much influence over him."

Horslei shrugged, "They're husband and wife. She'll always be his foremost advisor."

They were interrupted by the appearance of sails downriver. Eusari pointed, "There's *She Wolf*." The ship made a slow approach, dropping anchor just off shore. Soon the other ships in Robert's armada followed her into the lake. Eusari swung her leg over the side of her beast and dismounted, placing a hand on the mare's back to steady her balance. With a pat she said, "Thank you friend, but next time I'm riding my ship."

Amash suddenly pointed. "Eusari, if you want to speak with Robert, now's the time." He pointed to a tent the servants had hastily erected. "It appears that he's convening counsel." They watched as General Titus waved over an unassuming man with spectacles and the two entered behind Robert.

The old house steward stiffened. "Since when is Percy Roan part of his counsel?"

"That's a mystery to me. They met in Eskera, I heard."

"The man is knowledgeable for sure, but his friends are the wrong sort. They're snakes," Phillip warned, "the kind that will strike the moment you reach tall grass."

Amash patted him on the shoulder. "I'll keep an eye on him. In the meantime, make yourself comfortable and stay close. I want to speak with you more."

Eusari followed Braen's friend to the tent and entered without trouble. No one tried to prevent her entrance, meaning she had made her way into Robert's trust.

"Ah," the king said upon seeing her, "just who I'd hoped to see. How long until your uncle arrives?"

"Caroline said they are two days out," she answered.

"Good. I want to march shortly after they arrive."

Amash spoke up, "Which direction? To Eston, I hope."

"Not yet," the king said. "My army isn't big enough. I need to recruit loyalists from Logan." He turned to Eusari, "You hail from Loganshire, do you not?"

"Aye," she felt suddenly uneasy as she worked out his plan in her mind. "But it's been many years since I've returned."

"True," agreed Robert. "But your uncle is well known in the city and the surrounding towns. I need you and him to instigate a revolution in Logan. Draw as many of my supporters as you can from the shadows, and bring them to me south of Norton."

"I will try," she answered. But she knew better; most of the people of Loganshire were still thankful for the Empire's protection from Fjorik. *There will be few supporters in that town,* she thought.

"That's all for now," he said. "I'll summon you after he arrives."

With that she was dismissed from his counsel. She had not secured his trust after all.

Chapter Fourteen

Marcus Esterling stared at the Falconer stationed by the door. Its mere presence insulted the king, who felt like he lost more of his power each day. The eerie beast-like man stared back, watching him like a hawk. *Really,* he thought, *what kind of king requires a babysitter?*

All of a sudden, the specter jumped up from his seat and strode from the room. Marcus perked up. He waited a moment to see if he'd return, then leapt from the bed and raced to the door. It was unlocked. He moved to leave, but then remembered the beads. He rushed to his hiding place and drew one before the specter returned.

He stared intently. The spheres captivated his attention each time he gazed upon their perfection. They were marvels not only in the powers they gave to him, but also in their symmetrical roundness. Once again, he yearned to feel the effects and craved the omniscience. He desired the freedom to fly. He popped it in his mouth and swallowed.

The way the specter had rushed from his room left him wondering, and Marcus was not one to ignore curiosity. Knowing he still had a few moments before the effect took his mind, he hurried into the hallway. No Falconers stood guard. He ran up one level to confirm and found the same. *If they are called away, then so was Matteas,* he thought. Now would be the perfect time to search his mentor's quarters for leverage he could use against him later.

He moved quickly toward Brohn's chamber and lifted his hand to knock. If the captain general were present, he would need an excuse to be out of his own rooms without supervision. He hesitated, feeling a stir in his mind as the bead took full effect. His vision swam and his body swayed. *No,* he pleaded, *not yet.* He willed the effects of the drug to hold off and succeeded in existing in two places at once.

The door between him and the room seemingly disappeared. He reached out and touched solid oak, so he knew that it remained, but could not argue that he saw right through it. On the other side the Captain General slept in his bed with several empty bottles of 732 lying about. He had obviously passed out from an evening of drunkenness.

The man was stripped to the waist and his sword belt lay on the floor. Marcus couldn't believe his luck. He watched him sleep for a few moments, thinking of all the times Brohn had called him "boy" or "princeling." This pitiful excuse for a man had lain with his mother, dirtying and defiling her. Worse, he had left a bit of himself inside to create Marcus. This sot represented every failure in his plan to rule the empire. He opened the door and walked in.

Thinking of the two writhing around while his true father, the great Charles Esterling, slept in the next room sickened Marcus. He bent down. He could see Matteas' lips on his mother's tasting and leaving marks. He picked up the discarded sword belt. He could hear her moans of pleasure as Matteas coaxed her into betrayal. The blade slid from the sheath without making a sound. He visualized the moment when Matteas penetrated what belonged to King Charles.

Marcus hadn't realized he even held the sword in his hand. When he did, he released it and stepped back, staring dumfounded as it protruded from Brohn's back. The general writhed, groaning and trying to reach the blade but unable in his drunken state. He was pinned to the bed like a bug on exhibit. Marcus drew his own dagger and leaned in close.

"I hate you," he said as he drew the blade across Matteas' neck. He watched as the sheets turned crimson, bleeding out traitorous blood that dripped onto the floor below. The king reached down, balling up the corner of the bedding and stuffing it into the general's gaping mouth. Smiling, he dragged the blade, sawing furiously until the head rolled onto the floor. "Now you two finally deserve each other," he said as he stood over a shocked and very dead Matteas Brohn. "And your heads will be buried together. Your bodies," he said, "I will keep apart as you should have before."

Marcus turned from the room, aware that the bead had effect, yet somehow still sensing the world around him. His feet guided him down the hall while his mind sorted through every conversation in the palace. One in particular mattered very much to the king.

Lord Campton Shol fed Reaver a mouse. He marveled at how she loved to eat the heads first. He watched for a moment then went back to his business. Everything was falling apart around him, and he was out of time. There was no way to reverse the decision of his father. The troops were on their way.

The door to his office opened and he looked up to find Kestrel, his childhood friend. When they had both volunteered for the oracle, Campton's father had forbidden him from joining, and Kestrel had gone on alone. His friend had quickly proven powerful, thriving as part of the spring coven. When Shol learned that he transcended into a Falconer, he brought him to Eston straight away. It almost felt like he had his friend back. Almost.

It was Kestrel's Ka'ash'mael that gave the final clue to stopping the Destroyer, and his final words were written on the parchment Campton held in his hand at this very moment. He waved it in front of him now. "Our plan is working," he told the Falconer. When his friend said nothing he continued, "That drunken general has no chance of winning this war, not while the true Esterling heir marches toward Norton." He laughed at Brohn's ignorance, "That fool believes they're headed for Logan."

"And that boy," he laughed again, "can you believe his audacity? He truly believes that we've no idea he's stolen the oracle beads. He has no idea that we are alerted every time he consumes one within the palace or that you watched him eavesdrop on our planning."

Kestrel still said nothing, but his muscles had begun to twitch.

Shol asked his old friend, "What is wrong?" He didn't respond.

In a trembling voice Kestrel slowly replied, "The collective demands my attention, my brother, and I must suppress our connection while the murder convenes."

"What are you saying? The council has called a murder of the Falcons?" Campton froze in place, suddenly very worried. He and his friend shared a strong bonding, but he could never override the collective shared by the Falconers. As such, Kestrel would always be a slave to the Astian Council. "The council hasn't called a full murder in nearly seventy years, not since your brethren were called upon to aid in the south."

"I cannot protect you from what is about to occur," his old friend lamented, "but I will meet up with you again after our business concludes. Until that time comes, know that this is in accordance with my foretelling. No matter what," he insisted, "you must find your way to the Rookery."

At the mention of the prophecy, Campton's eyes fell to the parchment in his hand. He gripped it so tightly that his forearm began to tremble, causing him to splay his fingers and let the crumpled document fall to the table. He stared at it then, wadded and discarded like the time he had wasted in Andalon. When he again looked upon his friend, several other Falconers had joined him in the doorway. After a moment more, at least twenty stood in the hallway. They said nothing, only stared.

"Kestrel," Campton asked, playing along and thankful for his friend's warning, "what is going on?" He was suddenly very afraid in that moment. Even Reaver screeched uncomfortably. *What if it doesn't go as he predicted?*

"Campton Shol, son of Jakata Horn," they all said in eerie unison, "your trial before the Astian Council has commenced. They see through our eyes and hear through our ears."

"You can't be serious." He moved a couple of steps backward and they each took one forward. "I need their guidance, yes, but why did you say trial? I need an update on my father's decision to reset."

"There will be no reset," came a voice from the hallway.

Campton watched Marcus Esterling approach the entry. In one hand he held a bloody knife. His other held a severed head that suspiciously resembled Captain General Matteas Brohn. The boy had finally lost his mind to the bead.

"The troops will arrive in three days, but the Society has set up an ambush." The boy strolled into the room with glazed over eyes, looking but not seeing. "Your father's plan to destroy Andalon has failed, and I alone must correct the course of this war for the Astian Council."

"What are you talking about, you wasted piss pot of a king?" He eyed the boy, wishing that the hatred in his eyes could strike the imbecile dead. "You wouldn't even be king if it weren't for me. I could have chosen anyone," he said. "I could have even done the job myself!" Pointing at Brohn's severed head he added, "Kestrel, he's killed Matteas Brohn. You assured me the drunkard would keep the boy out of my way while we regained order." The lead Falconer did not move. "Kestrel! Do something!"

"I am no longer your puppet, Lord Shol," Marcus said with muscles twitching violently.

"He's…" Campton stammered, feigning sudden understanding. "He's taken a pearl."

In unison the murder of Falconers spoke once more, the reverberation of their voices causing Campton to place his hands over his ears. "You will listen to the boy," they said, "and you will know his words as truth."

The king suddenly fell to the floor and seized violently, dropping the head of Matteas Brohn. It rolled to where Shol stood, coming to a stop with open eyes staring up at the chancellor.

And then the boy entered Ka'ash'mael. "Two of water but one remains," he said from his trance. "Only the son of Esterling can slay him in time." The episode ended almost as soon as it began. The boy lay on the ground unmoving but breathing. He had survived the prophecy.

When the murder spoke once more it was in a woman's voice. "Your actions and the testimony from the boy speak of your violation. You seized power over influence and changed the prophecy."

Campton recognized the voice. "Councilor Praedor," he screamed, "that's not true!"

The Falconers spoke the judgement of the council in unison. "Campton Shol," they said, "You are found guilty and the punishment for insolence is banishment. You may never return to Astia."

Kestrel retrieved Marcus Esterling from the ground, scooping him into his arms, bearing him as he faced his former friend. In the voice of Praedor he said, "You nearly destroyed us with your arrogance."

Four Falconers seized Campton, dragging him from the palace and casting him into the streets.

Chapter Fifteen

The waning moon hung in the sky over Cargia, reflecting off the water that enhanced its shimmer. Other than the lapping of waves against the dock, the only other sounds came from the distant taverns. The soft music cascaded through the streets and provided a soft background for the hell awaiting the town. Lord Valencia watched as the pirate captain stepped off *Aggressor* and approached him on the pier.

He asked, "You have a message from Charro Valencia?"

"I am Charro Valencia," the duke responded. "I'm not accustomed to speaking with unnamed pirates. To whom do I have the displeasure with speaking?"

"I am Captain Adolphus Dominique," the man replied then chuckled with merriment. "How did my last shipment of laborers fare on your plantation, your lordship?" When Charro didn't answer, the pirate added, "Well, it appears that when Nevra calls upon the southern continent, you lords actually jump to his beckon." He stared at the man's clothes. "You aren't dressed like a lord."

"A lord generally wouldn't sully himself by walking the docks alone at night. Is he necessary?" Charro pointed to a sharpshooter in the crow's nest. Alec had shown him the new weaponry as well as its capabilities. The muzzle was pointed directly at the Valencia's chest.

The pirate laughed long and hard. "He's just watching." He stepped closer to the man. "Lord Nevra told me to pass on his deepest regards."

"Get to the point, Captain. What does he want of me?"

"Only the usual deal with the devil. You'll have supreme rule over the southern continent except in matters in which he feels need to intervene. You will pay his tax rate of twenty-five percent on all bribes you receive while in his graces."

"That's preposterous. He already owns everything you see here," he waved his arms at the harbor. I'll give him fifteen."

Dominique leaned in. "You'll give him twenty-five percent and that's that. If not, we'll attack tonight and take what we want. Then he'll leave me in charge of *everything you see here.*"

Charro nodded. "Twenty-five percent it is."

Adolphus smiled. Several of his teeth had loosened from his gums and dangled in his mouth. He added, "It just went up to thirty."

"Thirty it is," Valencia said with disgust as a tooth sprang from the pirate's mouth, landing on the ground between them.

"I thought so. Sign this." He produced a parchment from his jacket and handed it to Charro.

The lord signed it and thrust it out like he held a venomous snake. "If that's all, then I'll be making my way to the manor."

"That's all." Adolphus dismissed him with a wave of his hand before turning to make his way up the plank.

Before he made it across the brow, Valencia called out. "Why didn't he come himself?"

Dominique paused, "He said that if you asked that question, to reply that you know why." Once he was aboard, he waved his hand in the air and thirty pirates ran past him onto the pier. "Don't rough the place up too badly," he shouted to them, "just do enough to make our point."

Charro noticed that they each carried rifles. After the raiding party disembarked, he ran as fast as he could after them. When they turned right on the wharf, he turned left and slipped into the shadows.

Braen watched from cover as Charro Valencia approached. "Pogue," the man whispered loudly, "Braston!" With two large hands the Northman grabbed the Southerner, pulling him to the rear of a large crate.

"Quiet," he commanded.

Alec stepped out from behind a coil of mooring lines. In his hands he held one of Sippen's long rifles. He set it atop the box and covered the wharf, scanning for trouble. In a whisper he asked, "Did you sign the agreement?"

"I did. But he sent soldiers into the city to ransack."

"I saw that, but couldn't count how many there were." Braen reached for the axe at his side, slipping it from its holster and gripping with both hands.

"About thirty, I'd venture to guess."

Braen relaxed. "That's a small raiding party. He sent them to make a statement." He stood and tapped Alec on the shoulder. "Let's go," he said.

"Wait." Alec had lowered the rifle, but wore a worried look. "Where's Marita?"

Braen pointed to a stack of barrels. "She was behind those."

Alec rushed over, clutching the rifle as if it were about to be ripped away. Braen noticed that Pogue had a noticeable limp when he ran. He was losing a step with age. "She isn't here, Braen."

Braen felt blood rush to his cheeks as a moment of panic set in. "She wouldn't," he asked, "would she?"

Alec nodded, "She would."

"Ship or city," Braen asked?

"There's nearly a full crew on *Aggressor,* so that's my guess."

Charro stared at the two with a fearful expression. "Shall I wait by the wagon?"

"Not unless you want to be gutted," Braen warned. "Stay right here and don't move. One of us will return for you."

Alec pointed down the pier. "I see her."

Braen turned and raised a spyglass toward the ship. Marita strolled boldly across the brow.

Marita stepped onto the deck of *Aggressor*. The boards creaked, even under her light weight, and one of the night watchmen called out. "Intruder on the quarterdeck," he shouted, rushing forward with pistol pointed at her chest.

Six sentries rushed from their posts with pistols also drawn. Marita giggled. She liked these odds.

One of the men called out to the others, "It's just a wee lassie, mates! Stand down."

"A wee lassie with swords, Jerome!" The first sentry to alert her presence advanced, poking the snout of the pistol into her chest. "Place them on the ground, dearie."

"These?" She drew them out slowly and held them in the air. "Why are you afraid of these if you men have pistols?"

All the men on deck laughed except the one called Jerome. He appeared confused. "Wait a minute, fellas. She knows what pistols are."

"Yes," she said with a giggle, "I do." She suddenly sprung into the air, spinning with blades outstretched. Every topside man fired where she had stood, sending their projectiles below her boots. As they moved to reload, she continued to fly, this time in a wide arching circle. She moved so quickly they felt rather than saw the blur breeze by. The only evidence that she passed were their hands, still grasping the pistols and laying atop the deck.

Once the men were disarmed, she squatted into the stance Calm the Waters. She had once called this pose Shit your Britches, but that was before Alec's lessons. Now she was a journeyman in their art, and much wiser. She flowed across the deck like water, fluid in her motions and dancing between the men. One by one they collapsed on the deck, both shocked and surprised by the quickness of the tiny girl.

"Look out!" The call came from the pier and Marita saw Alec pointing to the crow's nest. *Oh yes,* she thought, *the man with the rifle.* She heard the shot ring out and stepped to the left. Time slowed around her as she did. The bullet buzzed by like a heavy bumble bee, lumbering to its next flower and too encumbered with pollen to bother with her.

A wisp of air shot toward the man, wrapping around his neck. He grasped at nothing with both hands, dropping his rifle thirty feet to the deck. She yanked and he tumbled after, landing with a thud. Marita still controlled the air around her and glided toward the main hatch before the man struck the boards. She squatted behind the lid and waited.

It flung open and several more men rushed out, each armed with either pistol or blade. Her swords rested in her lap as she waved at the newcomers. "Hi, boys!"

They stared back and forth between their dead shipmates and the little girl smiling and sticking her thumb into the air. The firearms exploded in unison as she slid across the deck, passing underneath the slow-moving bullets. When she popped to her feet her blades were ready.

"It's a Dreamer!" The shout came from the captain's quarters behind her. She turned to see Adolphus Dominique standing by the door. "Sound the recall," he ordered his men.

"How about we don't," she said with a grin, sending out wisps of air that securely bound his hands and feet. By then Braen and Alec, out of breath, panted their way onboard. They arrived just as fifteen more men emerged from the hatch beside her.

"Marita," Alec shouted, "this wasn't the plan!"

"No," she responded, quickly tying up the others to match their captain, "this is a much better plan, but you never asked my opinion."

Braen stepped forward and surveyed the scene. Twenty-three men struggled against their invisible bonds and eight lay dead on the deck. In a calm voice he asked, "What's your plan, Marita?"

"Well," she explained, "they never would have allowed *Desperation* or any other Cargian ship sail into The Cove. So now we can sail in on *Aggressor*. Surely they won't keep Captain Dominique out."

Awe passed between Braen and Alec as they exchanged nods. "Let's secure these men below decks and await the others," Braen said. "Nice work, Marita."

Chapter Sixteen

Moonlight illuminated the bay south of Estowen's Landing. The site was perfect for an amphibious attack. The beachhead was two miles wide and the swath of sand cut several hundred feet into the timber line. Just offshore the shallow waters abruptly fell away, easily accommodating submersibles. They arrived a few hours after midnight, their black hulls barely noticeable in the dark water.

"This is it," warned Cassidy. The man next to her nodded and shifted his weight. She raised the binoculars to her eyes and watched the marines place inflatable rafts into the water. The first wave would secure the zone, most certainly the bulk of their force armed with small arms. "Let them land and establish their perimeter. Under no circumstance will anyone fire without my order," she commanded. "I'll give it as soon as the package arrives but not before." The lieutenant gave a quick salute and hurried off to check the line.

The process was just as she planned. Soon one hundred men with tactical gear and rifles formed a perimeter in the sand. They quickly dug in. The soldiers would have night vision, just as she. As a precaution, her team burrowed under thermal blankets specially designed to hide their heat signature. She watched patiently as the recon scouts scanned the tree line. Seemingly satisfied, signal lights flashed toward sea.

Soon the boats answered back, and the second wave put into the water. This would be a small team heavily burdened with resupplies and heavy gear. They quickly loaded the boats and joined the marines on land. Cassidy couldn't help but respect their efficiency.

The final boat to land seemed different than the rest. Instead of one or two soldiers like before, a five-man team escorted the cargo. As soon as they hit the beach, they formed a circle around their precious gear. Cassidy raised the flare gun and fired. On her signal the charges she had buried in the sand exploded in a chain reaction. The line of marines forming the outer perimeter vaporized. Her team charged.

Simcor waited for the signal. As soon as the flare launched into the sky, a deafening concussion echoed along the beach. Thirty blasts exploded in a blinding cacophony that ripped through the outer picket, completely wiping out the landing force. The four men ahead of him dropped to the ground, taking up defensive positions around the devices. He fired three shots leaving only Bachir alive.

He trained the muzzle on his friend who pleaded, "What did you do?"

"Leave your rifle, Bachir. Head south and find a village. You've been a good friend, but our orders were to leave no survivors. I'll tell them that you ran as soon as the blasts hit, and that I couldn't get a shot on you."

Bachir stared up with confusion, eyes begging for explanation. All he could ask was, "Why?"

"I'm part of the Society, Bachir. Astia, if you ever make it back, will be different than when you left. It will be better. All people will be free to pursue their own lives, their own wealth, and their own way. We will finally be free from the collective." He looked up to see his comrades advancing on the beach. He ordered, "Go!"

The confused man scrambled to his feet and ran. Simcor fired three shots over his head, wildly missing but making a believable show for the soldiers finishing off the wounded. The traitor pulled a swatch of cloth from his pack and affixed it to his tactical vest. He laid down his rifle and knelt as previously instructed. Then he waited for his commander with the codewords at the ready.

Samani emerged from the forest. His sisters flanked him on both sides, and they were followed by Johan and Kali. "See?" He pointed at the carnage on the beach. "A complete success!" They walked past his soldiers as they looted the bodies, removing all gear and munitions that could aid in the coming battles.

It did not take long for him to find Cassidy. She stood over the devices and directed the clean-up. He pointed to the submersibles. "Are they ours?"

"Yes," she replied. "We sent squads to each and secured them one by one." She smiled widely, "With the several we already owned, the Dragon now has a fleet."

"Yes," Kernigan mused, "he does." He knelt beside the devices. "How many did they bring?"

"Five," she answered.

"Five…" His voice drifted off with his thoughts. He would be able to do so much with these, even accomplish the final goal. "Good work, Cassidy. Let's get everything loaded up so that you can head across the ocean." He looked around, "I love this place, but it isn't home."

Fatwana approached him as Cassidy and the children scurried off. She placed a hand on his arm and tenderly asked, "Sam, what are those?" She pointed at the devices.

"Nuclear bombs, my dear sister. They are a holdover from the pre-destruction period. The very instrument that destroyed the world of our ancestors and drove Dr. Andalon underground."

"That was twelve hundred years ago, brother. Are they functional?"

"Very much so. The Astian Council breaks them out every so often to aid in the reset. They haven't failed them yet."

"Wait!" Cassidy suddenly exclaimed, "This isn't right."

"How so?"

"The plutonium is missing from each. These are inert!"

Samani smiled at the cunning of the Council and waved for Johan and Kali. They soon arrived with a small, lead-lined box carried between them. "In here," he said, "you will find everything you need to complete the devices. Johan, you and Kali help them load."

Fatwana paled with realization. "You've been in possession of radioactive materials?"

Samani waited until the children had departed and said, "Have you never wondered, sister," he asked, "why the council searched for me so aggressively? Or even," he added, "why I had to fake my own death?"

"You've had these on you the entire time!"

"Folly! No, that would have been too dangerous and cumbersome. I've had it stashed in Estowen's Landing since my arrival many years ago."

Fatwana's face grew dim with concern. "What will you do with them, Sam?"

"I'm going to destroy the Council, Fatwana. I will kill them in their arrogant chambers and bring true equality to all. Every man and woman deserves to live their lives free of tyranny."

"Yes, but shouldn't they decide that for themselves? If you force it upon them, you're no better than the Council." She gestured inland. "Just like here, Samani. Pearl was right. A curtain of ignorance shrouded this world, and you had no authority to rip it down. What will become of the people of Andalon now that you've set their revolution in motion?"

He turned to her with sad eyes that betrayed some hidden regret. Placing a hand on her shoulder he drew her in. "Sister, please understand. I've taken every precaution for their future, and will ensure that our continents find balance as we cohabitate this planet." His free hand moved, quickly putting something in his mouth that he immediately swallowed.

"How?" She asked, "What precautions can you take? Unless..." Her eyes went wide with understanding. "Unless you control their future government in the same fashion the Astian Council does now." She tried to step back but he held on, jerking her closer. Suddenly afraid, she asked, "Who is it? Which of these people do you control, Samani?"

She was so focused on her brother that she did not see Ashima step up from behind. The knife plunged deep between the fourth and fifth ribs on Fatwana's left side.

"In a moment, dear sister," he whispered, "it will also be you."

Chapter Seventeen

Eusari spent the rest of the days in camp aboard *She Wolf*. She hid out, mostly to avoid Hester, but also out of disgust with Robert Esterling. If he didn't trust her as an advisor, then she had no reason to sleep on the ground when a soft bed waited aboard her ship.

A knock roused her from slumber. "Enter," she said.

Caroline opened the door and got straight to the point. One of the things Eusari liked about the girl was her straightforwardness. "They're arriving soon. They entered the lake ten minutes ago."

"Thank you." She rose and dressed quickly. She wanted to have their meeting and be done with Esterling and his turtle pace, even if only for a few weeks.

By the time she reached topside, Peter Longshanks was ready to lower the captain's gig. She recognized the ships dropping anchor and nodded her approval. Shon had brought twenty, each loaded with seasoned soldiers. Although his losses had been high, their experience would prove invaluable in the fight to come.

She spotted Shon rowing to shore with the contingent of Dreamers destined to join King Robert. She recognized the oldest as Cuyler. Even in the dark, Eusari saw the deepened hue of Caroline's cheeks when she noticed him too. Eusari raised an eyebrow at the girl questioningly, but she turned away embarrassed.

"Why don't you come along with us, Caroline," she said. "I could use the company on the ride over." The girl leapt at the opportunity and boarded the small vessel. Eusari smiled at her eagerness. *I was robbed of that innocent crush,* she thought. Remembering the way she finally found herself looking at Braen, she blushed as well.

Shon found her quickly once they were ashore. "What's he got in mind for us? Frontal attack on Eston? Take down her defenses?"

Eusari motioned for Caroline to join the others while the adults discussed the parlay. "Go, say your goodbyes," she ordered. She waited untill the girl had gone before answering. "None of those," she replied. "He's sending us on a recruiting mission."

Shon recoiled, "Recruiting?"

She nodded. "He seems to believe that you have pull in Loganshire."

He felt his neck and said, "The only pull I'd have there is a tug on my throat by the hangman's noose."

"Regardless, he needs us to infiltrate the city and identify loyalists by the time he makes camp. Then he plans to march through the city and board his ships like he owns the harbor."

"That's ludicrous. It serves no purpose."

"It serves much purpose," said a voice behind them. The pair turned to find Robert standing beside General Titus and Sarai. "Albeit a political purpose rather than military. If the people can watch me march unopposed, sparing the last city from either siege or conquest, they will get behind my crown after I win the final battle."

"You're assuming that battle will be against your brother," snapped Eusari.

"Why wouldn't it be?"

"You're forgetting Skander."

"He isn't the threat," Sarai interrupted. "Marcus stands between Robert and his throne, not your bogeyman from the north. As soon as we hold Eston, we'll be able to turn out all the empire's resources against him."

Eusari pondered the queen's words then said to Robert, "That's why you've been avoiding my counsel. You don't believe Skander a threat."

"No," answered Robert, "I don't believe him a threat."

"You realize he's built an army of emotants?"

Sarai cut in, "So you say." She clung to her husband's arm.

Wembley cut in, "Why are we really going to Logan, Esterling?"

"You'll recruit loyalists and then wake the emotants there. Prove to me that it's possible and then help me retake my throne."

"That's a tall order, Esterling." Shon shook his head. "We can't take that city without an army."

"That's the point," Eusari mused, "you'll have us quietly take the city, but if we fail, you won't be blamed. You'll have your clean victory."

"Thank you in advance for that," Robert said. "Oh," he added, "would you take the northern queen with you? I'm tired of her insisting upon an audience she'll never receive."

"I hope we're making the correct decision," Robert told Sarai after the pirates were out of earshot.

"Of course we are," she said. "So you finally believe my theory that Braen is alive?" She narrowed her eyes and added, "You believe that he's raiding those cities?"

"I do," replied Robert, "and once we hold Eston, I can either force him to uphold his vow to aid me or I can defend against his attack. But there's no way I'll believe that Skander has the same powers as he, nor that he's waking emotants from the Rookeries. Had it been that easy, Eusari and Wembley would have done it in Diaph."

She placed her hand on his chest and lovingly gazed into his eyes. His heart leaped as he thought, *I love her so much.* Despite her scarred face he would always find her beautiful. He reached out and softly touched her cheek, tracing where the flames had marked her forever. He touched a bald patch above her ear. *She's losing her beautiful hair,* he marveled.

She recoiled as if reading his thoughts. "Well we have no choice in it now," she said. "What's done is done, and they'll either deliver Logan or they won't."

"They're powerful allies, too powerful to risk losing."

"You won't lose them," she promised. She grabbed his arm as they returned to camp. Two figures blocked their way and she tensed as she recognized the pair. "Taros," she said.

"Lady Sarai," the boy bowed his head in greeting. At his side was a beautiful Pescari woman. He nodded another greeting to Robert. "King Esterling," he said, "I wish to introduce my wife, Flaya."

"You're married?" Robert exchanged a look with Sarai who was equally surprised.

"Yes," the boy replied, "and also expecting a child."

"Congratulations, Shappan. May Felicima bless you with a strong and healthy boy."

Taros and Flaya bowed in acceptance and she said, "And may your gods bless you as well."

Sarai walked forward and gently took Flaya's hand from Taros. She smiled broadly like a big sister about to help the youngest prepare for a ball. All pretenses or anger toward Taros was suddenly lost. "Well now," she told Flaya, "it seems that I've a new best friend." As she led her away, she told the men, "You boys have fun talking strategy. We're going to plan the real business."

The girl appeared confused and asked, "What business is that?"

The queen giggled, "How to plan our baby showers while marching to war of course!"

"What is a *baby shower?*" Flay appeared confused.

"Come along and I'll tell you," she said, dragging her toward her wagon, "you're going to love it!"

After the girls had scampered off, Robert turned to Taros. "I assume you wish to talk?"

"Yes," the shappan explained, "I wish to know how you will use my warriors in the battle to come."

"That's still a long way off. Sarai has convinced me to send the pirates ahead into Logan, to recruit others and maybe a few like me."

"That is wise," Taros agreed. "We need many more like you if we are to achieve victory."

"But I'm not so sure the pirates won't betray us," Robert cautioned. "Now is the time for your warriors to scout ahead. Search the roads for signs of ambush and meet me at Norton. Ensure they don't see you leave." He pulled a map from his pocket and handed it to Taros. "Count the ships in the harbor and make note of city defenses."

"You wish to attack that city?"

"I do not want to, but I need to take it if I'm to defend against both Braen Braston and my brother." Taros nodded his understanding and turned to depart. "No need to leave, Shappan. Come spend time with me. Let's talk about how our forces will combine in the battles to come." The Pescari man smiled eagerly at the opportunity, looking forward to the friendship Robert had offered.

Chapter Eighteen

Marcus enjoyed his newfound freedom by strolling the palace. With Campton Shol out of the picture, he finally felt that it was truly his. He would meet with the council in an hour, but a desire to relish this freedom overtook the need to practice his speech. He pushed open the door to the man's former office and entered. A falcon in the corner screeched its displeasure at the interruption.

He quickly lost himself in the dispatches on the desk. Many were related to the kingdom, and painted a bleaker picture than the king had been led to believe. The loss of Weston and Eskera had disrupted trade to an almost standstill, and profits had ceased rolling in months ago.

Worse, the loss of control over Pirate's Cove had cut into their tax revenue. Skander Braston continued to wage war on his coastal cities, and the sacking of Middleton and Soston had lost him precious troops as well as the trust of his people. His rough calculations showed a huge disparity between insurance pay outs and his ability to generate funds.

His empire had bankrupted within the span of a year, and he blamed the chancellor. Hopefully, so would his council. That was the purpose for the meeting. They planned to choose Shol's replacement.

"You may be able to bond with her," Kestrel said from the doorway.

"Who?" Marcus didn't look up. He was too engrossed in the missives.

"Reaver." The Falconer pointed to the raptor perched behind the king. "She doesn't understand why her master no longer connects with her, or where Campton has gone. But, since you have affinity for the bead you may be able to do so."

Marcus didn't understand. "What do you mean *may*, aren't our powers absolute?"

"No. There are many variations of abilities, and each have limitations. It's a pity you weren't identified and trained early on."

The Falconer lingered, irritating Marcus far more than the initial interruption. But the words held his interest. "I would like to try," he said. "I need to test both my strengths and weaknesses. But first I must meet with the council."

"Of course," Kestrel replied. "The son of Esterling has our full support and we shall do his bidding so long as it aligns with the orders from Astia."

Son of Esterling, Robert nearly laughed out loud at the phrase. He had gambled and it paid off. It was pure luck that they had fallen for his faked prophecy. He bathed for a moment in satisfaction then replied, "Of course, whatever Astia demands of me."

"We are happy that you understand the arrangement." After a pause Kestrel added, "My liege." Having said his piece, the specter turned to leave.

Marcus spent a few more moments flipping through the dispatches before turning to follow the Falconer. He paused at one that had been crumpled and discarded, recognizing it immediately as once held by Shol. *He was reading this when I faked the prophecy,* the king remembered. He read the dispatch over many times, each causing his heart to leap. *It can't be,* he thought. But there was no denying the prophecy. He read it one more time aloud, "Only the son of Esterling can slay him in time." *They truly believe me the heir!*

Chief Magistrate Boothe spoke for the council. "Your Royal Highness," he began, "where is the Lord Chancellor?"

Marcus smiled disarmingly. "I assure you that I do not know, Chief Magistrate."

"That's unfortunate because we do. It seems that you had him illegally removed."

The king shrugged, "If I'm the king, how was it illegal?"

Boothe made a show of rolling his eyes so the entire council wouldn't miss his show of frustration. Marcus had expected this behavior and assumed they would try to prey upon his ignorance. "By order of our governing document, the Grande Charter: In order to remove a member of the ruling council or a representative thereof," he read, "formal charges must be brought before the chamber."

"Okay," replied Marcus, "then I bring charges against Lord Shol."

"Unfortunately," continued Boothe, "he has already levied charges against you."

Marcus laughed. "I'm sorry, can you repeat that?"

The magistrate ignored his request and read on, "You are accused of murder in the first degree of Captain General Matteas Brohn." The pompous windbag scanned the room, waiting for the gasps to die down. "Please," he urged, "I must ask my distinguished colleagues to refrain from emotional outbursts so that I may read the other charges." He pointed at the paper, "That was only the first."

Marcus reached below his seat and drew out an hourglass. He made a show of his own by setting it upon the podium before him. "If you don't mind, Chief Magistrate, I have business to attend. Please hurry so that we may move on."

The portly man scoffed and read the second charge. "You are accused of insurrection against the Grande Charter by way of removing the chancellor from his seat of power without formal proceeding."

Marcus yawned grandiosely. "Is that all?"

"You are accused of abusing two Falconers during the administration of their duties." He turned to the council when he added, "I believe the penalty for that crime is death."

"I fully agree, Chief Magistrate."

The man turned toward the sovereign with eyebrow raised. "You agree to the charges?"

"No. I agree that the penalty for interfering or abusing a Falconer is instant death."

"Ah," the magistrate smiled, "then we are in full agreement of recommended penalty."

"Yes!" Marcus stood. "I recommend the penalty of death for all who interfere with the Falconers!"

Boothe ignored his comment. "Marcus Esterling, how do you plea to these charges?"

The young king leaned forward and said, "Not Guilty."

Boothe snickered and banged his gavel despite that no one protested. "The court enters a plea of *Not Guilty*. To which charge do I apply that plea?"

"To the last two."

The room exploded with anger and Boothe banged his gavel "So you plead guilty to murder?"

"Not at all. I plead guilty to beheading Matteas Brohn."

The dignitaries stood in unison and shouted their protest. Boothe banged his gavel a third time.

"Kestrel," Marcus commanded, "give me the fat man's gavel." A wisp of air shot out from the hooded specter and ripped the instrument from the magistrate's hand. Every voice quieted instantly. "On second thought," the king said, "I'll get it myself." A wisp of air extended from his own hand and wrapped around the mallet. Kestrel immediately dropped his, giving it over completely to the young man's power.

Boothe protested, "You can't do that!"

Marcus made a motion with his hand and the floating gavel struck the magistrate hard across the face. He was rendered unconscious immediately. "I think we've all heard enough of his incessant hammering, don't you?" He made a show of waiting for a reply from the gallery before continuing, "As stated earlier and agreed upon by the lard ass on the floor, interruption of a Falconer's administrative duty results in the penalty of death." The gavel crashed down a final time on the magistrate, punctuating the king's point. To the rest of the assembly he said, "Matteas Brohn likewise interrupted my duties as evidenced by the armies currently marching toward Eston."

Marcus left the podium and strolled out onto the floor, amplifying his voice with his newfound abilities. He fingered the beads in his pocket as he walked, thankful for their power and that Kestrel had given him more.

"As to the other charges, I must question Lord Cedrick Strader, Minister of Finance."

"Wha…. What would you ask of me, your highness?"

"How much revenue did our kingdom generate this quarter?"

"I do not have the papers in front of me, my lord!"

"It's okay. You won't need them." Marcus paused in front of an older woman in a black dress. "Ah, Lady Strommel… You wear colors of mourning. Is that for my mother?"

"No." She replied. "I wear them for our empire which you have run into the ground."

"I see," he said. "Would you say that our coffers are dry, and the enemy is at our doorstep?"

"You *could* put it that way. Yes."

"Then place your blame on Lord Campton Shol. I have proof that he knew of our situation and withheld the knowledge from his monarch. Furthermore, he used Matteas Brohn to keep me in the dark. Together the two conspired to prevent my rule." He turned to Kestrel, "High Falconer, who is the only person who can save Eston?"

"The son of Esterling," replied the specter.

"And who conspired to keep the son of Esterling a puppet, withheld from a seat of power?"

"Lord Shol and General Brohn."

"And what is your primary duty in regard to the sovereign of Eston?"

"To ensure that none interfere with his or her administration of justice and fair judgement."

"Both of which Shol and Brohn interfered with, won't you agree?"

"Yes, my liege."

Marcus wheeled on the council. "So there you have it. Matteas Brohn received the due penalty of interfering with the duties of a Falconer. So should, I might add, Campton Shol as soon as he is brought before me."

No one in the council argued. The point was reasonably made. The king returned to his podium and faced the dignitaries. "Kestrel, who approved selection of Lord Shol and gave him power to interfere?"

"The Estonian Council, my liege."

Marcus clapped his hands three times, and fifty Falconers strode inside the chamber. They quickly blocked each exit from the hall. "Then their penalty is death."

The guards outside the rotunda tried in vain to respond to the screams, finding the doors barred from within.

Part II
Natural and Unnatural Life

Marked by birth his fate is sealed.

- The Oracle of Astian, 50th year of order

Chapter Nineteen

The crew of *She Wolf* worked with the precision of cogs integrated in a machine; each anticipating the actions of the man beside him. Sails slackened as the vessel eased into a berth and the men scurried topside to prepare to tie off. On the boatswain's order the sailors cast lines from port, spinning the tightly wound knots in circles and tossing them past the linesmen on the pier. The waiting dockworkers caught the smaller ropes and pulled until the larger lines emerged. They hauled these easily and wrapped them around wooden chocks.

Eusari watched her crew work, diligently ensuring the safe landing of *She Wolf*. The vessel was their home, the weapon upon which they ate, slept, and fought. The crew would stain her deck with their own blood if needed, ready to sacrifice whatever necessary to keep her hull intact. These men were misfits and outcasts sent or run away from their birthplace, but atop this vessel they worked with purpose and found family. Just as they loved the ship, each would kill or die for their captain.

Eusari scanned the deck for her first mate and found Peter Longshanks speaking with Krill. The conversation between the peg-legged men was animated, with the crazy pirate waving his arms and pointing at the cannons. The two finally erupted in laughter after the one-eyed man strutted around like a rooster, braying into the morning sun. Eusari would never admit to anyone that he had grown on her. She understood now that his persona was made artistically extravagant to inspire the crew, and she did find him comical. They loved him and welcomed him aboard immediately.

Peter caught her stare and ambled over. He pointed a thumb over his shoulder and smiled broadly. "That man knows his guns," he told her. "It's hard for me to act as first mate, sailing master, *and* gunner. You should promote him to the role he served on Braston's crew."

She nodded, "Aye, but he annoys the shit out of me."

"That's part of his charm," the older man advised, "and part of why you need him. I believe he's adopted you. He knew Braen better than anyone except Yurik, and would follow you out of the mere reason of his captain's love."

"Gather the others," she said, changing the subject, "and meet me in my stateroom. We have much to arrange and only two weeks to pull off the impossible."

"Aye, Captain," he growled with a crisp salute.

She caught a glimpse of the town as she turned, an image avoided since their arrival. *This is where I first boarded this ship,* she recalled. The skyline had changed since her departure fourteen years prior, the buildings now taller and built with more permanence. Even the footprint had grown, spanning not only the harbor but reaching up the hillsides all around. Logan had finally grown into a city. A city she couldn't wait to leave.

She dropped the hatch on sad memories and made her way to captain's quarters. Gelert lifted his head and whined when she entered. He could feel the anxiety. Her thoughts turned to Braen. What would he tell her about the days to come? *You always knew how to calm me,* she thought. *I wish you were here now.* But he was not. Leaving the door open she rolled out a map and waited. Eusari would have to face her past.

Soon Shon and Marque strolled in discussing the woman Madelyn. She was Astian like Samani, also a member of the Society.

"I'm gonna marry her," the lead scout insisted.

"I believe you," Wembley replied, slapping his friend on the back. "Maybe Eusari can perform the ceremony."

She stiffened at the suggestion, although the ritual was in her authority as captain, uniting another couple's love affair was the furthest thing from her to-do list. "Congratulations," she muttered despite her hesitation. She was saved by Sippen Yurik and Devil Jacque walking through the door. She was shocked to see the engineer, since this meeting entailed the incursion into the town. "Can I help you, Yurik?"

"I wuh... wanted to ask if I cuh... could come along with the landing puh... party," he stated. "I nuh... need to wuh... work on some nuh... new designs."

"Blacksmiths in Logan aren't keen on sharing their forges, Sippen." She shook her head. "No, I'm afraid you need to remain on the ship."

"I'll tuh... take Krill wuh... with me," he promised.

"No," she insisted. She couldn't afford to lose his genius, and didn't have time to babysit. She watched him leave disappointed.

Shon read her thoughts, "You made the right choice, dearie. We can't afford to lose him in this city. It's not friendly."

"Right." She pointed at the map. "Here are the primary locations to set up operations. Shon, would you like to explain?"

"Aye." The plan to recruit the city was his and he knew it better. "The mayor's a pompous windbag, as corrupt as he is wealthy. We can't go to him or we'd be immediately outed. Our best bet is to connect with the local street gangs. Jacque will reach out to the sewer rats here. Marque, you and Madelyn will find the leader of the harbor sharks on waterfront. Eusari and I will contact the wolf pack in the market square."

Jacque asked, "What do we do once we find them?"

"Two things. First, use the gangs to recruit the rebellion. Second, locate the Rookery but don't engage. Record the comings and goings of Falconers and try your best to learn their strength size. Don't risk your own necks or you'll be swinging by them."

"How do we convince the gangs to help?" Marque appeared skeptical, despite it was his boss's plan.

"Money, my good friend. Lots and lots of money." He reached under the table and hefted three heavy sacks onto the table. "King

Robert's financing this expedition, and this gold is straight out of the coffers of Eskera."

"Mercenaries," muttered Jacque. "He'd hire mercenaries to fight his war?"

Eusari interrupted, "He's desperate. He lost much of his army and most of his hope when the deserters flipped sides in Eskera. Our job is to find him enough fighters to take Eston as he claims his throne."

"How will we contact each other? There's a lot of people in that city," Jacque pointed out.

"Every three days we meet at a different tavern," Eusari answered. "The pattern will rotate around a codeword. The first will be *Boar's Balls*, followed by *Rooster's Strut, Admiral's Dive, Estonian Alehouse, and Napping Narwhal*."

"B-R-A-E-N," Jacque remarked.

Eusari couldn't help but notice his disappointment. In Middleton he had professed his feelings, but she had thrown up walls immediately. It wouldn't be right for her to enter a relationship with one of her crew. "Yes," she replied. "Is that easy enough to remember?"

"Not as hard as it is to forget, apparently."

She ignored his quip and picked up the map off the table, folding and holding it to the flame of the lantern. She held it until she couldn't stand the heat on her fingers before tossing it into a pail. "You have your assignments. I'll see each of you in three days."

The people of Logan could rely upon very few things in their lives. Their crops may fail due to locusts, drought, or flood. Their animals may contract disease or fail to deliver healthy offspring. These things were up to fate. But some things were certain. Eston would keep them safe from Fjorik raiders, strangers would walk the harbor district and thieves would lurk in its shadows. Falconers would bless their children every fall. And, every day, the market district would be packed with buyers and sellers.

Eusari walked beside Shon with Gelert between them, navigating the rows of temporary shops and ignoring the wares and shouts from merchants. She had visited this square many times as a child. Memories flooded her mind of her oldest brother Franque trying to round up his siblings. Jean and Thom would chase each other around the hovels, playing a game of hide and seek unlike any they could experience on the farm. The market was a playground to all of the Thorinson children except Eusari.

If her parents were busy Franque kept her glued to his side, always within arm's reach. Despite her protests he watched her like a hawk, scaring her with tales of men who would steal a child and sell them to seagoing vessels in the harbor. She hadn't believed him at the time, just as she doubted the bogeyman. But later she learned just how dark and hungry the hearts of some men really were.

She couldn't help but feel homesick for Brentway as she strolled, forcing her eyes not to scan the crowd for familiar faces. The last thing she needed was to connect with this place and start referring to it as home. She needed a diversion for her thoughts and broke the silence with her uncle. She asked, "How will you contact them?"

"I won't," he said with a smile, "I'll catch them in the act."

Just as he spoke a boy of about twelve years broke into a run. His right hand gripped a heavy purse, no doubt cut from a shopper in the crowd. The victim shouted for a constable a few heads over, but Shon was quick and snatched the boy off the ground and placed him in a constable's hold.

"Let go uh muh arm," the boy shouted in gutter speech as he tried to wriggle free.

Shon grabbed the sack of coins and tossed it to the rightful owner. He leaned in close to the boy and whispered, "I'll let you go after you've taken me to Matt."

"Matt who?" The boy spit in the direction of Wembley's face but the man anticipated the move, dodging the spittle easily.

"Don't play dumb with me, Jeremiah. You were only ten the last time I collared you, but look closely upon my face and remember."

The boy stared back with furrowed brow as he searched his memory. Then he stammered, "Cuh… Constable Wembley?"

"Aye," Shon replied, "and you and Matt owe me a favor."

"Gaw," the boy said, "you ain't even a constawbul no mo."

"No," he agreed, "but that don't change the fact that a favor is owed. Now get up." He hauled the boy onto his feet and slipped a manacle on his hands. Then he connected a long chain as a leash. He gave it a tug. "Let's go."

Jeremiah led them away from the market square into a residential row. He pointed to an alleyway between two tenements, the upstairs windows of which were connected by clotheslines. Sheets and shirts aired in the breeze, high above the stench of the city. The alley ended abruptly with a single door, and the boy knocked three times before a hatch opened revealing two green eyes. The boy in chains nodded his head to Wembley. The eyes grew wide with surprise and the hatch slammed shut.

A few moments later the door opened to reveal three older boys, each with arms crossed and trying to appear intimidating. The eldest spoke, "Come in, Wembley, but leave the dog outside. Matt doesn't like dogs."

Wembley placed a key in the boy's manacles and turned it, releasing his hold. The boy stuck out his tongue and blew a raspberry, then darted inside. Shon followed.

Eusari pushed past the boys with Gelert trotting closely behind. One of them held up a hand to stop and she snarled, "He's not a dog, he's a wolf." Both boys recoiled with alarm and she added, "So he goes with me." Neither boy dared argue.

Matt turned out to be a skinny teen of seventeen summers. Too busy gnawing on a rib bone, he didn't look up from his lunch when they arrived. "What do you want, Wembley?"

"Just a moment of your time and consideration of an offer," replied Shon.

The boy lifted his eyes and began to speak. He took one look at Gelert and stood from his chair, waving the rib in the air like a sword. Matt shouted, "No dogs!" Gelert, of course, didn't care. He reached up and snatched the rib from the boy's outstretched hand. "That was my lunch," he protested.

"In all fairness," Eusari smirked, "you offered it to him." She knelt beside her wolf and asked, "Would you like to give that back?" Gelert responded with a human-like shake of his head. Eusari continued, "No? Would you rather his arm or leg?" Gelert shook his head to the affirmative.

"As I was saying," Shon said, "you have a debt to pay and I'll be needing the services of your *wolfpack*. Can I count on your assistance?"

"Aye," the boy said, eyes locked on the wolf and afraid to look away, "I'll do anything you say as long as that wolf is kept outside."

"Good," Shon replied with a smile. "Here are the full details of the job." He handed over a parchment. "You'll be well compensated, of course."

As Shon and Eusari turned to leave, Matt called out, "What turned you outlaw, constable?"

Eusari watched her uncle pause at the question, no doubt considering the many ways he could answer. When he did it was truthfully, "I'm tired of the little guy getting shit on every time he gets ahead. I'm also tired of the nobles getting fat on our blood and calling their scraps our reward. The real world isn't what we think it is, boy, and I aim to fix it."

Once they were outside Eusari asked, "How'd you know he's afraid of dogs?"

"Soldiers chat around the campfire, dearie, and a darling wee lass told me a story about how she outsmarted him and the entire gang." He leveled his eyes on his niece. "She's got the same powers as you, dearie. Made the trees dance and the vines tangle. She can even bond several critters at once."

"Same powers as me?" Eusari marveled at the possibility, she had felt so alone for so long and now found herself surrounded by a new family. "And she's from Logan?"

"Aye. I'll tell you all about Kali as we walk to the inn. You're gonna love this little girl!"

"Where is she now?"

Shon shrugged, "Stayed with Kernigan," he said. "She and her boyfriend were adamant that they had to help him with his own war across the water."

Her knees nearly buckled. "Samani Kernigan is launching his war on Astia?" She suddenly felt sick to the stomach and this time it wasn't morning sickness.

"Aye." His eyes narrowed. "I thought you knew?"

"I thought he would help finish ours first."

"Things changed when Braen died. He said something about having an 'insurance policy' in case he did.

"Shon," said Eusari, "I don't think we have all the facts about what we're really fighting."

"We never do, dearie." He shook his head. "I aim to fix that too."

Chapter Twenty

The only thing Skander loved more than raiding cities was finding them unprotected. Eskera had proved an easy target, with Robert Esterling only a few days ride up river. The fool left the city with crumbling walls, half a harbor, and a mere militia to protect his flank. In other words, the boy left it just the way the northern king preferred.

His Saber Cats fanned out in every direction, accompanied by Fjorik warriors. In Middleton he had sent them one to a team and the mistake had cost him dearly. Now he sent them three to a kill squad with five soldiers alongside. The battle was over in less than an hour.

He rested atop *Malfeasance* as his army made quick work of the city. With feet on the railing and a glass of rum in one hand, he watched the carnage through a spyglass. *Why waste energy on such a trivial conquest*, he thought, *when I can relax and still reap the benefits?* Artur approached and ended his revelry.

"Sire," his friend reported, "there's no Rookery in the city."

"Preposterous," snarled the king, folding his eyepiece and tucking it away. "Surely every city in the kingdom has a home for the feathered beasts?" He stood and poured the remainder of his rum over the side. "Bring me Pamplona," he ordered, sending Artur scurrying away. He drew out his knife and carved on the rail as he waited.

Artur soon returned with a young Saber Cat. She was tiny with round eyes and raven black hair. Skander guessed her age around five summers. "Look around child," he told her, "tell me what you see."

"I see a city of emptiness, father. The people are so tired of fighting they gave up without a fight."

"Yes," he praised her, "and they'll give up much more now that the fighting is finished." He gestured toward the city, "I've been told you're better than the others when playing hide and seek. Perhaps you have a trick you use when tracking down your brethren?" She shrugged. He placed a fatherly hand on her shoulder as he asked, "Can you find hidden brothers and sisters?"

The tiny girl nodded vigorously. "The sleeping ones are close, father." She grabbed his hand and said, "Come, let me show you." She led him down winding alleys in the shadows of the city. She held his hand the entire time, letting go only when they approached a smooth wall. "Here," she insisted.

Skander looked around, confused by her confidence in what most certainly was a dead end. He observed several crates and barrels scattered about while stray dogs gnawed on discarded garbage. "I see no entrance, daughter," he said with trepidation. He felt uneasy, a state that bordered on rage for the northern king.

"I will show you," she said, patting his arm to calm his fear.

His hair stood on end as she unraveled the pattern, removing first the shimmer then the outline of the crates and barrels. Even the dogs glimmered with translucency. Before the image reestablished its form, he briefly glimpsed a door. His eyes widened with surprise, but, as soon as it appeared the portal was gone.

"What is this you've shown me?" His mouth drooled at the possibilities.

Pamplona did not respond. She bit her lower lip and concentrated, finding the individual fibers of the fabric and untying each one until the air fell away. As the weave disappeared so did the illusion. The door stood before them.

"Congratulations, Braston."

Skander wheeled to find an old man, fit of body and seemingly as strong as his youngest warriors. The man wore a soldier's uniform, once stark white now tarnished and tattered. His rank insignia identified him as a general. The northern king raised his axe to swing at the newcomer, but the man did not flinch. Instead he strolled to an empty crate and sat, unconcerned by any threat.

"This is where we hid the Falconers and Jaguars when Esterling came," he explained. "Our army was concealed in the sewers using the same camouflage."

"Who are you?"

"I used to be Merrimac Lourdes," the general explained, "but now I am nothing but an empty husk through which to speak." Skander raised his axe a second time, ready to follow through with his strike. "Cut me and I will bleed," Lourdes explained, "but you will be without answers or allies."

"With whom," the king pressed, "do I converse?"

"You know me as Lord Campton Shol, Chancellor to the Esterling Empire."

Skander lowered his weapon. "Have you come to surrender before my army?"

The general made a show of looking around before answering. "Quite the opposite. I've come to aid you in your attack on Marcus Esterling."

Skander opened his mouth and then shut it immediately. When he finally spoke, the voice belonged to another. "You have my attention, Lord Shol."

The face of the general lit up at the change. He asked, "Well now, who do I *actually* have the pleasure of speaking with?"

"You speak with *Lord* Stefan Nevra. What is your proposal?"

"Taking the cities of Norton and Logan will prove difficult, but you will succeed. I will give you Eston. Most of Esterling's forces will turn against his loyalists during the battle and open the gates for yours."

"You would betray your own king?"

"He's not my king. I hail from a place far across the sea and represent a far more powerful force."

Nevra nodded Skander's head as he understood, "You are Astian?"

"Yes," Shol as Lourdes confirmed.

"If I have the cities then you forget that I will also have Pirate's Cove and the entire Southern Continent." He placed a hand on the terrified little girl standing beside him, pulling her forward as if presenting a prize. "And I have a host of emotants far more powerful than your Falconers."

"By all means take more," the voice of Campton Shol urged. He waved his hand and the door in the wall opened. "But don't forget that you'll need support of the Astian Council if you are to hold your empire."

"And you can provide that?"

"For a small fee," the channeled voice promised. "Attack Robert Esterling and destroy his army. Free those emotants as well. Use them when you march on Eston."

"What else do you ask of me," Nevra asked.

"Once the continent is yours, reinstate our system of acquiring beads. If this is acceptable, I will return to the Astian Council and bring them your terms."

Skander's head nodded agreement. "I agree," Nevra's voice promised.

The general's hand raised a sharp blade to his own neck. "But in the meantime, destroy everything in sight." Blood spurt from his throat as the blade sliced cleanly.

The girl in Skander's hands spun around, terrified by the sight. *Kill her,* the voice in his head insisted. *She heard too much.* Her neck broke cleanly with a jerk. *You will forget this conversation occurred,* the voice commanded, and he did.

Campton Shol broke from the trance, shaken by what transpired but emboldened at the same time. He stared at the five Jaguars swaying in their ministrations on the floor. The corpse of the sixth lay on the floor between them. He thought about the way his mind traveled and he shuddered. Before they placed him in Lourdes' body, they assured him the creature's death would be temporary. 'It was necessary,' they had said, 'to pass the conscious of his making into the mind of another.'

"My lord," Kestrel asked, "I'm assuming you have a plan for dealing with the abomination you just invited to Eston?"

"I do. We finally know for certain who holds the mind of the Destroyer. Kill Stefan Nevra and take control of Braston, his minions, and the zealots he leads. Then we will turn him against the other abominations and Marcus."

Kestrel asked, "Do you know where to find this Nevra?"

"No," Shol admitted, "but he will show himself before long. My guess is The Cove, which is why I need your other friends. Are they ready?"

"Come and see." Kestrel led him through a secret passage in the wall connected to the Rookery. Soon they emerged from another doorway and into a great hall.

All Falconers of Eston were assembled for his inspection. A brief count revealed two hundred or more, each standing eerily at attention. Across from them he counted at least twenty Jaguars, many of whom were still bonded with their beasts despite their losses. A closer look revealed that a multitude of the animals had been reanimated, with wounds poorly healed or left unattended. He was impressed by the show of force they would bring to future battles, but the specters at the far side of the room drew Campton's full attention.

"They've arrived," he exclaimed.

"Yes. Only just so."

"Good," the youngest son of Jakata said, "keep leading the boy along as if he truly rules. I did not expect that he'd show sensitivity to the bead, but since he does, we must use that to our advantage. We will let *him* face Skander if we fail to find Nevra."

"And the brother Robert?"

"Our agents will do their job as planned," Campton said. "I always plan for contingencies."

"What about the Astian Council? Do you have a plan for them as well?"

"Indeed. Praedor not only warned us of my father's decision, but she has a plan to stop my brother as well. After she eliminates him, I will rule over both continents, my friend."

Kestrel flinched against invisible pain at the words. "Careful what you say directly, my friend. The collective strains against you."

"But our bond is stronger, is it not?"

The specter nodded. "A piece of it still resists."

Shol reached out with his mind, seizing the part of Kestrel he controlled. "The best part of being a son of Jakata Horn is this, my friend. Our powers are unmatched." The lead Falconer and every reanimate in the room fell to their knees, holding their heads between both hands and screaming wildly against the pain. *You are mine,* his voice boomed in their heads, *and so is this world.*

Chapter Twenty-One

Artema rapped softly. The last time he had stood in this doorway he'd watched his father die. He grinned devilishly at the thought of Jakata drowning on dry land, choking on his own froth as he breathed his last. The door opened and an attendant stared expectantly.

"Artema Horn," he told the young man, "here to see Chancellor Praedor."

The doorman nodded and swept the door open with a grandiose wave. "She's expecting you."

He casually strolled into the room, eyes scanning and taking in the décor. "You've redecorated."

"I have," the Chancellor replied, reclined in an overstuffed chair. "The shrine to Andalon sickened my stomach," she explained. She gestured to a small chair across from hers.

Artema sat but immediately regretted the act. The seat was uncomfortably stiff and set several hands below her luxurious recliner. When he shifted his weight, he only made the situation worse. He smiled nonetheless, all the while cursing her in his mind. He would reward her handsomely for her insolence.

"Thank you for coming right away, Councilman Horn."

Getting down to the business he asked, "Your summons promised news about my brother. Did your inquiry sufficiently support my claim?"

"Yes," she agreed, "your assistance in the matter proved quite enlightening."

"What punishment has befallen poor Campton?"

"He's been stripped of his position and denied access to oracle beads. He's powerless and will live out a life of exile in Andalon."

"Thank you for sparing his life, although exile will feel like death to my brother." He nodded. "Thank you for the information." Artema rose from the horrible chair and turned to leave. "I suppose I will see you at the next session of council."

"That isn't all, Councilman."

Artema froze so near the door that he could almost reach the knob. He turned, careful to keep the fake smile believable. "My apologies. I assumed that you had greater things to attend than my grief."

"Not at all, Artema. Losing both brother and father in such a short span of time must be painful. That is why it is difficult to ask of you what I must."

"I assure you that any distraction will be most welcome. What can I do to please the Chancellor?"

"The Humanitarians have been a nuisance of late. Your father was plagued by their riots and bombings, and my tenure endures the same. I need to know more about their leader."

"Their leader?" Artema felt panic squeeze his stomach. *Surely, she doesn't know.* "I've been away in Andalon for so long that I couldn't possibly provide that information."

"Quite the contrary, there is much you can do for us. Tell me everything you know about Samani Nakala."

Artema blinked in unfeigned surprise. "I'm sorry, who?"

"You know him as Samani Kernigan. What kind of man is he? What motivates him? How do we anticipate his moves against the council?"

"Samani Kernigan?" Artema repeated the name several times in his head. "You believe him the leader of the Society?"

"We do. His sister, Fatwana, was the lead sister of the Winter Oracle. She recently went missing, and our spies believe she rode a submersible across the ocean and joined her brother in Andalon."

"If they're together in Andalon, then what's the problem? Surely they're no threat to Astia?"

"Your father ordered a reset and sent in a sizable force."

"How is this a problem? The soldiers will wipe the continent and him along with it."

"Our landing force has disappeared."

"How many?"

"All of them. They've missed five check-ins already."

"And you believe Kernigan has interfered with their landing?"

"We believe he is on his way here to attack Bergin. But there's a deeper problem than just the arrival of an army. The landing force carried special munitions. They were armed with some..." she broke off, obviously intent on keeping secrets. After a moment she added, "with technology."

Artema shook his head. "No," he said, "Samani is a schemer but he isn't a leader. I mean, he has a military mind, but he certainly isn't a general. He'd rather drink wine than rule Astia."

"So did your father, yet he pulled it off."

"True," Artema said. "Very true." He threw up his hands with exacerbation. "Well I never saw Samani as anything but a leeching boozer and a pirate."

Praedor nodded but seemed unconvinced. She waved him out and he stepped into the hall.

It took all of his composure not to break out laughing as he left the room. As long as they chased Kernigan, they would never suspect him as the true leader of the Society. It was time to commence the second phase of his plan. His *special* weapons against the council would arrive soon. *Yes, by all means, it is time to begin.*

Councilman Merek waited for Horn to leave and then eased open the door. Chancellor Praedor's stare lingered in the direction Artema had left, when she finally turned she wore a sinister smile.

"They play us for fools," she said. "Those two orchestrated Artema's arrival just as sure as they've directed the bombings and riots."

Merek avoided the chair across from the chancellor, choosing instead to lean against the window frame. In a low voice he said, "By feigning ignorance of Campton's true plan, you'll draw the true leader from among them. Overconfidence will show their hand," he promised. He gazed out the window as he spoke, the view of the city helping him think. "The final question remains, which is the one they call the Dragon?"

"Most certainly Artema," she surmised. "Just as surely as he's the one calling the shots." She paused and then added, "one thing bothers me though."

"What would that be?"

"How he maintained control over the Society from across the sea. He's been away for so many years that any contacts in Astia would have grown ambitious in their own right." She shook her head. "No, Horn must have sensitivity to the bead just as Campton does. That's the only explanation. He either controlled his lieutenants with spring abilities or he communicated with them telepathically through autumnal. We must determine which."

Merek stared down at the city. Dusk was setting fast and curfew would begin within the hour. He watched as workers hurried to the train depots so they could return to their districts in time. Without averting his eyes he asked, "Why not both?"

"That *is* a possibility," she agreed, "but, as you know, occurrence of polykinetic abilities is rare. It is found in only one percent of emotants and far less in those with sensitivities."

"Then you agree it is a possibility."

She nodded. "When we apprehend him, we'll take precautions against both."

"What of the nuclear devices? Aren't you concerned that those have fallen into their hands?"

"No," she replied. "After Shol informed us of his brother's departure from Andalon, I intervened and altered Jakata's orders. The devices carried by the landing team are inert. I bought him time to take control of the continent, and he has three months to pull off his scheme."

She doesn't know, Merek realized, breathing a sigh of relief, *about the plutonium.* He shifted his weight, feeling less anxious about her knowledge. He smiled slyly. "That was a cunning trick of his, to warn us and then step away from the limelight. What's his plan for Andalon?"

"He's learned the remaining Braston is controlled by the leader of The Cove, and is drawing him out of hiding as we speak. He'll allow the chaos to burn itself out rather than waste his time chasing emotants. No, he'll allow them to draw together upon the fortified city. In due course Eston will fall as well, and we'll no longer need to reset the society. He'll continue to serve as our chief agent as well as supreme leader over the experiments."

"You believe he'll be easier to control than the Esterling family?"

"Unlike his brother," Chancellor Praedor explained, "Campton Shol is loyal to our Council. And unlike Esterling, he'll ensure that his queen isn't impregnated by one of his generals."

"That certainly caused complications, didn't it?" Merek's thoughts turned to the heir of Esterling marching on Eston. "At least the son lives. Are we certain the final prophecy speaks of him?"

"Shol has no doubts. He spent the past decade deciphering texts, and believes the heir is the key to stopping the Destroyer. After that he is expendable."

"What if Samani interferes?"

"The invasion force included another safeguard," Praedor explained. "Even if Nakala manages to interrupt the heir, I found a descendent of Michael Esterling here in Astia. He was part of the invasion force."

"I see," Merek smiled with understanding. "Then marked by birth his fate is sealed."

Samani watched the submersibles dip below the waterline. It would take his invasion force a week to cross the ocean into Astia. Part of him yearned to be aboard during the eastward journey, but his trip would have to wait. It was time to enter the next phase of his revolution.

Delilah approached. "Gretchen is hitching the horses to the wagon," she said. We can depart whenever you're ready."

He stared ahead, taking in the faint line where the sky met the ocean. The rhythm of the waves soothed his mind, quieting his unnecessary thoughts. *I'm sorry Fatwana,* he sent toward the vessels.

It's okay brother, she responded. *I'm happy to serve your collective. I fully understand your mission now and will see it through to the end.*

Then I will retreat from your thoughts, sister. Your memory will know only the truth I gave you.

After closing the conversation, Samani sighed audibly and turned to Delilah. "Let's be off then. Eston is a long ride."

Bachir Dilek watched from the trees, pressed low to the ground. With no weapon he felt useless, unable to interfere as the enemy force loaded the submersibles. Not everyone boarded, however. He was surprised their leader remained behind with only two women and a teenage girl. They climbed aboard a wagon and drove westward, along the forest road. He let them get a fair distance ahead before following.

Chapter Twenty-Two

General Titus halted the column. The high ridge they rested upon overlooked a broad valley with soft hills and tall grasses waving in the breeze. The choice in vantage restored his faith in King Robert. The boy carefully chose the position after studying detailed maps found in the belongings of the late General Reeves. It was easily defensible, and the wind here felt good against his bald head, cooling both his skin and the fever within.

The sweeping hills cascaded gracefully toward the city of Norton far on the horizon. They were bare except for occasional trees that had survived the strong winds and storms prevalent in late spring. *Yes,* he thought, *the king chose a perfect location for our defense.* There was not a trace of water anywhere, the closest spring miles away.

He ordered the men to dismount. "Dig in here," he ordered. "Cut down any wood you can, find and haul it to this location. Use it to line the walls of your trenches and protect against erosion." Turning his destrier, he trotted to the edge of the embankment. The sheer walls were impossible to climb and would funnel a northern attack to the south. A row of marksmen positioned here would ensure the enemy made a wide advance.

His scalp itched and he raised his hand to scratch. When he pulled it away his nails were stained with crimson. Frederique quickly pulled out his handkerchief and dabbed at the wound. He was finding these more and more on his body and the discovery of one in plain sight concerned him. *No one can know,* he worried.

"What do we do with these?" The voice came from a young lieutenant pulling a cart filled with animal skins. "I've got fifty wagons full."

"Those are for collecting and storing drinking water," Titus explained. "A gift from the Pescari."

"Take a squad about two miles south and you'll find a fresh spring. Ensure that each one is filled, even if you have to shuttle them over several days. When the siege begins, we'll need every drop we can find if we're to last several days in battle."

The young officer saluted and departed. The general watched him leave and quickly gathered volunteers. *No questions asked*, thought Frederique. *They're my troops now and follow me as they did Max.* Maximus Reeves had been his mentor and friend since he had been as young as the lieutenant gathering water. *I hope that I can live up to your genius, Max.*

He noticed a group of soldiers placing shovels into the ground. "Not there! Over here," he shouted. "Look at the angle of the slope," he explained. He dismounted and grabbed a rifle laying nearby. "Like this." Titus put it to his shoulder and pressed his belly into the dirt as he took aim. "If you defend this position, they'll be easier to pick off. You're hidden from their view and they'll have to keep their bodies upright to keep balance." Once he regained his feet, he handed the rifle to its owner. "Dig the line here," he ordered.

Robert rode tall in the saddle. The bulk of his force moved slowly along the Misting River. Weeks earlier they had split away from the main artery, following the eastern branch through dense pine forests as they marched northeast. They had finally emerged into the region of Norton, a patch of fertile farmlands that bordered Loganshire in the west and north.

"Only a few more days before we can see the city," he told Taros. Despite their earlier confrontation, he had grown to respect and even form a friendship with the shappan. He found him a wise leader, far more mature than his actual years. "We're not far from our milestone," he told him. "There, we'll venture inland and leave the river behind us as we approach the city from the south."

Taros nodded his approval. "We must remain unseen. What will happen if we are spotted?"

"That is the reason we keep to the trees. We'll avoid most of the farm houses this way and all of the towns. The region south of the fork has been sparsely populated, but we're bound to engage settlers eventually. Even if they dispatch riders to Norton, we should rendezvous with General Titus before they can mobilize."

Arne screeched high overhead and the king snapped his mind to share the eyes of his eagle. "Your uncle approaches," he said.

The Pescari strained to see the riders, too far for him to make out. He relaxed atop his mount. "Does he trot or gallop toward us?"

"He trots."

"Then the news is not grave tidings," Taros explained.

"Good. Let's hope it remains positive."

They reunited with Teot an hour later. "The city does not suspect our arrival," he reported. "They go about their business with open gates."

Robert asked, "What of their defenses?"

"Most of their cannons face the sea to the north. They are not prepared for a southern assault."

Taros turned to Robert. "Is that what you desire? Will you attack the city?"

"I hope not. They are my own people and I need their support instead of fear. No," he explained, "I expect Braen Braston and his league of emotants to attack before we can siege Norton. We'll assist the city leaders, and they'll celebrate us as liberators."

"And if they don't, and he attacks from the south, how will we defend from two sides?"

Robert smiled. I sent Titus ahead to prepare a defensible position, one that affords protection from all sides. There, we'll make our stand against Braston if he indeed attacks. If he doesn't then we'll parlay with the city leaders and make our decision before venturing to Eston."

Taros nodded his agreement. "It is a good plan."

Robert turned his attention to a group of teens riding in the back of a wagon. *The Dreamers,* he thought, *are so young.* The oldest, a teenager named Cuyler rode alongside the others atop a black steed. King Esterling motioned for a nearby soldier to fetch the boy. He hurried over.

"You summoned me, your highness?" The teen was outwardly nervous, no doubt unsure how to address royalty.

Robert smiled disarmingly. "You are the young man named Cuyler?"

"Yes, my liege... I mean... your honor."

"Your highness or my liege is fine. Save 'your honor' for magistrates and constables." Robert gestured toward Taros and offered, "Won't you ride with us a while?"

"Yes, my liege, but I'm not worthy. How can I serve the crown?"

Esterling scolded, "None of that self-doubt and never minimize your usefulness before your king."

"I'm sorry, your highness."

The boy began to say more but Robert cut him off. He questioned, "But am I?"

Dumbfounded Cuyler asked, "Are you what?"

"Am I your king? Do you swear allegiance only to me or do you serve Wembley?" Understanding filled the teen's eyes. *Good,* thought Robert, *he is bright enough to think for himself.*

Sitting straighter in his saddle Cuyler responded with a slightly deeper and more assertive voice, "I'm no outlaw. Of that I assure you."

"Good," replied the king, "unless you consider yourself a pirate instead." He set his face the way his mother had taught him as a boy, stoically and betraying nothing of his private motivations.

"Absolutely not, your highness." After a brief pause, he added, "I'm thankful that Eusari rescued us from the Diaph prison, and with interest for knowledge I stayed on to learn our craft."

"Craft?" Robert hadn't expected the word. "You call it a craft and not a talent? Perhaps a better word would be powers? We all are quite powerful in each of our own rights, isn't that right, Taros?"

The shappan had slacked reigns to allow the two Andalonians to ride alongside, but spurred Falia to match step. "I once believed myself a god when my powers first manifested."

Cuyler understood the insinuation immediately. "Your highness," he promised, "I am but a humble servant."

"Bullshit," the king pressed, "you are nearly my equal in power as an emotant. What assurance do I have that the Dreamers are loyal to my crown?"

Cuyler fell silent, pondering the words and betraying just a tinge of ambition. When he finally spoke it was with confidence. "I am certainly not a god, King Robert."

"Then what are you?"

"I'm a soldier. I was trained first by Samani Kernigan, then by Shon Wembley and Eusari. I can fight, my liege. I only ask for a banner under which to stand."

"Well," Robert promised, "I can provide that." He pointed at the eagle and rose flying atop a bannerman's pole. "What do you ask in return? How do you see yourself serving my sigil?"

"Since we first began our training," Cuyler explained, "I've seen us as a special type of soldier. Our weapons are... they are unique."

"I'll agree to that."

"I would like to be an officer in your corps, an elite corps if you please, and I'll ensure the others follow you as well."

"That is easily done," Robert promised. "How do you know the others will follow? How do we know they won't follow Eusari or Braen Braston?"

"Braen Braston is dead, your highness."

"Have you seen the body? Has any among your number?"

The teen fell silent while he pondered, then answered, "Only Sebastian and Caroline."

"And to whom do you attribute their allegiance?"

"Sebastian loves the Northman like a father," Cuyler explained, "and Caroline loves Eusari as a mother."

"And where are these two now?"

"Sebastian rides with your fleet and Caroline is in Logan with Eusari."

"And you're certain the others will follow you?"

"Yes," the teen promised, "all except Marita, but she's in the southern continent."

"Well then, Lieutenant Cuyler. We'd better get you a uniform. You're dismissed."

Robert spurred his horse and Taros followed, leaving the smiling boy frozen in his tracks. As they rode away Taros asked, "Can you trust him?"

"My father taught me that inside every soldier is a willingness to serve. You heard him; he simply needed a banner under which to march." Robert paused then added, "And I'll watch him closely until I'm certain of his loyalty."

Skander ordered his boats to drop anchor. The signalman beat his drums in response, relaying the message. Soon, sails raised on every vessel. The northern king waited until the ship held firm in its place, then strode to the railing. As he waved his hand over the waters, they rose up to meet him, freezing in place and presenting an icy staircase to descend.

Where is the city? The watery expanse confused him. *I see a lake where there should be Weston.* He waved both hands before him and the waters split as if he had shoved them aside. Shimmering walls stood on both sides as the water held. "Children! Come to me," he shouted. Soon three hundred figures clad in white fur descended staircases of air to join him on the lake bed.

He gestured at the black rock beneath their feet and asked, "Where are they?"

In unison the Snow Cats pointed.

"Dig," he commanded Artur who had joined his side. "The walls of the rookery wouldn't have melted. Break this rock and dig until you find the entrance."

His crewmen dug for hours, swinging their axes against the porous rock and breaking it into shards. Night fell upon the working crew men, their progress illuminated by torch and moonlight. They worked tirelessly, and bit by bit they made their way downward until their blows no longer broke the surface. The sight of his men standing idly by infuriated the king. He demanded, "Why have you stopped?"

Artur pointed. They stood atop black stone as smooth as glass. The pressure of the rapidly cooling magma and the heavy water above had solidified the final layer into fine obsidian. They could dig no further.

Skander roared his anger into the night.

Chapter Twenty-Three

Hester stood upon the lee deck, shaded from the sun but breathing the fresh air. If you could call it fresh, given the stench of the harbor and the aroma of decaying fish. Regardless of the offense it brought her, it beat the reek of unbathed men and the rancid way their odor left their bodies. She wanted off *She Wolf* in the worst possible way.

Movement caught her eye and she watched as Cedric and Sippen made their way to the brow. *Those ingrates are up to something,* she thought. *They always are.* They waited until the peg-legged first mate was looking the other way and then they darted across, stepping foot on the pier and making a beeline to the wharf. She made up her mind quickly to follow. Whatever they were doing beat bathing in the stench of a stuffy boat. While Peter Longshanks' back was turned, she raced after them.

"Stop," came the cries from the ship. "Come back!"

With a devilish smile she ignored the calls from topside and soon caught up with the mismatched pair of misfits. With accusation in her voice she asked, "What are you boys up to?"

They wheeled around like children caught stealing candy. Sippen stammered as usual. "Nuh... nothing, Huh... Hester."

"Just a bit of a walk to stretch the leg," Cedric added with a point toward the only one he had intact. She couldn't help but notice he had drawn toes at the tip of the peg. Those, along with the painted eye on his patch, completed his ludicrous ensemble.

"Bullshit," she accused. "I know you two as well as I do Braen. You're sneaking off and I'm coming."

"But it's duh... dangerous," protested Sippen.

"It beats boredom." She gestured forward. "Lead on. You can explain your need for secrecy along the way."

"Awe," Cedric replied, "it ain't no secrecy. We're just leavin' without the Cap'n's permission."

"Wuh... what he means," explained Sippen, "is muh... my need for a workshop is muh... more important than her uh... orders." He led them a few blocks into the city.

Hester's eyes darted back and forth as they walked, searching for hidden dangers. For a moment she questioned whether she should have left the ship. The streets crawled with ruffians and miscreants, and thinking of these increased her anxiety. She straightened out her dress. *Maybe I shouldn't have worn such extravagant clothing,* she worried. Then, as an afterthought, she removed the brooch of House Braston, clipping it safely inside a pocket of her cloak.

The first two blacksmiths wouldn't spare even a glance at the trio as they sent them on their way. They had to walk down two more streets to find another. They arrived at the door to the third and Sippen suggested they try a different approach, one that wouldn't give them away as northerners. Before entering they decided to let Cedric do the talking. Hester's accent was too thick and Sippen's stutter would get in the way.

Cedric removed his eyepatch, blinking both eyes against the sunlight. Hester gasped, suddenly realizing he had played at having lost one. "What the actual hells, Cedric? Your eyes are fine!"

"Nah," he argued and pointed at the one he kept uncovered, "this one's for daytime and this one," he pointed at the other, "is for seeing in the dark." He pointed again at the first. "So this one's better than the other." He grinned wildly and added, "It's me special eye."

"You," Hester said with a huff, "are an absolute moron."

"A moron who's about to get us a shop." He transformed into a gentleman, straightening his hair and quickly combing his beard before pushing the door and strolling casually inside. Even his clothing appeared less disheveled.

A burly man eyed them suspiciously, obviously on alert and wary of northerners. He demanded, "What do you want?"

"My good sir," Cedric began with a perfect Estonian accent, "my wife and I," to her chagrin he gestured to Hester, "are in need of repairs to our carriage." He yawned as if the conversation were boring him and wiped a finger's worth of dust off the window-sill. "We'll require that you rent us your entire workshop for a week or two."

"Well, if you only need repairs then I can do them for you." He demanded, "What do you need with my entire shop?"

Cedric placed a sack of gold on the counter. "We are not your usual customers, good sir. Our needs are our own and the gold is yours. All else we require from you is privacy and silence. Take your wife on a vacation or something. Just give us two uninterrupted weeks with full access to your shop."

The blacksmith stopped eyeing the purse and decided instead to open the top. He poured some out on the counter and his eyes grew wide with disbelief. "That's enough to buy it two times over."

"Thuh... then that's what we plan to do," Sippen said. "Suh... sell it to us and luh... leave your tools."

They didn't have to ask twice. The broad-shouldered man shed his apron and threw it down on the counter, pausing only to shove the spilled coins back into the satchel. He nearly ran from the room.

Cedric returned his eyepatch, ensuring that it snugly fit his head. Then he said, "See? I done told you that I kin speak s'phisticated when I won't to!"

"Yes," Hester agreed, "you're a consummate thespian."

Cedric beamed at this, mistaking the sarcasm for a compliment. "Aye, that be so. I love the women so much, I do."

Caroline had watched as Krill and Yurik made their dash from *She Wolf.* Turning to Mr. Longshanks she asked, "Why didn't you stop them?"

"They're grown men, Caroline." He shrugged. "And knowing Yurik he has a good reason to defy the Captain's orders. My guess would be that he intends to conjure up some sort of weapon we can use in the fight to come."

She nodded, remembering the carcass grenades and the toxic fumes they used to clear the batteries of Diaph. "But what about the northern queen? Won't she stand out in a city like Logan? Eusari said they hate northerners here."

"Aye," Peter agreed. "That they do. But she's a queen and there's no arguing with any woman, much less one raised with regality." He returned to his work.

Caroline stared after the trio, watching closely until they finally disappeared into the crowd. She made a mental note of the direction they had departed.

Chapter Twenty-Four

The people of Eston lined the streets to welcome the return of their army. All along the road to Unification Square, the audience cheered and clapped their arrival. Old and young climbed atop buildings for a better look. Fathers hoisted their children onto their shoulders, women threw rose petals on the cobblestones, and priests stood on the steps blessing all who had gathered. The triumph belonged to their beloved Marcus Esterling.

He sat on a magnificent throne in the square, having discarded the simple chair that his mother had sat upon during her blessing ceremonies. Despite the season of harvest, he had dispensed with her old traditions. He chose instead to celebrate his victory over Estowen's Landing. The kingdom belonged to him and no one could advise him otherwise.

His new generals stood on each side of their king, dressed in uniforms that matched his own. "Caswell," he said to the young man with tightly cropped hair and broad mustache, "isn't this fabulous?"

"Yes, my liege," the man replied. Despite his youth, he had been highly recommended to Marcus. So far, he had proven dazzling with his plans to attack Robert.

"How many citizens showed up today? In your estimate, of course."

The young officer beamed. "Ten thousand, your highness!"

He turned to the older man, a crusty old soldier who looked like he had bitten a pickle. "What do you think, Underwood?"

"I think you're a damn fool with his cart ahead of the horse. We shouldn't be celebrating until your brother's head sits upon a spear."

Marcus smiled at his candor. This officer had also come highly recommended, known far and wide for his actions against the Pescari. "That time will come, General."

Horns announced the arrival of the army and Marcus stood. His excitement soon disappeared, replaced by a sudden feeling of bewilderment. The people gasped as the soldiers stumbled through the streets, staggering with each step as if each would crumble at any moment. Instead of a triumphant fighting force, the city beheld a downtrodden and bloodied assembly.

Underwood gasped at the sight before him. "That's all that's left?"

"No," a voice answered from behind. "That is what is left of the living. The rest are awaiting the king's orders in the forest."

Marcus turned to find Kestrel standing out of sight behind a curtain.

Underwood asked, "The living?"

His confusion pleased the king who explained, "They've been reanimated by Jaguars." When he spoke to the general it was like he taught a simpleton befuddled by common knowledge.

"Restored," the Falconer corrected. "They will be your true force when the fight begins."

"This won't do," Underwood insisted as he watched the crippled army return. "The people will see this as a weakness instead of strength."

"That is very true, General," Kestrel agreed, "but the triumph was the king's decision."

Marcus played dumb, going along with the lesson the Falconer intended to teach. "Why didn't you advise me against it, if you knew how badly we were beaten?"

"My job is not to interfere with the plans of the true leader of Andalon. I can only advise, and will only take action when commanded by the council."

By then the people had begun to disperse, muttering amongst themselves and whispering of incompetence. Marcus did not need to hear their words to know they grumbled against his throne. Testing his newly appointed commanders he feigned anger, letting it fill him as he wheeled on them. "Did you know the army was in this state?"

"No, my lord," Underwood assured him. "We were triumphant in the east, and no dispatches suggested otherwise."

The king turned to the younger man. "What of you, Caswell?"

"No, your highness. The Falconers had control of our army the entire time, and we are never informed of their progress."

"I see," Marcus said as he faced Kestrel. "But you knew and did not inform me."

"As I stated before, my duty is to the Astian Council and serve only the collective."

He still serves Shol, the king realized. Then he looked at his generals, each staring blankly at the Falconer and offering no plan of action. *And they're as worthless as Brohn.*

"Caswell?"

"Yes, my liege?"

"Order the city guard to gather those who are leaving. Don't let them cross the span."

"Right away, your highness."

The king turned to face the wretched soldiers looking up with tired expressions.

"Underwood," he asked, "how many soldiers would you estimate stand before me?"

"A little less than two thousand, my liege."

"And how many were held in reserve and can march against my brother to quell his rebellion?"

"Six thousand strong, your highness."

"That means one-third of our force is under control of the Falconers and their Astian Council." He held a hand out for Kestrel. "The true ruler of Andalon demands one of your beads, Falconer."

The specter complied and pulled out a black Astian pearl.

"No. Not that one. Give me a white one."

The Falconer did not move. He stood frozen as if considering whether or not to obey.

"Give me," Marcus said again slowly, "a white bead."

"That is not advisable, your highness."

"If it is not compatible, then what is the worst of the danger?"

"Your body will reject it or you will die," Kestrel explained.

"Well," Marcus said with a smile, "if I die at least I am finally free of everyone's incompetence." He shook his hand, silently reminding the specter of his order. Unable to refuse, Kestrel placed a single white bead in his palm. "Give me several," Marcus demanded, "this will require much more than the usual dosage."

Again the Falconer complied, placing a second pearl next to the first. "Your highness," Kestrel pleaded, "perhaps you should only take one at first, to ascertain your tolerance."

"To Cinder with tolerance," Marcus replied. "Tolerance is what allowed this revolution to grow." He tossed both beads into his mouth and swallowed them with a gulp of wine from his goblet. Nothing happened. Unlike the black pearls, which caused his mind to spin and his stomach to drop as if he had suddenly risen thousands of feet into the air, he felt no obvious changes. Even his vision held steady. He held out his hand.

"I cannot give you more, your highness," Kestrel protested.

"You will give me that entire bag at your hip," the king commanded.

With everyone on the stage now staring at the Falconer, he complied and handed over a large satchel filled with dozens of white beads.

Marcus snapped his fingers and pointed at a pouch on his other hip. "Now the black ones." Kestrel handed these over as well.

The king dug into the first and pulled out two more, swallowing them down to chase the others. All at once, a mild wave of cramps passed through his muscles and a rush of strength followed in their wake. Marcus Esterling suddenly felt invincible.

Abruptly, he experienced awareness of every lifeforce on the span. The heat of Underwood, the closest to him, was overwhelming and the stench of illness intruded the king's senses. "Kill them, General. Kill them all," he ordered.

"Who, your majesty?" Underwood didn't understand.

"Fine," Marcus replied with exasperation, "I'll do it myself."

The city of roses abruptly sprang to life at his command. Every thorny vine in Unification Square animated, twisting and curling around both citizen and soldier. Women and children screamed helplessly as they struggled against strangulation. The men tried to fight back, hacking with knives and axes or any other tool on their belts. Eventually the gathered crowd fell silent, choked off by the foliage.

King Esterling smiled with satisfaction as he gazed at the massive rose garden below, taking in the magnificent blooms starkly contrasted against a sea of green leaves. For that brief moment he considered that his mother had been correct in regard to the blossoms. The rose provided a splendid display of his power and wealth.

"Now General Caswell, tell me again how many citizens had gathered today?"

"Ten thousand, my liege."

"Good number," Marcus said with a grin. Now I'll lead with a clear majority, wouldn't you say?" As if in explanation, he shouted to the garden below, "Rise!" At first nothing happened so he poured his own lifeforce like sunlight over the flowers. They turned in unison to bask in his glory, absorbing his strength into their leaves. Realizing his previous mistake, he slowly wrung the life from the bushes and poured it into the scores of dead tangled within the vines. As the stems turned brittle and blooms fell discarded, the creatures within flowed with energy.

"Rise," he again ordered, "and obey my command!" Twelve thousand answered his call.

"Kestrel," he said, but no answer came. "Kestrel!" The king spun around but the Falconer had fled. Turning to his generals he said, "Well, I guess I've no need for either of you." As he turned his back and made his way to his carriage, the horde descended on the horrified and useless senior officers.

Chapter Twenty-Five

Marque and Madelyn found the harbor sharks without much trouble. Each of the brutes clad themselves with identifiable blue shirts. They placed no secrecy around their dominion over the port and walked in broad daylight. The pair of outlaws followed three of them to a warehouse at the northern end of the wharf.

Two heavily muscled guards prevented their entry. "Not so fast," one of them growled. "State yah business."

Marque drew back his hood, revealing his face. He asked, "Do you know me?"

The sentry laughed. "Do ya 'spect me tah know ev'ry stranger in Lah-gun?"

"No," Marque replied, "I expected not since both of you are new. But your boss will. Why don't you take me to Karla?"

"She's busy," roared the second guard.

"Well then," he pressed, "let her know that her *Letter of Marque* has been revoked."

The first man shouted, "Piss off!"

"Fine," Marque replied, "I'll tell her myself." He pulled a cudgel from his cloak with a sweeping motion, catching the second guard squarely between the legs. When the brute doubled over, he swung again, this time downward across the man's temple.

The first man drew his own cudgel and raised it above his head. When he stepped forward Marque placed a perfectly timed sidekick to the outer edge of his knee. The guard's heavy bodyweight did the rest. As tendons tore, he toppled over. The momentum of his swing arched harmlessly past Marque.

Madelyn rolled her eyes playfully, "There's no need to impress me anymore. You know that, right?"

"Aye," he told her, "but an older man's gotta keep up with the youngsters. They may steal you away."

"True," she said and kissed him on the cheek.

They left the two guards outside the door, one writhing in pain and the other peacefully passed out. "I hate training new guys," Marque said as they moved inside.

The warehouse hadn't changed since Marque had left a year before. The only difference was a sign hanging over the office door that read, "Karla's Kove."

Madelyn pointed to the sign and asked, "You know her?"

"Aye." We have a wee bit of history, she and I." Catching her scornful gaze he added, "But not like that. Don't worry. She's as chaste as a pastor's wife."

A shout from the gallery drew their attention upward. "Hey! You there!"

Marque smiled. "This fella I recognize," he said. Throwing back his hood he shouted, "Hey, Sully!"

"By Cinder's Crack! Marque? Is that really you?" The newcomer rushed down the stairwell, eager to see his old friend.

"In the flesh. Oh, and your new door thugs are lying down on the job."

Sully turned his eyes to the door. "Demon's Nipples! Please tell me you didn't rough them up too badly."

"Only one. The son of a tavern turner told me to 'piss off.' You really should've trained him better."

"What do you want me to do," Sully asked, "show every new guy your wanted posters?"

Madelyn interrupted, "What wanted posters?"

"She doesn't know?" Marque shook his head and Sully roared with laughter. "Your mate here is the most wanted man in Loganshire. Hell," he added, "he used to run this outfit."

The door to the office swung open, immediately stifling the man's revelry. "*Used* to," a tall woman with flowing red hair emphasized. "But now this outfit's mine." To Marque she said, "You've got a lot of nerve showing up here. The deal was that you'd stay away from Logan."

"Aye, and I'm part of a different crew now. You're position's safe, Karla. But I need your help." He hefted a heavy purse. "If you're up for hire, I have a job for you."

"Get in here." She stepped aside and pointed to her office. "I don't do business in the warehouse."

Jacque figured out quickly why the group of thieves called themselves "Sewer Rats." As soon as he dropped into the underground system he was overwhelmed by the stench of waste and the chittering of rats. He found that he could straddle the cesspool by keeping to the sides. The going was slow, but with the map given to him by Shon he eventually found their nest.

No guards watched their door. Presumably, no one would venture into their realm without a purpose or business to attend. Even the wrought iron gate was unsecured. He pushed it aside and stepped into a den of filth.

The Sewer Rats turned out to be the lowest of the low in Logan, shunned thieves and outcasts from the guild. Most of the crew lay drunken or completely passed out, too inebriated to notice his arrival. The others paid no attention to his presence. He carefully stepped over bodies until he reached a room on the far side.

He found this door unlocked as well, and pushed it open easily. An unimposing man sat at a desk, scribbling in a ledger and pushing his spectacles onto his face each time they slipped down his nose. The man didn't even look up when Jacque entered.

"Are you the rat king?"

The man laughed, "Only Shon Wembley called me that, but he's gone away. Are you a constable?"

"Not at all," the pirate replied. "I take it the two of you were close?"

"Far from it. That son of a tavern turner harangued my every move." He finally looked over his glasses to study his visitor. "You're not in cahoots with *him,* are you?"

"Would it be a deal breaker?"

"It most certainly would."

"Well, in that case I am, and I'm not." He hefted the heavy purse and slammed it on the table. "This is a down payment," he said, "for upfront costs."

The man straightened up, setting down his quill and pressing his glasses up his nose. "By Cinder's backside," he commented, "That would pay for a lot of things *upfront.*" He suddenly stiffened. "Does this payment require me to work with Wembley?"

"Aye," replied Jacque, nodding his head. "That it does." He hefted a second purse, heavier than the first, and slammed it down beside the second. "But this requires you to kill him."

The little man narrowed his eyes. "This isn't an assassin's guild, but I'm not saying no. All I want to know," he asked, "is why you want your associate dead?"

"There's a certain prize I hope to obtain, but it's far out of my reach."

"And killing Wembley helps you how?"

"Killing Wembley does nothing for me." Jacque handed over a piece of parchment with a list of names. "But the rest of the list gives me everything."

"This," the man considered, "is a very expensive job. It'll cost far more than you've fronted. How can I know you can afford this venture?"

"Each has a price on their head. What I can't cover, you can recoup with bounties."

The man grinned with greed. "Then we have a deal."

Eusari listened to the Wolf Pack's chatter as they worked. They had gathered around a printing press as Shon placed the typeset.

Then he demonstrated the pressing and how to pull the page without smearing the ink when hanging each to dry. Once he felt confident they knew what to do, he let them take over.

Surprisingly, their incessant talking didn't bother her this time. She placed both hands on her belly and imagined what it would be like when her own child reached this age. She wondered if she would have a boy or a girl. *I hope for a boy,* she thought. Watching them fight over jobs gave her another concern. *But only one.*

Shon beckoned her to the door. "Come on, dearie. Let's go for a walk."

She pointed at the boys. "Are you sure they've got this down?"

He cocked his head and scanned the room. "Sure," he said with a dismissive wave. "They've got it. Come along."

He led her across the street to a small tavern. It wasn't busy, and only a few visitors were inside. One family in the corner looked up as she entered. The father appeared to be a farmer by his clothing. His wife had a kind face, simply dressed and with her hair tied into a bun. The children were well behaved. The two older boys discussed the pending birth of a colt with so much excitement that even Eusari felt eager to know the gender. The little girl never looked up.

She sat quietly, clutching her doll with both hands. Her bright red hair was braided down her back with a single green bow tied at the end. Though her face was down, Eusari imagined her with stark freckles contrasting her white skin. She barely touched her food.

"Eat some of your meat, Anne," her mother insisted. "You need the protein."

"I'm not hungry."

One of the boys piped up, "You have to eat your meat. Otherwise Papa won't get you candy from the store."

"I don't want any," she protested.

"Don't push her," the father cautioned. "If she isn't hungry then let her be."

Shon led Eusari to a table in the far corner of the tavern, far enough that the rest of the conversation was lost to her. "Dearie," he said, "how do you feel, being so close to home?"

She shrugged. "*She Wolf* is my home, Shon. There's nothing for me here."

"There could be," he said. "Your brothers live, and they have families." He pointed to her belly. "Just as you're about to be a mother. Forget this war and go home to Brentway. Buy a farm and settle down."

"Shon," she warned, "I'm not interested. I've no desire to farm and I can raise my child aboard a ship just as well as I can on shore."

"Surrounded by pirates?" He made a good point, and she clamped her mouth shut. "Dearie," he pressed, "would you at least like to meet your family?"

"We've got business here in Logan, Shon. I don't have time for sightseeing much less a reunion."

The door to the tavern opened wide and a man entered. He looked very similar to the farmer sitting with his family. Something about their features caused Eusari to pause. She looked closer. At the sight of Shon sitting in the corner, the newcomer waved. Then he sat down with the others.

"No." Eusari shook her head, tears suddenly filling her eyes as she realized his game. "What are you doing, Shon? I'm not ready for this."

"And you never will be unless you get it over with." He stood and reached out his hand. "Come. Meet your brothers, dearie."

Despite her fears, Eusari's heart won over. She took his hand and allowed him to lead her to the table. Now that she understood who they were, she couldn't help but see traces of her father in both men and the boys. They all waited patiently, smiling kindly.

Shon nodded to the father. "Franque." He turned to the newcomer. "Jean."

"Hello, Shon," Franque replied. "Your letter caught us by surprise. Why've you asked us into town? You mentioned a family matter?" He gestured around the table. "This is all the family left to us since Thom and Mauri died. What business do the Thorinsons share with the Wembley's?"

Shon pointed to the little girl. "She's grown. Looks like a spittin' image of her mother. Dearie," he asked, "how old are you now?"

She held up four fingers and whispered, "Almost five."

Eusari, afraid to look at her brothers for fear of breaking into tears, stared down at the girl. The doll she clutched was worn but clean, adorned in a regal dress befitting a queen. The toy was not the usual kind carried by children of Brentway farmers. Eusari knelt beside her and asked, "What's your doll's name?"

"Lady Crestal," the girl replied.

"Like the queen?"

The girl nodded, clutching it tighter to her chest. "She gave it to me."

"She takes that thing with her everywhere," Franque explained. "She hasn't put it down since meeting Lady Esterling last fall." He turned to Shon and pressed. "So are we going to get down to this family business, Wembley?"

"Aye," Shon replied. "That we are. But to do so we have to wait until your family's assembled properly."

Jean gestured at those gathered. "We're all here, Shon. Get to the point."

"I'm getting there." He pulled up a chair for Eusari and she sat. "Eusari," he said to her, "Say hello to your brothers."

Chapter Twenty-Six

Marita slept soundly throughout the voyage south. During her many travels with Alec, she had grown accustomed to the soft lapping of waves against the hull, and the creaks and groans of the wood no longer frightened her. Rather, the chorus was a lullaby that soothed her tired mind into slumber. On this night she enjoyed a dream.

She and her mother walked hand in hand into the forest around Atarax. They hunted truffles. Marita carried a little basket and her mother held onto a leash attached to their best rooting pig, Snuffles. He was a fat oinker with a hunger for the 'shrooms. Whenever they ventured out with him, they had no problem filling their basket.

"Mama," she said, "I wish you didn't have to die."

"I know, sweet love. But you have a good family now," Floret replied. "Alec and Mattie are the perfect choice for parents."

Marita opened her mouth to answer but it abruptly shut. The air around her changed and her mother dissipated. In the blink of an eye the dream faded into ether. Then the forest fell away, and she stood in a black world. In the far distance the stars stared down, beckoning with different pathways on which she could travel.

Sebastian materialized in front of her. "Cuyler says you have to come," he said.

"Well that son of a tavern turner can kiss my butt," she said. "I'm not going. They make fun of me every time and they never believe anything I tell them. I've heard their whispers; the older Dreamers say I'm 'touched in the head' but I'm not."

"They make fun of me too," he sighed. "But Caroline said that we're a team, and teams have to work together."

"*They* are a team. I have my own team with Alec and Braen. I don't need Cuyler or Caroline, or any of them."

"What are you talking about? Braen's dead, Marita."

She clamped her hands over her mouth, suddenly aware of what she let slip. "Forget I said that."

Sebastian moved closer. "They don't ever believe you, but I do. And I don't think you're crazy. Marita, if you've seen Braen you have to tell me. Remember when that lady Falconer was scaring me? This could be another one of their tricks."

"It's not," she assured him. "This is really Braen." She manifested a fluffy caterpillar and climbed on its back to get comfortable. "He and Alec swore me to secrecy, but I trust you, so I'll tell the story." She started with the night Braen appeared in the vineyard and ended with the taking of *Vigilance.* When she had finished, she hopped off the caterpillar and poked a finger into the chest of Sebastian. "You'd better not tell anyone."

"He won't have to," a voice said from the blackness. Suddenly Cuyler and the others appeared. "We heard everything."

Caroline demanded, "Why didn't you tell us? Eusari has been miserable since he left, and she needs to know!"

"Don't tell her! Please!" Marita begged but Caroline didn't remain. In a flash she was gone, back to the awakened world. Bearnard shook his head and also left. Marita turned to Cuyler and pleaded. "Please don't let her tell Eusari! Braen swore me to secrecy."

"That's if he's really alive," the older boy replied. "When will you ever grow up and stop your storytelling? Everything is always a stretch of the truth for you."

In an instant they were all gone except for Sebastian. He kicked at the invisible dirt and apologized. "I'm sorry, I didn't know they were listening."

"It's okay," she told him. "They're nothing but assholes anyways." Then a thought hit her in the gut. "What do I tell Braen?"

"He's a nice guy, Marita. Just tell him the truth." Then, in a bright flash of light he was gone as well.

No, she thought, *I won't tell him. I can't admit that I broke the code!*

A thousand miles away Samani Kernigan roused from his own slumber. He blinked his eyes against the darkness and adjusted them to the forest canopy above the wagon. When he sat up, he carefully removed the blanket so as not to rouse Delilah and Gretchen. Convinced that they hadn't been disturbed, he slipped to the ground and poked at the embers of their campfire.

The coals had cooled during the night, but enough remained that he could detect a faint glow. On this he blew gently, adding dried leaves until sparks caught and the flame roared to life. The warmth chased away the chill of the dream as well as the bite of the night air, and he huddled close. He expected company, so he added another log.

He thought about the conversation between the children. *Braen is alive,* he thought. *This changes everything.* He went over the story Marita had described. *But he's naturally revived, so he's powerless. That means he isn't the Destroyer.* He stared a little longer at the flame and finally concluded, *It doesn't matter, he's fulfilling the prophecy and I have another opportunity to revive him.*

Movement nearby caught Samani's attention and he spoke into the night. "If you're here to kill me, Bachir, can you first let me get warm?"

A moment passed and then two before a figure emerged. "You know my name?"

"I do. I also know the reason Simcor spared your life."

"I don't understand."

"No," Samani let out a sigh, "most people don't." He poked the fire once more, stirring it to a fierce roar. "He spared you because I wanted to meet you. What do you know of your ancestry?"

"Dilek is my father's name. His grandmother told him that our people originated along the southern coast of Astia."

"Aye," agreed Samani, "That's correct. But it's your mother's side I'm interested in."

"She hailed from Bergin."

"And her name?"

"Osterlang."

"A variation of Esterling. Did you know that?"

"I never gave it any thought."

"No, but we have," Samani insisted.

Delilah's voice spoke quietly from the wagon. "Only the son of Esterling can slay him in time."

"That's right," Samani agreed. "That's part of the prophecy and the reason you're here." He stood from the fire. I wanted to know one thing first, will you remove your pants?"

"I beg your pardon?" Bachir took a step backward.

"Do you have a birthmark or a scar on your leg?" He pointed to his thigh. "Right about here."

The soldier couldn't believe his ears. "I do. How do you know these things?"

"Please be kind enough to show us." Samani drew the pistol from his belt and trained it on the young man. "Please hurry, I don't really want to waste the bullet. These primitive things are so cumbersome to reload."

Bachir complied and unfastened his belt. He let his trousers drop to his knees. There, just below his underclothing was a darkened area of skin that wrapped around his thigh.

"Marked by birth his fate is sealed," Samani said. "Thank you, you may pull them up." He never diverted his eyes from the man when he added, "Gretchen dear, did you already swallow the bead?"

"Yes," she replied dryly.

"Then you may do the honors," he commanded.

The campfire abruptly blinked out and darkness enveloped the site. The soldier immediately burst into flames as fire sprang from

Gretchen's finger tips. Her eyes turned amber, glowing like hot coals in the night as she burned him to a cinder.

"You see, Delilah? The only other son of Esterling is no more, and cannot interfere. Nothing will stop the Destroyer until we're ready."

The brush along the forest edge moved and he looked up to find Ashima approaching, leaving the sentry post that had alerted him to Simcor's arrival. He would miss the omniscience shared with her bond.

"Brother," she said dryly, "the collective calls and I must respond."

"Go then," he commanded, "rejoin your brethren for the final time."

Chapter Twenty-Seven

Caroline awoke aboard *She Wolf,* shaken by the news Braen Braston lived. She swung her legs over the side of her hammock and hopped to the ground, quickly rifling through Eusari's footlocker. She found her captain's leather armor folded neatly and set to the side until after her pregnancy. They slid on easily.

Although a little baggy, she found the buckles could be adjusted to fit her smaller frame. She returned to the chest and removed the rest of the contents, digging down to find another box nestled beneath the clothing. She pried it open to reveal several throwing blades which stowed quickly into the many sheaths throughout the outfit.

As she pulled out a black woolen cloak, another box tumbled from within its folds. She dropped the cloak and stared. Curiosity won out over her race against time, and she pried this lock as well. Inside were letters addressed and sealed but never mailed. She scanned the names. They were intended for a family in Brentway, each with the same last name as Eusari. *She'll want these delivered,* she thought, and tucked them into a pocket on her thigh before slipping the hooded cloak over her head.

Most of the crew was asleep except for the night watchmen strolling the decks. There would be two lookouts, one each aft and forward. She could avoid these easily, especially veiled in the darkness of her captain's clothing. Her problem would be the security manning the midship's quarterdeck.

She crouched from behind a coil of hemp mooring lines and watched. A single lantern lit the station, and two men guarded the single entry onto the ship. She waited until one of them walked twenty paces away to relieve himself over the side. While he was busy looking the other way, she crept forward, positioning her body so close to the rail she could hear the other man breathe.

With a wisp of air she toppled three barrels to her left, far enough away that the man had to leave his post to shine the lantern. The padded boots of her armor made no noise as she sprinted across the brow and onto the wharf. The second guard shouted for her to stop, but was too busy buttoning his britches to pick up a rifle. In a matter of moments, she was free of the docks and wandering through the shadowy streets of Logan.

The city wasn't as large as Eston, but it was vast and quickly overwhelmed the girl. She didn't know where to begin her search for Eusari, and finally understood the expression "needle in a haystack." Her search, she knew, would begin once she found Sippen Yurik. He was the smartest man she knew, and would figure out a way to rescue her captain.

The trades district wasn't difficult to find, she merely followed the sounds of clanging metal and the aroma of melted iron. Her challenge would be to figure out which workshop the engineer had set up as his own. Her first thought was to find him working late. Surely no blacksmith was as dedicated as Sippen, she figured his would be the shop open the latest and he could be found tinkering the night away. That turned out to be a dead end. Most of the shop owners worked diligently, even at this late hour.

Frustrated, Caroline nearly gave up and returned to *She Wolf* when she noticed a plume of yellow smoke escaping a chimney. She crept closer and discovered that, unlike the other shops, this particular foundry kept the windows shuttered. She looked up. Even the upper level was closed tightly. The building was perfect for an engineer hoping to keep his projects away from the prying eyes of Falconers. She boldly knocked on the door and waited.

Sippen sat across from Caroline, eyes wide at the news. "Tuh... tell me uh... again," he said.

"Captain Braston is alive," she said, repeating the story a third time.

"Nuh... no wuh... way that's puh... possible," he protested.

"I dunno," Krill argued, "I wouldn't put nothin' outta the reach of Braen."

Hester, who had said nothing up until this moment, broke her silence. "We've heard the same about Skander, and his wound was to the head." She didn't look at the others when she spoke, she merely stared at the wall with tired eyes and both hands on her round belly.

Sippen needed more information. "Huh... who tuh... told you this?"

"Marita. Apparently, she, Braen, and Captain Pogue are on their way to Pirate's Cove. They're taking on Lord Nevra."

Krill beamed. "That's our Braen," he exclaimed. "Always taking on the bad guys."

"Buh... but wuh... why wouldn't he tuh... tell us? Suh... certainly he'd luh... let us know he's alive."

"No." The single word left Hester's mouth in a whisper. "He's too selfish to tell us. He's always preferred to risk his life fixing the world's problems on his own rather than sharing the burden."

"Thuh... that's true," Sippen agreed. If the three northerners in the room had one thing in common, it was their love for his best friend. They knew him better than anyone else except maybe Eusari. "Huh... he'd truh... try to do it on his own, juh... just like uh... always."

"Aye," Krill nodded. "That be true."

"I have to find Eusari," Caroline blurted out, suddenly aware of how much time they'd wasted. "She needs to know before she does something stupid."

"Luh... like what?"

"Like fall for Devil Jacque. He's been trying to woo her for months, ever since we left Middleton."

"Suh... certainly shuh... she wouldn't," Sippen reasoned.

"She likes him. She admitted to me that he's good looking, and that she hasn't given in yet only because it's too soon after Braen."

Hester snickered and Krill and Yurik turned. "That would suit me just fine," she said.

"Buh... but not Bruh... Braen," Sippen argued. "Wuh... we'll huh... help find her," he promised Caroline.

The sun rose over the Islands of Deception, named for the treacherous reefs hidden throughout the chain. Braen Braston stood the late watch, so he had spent most of the night leaning on the rail and waiting for morning. Illuminated by the golden glow, the shoals revealed their true danger, with sharp outcroppings just below the waterline. Many dangers awaited and, like the passage, not all treachery would be visible.

The creak of boards alerted him to approaching footsteps. He turned to learn Alec and Charro had already risen from their slumber. "We'll have trouble navigating with just the four of us," he told them.

"Aye," replied Alec, "which is why you need to hear Lord Valencia's plan."

"Neither of you seem pleased with the option, why do I sense hesitation in your voice?"

Charro spoke up, "Because murder is never the favored option, Lord Kraken."

"I've done my share of killing," insisted the northerner, "and I expect to slay many more as the day wears on. Spit it out."

"Without your power over the water we need a full crew to clear the reefs. The men we need are tied up below decks."

Braen considered then replied, "Dominique's men would rather run us aground than betray their captain." He shook his head, "No. I'll take my chances."

"They won't be Dominique's men, Braston." Valencia's words had turned icy, betraying a darker man beneath the colorful clothing.

Realization crept in and Braen felt a lump form in his throat.

"This *is* cold blooded," Pogue insisted, "but our only option."

Braston steeled himself and turned to Charro. "You can raise them all? You have that much power?"

The lord nodded, the grave expression never leaving his face. "I can and I do. But you'll have to kill them cleanly or I'll have a more difficult time taking control."

Pogue chimed in, "If you agree, then I'd like to get the business finished before Marita awakens. She's already observed so much violence, but murder is not something with which she should grow accustomed."

"I see the reason," he agreed. "Bring the men topside and I'll do it on the fantail." He felt his stomach turn and fought down a bit of bile. "We'll need allies when the fighting starts, and this ship is our only way out if things go wrong." Alec turned to leave but Braston called him back. "I need a knife. Someone removed mine from its sheath before my funeral."

One by one he slayed every man. Once he had finished, Charro knelt beside each and restored their life. Soon they had fifty men under their control. They saved Adolphus Dominique for last.

The captain struggled as Alec led him to the main deck. He abruptly stopped when he saw his crew standing with Braston. He asked, "What's this betrayal?"

"Make him kneel," Braen ordered. Pogue complied with a kick to the back of his knee. Without a word Braston pierced his heart with the blade, then wheeled around and plunged his hands in a rain barrel, washing his hands, but not his heart, of the evil deeds of the night.

While Valencia worked his magic, Pogue told Braen, "It had to be done."

"I'd beg my gods for mercy, but they abandoned me long ago." He stared out over the rail. "What's done is done. Get us inside The Cove."

"Aye." Pogue quickly ordered the crew about, hoisting the anchor and setting the reef sails.

Despite his words to the contrary, Braen prayed. *Forgive me this day, as my actions were noble in spirit. Guide me the rest of the way.* His thoughts immediately turned to Eusari. He suddenly needed her at his side. *No,* he told himself, *I can never face her again, not after lying with Hester.* He fought back tears as he stared across the sea.

They made Pirate's Cove by midday and Braen was shocked that the harbor defenses never questioned their entry. They merely acknowledged captain and crew and waved them into the harbor. Their ruse had worked, and Valencia had puppeteered Adolphus convincingly. Braston hoped he could do so again.

Braen and his tiny raiding party waited until nightfall before venturing out, leaving Dominique and his men behind in case they needed rapid escape. Once they disembarked, they immediately recognized The Cove had significantly cut roving patrols. From the pier to the city they only laid eyes on one squad and easily avoided detection. "This is too easy," whispered Pogue.

"Nevra has no opposition to his throne," Valencia explained, "he's not concerned about invasion."

"Meaning I'm supposed to be dead and Eusari's busy running around with Esterling." Mentioning his love twisted his anxious heart. "I'm sure we'll see more as we approach the palace."

Marita pointed, "Look!" Another patrol emerged from the city square. The trio ducked behind a row of hedges as the soldiers marched by. "That was close," she whispered after they had passed from earshot.

Braen pressed onward and signaled the others to follow. As they passed through the merchant sector, they paused at a boarded-up shop. "This was Ralphe Station's shop," Braston commented. He read the words aloud, "Kraken Lovers." He moved to the door and tried the handle. A busted lock gave way and the oak swung inward. He surveyed the room with sadness. "They sacked and looted his shop for being my friend," he explained.

"Braen," Alec reasoned, "he knew the risks. Don't blame yourself."

"There's no one else to blame, Pogue." He led them up the stairs and peered into an open room. The crimson stained mattress told the tale. "They killed him where he slept," Braen observed. He thought for a moment then added, "He had a daughter." He hurried to the next room and found the tiny bed empty.

"She's gone," Charro remarked. "I'm sure one of the neighbors took her in."

Braen nodded sadly and followed his friend downstairs. They found Marita staring at the stairs leading to the cellar. The northerner began to speak, but the girl shushed him with a finger over her lips. She pointed downward. The dust on the landing revealed fresh footsteps and many of them. Braston drew his axe and Alec his swords. The girl led the way, gliding down the steps without touching them or making a sound.

Once they reached the bottom, they could tell that the pantry had also been looted. Braen sighed and then turned to leave, "We need to hurry. The sun will be up in a few hours."

"Wait," Marita said with determination in her voice. The big man paused. She pointed to a row of shelves less dusty than the others. Tiny fingerprints had disturbed the light film. She tested the planks with a tendril of air. Then she smiled broadly and flashed the men a thumbs up. A secret door swung open, revealing a cramped compartment and three sets of terrified faces.

The men gasped as they stared down at the tiny trio. They watched as Marita sheathed her swords and casually walked forward. "Hello, Neill," she said with a grin. "Hi, Nathaira!"

Braston recognized the third face immediately. "Charleigh," he said. She rushed into his arms and sobbed uncontrollably. "I'm sorry about your parents," he whispered, holding her close and patting her back while the others climbed from their hiding place to greet Marita.

After there were no more tears to cry, the merchant's daughter asked, "Where is Captain Eusari?"

"She isn't here," he told her. "She sent me to find and rescue you."

The little girl wiped her nose on her sleeve and said, "That's fair. I guess you had to make up for almost killing me last time."

Alec Pogue's voice drew Braen's attention. "Demon's nipples," he said, prompting a stare by the younger children. "Sorry," he muttered. Rolling one of the barrels from the hideaway he said, "Looks like your friend had a nice stash of gunpowder."

Braen leaned in and took a count. "By the gods," he said, "there's at least fifty barrels!"

Marita listened closely to the story that Neill and Nat recanted. When she realized how important the story was, she called out to Alec. "Captain Pogue," she said. When he didn't respond she called out again, "Captain Dad." The men ignored her call as they rolled out barrels for inspection. "Captain Braston," she added. They were too busy chattering among themselves to notice. She sent a gust of wind that shoved each man, pushing them over the barrels and onto the floor.

Alec cried out. "What in Cinder's name did you do that for?"

"Because you adults are too busy celebrating your gunpowder to even know how to use it," she said.

"You listen here, dearie!" Pogue picked himself off the floor. "I've been shooting off cannon since before you were born!"

Marita rolled her eyes, and another gust of wind pushed a second hidden panel aside. "You could roll one or two all the way to the palace," she told him, "or you could do it my way." She pointed a single finger into the darkness. "According to these two," she pointed at Nat and Neill, "this tunnel leads under and into the palace."

Both men leaned forward and peered in before exchanging a glance. "If only we had a sled," Braen said.

Marita rolled her eyes again, letting out an audible sigh. The younger children laughed at her comical display. Tendrils of air abruptly wrapped around and through one another, weaving a sled just inside the tunnel. "Well, what are you waiting for? I'm not going to load it." She and the other children burst out in laughter while Braen and Alec shrugged.

She heard Braston whisper, "You've got your hands full, mate."

"Tell me about it," her adopted father agreed under his breath.

Chapter Twenty-Eight

Johan stole a final glance toward the submersible, sad to leave its confines. Within those metal walls he had been surrounded by the sea, embraced by powers he could sense just beyond the bulkhead. It had fueled his mood the entire trip, pumping the boy with emotions he hadn't felt since leaving his home. For the first time since the emergence of his powers, he fully understood that water would always be a part of his life.

When he finally pulled his eyes away, he stole a glimpse of Kali. The moonlight reflected her face so perfectly that she glowed angelically. He loved her. He also worried at how much she had changed since the battle of Estowen's Landing.

She tugged at the outfit Cassidy had given her to wear. The agent had referred to the clothing as "coveralls," and Kali's were a pale bluish color. His own were dyed a dull yellow. They were durable and comfortable, but neither child felt at home in the foreign cloth. She had called it "cotton." No matter what it was called, Kali seemed displeased. *That's an improvement,* he thought, she had been mostly stoic and devoid of emotion for the entire journey.

His mind wandered to a conversation he had with the boatswain when he first pulled into Logan a year before. He had heard the other sailors talk about a thing they called "sea shock," a condition where someone's personality changes after their time aboard a vessel. When he had asked the old salt if they were pulling his leg like a polliwog, the old man grew very serious.

"Oh, it's real, boy. It don't only happen on the sea, neither." The sailor had leaned in so closely that Johan could see the glint of oil in the man's whiskers. In a whisper so low that the boy had to also lean in, the man added, "It can happen to you after a battle too." The crusty man had darted his eyes back and forth to ensure no one listened then said with a hint of foul-smelling tobacco on his breath, "It can claim your soul any time after any stressful time."

Johan hadn't pressed, eager to escape the close proximity of the boatswain's foreboding. But he did ask a simple question. "How does it claim your soul?"

The sailor's eyes had grown wide with caution as he advised, "Once you've had sea shock, you're never the same. You wander around with wisdom in your heart that flutters every time you feel urgency. Your heart pounds at first in your chest and then in your ears until the rhythm itself drives you insane." He suddenly appeared crestfallen as a long-lost memory jumped to mind. "My friend Antwan fought alongside General Lourdes and his cavalry. This was the first time they used cannons against the Pescari. He said that when he touched the powder and the ball first flew, he watched it rip a man's head clean from his shoulders. To his dying day, he felt the shock every time the sky thundered. He was utterly useless on deck during a storm."

By now Johan was certain that Kali had acquired a touch of the shock during the battle, but he was unsure how to approach her with the topic. He finally worked it out a week into the voyage and decided to bluntly ask her of her troubles. But then, one morning, she suddenly perked up as if she had simply been resting. He quickly dropped the subject and enjoyed her bubbly personality. She fully resumed her usual self just before arrival in Astia.

She caught him staring and shot him a sly smile. "What do you want, sailor boy? You ain't looking for another kiss, are you?" She hadn't kissed his cheek since that day in the tavern when he'd promised Samani he'd come to Astia.

"I wouldn't mind one," he replied honestly and with a little shyness.

"Well I don't know why I did that so get the idea out of your silly gourd. I don't even know why we're here in the first place," she said with a hint of concern.

"It was your idea, actually," he told her.

"Yeah well, I was stupid. We should be fighting alongside Shon Wembley, Cuyler, and the others."

"We all were stupid," the woman walking ahead of them responded, voice filled with bitterness. She too had changed during the trip, again irritated with her brother. "Samani is a damnable fool who will get us all killed with his revolution."

"But you're a part of it," Cassidy reminded Fatwana. The young woman had been leading them up the pier but whirled to address their mutinous talk. "The Dragon will have you killed if you betray the cause now."

"I actually doubt it," the lead sister replied. "Samani assured me that I can return to the oracle. I've been away too long and have much to catch up."

Cassidy shrugged at her insistence. "Suits me," she muttered. "I'm done being your babysitter."

Johan barely listened to the women bicker, focused instead on Kali's nearby hand. Several times he thought about reaching for it with his own but hesitated, afraid she would reject him.

"Just grab it," she said as if reading his thoughts. "Sheesh," she added, "do I have to do everything?"

He scooped it up eagerly, smiling ear to ear and happy that his Kali had shaken her sea shock and returned to her former self.

Cassidy left them to speak with four men. Johan recognized them as soldiers from the beach, even though they had exchanged their uniforms for coveralls. Before them stood five crates, presumably with the odd devices packed securely inside. Johan strained his ears, barely hearing the words "oracle" and "council." Whatever the instruments were, the soldiers would secretly carry them as they departed for their separate missions.

A whistle in the distance shook him from his eavesdropping, and he looked up to see a plume of black smoke bellowing into the sky. The low rumble of the ground shook his feet, and a whining of machinery stole his full attention. Soon the sunlight reflected off a magnificent metal beast riding toward them atop two iron rails.

With excitement in his voice he asked, "What is that?"

Cassidy glanced only briefly then explained, "It's called a train. That's what we'll ride to Bergin."

His eyes grew wide at the prospect. "On its back?"

"No," the woman laughed. "Inside of its belly." She nodded to the four soldiers who returned the gesture. "Good luck on your mission," she told them. "Don't get caught." At her direction, two more men picked up one of the crates and carried it toward the tracks. They set it down near a small pile of luggage.

A few minutes later the train arrived, and doors opened on the sides. Cassidy led Johan and Kali into one of the compartments where they found rows of empty seats. "Get comfortable," she told them, "we've got a couple of hours before we reach Bergin." But neither of the teens would sleep, they were too busy marveling at the amazing journey ahead.

Fatwana watched the boy and girl board the train with Cassidy. *My brother has ensured their deaths*, she thought. *Surely, they cannot survive his foolish plans.* Almost as soon as the Bergin bound train had departed, four trucks arrived. Not wishing to appear connected with the soldiers when authorities arrived, she moved to a bench near the ticketing station. From there she watched.

The drivers dismounted the vehicles and helped each soldier load their cargo into the back of each. Then they too drove off into the night, bound for unknown destinations. For a moment she pondered the contents of their crates, wondering what they carried within. *Probably weapons*, she pondered, *bound to join her brother's revolution.* Whatever he had planned she wanted nothing to do with him or the others.

She checked the clock on the wall and noted that the train to Oslot would arrive within the hour. She would ride it north and then catch a bus to the winter oracle. Hopefully Subba had returned during the months of her absence, and would allow her admittance. She decided that she would eventually report the truth to the Council, that her brother had kidnapped her and whisked her away to Andalon.

They would summon her to Bergin, and she would make the journey. Once there she would tell them every detail. Her outlaw brother deserved whatever he received, and she would have no part of him. But that was a journey for another day, and she felt compelled to return to the safety of her oracle to rest in her cell.

But she still worried over the future of the people of Andalon. *It is wrong to farm them for beads, but they are a doomed people,* she decided. They, like her brother, had no business stepping foot on Astian soil. Only destruction would follow if they did.

"Fatwana Nakala?"

The deep and commanding voice broke the night, causing her to jump. She turned to see eight uniformed men standing nearby. She responded with a shaky voice filled with uncertainty and asked, "Yes?"

"You are under arrest for conspiracy and the abandonment of your assigned post. You will come with us."

Suddenly very afraid she asked, "Where are you taking me?"

"You're to answer before the Astian Council," the man replied. He gestured to the bag at her feet and one of the soldiers picked it up.

Her knees trembled as she stood, and nearly stumbled when she took her first step toward a waiting car. As one of the men held the rear door open, her thoughts again turned toward her brother. *I'll tell them everything,* she promised herself.

She shivered when she heard his voice respond in her mind, *I hope that you do sister, exactly as I taught you.*

Chapter Twenty-Nine

Robert surveyed the entrenchment, pleased with the work of Titus and his advance team. The system of trenches was nowhere near elaborate by any means, but would do the trick against all emotants except those of spring. A quake would bury his defenders in a heartbeat, whereby attacks by air would pass over his sharpshooters.

"Good," he said, patting his commander on the shoulder. "You've done well. Where will you position Taros and his team?"

Frederique pointed toward a thick grove of trees in the east. "Those will conceal the cavalry, and he and Teot will accompany them during the flanking maneuver."

Robert watched with disgust as the general scratched at a sore on his neck. It had festered since they last talked, oozing pus that he wiped on his pants. "For Cinder's sake, General. Get that looked at."

"I have. The surgeon said that it's not like any infection he's seen."

"Then go see the Pescari. Surely they have herbs that you can rub on it." When the commander hesitated, the king shoed him away with his hands. "Go now, don't waste any more time."

The military man gave a quick salute. "Aye, sir," he said, but lingered longer. Staring toward the western horizon he asked, "How far away are the sails?"

"A few days at least," Esterling replied. "Arne watched them depart Lake Weston yesterday morning."

"And our fleet is safely near Logan?"

"Yes, as was planned."

The general pointed into the distance, "Then who are they?"

Robert strained his eyes, barely making out faint blurs of canvas beyond the trees. From somewhere in the camp and eagle screeched, then raced into the sky, beating its wings with determined speed. Bonded with the animal, the king seemed to no longer see on his own, and nearly stepped off the edge into a trench. Titus quickly caught his arm and pulled him toward him.

"Careful," he warned.

"I can see the flagship."

"And?"

"It's *Malfeasance.*"

Titus did not hesitate to quickly order his soldiers to their stations. "Dig in, men! Hurry with that spare water and food. Get comfortable and prepare for a week or more in your position."

Robert barely heard though, as he focused instead on the fleet. Fifteen of Braen's improved ships accompanied another dozen Fjorik longboats. Although it wasn't a massive fleet, it would rival his own.

He screamed a name toward the camp. "Cuyler!" When the boy did not answer he shouted again in his mind, forming a connection with the leader of the Dreamers. The image of Cuyler's face appeared before him.

"Yes, your highness?"

"It is time," he told the boy, "to prove your allegiance to the crown."

Malfeasance pushed north into Lake Norton, lurching as the hull resisted against the calmer waters. Leaving the Misting River behind, Skander bellowed his orders to Artur.

"Ready the cannons!" He pointed at sixteen fireships closing in on their position. "They won't aim to break our keel or board our decks," he explained. "They'll ram us hard and torch our battery."

Artur nodded his understanding and relayed maneuvers to the helmsman.

"Fire!" Braston watched as the first salvo sailed over the incoming vessel. "Reload," he ordered. "Lower two degrees and fire again!"

The second blast took the swift ship just below the waterline, forcing it to dip downward and splash into the smooth lake.

The second vessel in Skander's army was less lucky than his own. A fireship rammed it full broadside, piercing the hull and pouring liquid fire into the lower decks. The crewmen immediately rowed backward and readied for another target.

"No," the northern king protested. He raised his hands and screamed into the morning sky. Storm clouds suddenly appeared overhead. They swiftly grew black against the pale blue, swirling into a storm above. Lightning struck in rapid succession, striking each enemy vessel in turn.

An explosion from the northwest battery bellowed a retort, sending whistling rounds toward his fleet and striking three of his ships. The explosion echoed in his ears as they struck with deep impact, quickly finding munitions and powder. Skander reeled as several of his Saber Cats were consumed by the flames.

He pointed toward several galleons approaching fast. Artur nodded and ordered another salvo, this time with explosive rounds of their own. The lead vessels floundered as their masts collapsed, then crashed into their trailing comrades as the line was unable to change course in time. "Now," he whispered to a white-robed child standing nearby.

The boy nodded and closed his eyes, relaying Skander's orders to his counterparts in the fleet. An enormous windstorm immediately rocked the waves between theirs and the enemy ships. The maelstrom quickly devoured the enemy vessels, crushing their bulkheads and pulling them and their crews to the lakebed for a watery embrace. The city cannons fired once more.

"Hard to starboard," Skander shouted, tightly gripping the railing. The boy filled the sails and *Malfeasance* careened as it turned, dipping low against the now raging waters. Most of his fleet followed suit but many did not. As the hot shot flew overhead, not too distant shouting informed him that they had found wood to splinter.

"I've had enough of this foolery," Skander muttered over their pitiful cries for mercy. His wavering legs moved one before the other until he stood tall on the forecastle, arms outstretched over the waters. With eyes closed he searched the lake for his trailing companions. He frowned when he found them, weakened by the long journey in freshwater. *Weak like my brother,* he thought.

With a splash, six Krakens broke the surface of the harbor, climbing high onto the parapets and ripping the batteries apart brick by brick. Had the defenders of Norton seen the creatures anywhere but in legend, they would have noticed how they'd changed. The freshwater had scalded their skin with white swaths that freckled their appearance with translucency.

They lumbered about, flinging guns and fighters from the parapets before quickly succumbing to exhaustion. Skander roared, "No! Finish your task!" He reached out with his mind and securely gripped theirs, giving them strength to focus on the walls. Bricks flew as they broke the mortar with their heavy tentacles, battering them like their master banged his fists against the wooden rail of *Malfeasance.*

Giddy with excitement, Skander drew his knife and carved his sigil into the bowsprit. As the shape emerged in the hardwood, the ghastly sky darkened with storms. Once he had finished, he cackled with delight as lightning carved the same form in the clouds above. His army, having already been unloaded for an assault, charged the crumbling city walls. A mere twenty minutes later, Skander Braston left Artur to tie *Malfeasance* to the pier while he surveyed the fallen city.

Arne circled the ship in the harbor, dropping low enough that his master could get a closer view of the invading commander.

"I can't tell if it's Braen," Robert told Titus. "He wears a few more scars and his beard is shorn, but it could be him."

The general pressed him for certainty. "Are you sure? I hear that they're very similar in looks and easy to confuse. Eusari told me that she even confused them at first meeting."

Robert wheeled on his commander with anger in his voice. "Eusari said? Don't you get it, Frederique? She's his lover and they've set us up. If I'm to march on Eston, I must now go through him!" He gestured to the north. "He's cut me off from my ships."

"Your highness, please don't misunderstand. I only urge caution, just as Max would."

"Max is dead, and caution failed him as a strategy." He pointed toward the city. We should strike now, while they're weary and he stands on dry land."

Sarai's gentle voice carried into the tent. "Yes, husband. You must destroy him now while he's separated from his mistress. That wolf of his would double his powers. Deal with him so that you can handle her."

Robert agreed. "He'll take some time to plunder the city. I either attack now while his army is in bloodlust, or I wait."

Titus pleaded, "Don't give up this defensive position, your highness. Draw him here if you must."

"You must attack, Robert!"

The command in Sarai's voice reminded Robert of her father Abraham. Maximus and the former governor had often argued over temperance or overwhelming force, and Horslei had often growled in the same manner as his daughter had. Esterling looked upon his wife with worry, then ordered her from the tent. "Go, Sarai. Let us plan without interference."

"Interference?" Her eyes danced with rage as she grabbed his arm and spun him around. "I am your queen, and my place is at your side!"

"Your place is in your birthing wagon!" He didn't mean for the words to sound so scalding, but he could not take them back. He softened his voice a little and added, "That was cruel. I'm sorry. Please return to your wagon and prepare to egress. If I need you to retreat, I want both my wife and heir kept safe."

She did not answer with words, but her glare was response enough. Her eyes burned a hole into Robert's heart.

After she had departed, Taros cleared his throat. "I too suggest that you attack, but, like the general, I recommend you set a trap. Let me draw him to you."

Robert looked to Titus who nodded and said, "It is possible, hear him out."

"Explain it to me," the king ordered.

Frederique turned to a waiting captain, "Send again for Lieutenant Cuyler. He will be a part of this trap and needs to be at this table."

"I'm here, your highness!" The teen entered the tent out of breath and full of news.

Robert read his excitement. "What is it?"

"You were right! Braen Braston really is alive!"

Chapter Thirty

Eusari watched the faces of her brothers change from skeptical to shocked as they processed Shon's words. "Eusari," he had said, "Say hello to your brothers."

Franque was the first to truly recognize her. As children they had been close. He could always be found glued to the side of his little sister, keeping her out of danger and teaching her about life on the farm. "It's truly you," he said. "I didn't think I'd ever see you again."

Memories of them playing together rushed in and she smiled warmly. "It's me," she admitted.

Jean jumped right into the question that she had hoped to avoid. "Where've you been all these years, dearie?"

She hadn't expected to tell the story of her childhood, but the narrative flowed. She spared the children from the more sensitive details, skipping over but alluding to the adults the harrowing abuse she received. When she revealed her position of captain, the children's eyes bulged with shock.

The oldest, named Jhan, couldn't contain his excitement. "You're the lady pirate captain of *She Wolf?*"

"Aye," she said with a grin.

"That's amazing," he said. "Tales of your adventures have reached Brentway!" He looked around, scanning the room. "I've heard you're bonded to a wolf! Where is he?"

She had left Gelert to watch over the boys across the street, but sent him a gentle summons. In a matter of moments he pushed open the door and joined her side. She scratched his ears as her nephews scrambled to pet him like a common dog. But not Anne. She never looked up from the table, refusing to look at either the wolf or her newly arrived aunt.

Franque gave Eusari a rest from talking about her past and turned the questions toward Wembley. "And where have you been, Shon?"

"After Thom was hanged, I left my position as constable. Let's just say I've taken up a different line of work."

"I've heard of outlaws operating in the forest of Diaph," Franque noted. "In one of their raids a certain pirate with a black wolf attacked the town. I'm assuming you two were a part of that?"

"Aye, that we were," Shon admitted.

"So you are part of Braston's revolution against the crown?" The words came out accusatory, Franque apparently held no love for Braen.

"Whatever you've heard is false," Eusari explained. "Marcus Esterling killed his mother and blamed Braen out of convenience. But it doesn't matter now. Braen is dead and King Robert marches against his brother."

"Is that why you're here then?" Franque was outraged. "To gather support for that conspirator against the crown?" He spit on the floor when he said, 'conspirator.' "Sister and Uncle notwithstanding, I'll have no part of your revolution." He pointed at Anne, adding, "When you go against the crown you create orphans."

Eusari's eyes turned cold and she growled. "There is a war raging. It battles against an evil the likes of which your simple mind will never understand, Franque Thorinson." She stood from the table. "Marcus Esterling is the enemy, as are the Falconers. If you stand with the creatures who killed Thom, then you're no brother of mine."

"If you stand with Robert Esterling and the ghost of Braen Braston then you're no sister of mine."

"So be it," she said. She turned to leave but froze when she saw that Anne no longer stared at the table.

All of the girl's focus was on her aunt and she stared with an intensity that rivaled Eusari's. She held the doll into the air, as if warding off the evil that stood before her. "The queen gave me this doll. She was my friend and your friend killed her."

Irritated, Eusari reached to swat the doll from her face. She missed, and clipped only the head, sending it flying across the room. It rolled to a stop in front of the hearth, staring up with long locks of golden hair and eyes of blue that stared into the pirate's soul. The girl leapt from her chair and ran, not to retrieve the doll's head but out the door and down the street.

Franque and Jean raced after, calling her name as they rushed from the tavern. The two boys followed.

The farmer's wife placed a firm finger in the chest of Eusari, shoving her backward and then pointing at her pregnant belly. "When you hatch the child of that beast you'll understand. Children are off limits to the violence of this world, and there's no greater war than one against a mother!" She spat in Eusari's face as she shoved past, chasing her family into the city to find the missing Anne.

Shon handed her a cloth with which to clean her cheek. "Come, dearie. We've business to attend. I'm sorry about..." He gestured at the empty table. "I'm sorry about this."

Eusari thrust the rag into his hand. "You'd better be." Whirling around when she reached the door, she stated, "Like I said, my home is aboard *She Wolf*."

Franque Thorinson didn't have to go far before he found Anne. As he and Jean rounded the corner, he saw her reaching up on tiptoes and whispering into the ear of a constable. She still clutched the little doll against her chest, despite its missing head. The lawman's eyes were large with surprise, but his amused smile betrayed his skepticism.

Her father shouted, "Anne!"

"Is this your child?" The constable shoved a stick in Franque's stomach, poking as he asked. "Child," he said, "is this your father?"

She nodded that he was.

"She ran off, constable. I'm sorry."

"According to her story she had a good reason. Why are you consorting with criminals?" He had Franque off balance, teetering on a fall. "Well?"

"There was no consorting, constable! They approached my family in the tavern and we just now got away."

The constable was not convinced. He turned to Jean who had joined his brother "Is this so?"

"Aye, Shon Wembley is here. He's connected on our deceased mother's side, and thought he could appeal to us as family."

"What did he want?"

Franque interrupted, "Only aid. He's desperate and passing through town."

Anne had been staring down at her doll while the men explained to the constable. Upon hearing their lies she spoke out with anger. "He tried to get Daddy to fight against King Marcus."

"Well, it seems that the child is the only member of your family with a sense of duty." He again shoved the stick into Franque's stomach. "She also mentioned a lady pirate. Who does she mean?"

"Just some woman with whom he travels. I didn't catch her name."

"Yes, you did," Anne screamed, "she's your sister Eusari!"

The constable raised both eyebrows toward Franque. "You have many criminals in your family. Perhaps I should round up the lot of you and place the child in the care of an orphanage?"

"No, your honor," Franque pleaded, "we told them to leave! We wanted no part of it."

"Then tell me the name of the ship on which they sail," the constable demanded.

"It's called the *She Wolf.*"

The eyes of the lawman lit up at the name. He had obviously heard of her exploits. "Get on with your day," he said. "If you're finished with your business in Logan, then you'd best return home."

Chapter Thirty-One

Skander laughed with glee as his men picked through the palace, bringing him crate after crate of treasure. The riches of Norton were vast, rivaling only the capital city of Weston, and they now belonged to Fjorik. He ran his fingers through a chest filled with jewelry, freshly pulled from the hands, ears, and necks of the citizens. One fine golden necklace in particular caught his attention, and he felt the delicate braid with only the tips of his fingers. It would look fine on the neck of his Hester.

He rubbed harder as he stared at the delicate piece, intently focused on the individual links as they bunched within his fury. *Around her neck,* he thought again. *Wrapped around her neck and twisted tightly,* he smiled, *twisted until I deny the air to reach her lungs.* Disgusted, he threw the trinket into the chest and kicked the entire vessel over with his boot, spilling gold across the marble floor. Skander roared.

Horns blared in the distance. The northern king cocked his head at the sound, raising an eyebrow toward Artur. His first mate simply shrugged and walked to a window.

"I thought you killed every soldier in the city," Skander remarked.

"We did, my king. Riders are approaching from the south."

The younger Braston brother strode to the window and shoved his friend aside, gazing out. The warm sun hung high above the streets, forcing him to squint to see clearly. More horns sounded and the men watched a cloud of dust just beyond the remnants of a gatehouse. He cursed quietly. His army had been so consumed in sacking the city that they failed to post sentries or form a picket.

He flinched from the portal when more than one hundred Pescari raiders burst into the city, rapidly firing arrows into his drunken army milling about the streets.

He fumed as he watched a patrol of surprised Saber Cats fall to wooden arrows, such simple twigs felling his weapons of chaos. He roared. "Form a shield wall along the southern border! Kill those savage beasts!"

"Your highness," Artur pleaded, "Why are Pescari so far north and east? Weren't they pushed across the waste?"

Skander paused only a moment, then grabbed his first mate by the tunic. He shoved hard, pushing the man out the window, holding him with only his feet within the room. They danced against stone, searching for a footing as his hands clutched the forearms of his king. "I can send you flying from this height, Artur. Do not question my orders again."

Unable to speak, the warrior nodded.

Skander pulled him into the room and sent him sprawling onto the floor. With one finger pointed toward the city he screamed, "Form the shield wall and let's kill those barbarians!"

His raiders let out a whoop and ran drunken from the palace, streaming into the streets.

Teot and his scouts circled the palace, raining arrows into the emerging warriors. These men wore furs instead of the steel armor of the Westonian army and fell easily when pierced. It helped that these men were drunken, caught reveling in their plunder. Several emerged from houses, pulling on their breeches and fumbling with their sword belts. These were the easiest to kill.

He raised his bow just as a northern soldier raised an axe in his direction. Clamping his legs tightly around the neck of his steed, Teot swung underneath its neck just as the warrior released the steel. It flew harmlessly where he had previously been. Still using his horse as a shield, he nocked and sent three arrows in rapid succession toward the would-be assassin. The man fell as a heap of furs upon stone.

The uncle of the shappan sent a call to his scouts, signaling they should conclude their business. The raid was meant to remain brief and they were instructed to flee before the northern army could rally. A glance toward Felicima let him know that she had witnessed his attack and would display displeasure toward his people. As he and his horsemen raced through the fallen gatehouse, he flinched with his own worry over their audacity. The battle for the city had begun.

Robert watched as Teot and his scouts raced southward, fanning out into the trees and disappearing quickly from view. More Pescari quickly darted from their cover to sweep the tracks leading into the forest, trailing branches that cleared any trace. For added measure, King Esterling sent a gentle breeze to help swirl the dust and any tracks they missed. A few moments later, the northern army emerged, forming a shield wall just beyond the fallen rubble of the gatehouse.

Robert asked Titus, "Are you certain we're out of view?"

"Yes, my liege. From this angle they can only see a barren hill."

"Good. Amash, begin phase two."

Horslei saluted and jogged down the trench. When he reached the western edge, he raised a banner. Mere heartbeats later the infantry emerged from their position west of the hill. They were joined by two units of cavalry, each joined by several hundred Pescari warriors. Taros led the eastern contingent.

With his own shield wall formed at the base of the hill, the northern aggressors would rightly infer that Esterling held the high ground with artillery units. These rang out on his next command.

"Fire when ready, Titus. Let's see if the Kraken bites our bait." The explosion was deafening, and the Dreamers and riflemen covered their ears to muffle the cacophony. The first volley struck only dirt, well short of their true range. The roar of enemy laughter carried on the cool northern breeze.

Titus pointed to the shield wall. "To make this believable we'll need to sell it, your highness."

Robert nodded and shouted, "Shield wall... advance!" He watched as his line advanced toward the other, step by step toward the killing field in the middle. *Max, I hope you are proud of me,* he thought. *Whatever happens next is completely on my conscience and I'm fine with that. I only hope that I'm right to attack instead of hold.*

"Cuyler," he said, "Signal Sebastian that it's time to bring the fleet." *And time to expose any treachery Braston's boy may bring,* he thought. His orders given and plan in motion, Robert could do nothing else but wait. The die was cast.

Skander watched the cannon balls land harmlessly in the field before him. His warriors laughed at their puny showing, but he did not. Looking to Artur he asked. "What caliber is that?"

"Twelve pounders, sire. Those should have reached the fallen walls."

"He's toying with us then. Whoever this is thinks me a fool. What banner does he fly?"

Artur raised his spyglass and took a brief look before handing it to his king. "He flies the Esterling sigil, and his personal banner has the colors of the eldest son."

Braston confirmed for himself and returned the glass. "I didn't see his ships on the river. Where do you think he's hidden them?" Looking over his shoulder toward the harbor he frowned. His own fleet docked safely in the harbor. "Bring my Saber Cats forward," he ordered. "Have them dispatch birds to watch the armada. I'll reward any who find Esterling's."

"Right away," Artur obeyed. He relayed the command and quickly rejoined his side.

"Let's play his game but be wary. He's hiding more than artillery on that hill, I'm certain."

"Shield Wall!" Artur screamed, "Forward... march!"

Chapter Thirty-Two

Braen and Alec followed the children down the dark passage. The tunnel, it turned out, connected to an elaborate system that connected every street in the city. In his two years living in The Cove, he never imagined catacombs existed beneath his feet. They ran beneath each building, eventually leading to the palace. As his eyes adjusted, he marveled at the complex construction. Despite the obviously ancient composition, the system was an engineering masterpiece.

He paused at a branch that led away from the direction Charleigh led them. "What in Cinder's name is this?"

Marita and the others stopped pulling the sled of air and joined him. Alec was already there, staring dumbfounded at the statues. The sculpted figures were clearly of animals personified to appear human. Braen wiped away centuries of dust and grime to reveal a mouse with large eyes and ears. Its grin unsettled the large man. Its humanlike arm was held high, waving at Braen and his squad with large white gloves.

"Creepy," remarked Pogue.

"That's an understatement," Braen agreed. "Let's move on." The Dreamers resumed pulling the invisible sled and he followed, occasionally peering into the shadows of the branching corridors. Down one he caught a glimpse of more statues that had once depicted beautiful young women dressed in flowing ball gowns.

"That's the princess hall," explained Charleigh. Braen nodded, silently agreeing that she had named it well.

When they reached the end of the main tunnel the group paused. "We're here," said Charleigh.

Braen noticed that Nat and Neill huddled together, refusing to proceed. In a kind voice he asked, "What's wrong?"

Neill pointed into the shadows and said, "That's where the dead pirates guard the entrance to the palace."

The northern captain pushed by and paused when he found himself staring face to face with a skeleton army. Each wielded a cutlass, swinging it in the air but frozen as if they had died amidst a great battle. One of them had the face of a Kraken instead of a man's. Braen laughed hysterically when he saw that many of them had peg legs and wore eyepatches. *Krill would fit in fine with this crew,* he thought.

"These are only statues," he told the children, "like those near the entrance. See how the paint has peeled from these? Someone set them here long ago to ward off unwanted visitors."

Alec pointed to a door and asked Charleigh, "Is this the pantry?" She nodded and he went to work. The former Captain of the Guard knew every inch of the palace above. He pulled out a piece of parchment and scribbled a quick map of the castle, carefully pacing out and drawing the tunnels and the directions they branched. He indicated several places where he wanted charges placed and put the children and Braen to work.

After they had finished placing gunpowder, he showed Charleigh how to roll out the fuse. "Now, dearie," he told her, "You'll need plenty of room between you and the explosion. There's about one hundred feet on this spool, so use all of it. If we don't return by midday, I want you to light the fuse and run like hell to your Daddy's store. Then you get outside and cover your ears. You'll only have about ten minutes before it blows. Do you understand all that?"

The girl nodded confidently.

He turned to Braen. "The blast will take out the armory, the powder stores, and the king's quarters. The secondary blast from the powder should wipe the palace off the map."

Braen understood. He replied, "It's close to dawn, so we've got about five and half hours to find Nevra, kill him, and, if we're successful, cut this fuse on our way out."

Marita seemed confused. "And if we're not?"

"That's why we set the charges."

Her eyes rounded with understanding and shot a thumbs up, forgetting to smile this time.

Braen knelt in front of the merchant's daughter. "Charleigh, I need you to get the younger children to safety. Keep them hidden until midday."

She nodded and then surprised the captain with a tight hug. After a few heartbeats she pulled away and grabbed the hands of the two young Dreamers. "Come on," she told them.

Pogue patted the northerner on the back and said, "You'd make a wonderful father, Braston."

Braen's thoughts soured as he remembered that Hester bore his child, one he had no interest in raising. "Well, that's not in the stars," he replied. He took in a deep breath and held it while slowly pushing open the secret door. Once he was certain there was no ambush, he waved for the others to follow.

The pantry appeared exactly how the children described. Stores lined the shelves in glass jars and salted meats hung from the rafters. Alec frowned while Marita grabbed a sweet roll. "That's stealing, dearie," he warned."

"Only if I get caught," she retorted while licking icing from the top. "Until then it's a sweet roll." She smacked her lips and added, "A yummy, sweet roll."

Pogue sighed and asked, "You sure you don't want to be a father, Braston?"

The northerner grabbed a sweet roll for himself and took a bite. "Positive," he replied with a wink to the girl. She giggled. After licking icing from his finger he said, "Check the other side of the door, Marita."

She sent forth a strand of air that stretched through under the door. After a while she reported, "It's clear all the way to the main hall."

"Then let's go," Braen ordered, "but be careful not to make a sound." She nodded and pushed her way into the kitchen. Braen placed his hand on Alec's arm and whispered, "Shouldn't one of us lead?"

Alec replied, "Trust me, she wouldn't allow it." With a smile he followed his daughter, leaving Braen alone.

The large man grabbed a second sweet roll, wrapped it in a napkin, and slipped it into his pocket for later. Then he too followed the girl.

They crossed the kitchen fairly quickly and emerged in the great hall. The massive room was deserted except for a single throne on the far side. Braen took it all in. The last time he stood in this chamber, a feast was thrown in his honor. A gawdy banner had hung on the wall and Artema Horn proclaimed him the Kraken King.

So much had changed since then and, no matter how much he wished they could return to that simpler time, Braen knew that it was he who had changed the most. He lived only to reunite with Hester then, and Eusari was merely an enigmatic woman of shadows. Now he yearned to hold the shrouded she wolf, to retire on a hillside and tend grapevines while their children played in the meadow. And, if he ever laid eyes on Artema Horn again, he would flay the man alive.

A voice echoed across the hall. "You seem to have me at a disadvantage, Lord Braston. I am without my guards and you are accompanied by a wounded has-been and a child." The chilling laugh revealed that Lord Stefan Nevra reclined on the throne. "Have you come to kill me and free the world from your brother? Or are you here to join him as my champion?"

Braston's voice echoed off the walls as he replied, "I'm here to end this once and for all, Nevra."

"And how will you do that, Lord of Kraken? You have no power."

"But I do," answered Marita. She glided across the great hall on a cushion of air, racing toward the pox-scarred man on the throne. Halfway across the room she drew her blades and crossed them in front of her chest. *Ready and able stance,* she thought. Twenty paces out she crouched into Calm the Waters and raised her blades, now thirsting for the man's blood.

Three paces out Marita felt a crushing impact on her chest. The force sent her sprawling backward. She gasped for breath as she reached for her blades, each lying several feet out of reach. She rolled back and forth on the ground, desperate for air that wouldn't come.

Braen bellowed, "No!" He charged after the girl, a shimmer in the air above her catching his eye. He shouted, "Roll now!" With terrified eyes she nodded and rolled to her left just as shards of granite floor exploded where she had been moments before. The shimmer briefly appeared a second time, looming above Marita. Braen Braston threw his axe.

The blade turned end over end in the air, seemingly flying in slow motion as he sprinted toward the girl. It stuck in the air, floating above her with blood spraying outward from nothing. The form of Adamas Creech slowly appeared around the axe, a startled look of surprise permanently fixed on his dying face. He fell to his knees and slid into a heap on the floor beside Marita.

Alec watched in horror as Marita writhed on the floor. He called loudly to the southern lord hiding in the kitchen, "Now is a good time, Valencia! Do what you have to do!"

"I can't," the lord replied, "it isn't him."

"What do you mean it isn't him?" He pointed at the throne, "That's Nevra! Take control of him!"

But then Braen threw his axe and Alec saw the shape and face of Adamas Creech materialize with the weapon embedded in his chest. *No,* he thought, *Charro controls him and his entire crew! They wouldn't attack us!* Turning to the southerner he realized the truth. "You serve him, not the other way around!" He started toward the duke, but a blast of air made him stumble. Valencia ran toward the pantry and knelt to the floor. Alec could hear his rhythmic humming.

Braen grabbed the handle of his weapon, ripping it from the dead man's chest mid stride. He shouted, "Use your blades, Pogue! Look for disturbances in the air!"

Alec felt a soft wind rush past him into the hall, shimmering like water disturbed by a pebble. Then he remembered the moment Marita fell. *Someone's cloaked with invisibility,* he thought. Drawing both blades he spun into Dance with the Moon, slicing the air around him where he had seen the shimmer. His left hand felt something solid and he drove it through despite that his eyes saw nothing. Abruptly, the head of Nathaira rolled onto the ground. Her body appeared moments later as it swayed and then collapsed.

Terror gripped the duke as he recognized the girl. Remorse rushed in and bile rose in his throat.   He didn't mean to kill her, she was an innocent.

"Remember her story," Braen shouted, "and how they hid from Creech!"

Alec didn't answer, he stared down at the child's remains. He had once heard that a decapitated head could survive for thirty seconds after severing from its body. The evil look of hatred that stared back lasted only ten as she mouthed some silent curse. When the muscles finally stopped contracting, the air in the room unraveled, dropping her woven veil and revealing a small army of men loyal to Lord Stefan Nevra. Among them were Creech's crew. Across the room the illusion of the Pirate King dissolved into wisps of air atop the throne. Adolphus Dominique sat upon it instead. He stood, drew his sword, and ran toward Braen.

To Alec's immediate right Neill appeared, sending another blast of air that slammed the sword master into the wall. Alec felt tendrils form around his arms, trying to wrestle the blades free from his hands. He clung with all his strength. "Give in, Pogue," the voice of Nevra said from the boy's lips. "I would use your blades to do my bidding."

Through clenched teeth he snarled back, "Eat shit, pox-faced bastard." The boy's magic was weak, and Alec was able to turn his body around while still gripping the swords. They faced each other in this invisible tug of war, each vying for control over Pogue's weapons. Finally, the boy dropped to the ground exhausted and Alec gained the upper hand.

Braen shouted, "Kill him! He's no longer the child!" The captain put his back against Marita who had recovered her own blades. They stood with weapons ready, staring down the advancing soldiers from all directions.

Alec placed the swords to the neck of the child, ready to send him on his journey down the crimson river. Movement beside Braen caught Pogue's attention, and he turned to see Creech rising from the ground. "That's not possible," he muttered.

"What's wrong, Pogue?" The child's lips moved and Nevra's voice asked, "did you really think I'd allow another to have control over me?" A tiny hand shot forward and a dagger ripped through Alec's leather armor, slicing his side but missing vital organs. He acted instinctively then, and sent the boy on his journey.

In the center of the hall Braen and Marita fought, keeping the horde at bay and killing them one by one and sometimes two by two. Their styles of fighting were so different, he noted. She dealt death like a tiny spinning ballerina, flowing under and around while cutting flesh. The northerner made brutal strikes with his heavy axe, lumbering with brute force and anger.

Before his eyes Creech and his fallen men stood and retrieved their fallen weapons. Alec watched with confusion. *There are no Jaguars in The Cove*, he thought. Then he heard the humming from the kitchen. Valencia sat on the floor of the pantry, swaying to the rhythm. Alec rushed forward to interrupt his ministrations, but was suddenly caught from behind. Braen watched as a strong net of air enveloped his friend, tightening around his skin and squeezing a little more breath each time he exhaled.

Four teens stood in the corner of the kitchen. They raised their hands in unison.

Chapter Thirty-Three

The tavern reeked of rancid mead and putrid ale. Eusari could not help but also notice the patrons smelled even worse. She decided the late-night venue for their clandestine rendezvous couldn't have been better selected. No constable could hold his breath long enough to thoroughly search the establishment. She followed Shon to a back room.

Marque and Madelyn had already arrived and were accompanied by a tall and comely woman with determined eyes that seemed difficult to surprise. This woman had seen much in her life, seemingly at ease in any environment. They introduced her as Karla. The captain decided immediately that she liked this woman. She gripped Eusari's hand with a firm grasp and did not shy away as they met. When Karla stood before Shon, she took his hand as well. But slight hesitation betrayed a lack of trust for the former constable.

Once they had seated, Shon looked around. "Jacque's running late," he commented.

"Aye," replied Marque, "but we shouldn't wait for him to begin, don't you agree?" Eusari could tell by his darting glances that he felt uncomfortable and longed for the outdoors.

"You can begin then," Shon told him. "What's your status?"

"Recruitment on the docks is easy," he explained. "Most of them are drifters with no allegiance to Loganshire. But they're the seedy type, boss."

Karla sat up with surprise, something in Marque's words stirring interest in the way he addressed Shon. With understanding creeping into her voice she asked, "You're not in charge of this operation? How long have you worked for Constable Wembley?"

Marque shook his head. "When you came to the docks you didn't know the arrangement, Karla. I apologize that I couldn't divulge the truth when I handed over power to you."

"You were his deputy," she surmised, shaking her head with honest disbelief. "That's why you were able to keep the Tin Stars away from the harbor."

"Close," he answered. "But I was actually a full constable. I worked my way into the sharks under deep cover, using the gang to keep eyes on the guild."

"But you were our leader," she protested.

"Aye," he smiled, "worked my way up quicker than I would've liked. Shortly after Shon sent a message saying he left the constabulary, I followed suit. I guess I got too close to the criminals I rubbed elbows with, and his venture matched my own interests."

Eusari could tell that Karla didn't disapprove that her former boss had been spying on the guild. She was merely surprised by the revelation. "You were gifted as an outlaw," the woman stated, "and I had wondered why you left so abruptly."

Shon changed the subject, returning conversation to the mission. From Marque's expression he appreciated the shift. "So where do we stand? How many have we recruited?"

"Fifty so far," the lead scout replied. "The first bunch left this morning on a transport for Norton. They were instructed to head south to meet with King Robert and gather intelligence on the city as they do."

"That's better than we've been able to muster," Shon mused. "So far only twenty men have shown interest in mercenary work, but their prices are too high. It seems no one wants war against Marcus' Falconers."

"We decided to take a different approach," Eusari added. "We've distributed flyers around the city that reveal the truth of the featherheads. We're hoping that enough locals resent them for the "blessings" and decide to challenge their authority. That may help us find the Rookery as well, or stir up a riot or two."

Madelyn agreed, "That was wise, but they've hidden their nest so well. I doubt even the locals know where to find it. Without proof, the rumors will fade into myth and disappear from lips."

"Then we need to make finding the Rookery top priority," Eusari decided. She started to say more but was cut off by a knock at the door.

Marque was closest so he responded. As he pulled it open Jacque strolled in with a pint in his hand.

"You're late," Eusari scolded.

"I had some business to attend to," he muttered in response. He sat in the chair once occupied by Marque, who did not hide his irritation as he leaned against the wall.

"What've you got for us," Shon asked, ignoring the man's attitude and getting down to business.

"Nothing at all," he replied. "The Sewer Rats showed no interest in helping Robert Esterling. They sent me away without even a thought."

Eusari frowned. "What have you been doing in the meantime? Surely it didn't take three days to find them," she accused.

"No," he agreed. "I found them straight away. They put me up in their den and I spent my time..." he paused, choosing his words. With a grin he added, "I spent my time observing their ways."

Karla scoffed and all eyes turned to her. "Marque," she said, "you know what that means."

"Aye," Marque nodded sadly. "It means you got caught up with their drunkenness and debauchery."

Eusari held out a hand. "Where's the gold we entrusted with you?"

Jacque held out two empty palms and shrugged. "They must've slipped it from my belt while I slept."

"Passed out you mean," muttered Marque.

Jacque stood, whirling with a knife in his hand and ready for violence. "Keep your thoughts to yourself," he snapped, "or I'll cut you open right here."

The lead scout ignored the threat and sniffed. "Smell him," he said as he waved his hand before his nose. "He's drunk right now."

"Leave us," growled Eusari. "Everyone out except him and me."

Shon nodded and rose from his chair. Marque held the door open for Madelyn and Karla before handing it to his boss and turning to follow. Wembley cautioned his niece, "Clean your house, dearie."

"Oh," she agreed, "I intend to." Without averting eyes from the boatswain she added, "I'll catch up with you in the wolf den." After everyone had left, she pointed at a chair. "Sit," she commanded, and he complied. "Why in Cinder's name are you doing this?"

"Doing what," he responded casually, turning his palms innocently toward the air.

"You know damned well what you did," she pressed. "Why would you undermine my authority and embarrass me so?"

"Embarrass you?" He snarled and added, "like you've embarrassed me for the past three months? You've made it quite clear that you don't want me around."

"That isn't true," she protested. "I need you, Jacque."

"Need not want," he commented. "I'm in love with you, Captain. I'd give everything for you to return my affections, yet you pine for a ghost." He pulled his chair closer and leaned in. "Don't tell me that you aren't attracted to me." She said nothing, just stared unblinkingly as he went on. "You're worth so much to me, Eusari. I'd gladly pass on every treasure in this world just to be at your side."

"No," she whispered, averting her eyes from his. "It won't work, now."

"Why not?"

"Because I carry his child."

"You think I haven't thought about that? Come away with me. We'll start a life wherever you want, and I'll be the father Braen can't."

Good gods, she thought as she noticed his eyes. They misted with emotion as he awaited her response. "Don't do that," she said.

"Do what?"

"Promise me the world and then cry like a whipped cub." She let out a soft laugh. "You look stupid."

"I am. I'm stupid for chasing after what I can't have," he said, taking her hand in his. "Let me love you," he begged.

Shouting from the main room cut off what else he was going to say. Eusari jumped to her feet and moved to investigate. As she pulled open the door, she braced her foot in case it flung inward. Angry voices trailed in followed by sounds of a scuffle. "Demon's nipples," she cursed and flung the door wide just in time to witness Marque slumping to the ground. A dagger protruded from his sternum. She shouted. "No!"

No one turned toward her scream as they were focused on the fight. Madelyn tore her eyes from her dying lover and drew her own blade, putting her back to Shon's. They were surrounded by ten men, each with swords held at the ready and pressing in. In the confusion, Eusari saw Karla backing away into the shadows, trying to distance herself from the murder.

She betrayed us, Eusari thought, with hatred filling her soul. The knife flew from her hand before she even knew she held it. It flew end over end until it burrowed deep into the betrayer's breast. Eusari turned to aid her uncle when a pain in her belly forced her to suddenly buckle over.

The agony in her womb felt as if every muscle tore at once. She panted against the contraction, unable to stand and only able to lift one hand from the floor. When she finally looked up, it was just in time to watch Shon Wembley topple with a gash across his throat, dead in the blink of an eye. In less than a heartbeat, Madelyn joined him with her hands crossed against her sliced gut, trying to press in what protruded. The next blow took her life as well.

Jacque's hands grabbed Eusari beneath the armpits and he heaved her upright. "We've got to get out of here," he said as the assassins moved toward them. He tried to pull her into the kitchen, but she strained against him.

"No," she protested. "I can take them." She felt the world around her, searching for Gelert and finding him sleeping under the boardwalk across the way. He awoke the moment Eusari entered his mind.

The wolf's eyes opened with alarm and Eusari, bonded with her wolf, sprinted between frightened people in the street, ducking and dodging wagon wheels and hooves. The door loomed ahead, just beyond three wooden steps. She lunged into the air, meaning to clear the obstacle in a single bound, but the blast of wind pressed her just off course, sending her crashing into the doorframe. Two of her ribs cracked instantly and the sudden loss of breath toppled the beast to the ground. Inside the tavern, the woman fell as well.

While still sharing Gelert's mind, Eusari tried to stand but her legs failed to gain traction beneath her heavy frame. She lifted her head to see two Falconers strolling confidently toward the tavern. She quickly looked the other direction to find five more accompanied by two Jaguars. Their beasts showed no mercy as they converged on the wolf, tearing him apart with their long teeth.

Inside the building Eusari groaned against the pain, pulling back just as her wolf lost all lifeforce. Tears flowed from her eyes and anger raged within as she pushed to her feet. "Falconers," she said to Jacque between rapid breaths, "are coming." When he did not answer she turned to watch the tail of his cloak flutter as he raced through the back door. "Coward," she whispered.

She had to choose, follow Jacque, face the men, or get answers before the Falconers arrived. Her hesitation cost her the first two options so she rushed as fast as she could to speak with Karla. Kneeling by her side, she asked, "Why did you betray us?"

The woman's shocked eyes stared back with pain as she whispered, "I didn't," before she died.

Horror at her mistake coursed through Eusari's body. She pulled the blade and held it with an outstretched hand. The gang of men fled the way Jacque had run and she faced the Falconers alone.

The wisps of air wrapped her tightly. Feelings of vulnerability rushed in, filling her with a void of loneliness. The bonds closed tightly, stripping her confidence. She bent to their mercy, no longer the strong captain of *She Wolf.* Fear reduced her to the terrified girl who had been dragged aboard the merchant's vessel fourteen years before.

She felt the wriggling caterpillars enter her ear canals before she saw the Jaguar leaning over her body. She spotted one of the beasts lurking by the door, painted crimson from the bath in Gelert's blood. Reaching out, she tried to wrench control away from its master and failed as the larvae screamed in her head. Slumping down she gave in to defeat.

"Bring the child," the Falconer by the door ordered one of the others.

Soon a constable appeared with little Anne at his side. She clutched the headless doll in one hand while gripping her father's fingers with her other. The lawman asked the girl, "Is that her?"

She nodded and Franque turned away, unable to look at his sister the outlaw.

"Thank you," he said, handing a large sack of coins to the child. "Always remember that this is the side of law and order on which the righteous stand. You did the right thing and the empire always rewards those who remain loyal."

Eusari tried one more time to reach out to any living thing in the vicinity, but found only the screech of the larvae and a swift kick to the ribs. She was alone and not even rat nor roach would come to her aid.

Devil Jacque scurried out the back door and into the alley, nearly colliding with two constables rushing the opposite direction. One of them shoved him out of the way.

The law man narrowed his eyes and asked his partner, "Is this one of them?"

"I don't think so," the other replied, "but clamp him in irons nonetheless."

Jacque didn't give the man time. He drew his pistol and fired point blank into the constable's heart, setting his coat on fire with the muzzle flash. While the second man stared wide-eyed with fear, he ran, fleeing the alley and racing toward the docks. He didn't slow until he was certain no one had followed.

"There he is," a voice came from a sewer tunnel. A hand reached out and gestured while a second voice called, "Jacque, over here."

As his eyes adjusted to the darkness of the catacomb, he recognized the rat king. The pirate growled his questions. "What the hell happened? Why did you do it there?"

"Because the constables arrived. They planned to arrest Wembley and your captain, so we acted quicker than we would have liked. Killing that bastard felt good, and I'll be damned if I'd have let them dangle him before I had my revenge." Narrowing his eyes he added, "and now you owe us for our trouble."

"How much," asked Jacque.

"The full amount."

"I don't have it," the pirate protested. "But if you help me take *She Wolf,* I can pay you double."

The king snarled, "Why would we do that?"

Jacque held up his pistol for inspection. "Because I can get you these."

The first man eyed the weapon suspiciously. "What in Cinder's name is that?"

Jacque smiled devilishly and said, "The advantage you need to own this town."

Chapter Thirty-Four

Frederique Titus stood beside King Robert as both armies marched slowly toward a bloody meeting. Max would be proud of his son and so would General Lourdes. A boy no longer, the king commanded the field with confidence. He pointed to the enemy line. "The timing was good, and they'll meet where we planned. We should ready the Pescari for a flanking run."

"Not yet, General." The king held his head with poise and confidence. "They can still retreat into the city, so let's wait until they commit to engage."

Titus nodded and waited. He wasn't having a good day, and he yearned for the battle to end. The pain in his head had returned with the pounding of the cannons, crushing his temples and blurring his vision at times. He absently scratched at the sore on his neck, catching himself and pulling away bloody fingers. Not wishing to mar his white uniform, he wiped them instead on his water pouch.

The king stands so close, he noticed. Close enough that, if he were an assassin, he could easily do the deed. No one else watched the king since all eyes were on the pending battle. He diverted his eyes and his body trembled slightly with a chill. *This is wrong*, he thought. *I shouldn't have these thoughts.* He was sworn to protect King Robert and would do so always.

The northern army suddenly shouted, and Titus lifted his head toward the noise. They were running, committing to the attack and pressing hard to end it swiftly. They slammed against Robert's line with force, and the sound of steel clashing against steel informed the general that the shield wall held.

"Look how balanced our line is," King Robert pointed out.

But Titus didn't notice. His eyes had returned to the boy's neck, *exposed to a blade if one chose.* He pried his attention back to the battlefield. "You should signal now."

"What in Cinder's name are those?" Robert pointed at a line of brilliant white cloaks emerging from the southern entrance of the city.

Titus raised a glass and peered. "An odd assortment of men, women, and children," he replied. "Wearing white furs with hoods that resemble snow cats."

"That must be his army of emotants," the king surmised. "Braen certainly has showmanship." He waved his hand and a gust of wind blew through the trees on both sides of the battlefield, shaking the leaves and rattling loose branches. On his signal, movement from within the forest awakened, and hundreds of mounted Pescari whooped out to flank the enemy army. "We'll focus on the infantry and draw the rest in. Taros should blind them for a quick finish."

As soon as the words had come out, the shappan could be seen whirling his horse around to the rear of the assault. Flames shot out from his hands, lighting pools of pitch dumped on the soil in the weeks before. The king gave another order to Amash who darted off. In moments several large bonfires raged behind the hill, ready to fuel the shappan's fury. The fire cut off Braston's army from the line of emotants, all of whom flinched from the heat.

Titus looked around for Amash. He would be gone for a while, since his crew had a difficult task of keeping the flames blazing. It was only him and the king. His hand moved absently to the knife at this side. *No,* he fought against the urge.

Yes, a voice in his head insisted, *after he is dead you will be rewarded handsomely.* He staggered at the sudden arrival of the strange voice. It had sounded clear, unlike a thought and more like someone had whispered in his ear.

I'm going mad, he reasoned. *I must be feverish from the wound.*

"How is it going, husband?" Sarai's voice caused both men to turn. King Robert appeared irritated that his bride had joined them, but Titus felt private joy at her arrival. He removed his hand from the dagger.

"You can't be here, Sarai." Robert turned to face the battle. "Please return to the camp. If something were to happen, I might not be able to protect you. I need all of my attention here."

"I'll remain," she retorted. "My place is beside my husband wherever he stands." Titus breathed another sigh of relief when she stepped between him and the sovereign. The queen pointed to the field, "Why are the flames dying down?"

"They're trying to remove the air around the fire," Robert noted. "I'm doing the opposite from here, pouring more into it but not so much that it snuffs completely. It's tricky."

Kill him now, the voice returned, louder than before. Titus clamped his hands to his ears, reeling from the pain it brought.

"Are you well, Titus?" The king placed a hand on his general, and his voice carried genuine concern.

"Yes," Frederique backed away, resisting the sudden urge to draw his knife. *I could do it now,* he thought, longing to strike down the boy he was sworn to protect. Instead he said, "It's merely a headache."

But the king himself was suddenly not well. The enemy emotants ripped apart his hold over the air that fed the flames. As soon as they did, the fire abruptly snuffed. When they gained control, he had staggered to his knees, stunned and reeling from shock over the turn of events. "I'm okay," he said as he regained his footing.

Titus could tell that he was not. He could also tell that the queen hadn't moved to help her husband when he fell. She, like Titus, held her hand to her temple and closed her eyes against a raging pain within.

A fierce blast of wind caught them off guard as the white clad emotants joined the fight. Robert again stumbled and Titus pulled him down into the trench. The air swirled above their heads, seeking out the sovereign as if it were a dog on a hunt, biting with ghostly tendrils.

Cuyler and the others acted quickly, fighting to pry wisps of air from tangled marksmen hidden within the crevices. "They're stronger than Falconers," the lead Dreamer shouted to his king.

"Aye," Robert replied, fighting to shield the enemy from finding them below the surface. "But they're feeling around like a blind man in a satchel. They've no idea who or where we are."

Titus managed to wriggle back to his original spot, eyeing the battlefield with concern. The enemy blast had broken the shield wall, and Braston's men were cutting Robert's apart with fury. One of the beasts frenzied and foamed among the northerners, hacking and chopping with glee. The general raised his eyeglass and peered closer. "Your highness."

"What is it, Titus?" Robert had managed to rejoin him at his side.

"That isn't Braen Braston." He handed his king the spyglass and waited.

"No," Robert's face dropped. "He wears the sigil as King of Fjorik, but that isn't Braston."

"They're similar, but different," Titus said. "This man's beard is shorn, and his face is gaunt, but he surely isn't Braen." He lowered the glass and added, "And he's missing his right eye."

"Then I've foolishly risked our army," Robert remarked. "Sound the retreat, Frederique. We'll regroup and hold the hill."

"Aye, sir." Titus drew his horn and blew the notes that sent the survivors racing up the incline.

Skander's men tried to pursue, but the first line of rifles rang out, dropping their advance as soon as it began. The northern king roared his displeasure and signaled for his emotants to join his soldiers on the field.

"The ships!" Sarai eagerly pointed to the harbor. Robert's fleet had finally appeared in the bay. Soon cannons roared as they began picking apart the Fjorik fleet tied off within.

Skander watched as his men fell to the hand cannons. They had faced them once in Middleton, and caution urged him not to send a second wave up the hill. *But Robert Esterling is in your clutches,* the voice urged.

With a shout, he turned to call forth his Saber Cats and caught a glimpse of sails in the harbor. *The boy's fleet has arrived,* he told the voice.

Then you must retreat and bear me from this place! They will kill me if they find me hiding in the harbor!

Skander had another idea and shouted orders to his soldiers. As they regrouped, he commanded his children to turn the winds with force, blowing the enemy ships out of cannon range. "Hold them, my children!"

Returning his attention to the fight, he calculated. Esterling's force held the hill, and any attempt to take it would result in the loss of more men. Although Braston cared not how many he lost, he needed every man he could save for the coming assault on Eston.

"Arrows!" Artur gave the warning and Skander raised his shield just in time as hundreds rained down. The Pescari had returned. One of them, a young man, rode in front of the others. He raised his hands and fire raged as it flew toward Braston's army.

The northern king ducked behind his shield, feeling the searing heat wrap around. The boy attempted to cook him where crouched. Desperate for a source of water he reached out and found it surprisingly where he least expected, on the hip of every enemy soldier. He bled their waterskins dry, as well as all fifty thousand they held in reserve.

Robert could only watch as Taros directed the flames toward Skander. Yelling to Amash he shouted, "More flames! He mustn't run out!"

"We're trying," Amash promised, "but they're stealing our air!"

Cuyler, hearing the concern, scrambled from his trench to aid the bonfires. "I'm on it," he promised the king.

The white-clad emotants were busy holding Robert's fleet from the harbor, but several turned, and wisps of air sprang out, ripping Taros from his horse and spreading him like an eagle. The animal reared on hind legs then sprinted to the safety of the forest. But the flames of the shappan did not cease. With his hands outstretched to the sides, the flames flew from his eyes as he tried desperately to burn the northern king hiding behind his shield. Robert could see the edges melting from the searing heat.

"Your highness!" Esterling turned to see Titus holding a limp waterskin. The general pointed to the king's belt.

Robert untied the curiously dry bladder and held it up, inspecting it for holes and finding none. The water within had been drained. *Absorbed,* he realized. He asked with sudden alarm, "How many do our men carry?"

"Fifty thousand, my liege."

Robert leaped from the trench, climbing to the surface and shouting orders to the dreamers. "Get Taros untied! Drag him free," he screamed. "Focus on him!"

But it was too late. Once they had turned their attention from the bonfires, the boy's flames abruptly ceased along with every fire behind the hill. The enemy emotants had won. They held the shappan, wrapped in their shimmering ropes of air as Skander rose from his place of safety.

He tossed aside the shield, now glowing red with heat, and strode casually toward the boy. He bent over Taros and placed his mouth over the boy's. In a single moment the water filled the lungs of the bravest of the Pescari. He drowned on dry land while Robert watched helplessly.

Amidst the shouting, a single cry of alarm caused the king to turn. He recognized the voice as that of Amash warning of danger, and turned to find that Sarai had joined his side once again. In her hand she held a knife and she shoved it deep under his sternum.

On her face she wore a smile, evil as the mind that controlled her own. In a man's voice she said, "My name is Lord Campton Shol, and you can finally die, Robert Reeves."

King Esterling slumped to the ground as he stared at his wife's pregnant belly. Reaching up he touched the roundness that held his heir and begged, "Is he alive or as dead as she?"

"Only your wife is mine," Shol replied. "But killing the false heir will be her next act."

Titus watched as the queen slayed her husband. He heard her words clearly as she spoke, but his ears refused to accept their meaning. When she raised the knife over her head, ready to thrust it deep into her womb, he sprinted forward, tackling Sarai and wrestling away the knife. With it held tightly in his own hand, the voice in his mind rang as painfully as before. *She was our second option after you, General Titus. But you will do fine to destroy the heir.*

He no longer had control of his body as his arm raised the blade above Sarai's pregnant belly. Tears flowed down his cheeks as he fought against the unseen force, pouring all of his strength into holding it there instead of plunging it deep. *I won't let you,* he told the voice, *my job is to protect the king and his heir.* When the blade came down it found its way up and under his own sternum, piercing his heart, but never taking his free will.

His eyes, now glassy and seeing nothing but the ghostly image of Maximus Reeves, blinked twice. In a shaky voice General Frederique Titus spoke his final words. "I tried to keep him alive, Max. But at least your grandchild will live."

Amash rushed to his sister, holding her arms away from blade inside the dying general. Neither his eyes nor ears could believe what he had witnessed. To the Dreamer he shouted, "Tie her, Cuyler! We've got to get these bodies off this hill! Send for Sebastian!"

Amash flinched as wisps of air bound Sarai's wrists and ankles, scooping her into his arms and racing toward the rearguard. Searching for a friendly face, he found Philip sitting in the rear of a wagon. The quiet man calmly peeled potatoes while the battle raged on the other side of the hill.

Amash shouted, "Philip!" When the steward looked up his face instantly filled with worry for the bound queen.

"Yes, my lord?"

After heaving his sister onto the wagon, Horslei commanded, "Load the king as well. Bring more wagons and help me get the Dreamers to the river!" He checked the horizon, praying Sebastian hadn't frozen from fright as he had in the past. Off in the distance a single ship turned away from the others and made its way toward the mouth of the river. Amash breathed a sigh of relief.

Hearing the commotion, Percy Roan rushed forward. "Did you say to load the king? What happened?"

"The king is dead, Roan. Help Philip load the body!"

"What of the boy," the clerk asked. "What of Taros? Is he retreating as well?"

"He's also fallen."

A scream made him turn. He hadn't realized that the boy's wife, Flaya, had been standing nearby. She sprinted toward the battle and he gave chase.

To Cuyler he shouted, "Stop her!" A net instantly formed in the air, wrapping her tightly just as she neared the trenches. She fell to her knees and sobbed, staring down at the body of her husband left abandoned on the field.

A rider on horseback approached. "I must deliver him to Felicima," Teot said to Amash. "We cannot leave him to rot or his soul will never rejoin our goddess."

Horslei shook his head, "You won't reach him. We must all flee before this line breaks."

Teot understood. "You speak wisdom, but I will not join. I will take my nephew to the caldera." He pointed to Flaya. "Take her with you and protect the child in her womb. There are many who would like to see his child destroyed for his sins."

Amash stared up at the man with confusion. "Sins? What sins has he committed?"

The shappan's uncle pointed a single finger at the sun high above. "He showed his strength under the eye of Felicima and she has punished us all for his insolence. Do not forget that this attack was his idea."

Amash nodded, "We'll keep her and the child safe." He surveyed the losing battle, dismayed by the continued advance by Skander's force. "Cuyler," he shouted.

"Yes, Horslei?"

"Get your Dreamers to the wagons. Go now before it's too late."

The boy eyed the battle, obviously weighing the legitimacy of the order. He hesitated.

"Son," Amash said, "go with the king and protect the heir. That's your mission now! Protect him at all cost!"

Finally the teen nodded and rounded up the others. They hurried toward the rear and Amash followed. Once they had all boarded the wagons, Amash gave the order to leave with haste. Exhausted and anxious to leave the cursed battlefield, he collapsed between Philip and Percy. He stared down for a long while at the body of Robert Esterling.

A chuckle made him lift his eyes toward his sister. He was amazed to find her smiling as she tittered at the dead body at her side. "What," he asked, "is so funny?"

"It's even more amusing that you should ask, Son of Esterling."

"What are you talking about, Sarai? Have you gone so mad that you've forgotten your brother? We're both the son of Abraham Horslei."

"No, stupid man," the voice of Campton Shol jeered, "you're the only true born son of Charles Esterling. Have you never wondered why Abe hated you so?"

Chapter Thirty-Five

Braen caught his breath, panting against exhaustion. For a brief moment he marveled at the fluidity with which Marita fought. The girl was a natural killer who moved more like a dancer than a blade wielder, yet she had learned the art well from Pogue.

The thought of Alec returned his thoughts to the rest of his party. He wondered, *what is taking so long?* A glimpse of the kitchen revealed a bound Alec on the floor. Four Dreamers stepped over his form and entered the great hall. Behind them Charro Valencia swayed like a Jaguar. "Marita," he shouted, "we have company!" He pointed at the newcomers. She nodded and leaped into the air, clearing several enemy soldiers to reach her quarry.

Braen faced the advancing army alone. As soon as he dropped one or two, several more would rise from the dead and join the fight. He was hopelessly outnumbered and certain to lose. He would die a second time, only without Eusari nearby. He agonized, *why did I let her down?*

A blade whirred, just clipping his ear. He roared at the attacker, punching with the pommel of his axe and striking the man's nose. Anger seethed inside. His heart filled with hatred for Nevra and Artema Horn, the men responsible for stealing the peace from his exile to The Cove. Disgust usurped the hate as he added feelings for Skander, his pitiful brother who robbed him of his father and plunged him into a life of chaos.

Their mother had been a Berserker, that was the secret his father had confided in Braen the night she had died. "Rage is in your blood, Son, control it and unleash it only when you face the enemy," Krist Braston had advised.

At the time he had asked his father, "Does Skander know this?"

"Your brother blames your mother for his anger. He's convinced that she is proof that it cannot be contained, and that his own will burn forever unless he learns to contain the beast within. He'll never control it like you can."

"I wouldn't call my anger controlled, father. Especially after... what happened."

Krist had placed a supportive hand on his son's shoulder. "You do well enough, and it only comes out when it is needed. Love him no matter what. Treat him with kindness and never turn your rage toward him for he is your brother."

His opponent swung at his neck, forcing him to bob and weave out of striking distance. "He is my brother no longer," Braen said to the frustrated attacker. The axe caught the pommel, and he swung, wrenching the weapon from its master. In a single motion he sent it flying across the room then roared at the defenseless man. "He is not my brother and you are not Adamas Creech."

In that moment he gave in to the rage, embracing the destruction residing in his blood. He killed mercilessly, hacking and chopping his attackers as generations of Berserkers fueled his killing spree. He did not rest until every man in the room had fallen under his axe. He did not have long to catch his breath for as soon as the last man fell, the first began to rise.

Across the room, Marita squared off against Hallbera and the younger Dreamers. They had positioned themselves in a way that blocked her access to Alec. Just beyond him she glimpsed Charro Valencia kneeling on the floor and swaying like she had seen the Jaguars. The fight would be four against one and she liked the odds.

"Hello, Magnus," she said, pointing at the head of Nathaira on the floor. "I see you're still bullying littler children." The boy said nothing in response.

Kadlin and Hallbera wasted no time, sending wisps of air in an attempt to trip her up. She slid between these, tying the ends together with her mind, forcing her attackers to either take the time to untangle the pretty bow or dissipate the threads and try again. While they chose the latter, she sent a concussion that forced them hard against the wall. Without hesitation she attacked Olafur with a flurry of steel.

He tried desperately to defend against her attack, but he lacked any weapon except his power over air. She won quickly by forming a bubble around him, sealing him in and then plunging her sword deep. She made a popping sound with her lips as she poked his heart with her blade. No sooner did he die then he reanimated, striking out and forming a net with the others.

She sliced the invisible bond with a different kind of sword, one that she formed out of a tight weave of her own. This she wielded with her mind, spinning it around her body as she ran toward Lord Valencia. The others flung every weapon imaginable with their air, but her invisible sword cut down every attempt. She flew the final stretch, leaping over Alec and flying twenty feet in air, spinning as she did. As she reached Charro, she plunged her swords deep into his back, driving them in and collapsing on the floor. She stared up at the four Dreamers and waited.

The death of Valencia aroused the wrath of the four Dreamers. They roared with anger and threw a net toward Marita. She rolled out of the way, just dodging their prison of air. Abruptly an explosion rocked the great hall, sending a shockwave through the kitchen. All four teens slammed hard against the wall, and Marita quickly secured them with wisps of her own. Alec scrambled to his feet, pulling the swords from the fallen Duke of Cargia and handing them to his daughter. Together they rushed to check on Braen.

All at once each of Braen's attackers had frozen where they stood, encircling him and speaking in unison. Each bore the voice of Stefan Nevra, "No, Lord Kraken," they said, "he is no longer your brother. He is my special plaything." They each licked their lips lecherously and added, "You could have been as well, had your wolf not dragged you away. Once again, your life is mine to take. Only this time your life will be restored unnaturally."

The corner of Braston's eye caught a glimpse of Marita flying through the air in the kitchen, both swords outstretched as she pounced on a foe. As she landed, the men surrounding Braen screamed.

They rushed him all at once, intent on crushing him beneath their combined weight. He felled the first three to reach him, but collapsed under the weight of the others. They lay atop his body, crushing and clawing at his throat. *Not like this,* he thought, *I won't die this way.* He felt them squeezing hard and cutting off his air. His vision swam and flickering lights blurred the room as darkness took over.

An explosion of fire filled the great hall, flinging the bodies of his attackers and tossing them about. The heat scorched the hairs on his body, singeing them into curls. He blinked his eyes as he stared at the ceiling, the whooshing beat of large wings meeting his ears. He rolled his head to the side, searching for the source of the explosion.

Six enormous birds hovered just inside the large window that overlooked the harbor. Their feathers were boldly colored in red and orange with splashes of yellow tinging the ends. Their eyes glowed like burning embers, seemingly like fires set into the splayed feathers adorning their heads. *No,* he thought, *these are only legends.* But so was the Kraken, before Braen first called them to his side.

Voices shouted from across the room. "Braen! Come quickly!" He rolled over to see that Marita and Alec stood in the kitchen, waving him to join them.

Yes, he reasoned, *these beasts are not my saviors, and will destroy me as well.* He clamored to his feet just as the magnificent birds screeched, bellowing fire from their beaks as they beat their massive wings and fanned an inferno. The bodies of the fallen men burst into flames as he sprinted toward freedom. *I'll never make it,* he thought, feeling the searing heat on his back.

Marita screamed, "Hurry!" She stood near the pantry door with arms outstretched, knitting a web of air around him and deflecting the worst of the heat. He raced past and she followed, both slipping inside the secret door just as Alec slammed it shut. Together they hurried into the tunnels. They paused only when they heard groaning in the dark.

Kneeling, Braen found Charleigh laying semi-conscious on the stone floor. He scooped her into his arms and shouted to Alec. "Cut the fuse! We need those barrels to blow now, not in ten minutes!" Alec nodded and went to work.

Marita picked up the discarded torch, dropped by Charleigh when the Dreamers had turned on her and followed the others inside. With a nod from Braen she lit the fuse, and they ran, counting heartbeats in their ears as they rushed to Ralphe Station's store. The explosion behind them was deafening, as the castle in the center of The Cove collapsed.

Part III
Life is Love

Only the son of Andalon can slay him in time.

- Samani Kernigan, 806th year of order

Chapter Thirty-Six

Rough hands tossed Eusari into a wagon. Bound tightly, she could not move, forced to stare at the fluffy clouds clinging to the blue sky above. *Strange,* she thought, *how it's always the most beautiful skies that bring the worst storms.* Utterly powerless against her fate, she relaxed without a struggle. There was no sense wasting energy, she knew where they traveled. She had become a mere specimen, a new addition to the Falconers' Rookery.

Her mind replayed the death of her uncle, Shon. *I was just learning to trust him,* she lamented. *He sincerely cared about family, and I never allowed him to get close.* The images of her brother's faces raced through her mind as well. *He wanted so badly to bring us together, but I pushed them away as well.*

And poor Karla, she thought. The old Eusari had killed her, the impulsive and emotional pirate hell-bent on revenge. *I murdered that woman without knowing the truth of her involvement. Why have I always been so quick to rush to judgement? Where has assumption ever taken me except to despair?* She was suddenly very thankful that Braen had not lived to witness her shame.

During the brief time he shared her life, she had drawn strength from his wisdom. Except for killing Karla, she was no longer petulant or impulsive. She was no longer alone in the world. She had learned to trust, and after trust had followed love. Her disappearance into the rookery would be noticed by her friends, and, for the first time in her life, she would be missed after she was gone.

They will worry, she realized with pangs of anxiety. *No,* she thought, *they mustn't try to find me. Especially not Caroline. She'll surely risk her life to come, and they will capture her as well.*

Peter Longshanks would most likely assist the girl. That man had become Eusari's most trusted confidant, and she imagined her first mate putting together a rescue plan that very night. But they weren't the only ones who would act foolishly. Sippen and Krill would search purely out of a need to preserve Braen's love and also for his child. His child. Her child. *Our child,* she realized. *I must escape my bonds and live for our child.*

The cart came to a stop and Eusari feared they had already reached the Rookery. But, after several heartbeats they moved. The clouds hadn't changed, and she had no way to know where in the city she was. That is, until branches passed overhead, tied with beautifully colored ribbons that announced the festival. They passed through the city square.

She tried once more to reach out with her powers, attempting to bond with the tree. The larvae in her ears screamed and hissed until she lost focus, forcing her to abandon the effort. Whatever these worms were, they had attuned with her ability to channel lifeforce. It was as if they were controlled by another being, one with full knowledge of her skills and with the ability to preempt her attempts. *A Jaguar, perhaps?*

She thought about the way the creatures had reanimated King Robert's soldiers. From the stories she had heard, they raised them from death in the same way she had thought to raise Braen. Of course, she had hesitated at the thought, choosing instead to let him die instead of stripping his free will forever. These simple caterpillars must serve their masters in the same manner and as part of a collective bond. As such they could be separated from their master.

Eusari was careful not to alert the collective to her plan. She could not take them by force, and for this she would need a gentle touch, one similar to the approach she would use as a mother. That depended, of course, on whether or not she lived to birth her child. The results of her next efforts would decide that fate.

Her tender probing discovered that the larvae had simple consciousness, barely sentient and only aware of their immediate surroundings. She tested them, reaching out to wiggle a single leaf loose from a low hanging branch. Pain instantly shot through both nymphs, amplified as if she had attacked them directly. *These poor worms,* she thought, *only act according to their simple need for comfort.* She realized they were no different than a baby inside a womb.

She probed again, this time soothing them as she did. They responded differently this time, relaxing their sinewy muscles and eventually their hold. She sang to them with her mind, a sweet lullaby her mother had sung to her as a child.

> *"Over hill, a rushing spring,*
> *swiftly flowing oft to bring.*
> *A mother's love that's ne'er lost,*
> *Always found within your heart."*

The horns of the larvae retracted as their bodies slackened, no longer held by the foreign Jaguar. Just as gently she soothed again, this time coaxing their attention toward her own mind. Oh, the love she felt then, as the tiny caterpillars accepted her beckon. *I never believed myself worthy of love,* she realized. *I thought that ability had been stripped away by the evil men, but instead it was there, forever sealed in my heart even as I watched my mother die.*

Understanding filled her. *She died so that her body would endure the worst of the pain so that my young body would survive. I am alive because of her sacrifice. What was done to me was done, and cannot be undone, but I can ensure that my child is raised with tender love.* Another thought occurred to her then, more faces upon which her life depended. *I must survive so that the Dreamers will endure as well.*

No longer constrained by the will of the Jaguar, she reached out to the trees above the wagon. She paused momentarily as a tiny sparrow fluttered overhead, circling as if to say, "I see you." She smiled softly at the creature, then winked. *Caroline,* she thought, *if that is you, then here is something to watch.* The limbs of the tree came to life, reaching to grab ahold of the Falconers riding atop the driver's seat. They writhed and kicked against the pressure as she squeezed, caught completely off guard, and dropping the bonds that tied her hands and legs.

Eusari scrambled to her feet, ready to jump free and make her escape when the grip around her neck slammed her hard against the buckboard. As she fell, she turned and saw five more Falconers and two Jaguars riding atop a second wagon behind her. They laughed in unison at her futile attempt.

Across the city of Logan a group of hard men approached *She Wolf*. Most of them remained on the pier, but three wasted no time crossing the brow.

The midday watch asked the man in the lead, "Who're your friends, Jacque?"

"Eusari sent us, said we need to arm some of the street gangs," the pirate replied as he pushed past.

"You're crew so I'll let you board Bos'un, but they need to hold fast while I call for Pete."

Jacque shrugged. "Do what you must, Porter, just be quick about it."

The man guarding the quarterdeck turned to the messenger. "Go tell Mr. Longshanks that his presence is requested. Tell him he should hurry." The other man nodded and hustled off to relay the order. When Porter again turned to face Jacque, he felt steel pierce his breast. He slumped to the ground, helpless to stop the other men as they boarded.

"The armory is this way," Jacque told the others.

Peter Longshanks hadn't run since he'd lost his leg. That was when he bootlegged rum from the southern continent. Although the crew liked to whisper that he'd lost it to a cannonball fighting the Imperial Navy, he'd actually lost it to a far more dangerous foe. Infection took his leg and barely left him his life. He had been fine with the exchange at the time, but on days like this he wished he could run instead of hobble around.

As he rounded the lee deck, he halted so abruptly that the messenger of the watch rammed him from behind. "Go, Giovanni," he said, "gather the others working aft. There's a mutiny afoot!" As the other man sped off to gather help, he crept around to the forward hatch and drew his pistol to the ready. His other hand drew a short cutlass from his waist and held it aloft, ready to counter the first sign of trouble.

When the hatch flung open, he called out, "You'll be halting where you stand, Devil Jacque. Where you be takin' those guns?"

The scum turned slowly with eyes that danced of mischievous victory, dropping a crate as he drew his own blade. "So it's a fight then, Pete?"

"Aye," the first mate agreed. "It's a fight." He only took his eyes from Jacque for a moment, as six more men joined the mutineer. Peter frowned. He did not know these men. "You're enlisting rabble, as well?" He spat with disgust and fired his pistol at Jacque, missing wildly as one of the newcomers fired his own at the same time. Thankfully, he missed also.

A few more shots rang out from both sides as the deck seamen arrived, joining their first mate to defend the ship. Surprisingly only three men fell during the brief firefight, and the clash of steel against steel announced an old-fashioned melee. Pete's blood boiled with excitement during the fray, he had long ago tired of Jacque's attitude and the thought of splaying the shitpot's gut brought young life to his old bones.

He found an opening and attacked, arcing his cutlass and making contact with the boatswain's head. Unfortunately, the man shifted his weight and stepped at the last moment and Pete only succeeded in cutting away his ear and part of his devilish good looks. Jacque roared with rage and lunged, taking advantage of the committed attack. The blade caught Longshanks in the arm and forced the older man to step back.

As he caught his breath, he surveyed the scene. Most of his crew either lay on the deck losing blood or knelt and begged for mercy from their enemy. He turned back to Jacque who tenderly touched his head and pulled away a bloody hand. There would be no mercy from him. *I've nothing left to do,* the older man thought. He grabbed the rail and swung over the side, hitting the water with a splash of cowardice as he abandoned Eusari's command.

She Wolf had a new master behind her helm, and his name was Devil Jacque.

Chapter Thirty-Seven

Captain Santos barked orders at his crew, but each command proved futile against the forceful gale pushing them away from Norton harbor. Even the boy was useless, hiding in the lee deck like a craven, afraid to even attempt to fight back. He scanned the shoreline, watching the battle unfold south of the city as the enemy army pushed closer to the hill. King Esterling was suddenly losing the day.

The screams of the boatswain relayed the commands, sounding oddly strange amidst the odd silence atop the lake. "You heard the captain, raise the sails and row, you sacks of blood!" He and the coxswain were doing everything they could to move the ship closer to the city.

A tug at Santos' sleeve made him look down. The sight of the useless Dreamer made him sigh. "What do you want, boy?"

"We have to sail the opposite direction," the child said. He pointed toward the mouth of the Misting River. "They're telling us to meet them along the bank."

The captain shook his head and pointed at the battle. "The fight rages and we have the king's orders. We have to take out those ships."

The boy, Santos remembered that his name was Sebastian, was timid, but suddenly found his voice. "The king is dead and they're taking his body to the riverbank. We must be there to help them escape."

"Dead?" The captain shook his head and tried to fathom the boy's words. "The king is dead? How?"

Sebastian shrugged and then insisted. "Lower the sails and I'll get us to them."

"By Cinder's Crack," the captain swore, "then the war is lost." He chewed on his next words for a few seconds then turned to his crew. "Stow away those oars and unfurl the mainsail! Hard rudder to starboard with the sails turned to port!" To Sebastian he added, "That'll turn her belly, but the rest is up to you."

The wagon bounced dangerously along the road, tilting and careening as they avoided washed out sections and rocks. Amash had been quiet since their escape, mulling over Philip's earlier words. *My father was Charles Esterling,* he thought, *not Abraham Horslei.* He looked down at the lifeless body of the king. *He's my brother?*

As if reading his mind, Philip spoke up. "He was a sweet boy, but wasn't the true heir. I wish Charles could have known him; he reminds me a lot of him."

Amash looked up, "You knew King Esterling well?"

"I did. I was his valet for several years. After his affair with Lady Horslei, I was strategically placed in the governor's quarters to… watch over any developments."

"Meaning me?"

"Yes. Meaning you."

"This was when he fought the Pescari?"

"Yes, and before his accident."

Amash was at a loss for words. He had known that Abraham and Charles had worked closely together during the Pescari wars and that he had housed in their palace. What he didn't suspect was the affair. "Did he know about me?"

"Yes, but he kept you a secret from Crestal, or you would have been killed. After he died, Abraham and I were the only two in Andalon who knew the truth, but you had already fled the academy. We had no idea where you had been hiding, but it didn't matter, because Crestal had already stolen the regency. Even if we'd found you a bid for the witan it would have been pointless."

Percy Roan was squeezed into the rear of the cart. He interjected. "You mentioned an accident, Philip?"

"Yes," The old steward smiled at the secret knowledge and some private joke. "He, Reeves, and Abraham had been drinking heavily one night, and passed by the stables on their way to the palace. The king told them that he'd been teaching his new destrier tricks, and they stopped to place wagers on whether or not he knew dressage."

Amash frowned. "A dancing horse?"

"You can call it that. General Lourdes certainly did after he found out what had happened. Everything was fine until he drunkenly gave the wrong command and the horse reared instead of bowing. Charles was already off balance, and fell to the ground beneath its spooked and panicking legs."

Horslei paled. "Was he hurt badly?"

"One misstep of an errant hoof ended his ability to sire more children after you."

"That's awful," Roan remarked. Then a thought struck him, "So, King Robert?"

"Is the son of Maximus Reeves."

"I thought he and the king were best friends," Amash pointed out. "Why would Max lay with the queen?"

"Because it was Charles' wish that the boy be sired by his closest friend and confidant."

A thought lit Percy Roan's face. "And the other? What about Marcus Esterling?"

"I've no idea. He could also belong to Max, but knowing Crestal he could belong to any

of the generals in the court." Philip watched Amash for quite a while then added, "You could challenge him now, if you wish. I would testify for whatever good it would do."

"What's the point?" He pointed at the king's dead body. "I don't have an army and his was left behind to die by Skander's hand."

"There are other ways to become king, young Esterling." The voice came from Sarai's lips, but the deep baritone was certainly not hers.

"What do you mean, Shol?"

"With my support and that of the Astian council I could place you on that throne. I will back up the steward's story, and confirm your claim over Marcus."

"Why would you do that?"

"Because we will need to rebuild after Nevra and Braston destroy Eston."

"Nevra? Braston? What are you talking about?"

Sarai laughed a deep and hearty laugh. "Did Kernigan not tell you about the final prophecy of the Destroyer?"

"No. He didn't."

"Pity, since it involves you."

Cuyler, who had been sitting nearby listening, replied. "Only the son of Esterling can slay him in time." When all eyes turned to him, he explained, "Samani told me."

"Slay who," Amash asked. "I thought the prophecies were about the Destroyer, but Braen is dead."

"No," Cuyler revealed. "He's alive and currently fighting in The Cove. He's trying to kill Nevra to end his control over Skander."

"Oh you pitiful Andalonians," the voice that had taken over Sarai proclaimed. "You've no concept of the Destroyer." She made a 'tsk' sound with her teeth. "It isn't our continent he will destroy, but your own. No, Amash Esterling, when the time comes you will have no choice but to slay him. Just hope you do it in time."

"Gag her," Amash ordered and Cuyler complied, wrapping her mouth full of wadded wisps that worked as well as a rag.

"Is it true then?" The lead Dreamer stared at Amash with wide eyes. "Are you the true heir to the kingdom?"

"No," the pirate replied honestly, "I'm merely a guardsmen for Pirate's Cove."

Sebastian spotted the wagons and directed Captain Santos to a spot to which they could easily tie off. The crew quickly tossed cargo nets over the side, upon which the party could climb. He watched with wide eyes as the other Dreamers lashed Queen Sarai and the body of King Robert, pulling them gently aboard without ropes.

He stared at the lifeless king and sadness filled his heart. This body was just one of many in the young boy's life. He was tired of death. He was tired of the killing. Once they were all aboard, Santos gave the order and they cut lines and Sebastian filled the sails to speed south, mournfully giving life to the canvas in order that those aboard would live.

Both the king and queen were taken below decks, him to lay in state and her to await judgement in a cell. Once she was out of earshot, the motley crew gathered on the forecastle. They were a sad lot. All that remained of Robert Esterling's army were a grouchy captain, a pirate, seven dreamers, a house steward, a pregnant Pescari woman, and an accountant. They were a miserable lot indeed.

"Where do I drop you off," Captain Santos asked Cuyler, addressing him out of respect for his rank in Robert's army.

"We are all headed to Logan," Amash replied before the boy could utter a response. "We need to meet up with Captain Thorinson and the others. Then we'll decide where you'll take us."

"I most certainly will not," the captain objected. "I'm an imperial officer and loyal to the crown. I won't cavort with pirates."

"Actually," Cuyler answered with wisdom beyond his years, "with the king dead, you are now a deserter to the ruling imperial navy, and they'll hunt you down as a renegade."

Amash nodded his agreement. "One without a letter of marque," he said. "Whether you like it or not you're now an outlaw. At best we're pirates, and Captain Eusari is the closest we have to a pirate queen unless you want to swear fealty to Nevra." He shuddered when he mentioned the pox-faced lord. "If you have any sense, you'll take us there to regroup while we figure out how to survive this debacle."

Sebastian watched Captain Santos and could almost see the words sinking in. He wasn't a fool, this captain, and he quickly saw reason.

“Okay,” the man agreed. “We sail for Logan. I’ll treat with this Captain Thorinson, and decide the fate of myself and my crew after. I hope she is truly the queen that you describe.”

Chapter Thirty-Eight

A mounted Teot watched the others depart, sadness filling his heart for his nephew's bride and the journey she must endure with her unborn child. He surveyed the battlefield, studying the line and trying to determine how long Esterling's abandoned forces could hold back the northern horde. Despite their high ground and weaponry they would soon fall, overrun by the relentless foe and the madman who led their charge.

He scanned the surrounding Pescari faces. Only a few dozen of his scouts remained, the rest slain and strewn across the scorched grass and already attracting flies. His nephew lay among them, discarded like the bones of a horse lost crossing the Forbidden Waste. *This will not do,* he thought, and readied himself to recover the body and commit Taros' soul to Felicima.

She had already set in the western sky, and would not see his boldness. *That is good,* he knew, *and improves my chances to succeed.* His hand flashed signals to the others. *Cover me,* he said, *and draw their fire. I will gather the shappan.*

They replied, *Render him to Felicima, Shappan.*

Teot paused and signed, *Why do you call me that? There has been no shapalote.*

You are the agent of Felicima, they replied. *None shall challenge.*

I do not want it, he pressed.

No other will take it. It is yours.

He scanned the enemy line, searching for the demon who led them. He stood close to Taros, ordering the white clad men, women, and children to the rear guard. *They are powerful,* Teot knew, *and there are many.*

He flashed another order to the scouts. *Charge as soon as I hit the tree line, attack from the west so that I may have their backs toward me.*

Go, Shappan. We will do as you say.

He spurred Ciro beneath him, pushing the steed hard as he raced down the hill to the east. The trees and brush were thick in this part of the forest and forced him to slow as he moved again northward. Through occasional clearings he saw the enemy line shift toward the west, and a war whoop in that direction let him know that his people had engaged. With a final spur he leaped from cover and charged to the spot where his nephew's body lay.

He swung over the side, gripping the horse with a strong leg and using its body for cover as they sprinted to the fallen shappan. Every Pescari practices horsemanship at a young age, and Teot held firm without trouble. The problem would come when he had to halt the animal without flying underneath his hooves. He would have to come to a complete stop to recover Taros.

He neared the body and shifted balance, placing more weight over the neck and clicking his tongue in the horse language. Ciro slowed to the Pescari calls. At the last minute Teot swung his body squarely onto the horses back, squeezing with his knees and giving the final cue. He stopped abruptly.

Teot stole a glance toward the enemy forces, then dismounted while taking note of a small group of white robes making their way toward him. He hoped they were out of range as he heaved his nephew's son over the shoulders of Ciro. The white robes lifted their hands in unison, stirring up wind around them and weaving them into a gusty tornado. This caught the attention of their demon lord, who quickly commanded others to join in halting the Pescari scout's escape.

Without a source of flame to draw upon, Teot would have to strictly adhere to the ways of his people, relying upon cunning and his mount to survive. Leaning low over Taros, he spurred forward, keeping out of the vacuum of the vortex, but only barely. He raced along the northern edge, circling and making for the trees lining the eastern edge. He nearly made it free when a gust of wind sent him flying from atop Ciro.

The ground met him with breathtaking pain upon impact. He rolled, hand over his ribs, willing his legs to work. He scrambled to run after his horse, but the beast was at a full sprint with a draped Taros bouncing as if he were about to be bucked. He pushed down the pain and chased after the steed, the sound of the roaring cyclone racing after him from behind.

Ahead six riders emerged from the trees. Two split apart from the others, riding along both sides of Ciro and bringing him under control. The others raised bows and pointed them in Teot's direction. *Is this deception?* His heart raced as he suddenly worried his own scouts would kill him upon this battlefield. His pulse pounded in his ears as he continued his sprint toward them. He stole one glance over his shoulder, the cyclone had gathered strength as it chased him down.

Four flickering lights flew toward him, flaming arrows arcing through the air and landing several strides ahead. He grinned, proud that his scouts had not doomed him to die. The torches extinguished cleanly without a hint of smoke, granting him just enough strength to face the vortex.

It spun violently, building an orbiting cloud of dust as broad as one hundred horses. He felt the winds pulling at his buckskins, tangling his hair and forcing him to lean backward to resist the pull. That massive draw grew stronger with every breath he took, but he patiently waited.

Teot swirled a pattern of his own, twisting a small flame between his hands that slowly grew into a whirl. He set it upon the ground like a spinning toy, sending it toward the bigger vortex. He felt other sources of heat now. The battlefield was full of it, emanating from each man as they burned the energy of their bodies. *This heat is different,* he realized, *but will fill me the same.* His cheeks flushed while the men fighting upon the hill grew paler, chilled air puffing like clouds with every breath. His eyes burned like fiery coals within their sockets, as he poured this source into the spinning flame now standing as tall as he.

The winds of the torrent fueled his own, raging the red and yellow tongue until it grew blue with searing ferocity. Now spinning with life of its own, Teot gently guided the whirl toward the cyclone of air, sucking more fuel from the dry fields. When they crashed together, he gained absolute control over the newly formed cone of fire reaching into the heavens. He directed this toward the demon's army and sprinted toward his waiting scouts.

Once again mounted, he called for the retreat of Esterling's remaining forces. Having witnessed the break in Braston's line, they eagerly followed the Pescari shappan and raced southward alongside his scouts. The enemy, scattered by the flaming vortex, did not pursue.

Skander Braston watched as the Pescari horsemen escaped with the body of their leader. *He was a prize,* the voice said, *and you let both him and Esterling slip away.*

"Shut up," the northern king said aloud, causing Artur to turn around confused.

"No one said anything," the first mate responded.

The sword flashed too quickly for Artur to react, taking him in the belly and buckling his knees. Skander placed a boot against his friend's chest and pressed him to the ground, pulling his blade free as he whirled around to face the vortex. The heat from the spinning torrent of fire seared his hairs, causing him to chase after his retreating army as they returned to the safety of their boats.

The voice remained quiet until after he had returned to *Malfeasance.* As soon as he stepped aboard, it commanded, *Deal with those ships.*

Skander stared past the rail. Esterling's navy held fast, unable to pierce the wall of opposing winds made by his children. *I had forgotten about those,* he realized. He called for his first mate, "Artur!" No one answered, and so he called again, "Artur!"

A brutish warrior with more brawn than sense timidly replied, "He's dead, sire."

"Dead? How? Why was I not informed?"

The man stared dumbfounded at his king, stammering and unable to find the words to answer.

See? They fear you, the voice explained, *but they respect you as well. Show them the true magnificence of your power. Destroy the boats yourself, my love.*

"Yes," Skander replied. "I should do it myself."

"Do what, my lord?" The brute stepped out of his way, and Braston leaped over the side, landing firmly on the water and walking casually toward the enemy ships.

His army, still reeling from their hard-fought victory, manned the rails as he approached the vessels.

"Father," he asked, "why did she die?"

Everyone dies, Skander. Focus on the task at hand so that we may pursue Esterling's body. I need it.

"I'm not asking you," he said to the voice, "I am asking my father."

Your father is dead, the voice replied. *Focus on the ships. Destroy them so that we can be free of this place.*

"Father," he asked again, "why did mother die?"

She died because of you, son, the deep voice of Krist Braston replied, *because you had a habit of discovering her secrets.*

"How did she die, father?" Skander had reached the first of the ships. He clapped his hands and the water around them abruptly crushed their hulls, sinking five vessels with a single motion. He continued on. "Tell me again," he pleaded, "how she died. I cannot remember."

I vowed never to speak of this again, the voice of Krist Braston boomed in his ears.

He reached outstretched arms toward ten more ships, waving his hands like a conductor and closing his eyes to listen to the beautiful music of the orchestra. The current beneath them spun in opposite directions, swirling and sucking them downward to the muddy floor of Lake Norton. In his mind the music intoned, the horn section replaced by the deep baritone of screaming men, and the flutes were substituted by a crying infant.

Skander, the voice begged in the distance. *My love, come back to me. Push these other voices from your mind. You belong to me,* Nevra commanded, *you shall listen to me alone!*

"Father," the younger Braston asked a third time, "how did my mother die?" Five more ships sunk beneath his power, torn apart by the waves and thrashed against one another.

She died at your brother's hand, Skander. Braen killed her to save you.

"What did he save me from," he asked as the final ship sank beneath the waves. "I can no longer remember."

The voice interrupted, answering before his father. *You cannot remember because I alone have purged those memories from your mind. Come back to me and push these ghosts from your mind. Only I have answers for your questions.*

"I am speaking to my father," Skander roared. "You shall remain silent!" He asked Krist Braston once more. "Father, what did Braen save me from that resulted with her death?"

He saved you from your mother's rage, son. She learned what you had done and also panicked over her own mistake, unable to hide her sins. She hated you then and fell into her berserker madness. She beat you like a cowering dog while you wet yourself and cried on the floor.

"But Braen loved me enough to stop her."

No Skander. He proved to the world that you are a craven who cannot fight your own battles. That is why you killed me and blamed him for my death. That is why you stole his woman. All to redeem your dwindled masculinity.

"But I am a man now, father."

No. You allow Stefan Nevra to control you because you will always be weak. You carve others like a snow cat marks its territory, weak and hoping the world sees you otherwise.

Skander wheeled around, sprinting across the water toward *Malfeasance.* He leaped high into the air and pulled himself over the rail, muttering words that were incomprehensible to his crew. He threw open his stateroom door and charged in, staring down the pox-faced man huddled in the corner and filled with fear. "No one controls me!"

The horrible man screamed, "You cannot kill me! Not while I am in your mind!" He turned his back and curled into a ball facing the corner, his disgusting rat hissing angrily up at Skander.

"There are things far worse than death," Skander promised. He drew his blade and stabbed it through the animal, pinning it to Nevra's back. With it still clinging to his blade, he carved deeper than he had ever attempted, leaving one more bit of proof to the world that he was the rightful King of Fjorik. "My father is correct," he said above the cries, "I mark what belongs to me."

Chapter Thirty-Nine

The boy stared wide-eyed and amazed by the sights just beyond the glass. The city outside the train window was larger than Eston and Middleton combined, far larger, he imagined, than all the cities in the Esterling Empire. Each building was perfectly shaped and of single stone, almost as if each had been carved from a single source. *Impossible,* Johan thought, *some of those buildings are forty stories tall!*

Cassidy, who had watched the children marvel for quite some time, commented, "Welcome to Bergin," she said. "The capital city is ancient, built upon the ruins of what survived after the Great Destruction. See that river?" They sped across a massive bridge, easily the size of fifty or more of the Span of Eston. "That is the Spree, and is one of eight total within the city itself. You can literally travel anywhere in the city via waterway if you choose."

Kali pointed out the window with excitement, the most she'd shown since leaving Andalon. "Look, Johan! There's a lot of lakes too!"

Cassidy nodded. "Three thousand to be exact."

But Johan did not need either of the girls to point out the waterways. He already felt their power coursing through his body. The stimulation electrified every nerve ending. He squeezed Kali's hand with satisfaction as he bent his neck to get a better look at the scenery ahead. A round building, easily as large as Eston's entire Unification Square, sat upon a tiny peninsula jutting into the Spree, surrounded on three sides by the river. To the Society agent he asked, "What is that building?"

"That," Cassidy said with a smile, "is where the Astian Council meets. We call it the Rotunda."

The squeal of brakes indicated that the slowing train would make another stop. They had been through the process several times during their journey, but Johan's heart raced just as much as it had the first.

Cassidy sensed his anxiety and spoke calmly, saying, "Just do what you did before, show your identification and don't smile. No one smiles in Astia."

Two soldiers approached, just as the other times, armed with scary black weapons that made Shon Wembley's hand cannons seem archaic. He tried to follow the agent's advice, but found that he couldn't stop fidgeting. He fumbled his identification card, dropping it to the floor and bent to pick it up. One of the soldiers jabbed him with the buttstock of his rifle.

"What's wrong, citizen? Are you up to no good, child?"

Johan quickly retrieved the document and held it aloft, shaking his head to the contrary and avoiding eye contact. He didn't know which terrified him more, the intensified drumming of his heart in his ears or the thought of the men dragging him from the train.

"Leave the boy alone," the other soldier said. "He's just a child." The first man grunted, and the pair moved on.

After they had left, while reflecting on the situation, Johan realized they were only men, bored with their duties and only half paying attention to the passengers. He had panicked over nothing.

Kali asked Cassidy, "We're not stopping here?"

"No," she replied, "our stop is further up river."

"Why are the others leaving?" The girl pointed to the platform. Four of the disguised Society agents were offloading their crate onto a waiting truck.

"Never mind them," Cassidy warned. "They've other business than ours."

Her words made Johan perk up. Nothing about this trip made sense to him. Samani had insisted that the Society couldn't do their job without Kali and him, as if they'd be fighting in a war. But the city surrounding the train was peaceful. Other than the soldiers checking faces at each stop, there was no sign of any army, nor of oppression. The citizens appeared healthy, going about their business carefree despite their lack of smiles.

With a shaky voice he asked, "What is our business?"

"You'll know when you meet with the Dragon."

Kali suddenly asked the question both children had pondered since the first mention of the mysterious stranger. "Does he breathe fire?"

Cassidy, despite her caution against smiling, almost laughed out loud. "Hell no," she said. "We call him that because it's the best description of his fiery red hair." She took a moment to collect herself and added, "No, he's just a man. I don't even think he's sensitive to the beads."

The train lurched as it resumed the journey through the city. Johan stared out the window at the Rotunda, wondering silently if he'd ever see the inside.

Johan asked, "What's wrong with Astia? What's so wrong that the Society wants to overthrow their government?"

Cassidy grunted. "Can't you tell?"

"No," he replied.

She pointed to a row of mansions sitting on a hill just a few miles from the Rotunda. "Do you see those buildings? The ones with perfectly manicured lawns and trees all around?"

"Yes."

"Those are homes," she said.

"They're very nice," Kali remarked. "Why is that a bad thing?"

"That is where the members of the Council live."

Johan still didn't understand. In a timid voice he asked, "Where do the people live?"

Cassidy pointed. They crossed into a section dwarfed by tall buildings, each unadorned and without trees or bushes. The streets were quiet, dark and gloomy with no life anywhere to be seen. "There," she said. "They live in those tenements, crammed in with several families to an apartment."

"Why don't they work harder," Kali asked, "to get a better place? Why don't they move away from the city?"

"Because they cannot get away. They receive a state designated salary based on their assigned duty. If they reject that duty, they're sent to reeducation camps, forced to comply with their caste or sent down to an even worse sector." The anger on her face was obvious when she added, "There's no freedom anywhere in Astia."

Johan asked, "Why not?"

"Because of a thing called the Collective." She turned her gaze away from the window and faced the children. "You Andalonians are slaves to Astia, farmed against your will, but you have no idea how much worse it is being part of the Collective."

Johan still didn't understand. In a quiet voice he asked, "How do we have it better?"

"You have choices."

Simcor Bralog spied headlights on the road ahead. "Pull over," he instructed the driver. Just as they had done several times before, they ambled off the road and parked in a way they wouldn't be easily spotted by the other driver. They had to be careful on this road, especially at night after curfew. He waited with bated breath. An electric car silently rolled past, markings on the side indicating that it belonged to the Oslot local council. Most likely a member of the party conducting unofficial business while the enslaved citizens lay trapped in their communes after dark.

That was only one aspect of Astia government he resented, one of hundreds he could list that drove him to join the Society. Those officials, while acting in the name of what's best for the citizenry, each lived above the law. He knew, because his own father had been ranked highly in Bergin.

His life had been easy, so easy in fact, that he had no idea how the other children his age lived. For the longest time he believed that they also had opportunities to play and learn while surrounded by luxury. While he spent his school age years playing sports and attending recreational events on days there were no classes, his counterparts in the rural communes worked tirelessly beside their parents to tend the crops and manage the harvested electricity. He had already passed many of those on his journey north, and pitied each family trapped within.

Those citizens in the urban zones fared even worse. Although they actually received an education, theirs was focused on learning trades, denied access to the arts and music that he personally believed coaxed civilization out of prehistoric caves. At some point those citizens, after learning only enough reading and writing to function as a labor force, were sent to toil in the thousands of factories in the larger cities.

Confident that the vehicle had passed, he motioned to the driver to continue. The rest of their journey passed without incident, despite the steady rain. They soon turned off the main road and onto a winding drive leading up a mountain. Steep drops loomed just beyond his door. Normally this approach would not have bothered Simcor, except that the driver's night vision devices limited his depth perception. A single miscalculation could send them tumbling over the side and thus end their mission. Thankfully, they arrived at the Winter Oracle without incident.

Breaking into the convent proved more difficult than the drive. Simcor and his team had thoroughly studied the layout of the complex, but those documents had been hundreds of years old. Needless to say, upgrades and repairs to the building were oftentimes only partially recorded or left off entirely. The maintenance entrance, unfortunately, fell in the second category. Leaving his team by the vehicle he crept closer to the southside of the outer structure, digging through vines and thick mud for several minutes before locating the seam in the concrete.

He was at a loss for ideas at this point. They couldn't blast a hole in the wall, that would attract too much attention when the entire operation was meant to remain clandestine. They could try chipping away at the old doorway, opening it enough to slip in, but that would leave evidence of their visit. *No,* he reasoned, *we must find another way in.* But entering a building with no windows would be a challenge. He flipped on his night vision and lifted his head upward, searching for a ledge they could grapple onto. Of course there were none. He rejoined his crew.

"There's no way in," he informed them, pulling off the device.

"May I help you, gentlemen?" The voice from behind caused Simcor to freeze.

"I'm afraid we're lost," he replied, hand slowly reaching into his coveralls for a weapon. He dared not turn around quickly, lest the speaker be a soldier. With his left hand he held up the building schematics. "This map," he lied, "places us at the water storage well of compound sixteen."

"I'm afraid that's on the next mountain over," the voice replied. "My name is Subba, acting lead brother of the Winter Oracle. Since it's after curfew, why don't you come inside and rest here for the night?"

Simcor released his grip on the pistol and turned. "Thank you, brother. Since it could possibly rain, do you mind if we bring our equipment inside as well?"

"Not at all. I'm afraid that my brethren and initiates are already resting for the night, or I'd send assistance."

"No bother," Simcor responded. "We're thankful that you saw our approach. How *did* you since the building has no windows?"

"I didn't," explained the coven leader. "Since the disappearance of our lead sister several months ago, I have a ritual of walking the grounds at night." He frowned at some not so distant memory. "We once lost a coven member who ventured out on a night like this, so I like to honor her memory with solemn remembrance and reflection."

"Well," said Simcor honestly, "I'm very happy that you did so tonight." He pointed to the single crate in the bed of the truck, "Let's carry that inside, gentlemen."

Subba showed the crew to their guest quarters and left them alone to rest. "I'll make sure you're brought breakfast in the morning," he told them as he retired.

The toughest part of the evening was lying awake long enough to be certain everyone in the coven was asleep. Once he dared, Simcor drew out the building plans and studied them with his crew. The stairwell to the utility basement was right around the corner. Further investigation found it conveniently unlocked. They placed the device and returned to their quarters, awaking early the next morning and reloading the now empty crate onto their truck.

Subba, the kind and generous lead brother asked over breakfast, "What kind of gear is that? What's so special that you didn't want to leave it out in the rain?"

Simcor answered truthfully, "Just some old machinery that we needed to fix some problems with the infrastructure."

"I understand," Subba replied.

No, the Society agent thought, *you most certainly do not.*

Fatwana awoke to rough hands shaking her in the back of the van. They had locked her in tight wrist restraints and then placed a dark hood over her head. They dragged the lead sister from the vehicle, tossing her to the ground. She grunted as the same hands grabbed her armpits and heaved her to a standing position.

"Walk," a sinister voice commanded, and she dutifully complied.

In what she hoped was a commanding voice of her own, she asked, "Where are you taking me, that you have me blindfolded?" When no response came, she pressed, "If I'm under arrest, then why the secrecy?" The returned silence told her all that she needed to know.

A heavy crash of steel doors caused her to jump, pausing briefly and losing step with her captors. When they tugged, she lost her balance and fell to the ground.

"Be careful with her!" The voice echoed through the chamber, suggesting that she was in a tunnel or a cave.

The hands were gentler when they helped her up the second time, but directed her to a small room and a single chair. Only when she was seated did they remove her hood. She blinked against the sudden burst of light and heard a heavy door slam behind her. When her eyes adjusted, she was not surprised to face Artema Horn.

"So, you're behind this?"

The redheaded man laughed at her words, then turned very serious. "I believe you have a message for me from Samani?"

"I most certainly do not." She looked around, finally taking in the room with her eyes well adjusted. "This is a bomb shelter," she remarked. "One of the ancient cellars from the time of the Great Destruction." Wonderment filled her and she asked, "Is it the same one?"

"Gods no," Artema replied. "That bunker is several hundred miles to the southwest."

She smiled slyly at his slip. "So we're in Bergin. Thank you."

The son of Jakata seemed amused by her trick and shrugged off the slight. In his usual jovial manner he asked again, "What message do you bring from Samani?"

"I assure you that I have no idea what you're talking about..."

"Fine," he said with a dismissive wave. "I'll talk to him directly."

At his words Fatwana froze, unable to move any muscle as her thoughts blurred at the edges. Abruptly she felt her consciousness slip as her head collapsed on the table and her vision swam into blackness.

When she awoke, Artema was gone and she was locked in a cell. It was cool and a bit too musty for her liking, but the size was very similar to her room in the oracle. Thinking of home brought thoughts of her brethren. *I wonder how Subba is managing things since I've been away,* she thought. *I hope he hasn't thoroughly screwed everything up.*

Chapter Forty

They found *Aggressor* still tied where they had left her in the harbor. The frigate, devoid of movement, loomed like a ghost against the pier, eerily quiet and beckoning like a siren. She was lifeless, without even a security watch posted. The trio ran aboard without even noticing.

Braen carried Charleigh in his arms as he rushed aboard with Alec and Marita close behind. He put her down in the captain's quarters then raced topside to aid the others. The tiny crew immediately went to work getting the ship underway. Never before had a team of three sailed a frigate across open seas, but they somehow managed to clear the harbor.

Marita worked the sails, untying and hoisting several at once with her adept powers. Tiny slivers of air reached out in every direction as she worked the rigging as well as any crew she'd sailed with. When she pulled the mainsail she giggled, proud of her cunning and causing Alec to turn and laugh. But launching from the dock is difficult even with a full crew, and she found herself unable to back the sails into the wind. Always resourceful, she instead moved it to match their position, and they launched toward open seas with Braen manning the rudder and Alec charting their course.

The makeshift navigator asked Braston, "Where to now, Captain?"

"To find Nevra, of course."

Alec considered the myriad of possibilities ahead. They had little time to find the scoundrel, and what they had was running out. "He must be aboard *Malfeasance.*"

"Yes," Braen agreed, "But where in Andalon?" He called out to Marita. "Dearie, ask the others if they know where to search for Skander." To Pogue he added, "One of the Dreamers has information, especially if he's sacking towns."

Alec thought about the conversation he had with the child in the palace. "Braen," he said. "Valencia didn't control Nevra. I believe it was the other way around."

"I was busy fighting off the mob, but I figured that was so."

"How'd you figure?"

Braen raised an eyebrow. "Well let's see, maybe when I realized Dominique and his crew stood against us?"

Alec laughed, "Aye, there was that." He pressed, "Doesn't that go against what he told you? The rules of your restoration, I mean."

Braen frowned, "I don't understand."

"He said that those unnaturally restored can be puppets or shadows. If one's been raised himself, then whatever he raises in turn are shadows."

"I don't follow, Alec. Speak plainer."

"If Charro raised Nevra, and then in turned Valencia raised him, then he would have been a shadow. Other than the pox scars he looked healthy to me."

"Aye," agreed Braen. "To me as well. But that simply means that he lied. Nevra could have raised him at any point after. As for what he remembered, he repeated the reality that Stefan taught him upon restoration."

"But Braen," insisted Pogue, "That would suggest that killing Stefan wouldn't kill Skander. I don't think he lied about that." Both men stood in silence for a while, contemplating and considering the implications. Finally Alec asked, "Did you get a good look at Creech and Dominique?"

"Aye. They looked like hell."

"Worse, they looked like they were reverting to corpses. Their teeth were falling out, their hair was missing in patches..."

"And those sores reeked like rotten flesh," Braen agreed.

"Meaning Nevra's been restored since *after* raising Valencia."

Braston turned, wide-eyed with understanding. "Someone else controls all of them. But who could it be, Alec? It had to be someone from The Cove!"

"Aye, that's true. But who?"

"No," Braen shook his head violently, "it can't be Eusari! She's the only one I know of with that power!"

"Captains!" Marita's voice suddenly interrupted. They turned expectantly, only to find her staring at the decking with arms crossed behind her back. "I need to tell you something about Eusari."

Alec knew his daughter well and interpreted her tone. Her entire body language betrayed some dire secret. Braen started to speak but Pogue raised his hand and quickly silenced his friend. With love and compassion he walked toward her. "What is it, dearie? What do you need to tell us about Eusari?"

"She knows about Braen."

"What do you mean," the captain asked, "that she knows about me?" He hadn't intended to come across menacingly, but the words growled from deep in his chest.

"She knows," the girl said, "that you're alive."

Alec placed a tender hand on his daughter's shoulder. "How does she know that dearie?"

"Because I accidently told Caroline." She suddenly lifted her eyes to meet theirs. "But she needs us right now! She's in trouble and we have to go to Logan!"

Her father shook his head, "But where is Skander?"

"He's in Norton," she said, "and he killed King Robert. But we need to go save Eusari right now!"

Alec turned to Braen. "That's a tough spot, mate. Save the woman you love or kill your dead brother."

"You know my choice," Braen answered, gripping the helm with all his might and willing the ship faster winds.

"Aye. That I do. Setting course for Eusari."

Caroline's eyes snapped open and she bolted upright, eager to share her news. "I found her!"

Sippen and Cedric took immediate notice, leaning forward with anticipation. They were anxious to rescue Braen's lover. Hester, who cared not what happened to the woman, simply grunted at the news. She reclined in her chair and closed her eyes, dreaming of the day she could return to Fjorik.

Sippen bubbled over with questions and asked, "Wuh... where is shuh... she?"

"The Falconers have her in a wagon," the girl explained, "and I'm following above them. They just left the Market Square and are turning west. She tried to get away and nearly did, but they captured her a second time."

"Kuh... keep following. Wuh... we don't know where the ruh... Rookery is!" The engineer hopped to his feet and grabbed four satchels. He handed one to Krill and reached another out to Hester. "Tuh... take this," he said.

She eyed the filthy bag with disgust and refused to take it. "I most certainly will not," she declared. "And if you think that I'll help with your suicide mission, you are sadly mistaken."

"Wuh... we all hah... have to work together tuh.... to save her."

"Yeah, Hester," Cedric agreed, "we need your help!"

"Most certainly not!" She averted her eyes from the offered satchel, but Sippen held his arm outstretched. When it was finally clear that she refused to take it, he placed it on the ground next to her chair. With a soft sigh he returned to the others.

What do they expect me to do against Falconers? I've no powers. For that matter, she mused, *neither do they, except for the girl.* She watched them for a while, scheming and planning how to enter the Rookery once they found it. *Sippen has his wits and his gadgets, and Cedric has... well, he's Cedric. Each of them makes sense in a fight. But to bring me along? I'm pregnant, for gods' sakes. I've lived a life of privilege and I've never even learned to hold a weapon,* she thought as she felt inside her shawl. There, close to her breast she felt the blade. Braen's blade.

Krist had given the piece of polished steel to his eldest son as a fifteenth birthday present, marking him as both a man and a warrior. Braen had worn it proudly ever since. "The knife," the king had explained, "belonged to your mother's father." That made it a Berserker's Blade, meaning the tempered steel was cooled with blood instead of water each time the maker heated and folded it over. "Keep it sharp," he commanded, "and bathe it in blood every full moon. If it goes too long without," the elder Braston said, "it loses its soul."

Hester, of course, had laughed at that when Braen relayed the rules of owning such a blade. "Knives don't hold souls," she had said. But that belief hadn't stopped her from removing his blade that day he was murdered. At the time she had been ravaged with hopelessness, angry at the cruelty of her northern gods, and holding his lifeless body as he lay upon the deck of *Malfeasance.*

As Eusari ran toward the ship to steal Hester's time to mourn, the northern queen had drawn the knife, balancing its weight and considering her next move as she left behind a sheath as empty as her options. With Braen gone there was no longer hope that his goodness could overcome the nature of Skander's child, not after witnessing the true darkness of her husband's illness. That alone was reason to destroy the life in her womb.

She had tipped the knife into her breast as she knelt over his lifeless form. *Skander's spawn cannot be born,* she had decided. She meant to bathe the blade with her own, but hadn't. She was a coward and hid the knife in her furs the moment Eusari had boarded the vessel. *I keep it on me now,* she thought as she ran her finger along the sharpened edge, *for when I finally work up the courage.*

"Suh... so it's agreed?"

Hester broke from her musings. "What's agreed?"

"We attack at nightfall," Cedric chimed in. "Haven't you been listening?"

"Or," she said, "you wait until Braen arrives and then do it." She pointed to Caroline and asked, "When will they arrive?" When the girl merely stared blankly the northern queen accused, "You didn't even ask. You nitwits were planning to rush into a Rookery to save your friend when Braen could arrive any moment with powers beyond imagination." She shook her head. "For such intelligent people you are all three very dumb." She removed her hand from the blade and stood. "Let me know what you decide in the morning. I'm retiring for the night."

As she walked up the stairs, she heard Caroline say, "Marita said they're pushing *Aggressor* to splinters and will be here tomorrow."

The queen paused at her door. *Tomorrow,* she thought. *Braen will return and I will have one more chance to win him over.* The thought of him rushing into the Rookery to save his wench turned her stomach, sending bile into her throat as she choked back sudden realization. *And he will rush to her and once again abandon me.* She touched the blade one more time then called out, "Sippen?"

"Yuh... yes, Huh... Hester?"

"What kind of gadgets do you have ready if we did sneak into the Rookery tonight?"

"Luh... lots," he replied with a grin. He rushed to a workbench and grabbed a long bundle, heaving it into his arms and spreading the contents so all could see.

Hester leaned over the railing, peering down with genuine interest that surprised even her.

"Thuh... these," he said as he held what appeared to be a shorter rifle, "shuh... shoots buh... bearings. Thuh... they spruh... spread out like grapeshot."

"That be my idea," Cedric boasted, pointing at his chest and grinning like a lunatic. "Those featherheads be seein' the future, but can't get out of the way of grapeshot!"

Sippen nodded his large head with eager agreement and set the weapon down. He bent down and picked up a satchel, reaching in and pulling out a rounded object. "Thuh... this does the same thuh... thing, buh... but like the cuh... carcass grenades, these are thrown."

Cedric cut in, obviously ready to claim this idea as well. "But instead of gas, these bastards shoot out shards of metal in every direction! The blokes won't know what hit 'em!"

"Interesting," Hester remarked with a glimmer of hope in her voice. "Then we shouldn't wait for Braen! Anything could happen before he arrives, and time is running out for Eusari. Caroline, go find me some breeches and I'll come along."

The girl scampered away while the men went to work, loading the satchels and planning the attack.

And I'll help them fight, she decided. *It's about time I stood up for something instead of always taking the easiest road. I should have stood up to Skander when he first hatched his plan against Braen. I could have done more than warn my love, I could have helped him defeat his brother.* She touched the Berserker Blade. With her hand on the hilt she also realized, *after Eusari bathes this steel, I will help him finish the fight and take my rightful place at his side.*

Chapter Forty-One

Gaius Wilman rested in his parlor, watching as his many grand-children raced around the backyard, playing a game of tag and bringing joy to his old heart. Out of his seventy-five years, he had served the Council for fifty, proud to discharge his duty and eager to remain steadfast in his devotion to ethical service. Despite the pleasure he drew from his commitment to Astia, the delight of all his years came from watching his grandchildren grow to become citizens themselves.

Gaius believed in Astia, both in its founding principles and the benefit to the collective. Privileged to have born into the ruling party, he had built upon his father's reputation and secured a picturesque chateau overlooking the city below. The disheveled hive of labor scurried to their duties daily, all the while safe beneath his shadow of service. Today he faced the splendid garden and its magnificent blend of color.

His house steward rapped on the floor with his heel.

"What is it, Martin?"

"Artema Horn has arrived, sir."

"Let him in at once! The newest, most junior member of the Council must be treated with respect!" He turned to see that the man with fiery red locks stood behind the steward, head properly bowed in humility with eyes firmly locked on the floor. *Good, his nerves guide him today, unsure why he was invited to the home of the second most senior official in the council.* Gaius failed to see any hint of threat as suggested by Praedor.

"Thank you, Councilor Wilman, for the gracious invitation." Horn lifted his eyes and donned an air of fake confidence befitting a rising star in politics.

That ability to act confident will serve him well, Gaius thought. "Of course," he said, dismissing any concerns regarding the visit as anything but friendly. "Your father was a dear friend to me, after all!" He pointed to a stately home atop the next ridge. "Don't you remember that we were neighbors in your childhood?"

Artema peered out, taking in the row of color between the two estates. "I do," he said with an air of nostalgia. "The garden was much smaller then, and there was a creek that ran through the valley. Campton and I fished and swam there many times."

"I remember your father caught you one time," Wilman recollected. "I lounged in this very parlor and listened to the anger that wafted in from these open windows."

"Did that breeze carry also the beating that we both received?"

He holds resentment, this man, with fire in his belly as well as atop his head. "It did, and I spoke with your father with great concern. I never understood why he wouldn't allow you both to act as boys do." He gestured affectionately toward his grandchildren, now splashing in a grand fountain where the creek had once run. "Children deserve freedom to frolic and experience life without boundaries," he said. "Our duty as Councilmen grants station that greatly improves their living, something they should be allowed to experience. Don't you agree?"

"Jakata believed differently. He preached that the citizens were rabble, and that our sector held the last remnants of civilization. They toil their lives away so that we can enjoy the art and luxury provided by the duty to state. The thought of us playing instead of learning the art of politics riled him and was seen as wasteful of our gift of status."

"He wasn't wrong," Gaius agreed, "only too hard on his boys. Perhaps your brother would not have defied him, or worked his subterfuge in Andalon had he been allowed to frolic?"

"Perhaps," Artema said, the look on his face betraying a longing to relive those days. He turned to Wilman and got down to business. "I appreciate the invitation. Might I ask why you've bothered with a lowly upstart like me?"

"Oh, please," the senior politician said dismissively. "You are certainly no upstart, only junior in your seasoning." He took a seat next to the open window and offered Artema one as well. Once the young man was seated, he continued, "Your name ranks you above most, forcing most to accept your appointment. Many more will follow you, even, once you've established a track record of duty. I would like to offer an opportunity for you to grow that experience."

"I assure you that I'm adept at politics," the young man said, sneaking a grin.

"In Andalon, sure. I heard you were a pirate king, or some sort of nonsense." He swallowed distaste for the obvious waste of time. "Here you are ignorant of procedure, and I wish to offer training while you legitimize your hold. Eventually, after ten or so years, you may be ready to challenge the seat of Chancellor."

"And you would have me continue the agenda that you have built for your own family?"

"Yes. I am old, and my son will fill my seat. Unfortunately he does not have your name, or he'd serve as Chancellor himself. When the time comes, I will expect you to elevate him to your trust as I will instruct."

"Why not now," the son of Jakata said slyly, "when the hold by Praedor is tenuous at best?" The redheaded fool sat forward in his seat, his smile no longer cautious, but instead raging with arrogance. "With your support I can reveal evidence against her that will prove damning, forcing a vote for incompetence. Then, you can nominate me for Chancellor, and we can begin the new order now instead of later."

The laughter burst from Gaius' throat before he even knew it lurked in his belly. "You've a glorious sense of humor, young councilman, and I thank you for the joke."

Horn's face changed in that moment, briefly sending a chill of anxiety through Wilman's body. "I assure you that I do not jest, old man. I scheme. Most importantly, I always get my way. You can get behind me now, while I am assured of success by forces you cannot even fathom, or you can remain a roadblock to my rise."

The sudden rise in blood pressure dizzied Gaius. His face flushed and his pulse quickened. He tried to stand, but Artema blocked his balance and he tumbled into his seat. "Such insolence," he spat, "will not be tolerated. You're nobody without a patron to aid your rise!"

Artema stood and resumed his casual air, projecting power by his mere presence. He waived his arms, indicating both the parlor and surrounding villa. "All of this," he said with a sneer, "is a fine legacy to leave. But you forget that this entire sector is a daily reminder of my father's cruelness toward his children." He leaned in with madness behind his golden eyes. "I would hate for you to outlive your grandchildren, or the council would send your legacy to the state." He was so close that Gaius shut his eyes against the heat of the man's breath. "And I *will* become the state, old man."

Councilor Merek ascended the stairs to the council archive, anxiously wondering if his mistake could be corrected. He had only been a young intern at the time, fiercely loyal to Praedor and with access to procurement and her endless treasury. Well trusted by his mentor, anything he routed came with her automatic approval. He never took advantage of her signature stamp, well, except for that one time.

His friend had been away at the oracle for quite some time when he suddenly appeared, accompanying the lead brother when summoned to the Rotunda. Merek had been surprised to see his childhood friend, the son of Councilwoman Nakala, when he knocked upon his office door.

"Samani!" He was overjoyed to see his friend.

"Mathieu!" He looked around the tiny office. "Is this where they keep you? Locked away pushing papers around for perpetuity?"

Merek had laughed, always appreciative of his friend's humor. "Actually, my internship expires in a few months. I will be elevated to associate. Can you believe that? An actual assistant to Praedor! Mark my words, she'll be Chancellor one day!"

"Oh heavens," Samani feigned shock. "Don't let Jakata hear you say that!"

Merek had laughed, but deep down he yearned for the day Jakata Horn was usurped. He changed the subject. "What brings you up a dozen flights of stairs to a dark procurement office? Certainly not only to see me?"

"Well, truth be told, the lead brother had an errand he needed run while addressing the Council. Since I knew you were here, I thought I'd take advantage of a personal request and visit with you at the same time."

"What does he need?" Merek reached out a hand for the requisition.

"Not much, just several ounces of an element."

"Samani!" Mathieu read the parchment several times. "This is controlled. Why does he need this?"

"I'm not sure," Nakala had replied. "Something to do with the energy reactor and the cold storage. I really don't know much about it, but lead brother stressed the specific amounts."

"I'll need to check his clearance against the database," Merek had insisted. He leaned over the faintly glowing monitor, such an archaic device, and typed in his code. After a few moments he shrugged. "Well, it checks out. Each oracle is allowed an allotment of this size one every fifty years. He isn't due for two more, but I think we can make an exception." He pulled the order and stamped it, placing it in a pneumatic tube and sending it to the disbursing office. "Give it an hour for them to cut the funds, and then you can pick it up from supply. Here, you'll need this since it's in the lead brother's name." He handed him a voucher with Praedor's seal and signature.

"Thank you so much, my friend! So," Samani changed the subject, "tell me about your family! How are your parents?"

The rest of the conversation was lost to time, and Merek hurried his pace, suddenly fully aware of the trickery his friend had pulled. *With those devices in Samani's hands, I cannot leave any trace of that plutonium leading back to myself or Praedor.* He entered the vault, showing his access card to the attendant who released the magnetic seal on the door. Making his way to the correct file, he searched by date and thumbed through. It was gone.

He hurried to the archive clerk and handed over the document number. "I need to know the whereabouts of this record," he said with causal disinterest, not wanting to alert the intern to his urgency.

The girl scanned the files and frowned. "That record was checked out last week," she informed him, "by Councilman Artema Horn."

Merek felt the entire Rotunda shift around him as his stomach dropped into the depths of his anxiety.

Chapter Forty-Two

Marita hadn't exaggerated when she told Caroline they were "pushing *Aggressor* to splinters." The ride up the river literally cracked the mainmast as they sped north, and she held it with a tenuous lashing of air. She frowned as she felt the ship lurch, sending subtle messages that the damage had also affected the other rigging.

In a worried voice she called over the winds, "How much further, Captain Braston?"

He replied with a confident smile. "We made it to the lake, dearie! Hold on for another thirty minutes or so."

She arched her neck to get a view over the side, just as the ship jerked against the smooth waters of Lake Norton. Losing her balance, she also nearly lost her grip on the lashing. She hurriedly threw a net of tendrils to pull it tighter. Thankfully it held.

Alec was also topside, staring absently at the western horizon. "Dearie," he said with ominous worry lurking in his tone, "think you could push us a wee bit faster?"

Sure, she thought, *give the sweet dearie all the work,* she thought as she counted her lashings. Currently she held the helm, six lashes around the mainmast, four around various portions of the beam, and one on each of the two halyards that operated the three sails. Those she filled with three more continuous bonds, each pumping as much air as she could bellow into their canvas. She held nineteen connections, a personal record.

Braen immediately jumped to, sensing the worry in Alec's voice and rushing over to get a look past the rails. Marita frowned at his selfishness and lashed onto the helm he vacated. *Twenty,* she thought. The other Dreamers had once competed to test their strengths, and she had only accomplished fifteen at the time, with Cuyler and Beth coming in a close second with thirteen each. *I wonder how many King Robert could do,* she pondered. *He's surely stronger than me.*

"Marita," Braen called with the same urgency as her father, "can you give us more speed?" He only paused a moment before adding, "Now!"

She turned her head to give him a tongue lashing and a lesson on the limits of emotancy when she realized their cause for concern. An Imperial Galleon loomed ahead with full broadside at the ready. She let out a single word. "Shit."

Alec promptly screamed, "Marita!"

"Don't get your britches in a bunch," she hollered back, "Mattie said I can say it when I'm pirating, and that's exactly what we're doing! So stand the f..."

"They're coming about! Marita, give us more wind," Braen ordered. "Now!"

She tried to comply by conjuring one more connection, but lost all that she held at once. A creaking mainmast prompted her to cuss one more time. "You boys had better move out of the way," she warned.

The top lookout called out suddenly, announcing a distant sail. "Ship on the southeastern horizon!"

Amash was the second to see it, since he was currently bent over the aft rail and tossing the morning's breakfast over the side. *I hate ships,* he complained to himself. The other vessel was moving fast, dangerously so, as it rounded the bend into Lake Norton. "Cuyler," he called out, "Is that one of Skander's?"

The teen turned his attention from tending the sails. "I don't know yet, my lord! I need to be closer."

"Stop calling me that!" He wiped his hands on his trousers and sent one of the deckhands to find Sebastian. The boy had spent more time in The Cove than the others, and if this were a friendly vessel he would know. By the time the boy arrived, the ship had closed the gap considerably, blown by winds that were no doubt stronger and as unnatural as their own. Amash pointed toward the vessel. "Can you identify that ship? Is it one of ours that Braen lost to Skander?"

Sebastian squinted then shook his head. "No, but it does hail from The Cove." With a trembling voice he added, "That's Captain Dominique's ship."

"*Aggressor*?" Amash frowned. "Last I saw this vessel it was in the wet docks. Sippen's crew had it in line for refitting and renaming, and a new captain hadn't been chosen." As it drew rapidly nearer, he recognized the sleek line of the hull. "Aye, it's definitely *Aggressor,* but who's at the helm? We all watched Adolphus hang, so I know it isn't him." He trailed off, impressed by the unholy speed it harnessed. "Who's blowing the sails and who in the name of Cinder would bring this particular ship so far north?"

Sebastian suddenly shouted, pointing wildly and hopping up and down with joy. "It's Marita!"

His excitement brought Cuyler closer, and the teen raised a spyglass to confirm. "Yes, it's her alright."

"How can you be so sure," Amash asked.

Sebastian grinned and replied, "It's a Dreamer thing."

Cuyler rolled his eyes and pointed. "Count the bindings of air, Lord Horslei. Only she and I can manage splitting our power more than a dozen times." He handed the glass over to Amash.

"I see the wind in the sails, but what else should I look for?"

"Look for shimmering along the planks," the teen explained. "She's losing her mainmast and several of her riggings have torn free. The ship is literally falling apart beneath her feet."

Amash turned and shouted toward the helmsman. "Captain Santos! Bring us on an intercept course immediately!" To the Dreamers he added, "If Braen is aboard there'd have to be a damned good reason to push a ship to splinters."

"Twenty," said Sebastian.

"Twenty what?" Amash looked down upon the boy with wonder, but Sebastian only stared wide-eyed with mouth agape toward the other vessel. Captain Santos had warned Horslei in private about his concerns over the boy's stability. *He's so odd,* he thought, *a mixture between bravery and cowardice. I can see why Braen took a liking to him.*

Cuyler answered for him. "Twenty connections," he said. Awestruck he added, "Cinder save us, but she's as strong as Sebastian and me combined."

"But not strong enough," Amash noted as he returned his gaze toward *Aggressor*. The mainmast abruptly tumbled, and the entire ship fell apart before their eyes.

The deck boards split beneath Braen's feet, splinters flying about and one catching him on the cheek. The wooden projectile barely missed his eye as it left a streak of blood the length of his hand. The metallic taste burned his mouth as blood mixed with sweat.

"Abandon ship," he ordered Alec and Marita. "Swim away immediately or she'll suck you down with her!" They both nodded and complied, swinging over the side and splashing deep into the lake. He grabbed the rail to follow and lifted his leg to jump when he suddenly froze, remembering another life aboard *Aggressor* and in his charge. *Charleigh!*

He raced toward the hatch as the rest of the planking ripped down their seams, folding and rippling like waves on an angry ocean. When he grabbed the door he tugged, but the boards held tight, squeezed together by the pressure of the disintegrating ship. He braced his feet and pulled upward as hard as he could, feeling the resisted effort in his legs and lower back. Beneath his feet he heard the child screaming for help.

He bellowed at the unmoving hatch. "Charleigh! Can you hear me, dearie?"

Her tiny voice answered back, muffled but easily understood. "I'm trapped," she shouted, "and it's filling with water!"

"Move away from the hatch," he told her. "I'm coming!" He drew his axe from his belt and held it high in the air. He brought it down hard, muscles in his forearms shaking from the vibration of steel splitting wood. Then he furiously chopped, frantic to save the girl and trying not to watch the rising waterline now splashing under the rails. Despite his efforts the hatch held longer than he expected, but he was finally able to reach the axe handle into the hole and he pried. Relief filled his heart as it came loose.

Charleigh was huddled on a stack of barrels in the hold, so only her feet were submerged in the freezing lake water. Braen shouted to the girl, "Can you swim, dearie?" He reached out his hand, but the violent shaking of her head let him know that she could not. He hopped into the void with a splash, then waded toward her. She crawled into his outstretched arms.

Poor child, he thought, *to venture near death so many times and always of my doing.* He made his way to the ladder and with one arm hoisted them upward. Just as he raised his head to the opening, the hatch slammed shut. He pressed his back against the splintering planks and pushed with his legs, trying to force it open, but finding himself unable. Something, most likely the mast, had rolled atop the portal and sealed them inside.

The slow sinking of the ship suddenly gave in to the gravity of water all around. Braen felt the vessel lurch as buoyancy escaped, their wooden tomb eager to meet the muddy floor of the lake. Charleigh whimpered in his arms and pressed her face into his chest, too terrified to watch the rising death that had reached their chins. *No,* Braston thought, unwilling to accept death a second time. *At least not yet,* he considered, *not until Skander is stopped and the Falconers and Jaguars are destroyed.* Another darkness crept into his thoughts, in the image of the fiery birds he faced in The Cove. *Air, Land, and now Fire,* he mused, *leaving only Water.*

He was surrounded by water. *The element I once commanded,* he lamented, *but no longer.*

"Simple, Lord Kraken," Lord Charro Valencia's words resounded in Braen's memory, "whatever revives itself loses power until killed again and revived unnaturally."

But Charro Valencia had proven an enemy and not a friend, a pawn of Stefan Nevra sent to dissuade them from their true goal and lead them into his deadly trap. *An enemy full of lies, perhaps?* The water surrounding Braen was cold and sapped his strength as he considered his former bond. *I always found it strongest when I fought to save those around me who I loved.* The little girl in his arms was in his charge, facing danger as everyone around him eventually did. *In my desire to build the world better, I always bring them to destruction,* he realized. *I alone must right these wrongs, and I will need my powers restored.*

He reached out with his mind, giving in to the coldness wrapping his muscles with despair. Images of Eusari, trapped in the Rookery, rushed past his eyes. He could see Sippen and Krill, planning a raid to free her. He suddenly knew that tragedy had struck the rebellion, and, though Robert Esterling was dead, his growing child lay trapped in Sarai's lifeless womb. Although nourished by the body of his mother, the infant boy would never know her love nor that of his father.

He saw the face of his friend Amash, standing upon the deck of an Imperial Galleon and racing to rescue Marita and Alec as they bobbed in Lake Norton. *Then there is hope,* he realized, *for a rescue that could bear us the remainder of the way to Eusari.* His powers had indeed remained, but had changed from a weapon of destruction into something more profound. They opened both his eyes and his mind to millions of possibilities for the people of Andalon, each as dark and dreaded as he had feared. *There is one way,* he realized, to destroy the Astian hold over our lives.

The water would not save him and the child from this deadly voyage to the depths below. For that, he realized, he would need to rely upon strength and a bit of luck. He took a deep breath from their rapidly depleted supply, now only a small pocket that leaked away, bubbled through the decking above. He positioned his back to the hatch and pressed with his legs against the ladder, crushing every bone and muscle against the immense pressure that fought to hold him in. It would not budge.

"Take a deep breath, dearie," he whispered to Charleigh, then tried once more, ignoring the pain that traveled down his spine and into his knees. With a last push he managed to break the seal, letting the water rush past the fleeing air that had promised them a few more minutes of life. The hatch, no longer burdened by the unequal pressure, flew open.

His strong hands gripped Charleigh despite their chilled desire to give up and accept the promise of sleep given by the cold. He pulled her close and kicked toward the glowing sun above the water. *It's so far away,* he realized. *We'll never make it.* He looked down at the girl, her tired face wide-eyed and fearful as she struggled to hold her breath. *She is only moments away from death,* he knew.

He turned his attention to the distant surface looming above and kicked harder, using his free hand to pull the water downward. But he found that they were too heavy to swim against the force made by the sinking ship. He reached down to find his axe, looped in his belt but trapped against his side by the weight of the girl. He would not pull it free as it had become the fateful anchor of their doom. With a sigh the air in his lungs escaped into the shimmering void, racing to the surface and away from the drowning pair. He sadly closed his eyes and prayed for the lives of those he loved, gripping the axe so that he could join the heavenly feast.

His next instinct was the sudden need to breathe and he opened his mouth and lungs, sucking in the freshness of air. *No,* he thought as his lungs filled with the sweetness of spring, *I am dead.* But when he again opened his eyes his face was surrounded by a glimmering bubble around his head. Through it he could make out two smiling faces. One belonged to Charleigh and the other to Marita.

Each wore a similar pocket of air around their heads as the older girl pointed up and swam away, leaving behind a trailing rope of braided air for him to grab ahold.

When they reached the surface he roared with victory and held Charleigh aloft. She wrapped her tiny fingers around the cargo netting dangling over the side of an Imperial Galleon, and climbed. Beside them, Marita treaded water with one thumb thrust in the air and her cheeks turned upward with a broad smile. When his eyes met hers, he laughed and so did she. Together they scrambled after the little girl and fell in a heap on the deck of the ship. Alec was already there, calmly drying his body with a towel and standing next to a grinning Amash.

"Get us to Logan," Braen commanded his friends, "we've got to rescue Eusari." He thought about the future revealed to him beneath the lake and added, "She is the key to victory."

Chapter Forty-Three

Fatwana awoke amid a violent coughing spell that wracked her ribcage and spread to her body, muscles tightening along her back and belly contracting into a pain she had only ever felt during Ka'Ash'mael prophecy. The spasm left her breathless, gasping for air that felt just out of reach and taunting her with life. Once she finally felt the flood rush into her lungs, she fell from her cot, dizzied by the countless black and brilliant spots spinning in her eyesight.

Sputum fell on the floor, green as the moss growing under her metal cot and fed by the same moisture weeping from the walls of her cell. Touching those reminded her of a cave she and her siblings had explored as children; she had dragged her fingers along that smooth limestone, almost tasting the metallic chime of sulfur in her nose. She could smell the humidity of this place just as well, cold except for the mattress where she had lay upon for the past week. It steamed from her feverish sweat and reeked of sickness.

Artema Horn had only met with her that one time, leaving her to the merciless neglect of her unseen captors. Occasionally a slot in the door would open and a food tray would slide through. At first, she had ignored the bowl of slop with the side of mold-tinged bread, but after the third day she had leaped upon that life-giving manna with ferocity. Lately she even licked the bowl dry.

Tears broke free from her soul and gave way to sobbing as she rested on all fours, suddenly angry at the world and her brother. *Why did he drag me to Andalon? I was happy leading my oracle, guiding others toward transcendence.* Her eyes suddenly grew wide with realization. *Is that what you wanted me to see, Samani? Why you revealed to me the plight of the Andalonians?*

His voice rode gently within her mind, clearly his and not unlike hearing it with her ears. *What did you see, sister?*

"I saw slaves," she replied in a whisper. "Slaves controlled and manipulated by the Astian Council."

But you witnessed that they enjoy more freedom than the people of Astia, how is it that they are enslaved?

"They are enslaved by a false image of freedom," she replied. "They believe themselves free, but are instead living in a box. No," she corrected herself, "a maze constructed by their rulers. The overseers we placed over them. They are free within the confines of the maze, free to find the cheese and even to enjoy its tantalizing flavors if it is found."

But it's rarely found, isn't it, sister? What fuels them to wander the maze for a lifetime, if the statistical chances are more in favor of them passing the same fate on to another generation?

"The smell of the prize is one they can almost taste, and the craving draws them forward, blinding them to the surrounding labyrinth."

Do any find the cheese?

"They must, or the others will stop searching." She paused, digesting the knowledge revealed by her brother. "Like the people of Astia have given up. We're content there is no prize except the privilege to work for the state, grinding away without a hint of reward."

But you are an oracle, and your reward is transcendence. Haven't they promised the most special among you the possibility to transcend to a higher plane?

"Transcendence," she laughed, sounding just a little like she had lost her mind. *I probably have lost that prize by now,* she thought, *after everything I've seen and learned in these past few months.*

You haven't, the voice promised, and they laughed together at the knowledge that she had.

"You took over my mind, didn't you brother?"

Only a part of it. You are still you, capable of independent thought on your own.

"How much of this understanding was planted by you?"

Not a bit, he promised. *I have only granted this direct connection and the words you will need to speak to the Astian Council.*

"Can I choose when we communicate?"

To an extent, but I can intrude if I wish. I will try not to unless the situation warrants.

She accepted her fate. "So my mission is to pass your message to the Council. What is yours?"

He ignored the question. *Events are unfolding here that require my presence. I must be here when it happens.*

The heavy bolt locking her cell door slid from its place and the heavy steel swung open. Two men dressed like soldiers stood in the opening.

She pleaded, "When what happens?" But he did not answer. "Samani," she sobbed, "when what happens?"

"She's gone daft," one of the men said aloud.

"Aye, and she stinks like vomit and piss," the other replied.

"We've got to get her cleaned up and presented to the Council. The Dragon said she's the guest speaker."

Rough hands pulled her forcibly from the ground and pushed her forward, chuckling and sobbing along the way. They led her down a stark corridor, pushing open a door at the end of the hall. Inside were rows of porcelain toilets and sinks, ancient in their construction, with crumbling ceramic tiles on the walls. If there were doors to the stalls or mirrors on the walls, these had long ago fallen off or were taken down. Just past these was another door that led to a long row of shower heads.

Once inside, she noticed that a towel and bar of soap had been set in a chair, along with a fresh robe. She eyed the clothing curiously. *They keep me locked as a prisoner, but will present me as a lead sister of the oracle?*

Samani's voice returned. *You never lost your status, sister.*

The sight of the robe emboldened the half-broken woman, helping her to find her voice and station. "Where is Cassidy?" The guards eyed each other with confusion. "Are you Society agents or soldiers for the Council?"

"Society," the taller guard answered.

"Then where is the agent called Cassidy?"

"She's away on a mission," the shorter man answered. "Now get on with your shower so we can take you to the Council."

"You will both either leave, or find a woman to guard over me while I prepare. But I am the lead sister of the Winter Oracle. I will not be gawked upon by the likes of you." She folded her arms across her chest and stared defiantly until the taller man shrugged.

"Sure," he said, and nodded to the shorter man who left to fetch another attendant.

She was tall and raven-haired with stern features. She appeared very put out by the sudden babysitting duty. Once the men had left, Fatwana asked again, "Where is Cassidy?"

"Who?" The woman was obviously bored, but her honest confusion in her expression confirmed what the guards had said.

"Never mind," Fatwana Nakala replied. "If she is important, I will see her again."

Kali walked along the edge of the storm drain, careful not to drench her feet in the flowing water. There was a lot of it, she noticed, runoff from the frequent rains and all of it flowed into the river they saw from the train. They were under the city, with muffled sounds of strange Astian vehicles echoing through the tunnels. Horns honked and train whistles blew, otherwise she would have felt at home as if she were in the cistern under Logan. Cities, it seemed, weren't much different even across an ocean or a huge gap in technology. She loved it.

"Where are we going," Johan asked Cassidy.

"We're almost there," she replied, pushing them forward as if it were normal to trudge through underground streams and caverns.

"Seems screwy to me," Kali admitted. "I still don't understand why Samani would insist we come along. All we've done is travel on a train and crawl through sewers since we've arrived. Maybe we should turn back."

"Don't be silly," Cassidy insisted, "it's right up here."

Johan frowned, "What is?"

The trio rounded a bend before the woman could respond, and they emerged to find a crack in the wall just large enough to allow a slender woman and two children to slither inside. The children instantly grew wide-eyed with fear.

Kali crossed her arms, suddenly wishing she were back in Logan. "You want us to go in there?"

Cassidy grinned and shined her lantern inside, revealing a second opening just a few feet beyond the fissure. "Come on," she urged, and slithered inside.

Johan waited a few moments for the woman to clear the entrance then shrugged at Kali. "Why not? We won't find our way out of the sewers without her, and she seems to know where she's going." He slid in easily, pushing himself along the walls with his fingertips.

Kali seethed with irritation. *Something is wrong about this entire ordeal,* she thought. *Ever since the Battle of Estowen's Landing, this entire world stopped making sense.*

A shout of excitement rang from the other side and she pressed her face to the crevice. Johan stood on the other side, holding Cassidy's lantern to his smiling face. "Hurry," he begged, "you've got to see this!"

She sighed and took a deep breath to steady her nerves, then slipped inside. It was tight. She didn't mind that because small places never bothered her. Even though it was foreign and she had no idea the outcome of their journey, she loved adventure. What she resented was that they were led by someone they barely knew or trusted. That bothered her immensely. As she wormed her way in, she thought, *this all started when I met Samani.* She suddenly found him unsettling as well. *He's behind all of this somehow, I'm certain.*

The crack in the wall opened into a world unlike any Kali had ever imagined. They were suddenly in an underground city, with streets very similar to those above. Here and there were hulking remains of abandoned vehicles, rusting away where they stood. She marveled at the buildings, constructed for beauty in a far-gone age, aesthetically calling her to stare. "What is this place?"

"This is the old city once called 'Berlin.' Ever since the Great Destruction, the bones of the old world have existed beneath our feet. Most was covered by ash or leveled by the nuclear blasts, but here and there you will find pockets of a civilization that built things with reason as they conquered the land around them. Their reason was beauty, while ours has fallen to function." She led them onward. "What we seek is further down. Come," she urged.

The children followed, taking in the sights with lantern light and trying to picture the people who once walked in this beautiful place. Eventually, however, the cavern ended abruptly with a massive stone structure that resembled those above. Kali ran her hand along the seamless stone. "What is this rock? I noticed the ancients used it for their sidewalks along their streets."

"It's called concrete. It is poured as a single unit, instead of chiseled and laid like the granite of those other buildings."

"So Astians cut into this other world to lay the foundation of this building? Without bothering to reveal the beauty that was already here?"

"That's exactly right. The Astian Council wished to destroy any trace of history that conflicted with their own, and, that which they couldn't, was instead hidden from view and forgotten."

Johan scrunched his face with confusion. "Why would they do that?"

"It's another form of slavery," Cassidy explained. "If you want to enslave large populations you must remove their connection to any identity they possess. You first take away religion, leaving them feeling alone and without hope. You then replace that hope with fear. The terrifying anxiety that even their own family would hand them over to the state if they opposed the chosen views. Eventually people will even doubt morality if they feel that sense of right or wrong goes against the ideology of those feeding them.”

“That’s awful,” Johan remarked. “Is that what happened on Andalon? The Pescari have religion, and so does Fjorik, but everyone laughs at theirs as superstition. It’s obvious to the rest of us that Felicima is the sun, and that there’s no heavenly feast after you die.”

“That’s because the rest of you live in the empire and have the luxury of blaming the Esterling family for your troubles or to celebrate them for prosperity.”

Kalie understood and muttered, “You don’t need gods when you have the state.”

“Exactly, but that’s just the first step to enslaving society. Next, you remove history, replacing fact with lies about the characters who shaped the original culture. Expose the flaws of those brave people who have a lesson to teach other generations, replacing respect with hatred and criticizing them for decisions made on a different set of morals, and in a remarkably less enlightened time. You replace lessons of humility with promises of lavish lifestyles, all the while condemning wealth.”

Ask her why she joined the Society, a random thought suggested, and Kali did. “Why did you choose to fight against the Council?”

Cassidy did not turn around when she said, “I had no choice.” She searched along the wall until she found a crumbled section at the base. Someone had long ago scraped the concrete away, leaving a narrow section that led underneath. She sat down on a nearby rock and told her story.

“My parents were members of the coven at the Summer Oracle. They fell in love, and I was the result. My father died during Ka’Ash’mael not long after my conception, so my mother fled on foot. Somehow, she made it to one of the nearby communes, and they hid her away until after I was born. Then she made it to Bergin and searched out the family she had left behind to enlist in the oracle.

"Were they happy to see their daughter returned? And that she had a child?"

Cassidy shook her head. "Just the opposite. They rebuked her for leaving her sworn duty to the state, and for walking away from the gift of transcendence." They turned her over to the authorities. They killed her in a public display, an example if you will, of what happens when you choose self over the collective.

"And you," Kali asked, "what did they do with you?"

"I was placed in a reeducation center, forced to live my years as an orphan."

"How did you learn about your mother's fate, if you were so young?" Kali finally understood the reason she trusted Cassidy so easily, having been raised parentless as well. From the look on Johan's face, she could tell that he too missed his family and shared the sadness of being an orphan.

"The headmistress at the school force-fed me those details every day of my life, as part of my conditioning into the collective. Then, when I turned eighteen, they offered me the opportunity to join the same oracle as retribution for my mother's treason."

"But you said no?"

"Actually, I said yes and waited at a train station with honest intent to board. The train pulled up to the concourse when a woman approached me. She sat down and called me by name, begging me for a few moments of my time. Since they hadn't called passengers I decided to listen."

Johan asked with a timid voice, "Who was she?"

"She was my mother's sister. She told me that she was the person who turned my mother over to the authorities, and that I was an abomination. That she wished I had been killed as well, and that it was a mercy to allow me the opportunity to transcend through the oracle. She then spat in my face and left me at the terminal."

Both Kali and Johan's faces lit up with surprise and the girl asked, "What did you do?"

"I threw my identification in the trash receptacle and walked away. I wandered the streets for a few years avoiding the authorities and staying out of trouble. When the Society approached me, they somehow knew my life story and where to find me. It was as if they too had the power of foresight like the oracle." She grew quiet for a moment, considering some other memory she wouldn't reveal, then added, "I've been a member for three years and my entire training has been for this mission. When the Dragon appeared last year, he revealed to me my true purpose, and how I will fit into the fulfillment of the prophecy. He knew me as well as if he had been next to me all those years. He spoke to me as if he had witnessed it all."

"Cassidy," Kali asked, "what is your mission?"

"Come," the woman said and laid flat, slipping her feet into the crevice. Before her face disappeared to follow her body, she added, "And you will see."

Chapter Forty-Four

The gates of Eston City loomed high above the eastern road. The first thing Samani noticed was the heightened guard, with more soldiers than usual checking wagons for entry. *It's begun,* he thought, *just as I believed. The final battle will take place here.* A soldier approached and reached a hand for their papers.

"The city's closed to visitors," he growled. "Only residents are allowed." He eyed their cargo suspiciously. "What's in the cart?"

"Cabbage," replied Kernigan with a shrug. "I'm hoping to sell it for enough money to purchase asylum during the battle."

The man lifted the tarp and peered in. Satisfied, he called over a sergeant. "He's got enough cabbage in there to hold a regiment for a week, Sarge. Same as with the others?"

The seasoned veteran nodded and scribbled something on their papers, then waved them through. "Head inside and take a right. There you'll find a commissary officer who'll purchase your goods."

"Thank you, Sergeant." Samani smiled his warmest appreciation. "Where could my small family seek refuge once inside?"

The gruff soldier laughed and replied, "This isn't the same city since... since things happened, and word of battle spread. If you stay, then wherever you land is up to luck and your ingenuity." He frowned. "But I'd leave if I were you, citizen."

"Thank you for the kind advice, Sergeant." Samani flicked the reins and guided the horses inside the walls.

The commissary officer was exactly where promised, seated at a purser's table and scribbling numbers into a thick ledger. Samani dismounted and approached, holding the sergeant's note in an outstretched hand.

The man never looked up. "What are you selling?"

"Cabbage," he replied simply.

"How much?"

"A standard wagonload. Also," he added, "Two horses and the wagon."

"We've no use for the equipment," the clerk replied. "No one's leaving and the extra horses will need hay. Best if you set them free outside."

"Horseflesh makes a wonderful stew during a siege, Lieutenant. Why don't you go ahead and take them for the butcher?"

The officer paused as if considering. Finally he smiled and looked up. "Well," he said, "we do have to feed the populace. I'll give you twenty talents, ten for the produce and five for the wagon and horses."

Samani hesitated, "And the other five?"

"You're of fighting age. You'll serve as a buck private and earn five talents a month for the duration of the siege." He handed back the papers and held out the silver which Samani took without question. "As soon as you say goodbye to your family, you're to report to the outfitter over there." He pointed to a tent where several other middle-aged men and teens tried on uniforms. "What's your name again?"

Samani read from the papers and replied, "Lyn Murdock."

The commissary officer returned his eyes to the books and muttered, "Welcome to the army, Mr. Murdock."

"I'm looking forward to it," Samani replied with a warm smile.

He strolled casually to the wagon and helped Delilah step down. Gretchen grabbed their personal belongings and joined them at the rear of the cart. "Look at the rose bushes," she observed. "They're everywhere."

Kernigan shrugged. "It's called the Rose City because the queen insisted on planting them everywhere." He turned so that he headed the opposite direction of the outfitter and motioned for the others to follow.

"Samani." Gretchen hadn't moved. Her feet remained planted where she stood. "Look at them closely," she insisted.

He turned, noticing for the first time that the common areas were clogged full of the bushes. Tangling vines hung everywhere, draping statues and even stretched across the busy streets. "That *is* peculiar," he remarked. "The gardeners must have been pressed into the army already. Normally they're groomed to perfection. Come now," he waved them to hurry. "We must get away before they press me as well."

The trio made their way down the road, pushing deeper into the city. Other than the overgrown state of the roses, the city hadn't changed. Samani knew the layout, despite that he hadn't visited but twice since its construction. He led them to The Shadow, a sunken area of the city beneath the middle-class homes and shops named for the perpetual darkness from the looming hulk of the palace above.

"When was the last time you visited, Delilah?"

She stole a glance at Gretchen, remembering that she was born a mere nine months after that trip. "It was the last time we met here together," she replied.

"Ah yes," he mused. "That was right after it opened. I believe they were still working on Unification Square."

"The scaffolding remained, yes." She remained thoughtful for a moment then added, "I remember more people walking around than this."

"Most likely the pending war," he noted. The rhythmic clanging of armor announced that a squad of soldiers approached. Samani held out his arm and pushed the women against a wall to save them from trampling. A strong shoulder struck his back and pressed him against the others in the narrow street.

"Odd," said Delilah.

"How so?"

"There were children in that formation."

Samani spun around, peering the way they'd gone and trying to get another look. "I missed that," he admitted.

"There were women too," Gretchen offered.

"Well," Kernigan offered, "then that *is* peculiar." He chewed on something for a moment then spoke his thoughts aloud. "The streets are empty except for soldiers making preparations. That's not surprising given the pending battle. They're enlisting every man of fighting age, but not women and children or they'd have tried to press you both back at the gate." His eyes shot open with alarm as he suddenly formed a thought. "We need to get to my contacts. I believe Jaguars have expanded the ranks of the Estonian army."

They quickened their pace until arriving at an inconspicuous tavern named the *Prancing Puck.* Samani pushed on the door but it wouldn't budge. He pounded with the heel of his hand, rapping several times before stepping aside to wait. He heard movement within, but no effort was made to open the door. "Gretchen," he asked politely, "if you wouldn't mind letting us in?"

The girl stepped forward and placed a black bead into her mouth. Her eyes dilated at once, and she sent a whisp of air into the lock. With a click the lock sprung and the door swung open. Samani entered first, smiling warmly to the family huddled in the rear of the tavern. The others followed, and Gretchen locked the door behind them.

"We don't have anything to steal," the owner of the tavern protested. "The soldiers took the ale and beef. We've nothing left to take."

"Oh, Gus," Samani said, "bust out the good stuff you keep in the floorboards. And grab the salted pork hidden behind the false wall in your cellar. We've much to celebrate my old friend."

The tavern owner's eyes narrowed then rounded with surprise. "Samani?"

"In the flesh. Now go get that bottle of 754."

Chapter Forty-Five

The Dreamers worked the sails while the adults talked business below decks. Learning a lesson from the loss of *Aggressor,* they were careful to push for speed without tearing the ship apart. At this rate, Captain Santos would have them and the others in Logan within the hour. Cuyler watched as the sun fell low on the horizon.

Next to him on the stern was a gig ready to lower over the side. The small boat had been piled high with kindling recovered from the lost pirate vessel, and doused thoroughly with rum. When Marita had asked why they wasted the rum, Alec had commented that it was accelerant for the fire. She had then asked if she could get accelerated and that had been the end of the conversation. Thinking of her, Cuyler pried his eyes from the king's shrouded body. It looked so lonely atop the pile of wood.

When she darted by, he said, "I'm sorry, Marita."

"Sorry for what?" She was busy tying off lines to look up, intent on finishing the task. He watched her work the sails with precision, like a seasoned sailor with decades of sea time.

"I'm sorry for doubting you. We've all been hard on you, bullying and making you out to be a liar."

"I see," she said. "So Alec told you he really is a duke?" Just to dig another point she slid several inches above the deck, racing aft to slacken the luff. "Or did you see me flying?"

Cuyler laughed. "Yes. He also told me everything you've done for him and his family."

"My family," she corrected. "They're *my* family." This time she whirled around to face him. "My *only* family."

"I know," he replied. "I'm sorry we've pushed you away."

"It's okay," she said with sincerity in her voice. "I never fit in with you guys anyway. This way I get to do my own thing after the war. Alec said that when I'm older I can start taking down the Jaguar dens. I'm thinking I'll start next year, since I'll be older by then." She winked, but Cuyler could tell she wasn't joking.

"What about you, Sebastian?" The boy was sitting on a barrel, staring out across the lake. "Will you come with us after the war? I'm thinking that I'd like to start a school, even if Eusari doesn't."

Sebastian shook his head. "I'm going where Braen goes. Piss on your school."

"What's wrong with you?" Cuyler took a step toward the boy, looming and putting him in his shadow. "You're such a coward any time we need you, but then you talk to me like you're something special?"

In a flash Marita had appeared between them, dual swords drawn and ready to attack. "Back off," she growled.

Cuyler raised his hands in a sign of surrender and retreated. Tired of being around children, he headed down below to talk to adults. He found them in Santos' stateroom, seated around a table and discussing Amash.

Percy Roan was talking about rite of succession. "It's simple," he said. "With Robert dead the only challenge is proving Marcus is illegitimate."

"There's no proof of that," Amash countered. "Besides, I don't want it." He pointed to Braen. "I want you to take it. You were born to be king. I was born to be an accountant."

Percy laughed, "You say that like it's a bad thing."

"I can't do it," Braston said with a hint of melancholy in his voice. "When I was at the bottom of the lake something happened, I saw something that I can't explain. I can only say that I have a different path."

Cuyler spoke from the doorway. "Only the son of Esterling can slay him in time."

"Yes," Braen agreed. "So the prophecy goes."

"Only," added Amash, "I won't kill my friend. That's out of the question."

Darkness clouded Braen's countenance as he considered a thought. "You may have to, if Eusari refuses. You'll have to do the deed in a way that gives her no choice but to restore me."

"I won't."

"You will, and you may need to kill me twice. After I do battle with Skander I will be subject to other forces, possibly taken over by Shol or someone more sinister. I'd rather you kill me before that possibility becomes reality."

"And if your brother wins?"

"Then we know that he was the Destroyer, and you slay him in time."

"All this talk of death is so dark," Percy remarked.

Philip, who had been sitting out of the way of the others, agreed. "Dark, Mr. Roan, but necessary. You've been involved with politics so long that you've forgotten that after the back-room dealings are done, someone has to conduct the dirtier business."

Amash raised an eyebrow. "You've carried out that kind of business?"

"Aye. There was a reason Charles Esterling chose me to watch over you as an infant. I was more than a mere nursemaid, my boy. To catch an assassin you must first think like one. Once you can do that the only requirement to become one yourself is to plunge a piece of steel."

Braen wasn't surprised, but he asked, "You've killed for the former Emperor?"

"Many times over, Lord Braston."

Braen and Amash replied in unison, "Not a lord, barely a Braston." They broke out in laughter after that, and the meeting was unofficially adjourned.

He placed a hand on his friend's shoulder and begged, "Just promise me that when all of this is over, you'll lead the rebuilding efforts."

"I can't do it alone," Amash argued.

Braen pointed to the two men from Weston. "You won't have to. Roan knows politics and Philip can teach you the finer points of intrigue. Everything else you need you already know." He pointed to Alec, quietly sharpening one of his blades in the corner. "And you've got allies in the south. With Charro Valencia out of the way, he should be in charge of the entire continent by the time he returns."

Alec grunted. "So much for retiring to make wine."

"You'll have time for that, my friend." That same dark thought from before returned to Braen's eyes. "I only wish I too had time for that."

Cuyler cleared his throat, "Lord Horslei," he said.

"Not a lord!"

"Amash then. You'll have the support of the Dreamers if you do take the throne. All I ask, is that when all this is over, you help us build a school."

"Like the academy? But for dreamers?" Amash smiled and turned to Braen. "I like this kid. He dreams big." Suddenly serious he added, "No matter who takes the reigns, you should have your school. Such power is dangerous without knowledge and understanding to guide those who wield it."

Braen pointed above and asked Cuyler. "Is everything prepared?"

"Everything's ready."

"Then let's go bury a king in the northern fashion."

Sebastian helped the boatswain lower the gig into the water. Once it was afloat, they let it drift slowly away. With nighttime gloaming, it was difficult to see as it distanced itself from the larger vessel. The Dreamers manned the rails beside Santos and his crew, and Alec Pogue stood with a bow at the ready.

Braen stood behind them all, reading off words from the book of the gods. "And we shall commit his body to become cleansed by flame before succumbing to the watery depths of the ocean below," he said before closing the book.

Marita interrupted the silence that lingered after his words. "Except that it's a lake, and Dad doesn't have any arrows."

Everyone turned to look at Alec. He bent down to pick up an empty quiver and then wheeled around to face his daughter. She shrugged. "How did you know there were no arrows, dearie? And why didn't you tell me before we lowered him over the side?"

"Well," she said, "to be perfectly honest, I didn't realize we were going to shoot flaming arrows at him until Captain Braston read those words just now."

"And where did my arrows go, dearie?"

She pointed at the little vessel bearing the king's body. "We needed kindling and that looked like the closest thing."

Braen laughed, despite the somber moment. Soon every man topside joined in as well.

Amash asked, "What will we do?"

A voice from the hatch leading below spoke up. "I think I can help." Everyone turned in unison toward the Pescari girl, Flaya. She had remained locked in her quarters the entire trip, not breaking her mourning over her husband.

Sebastian had nearly forgotten that she was still aboard. He asked in a timid voice, "Do you have the same power of your husband?" Realization set in before she could answer and he pointed to her belly and asked, "Does your child have powers as well?"

This made the girl laugh, and she shook her head to the contrary. "No," she said with her deep Pescari accent. She drew a long blade from her buckskins and grabbed an oar from off the deck. In mere minutes she had shaved off a splinter just about the right size as an arrow. She pulled two feathers from her hair, splitting the shaft of each and cutting them to size. These were slid into grooves she had carved in the shaft, and she carefully notched the rear for easy nocking. Once she wrapped the blunt tip with a rag, she held it out for Alec.

He looked it over, then handed both the bow and arrow to the woman. "I don't know, dearie. He's drifted pretty far, and I don't think I should be taking that shot. Besides, we're also celebrating the life of your husband tonight."

"Teot will take Taros to Felicima," she said matter of factly, then the Pescari queen took the weapon and held the arrow out for Amash. He doused the wadding with rum and lit it aglow with flint and steel. She raised the tip and closed one eye. Before loosing the arrow, she said, "Felicima claims you, Andalonian Shappan." The arrow flew true and landed square in the kindling. The pyre erupted with flames as the silent onlookers considered their own mortality.

Chapter Forty-Six

The crack under the wall opened into a strange room full of metal pipes and wires. Johan examined these as he followed behind Cassidy, exhilaration coursing through his body while sensing the cool water running through the building. Each led to a different section, some bringing fresh water in and others taking waste water out. The maze was dizzying, but he traced it out with his connection to the flowing liquid.

Just within his mind's reach, he sensed energy unlike any he'd felt since the ride in the submersible. The power surged everywhere with fast moving energy. Beyond the Rotunda's water supply, he even detected the city's storm drain, realizing that it flowed directly beneath the center of the building. He thought back to the train ride and the beautiful river surrounding the peninsula. "We're inside the Rotunda," he said aloud.

"Good job!" Cassidy grinned broadly at his deduction, suddenly excited to clue the children in on the mission. "The Astian Council is meeting today and are gathering above us right now. The Dragon left a surprise that we're supposed to deliver.

Kali suddenly appeared worried. "What kind of surprise? This isn't dangerous is it?"

Cassidy smiled disarmingly. "Of course not," she promised, "but it will make a lasting impression."

Johan tore his eyes away from the pipes as the trio emerged into a large room. They stood on a metal gallery suspended over a large cistern below. Inside, the water churned and flushed out impurities. He could sense that the water pumped from the pool was pure, ready for drinking as if it had bubbled from a crystal-clear spring. "Is this where they clean the water?"

"Yes," Cassidy replied, smiling as broadly as before. "The council doesn't just meet here, they sometimes spend weeks living in their apartments within the Rotunda. Their water supply is kept separate from the rest of the city to prevent contamination, and also to prevent a mass assassination through poisoning.

Johan felt the blood leave his face as he paled. "We aren't doing that, are we?" His stomach dropped, appalled by such horrific killing.

"Heavens no," she assured him, "nothing like that at all. You have power over water, and will use it to create a diversion. Our job is to divert their attention away from the real plan. If you do exactly as I say, we'll be in and out without any trouble."

Johan stared down at the pool swirling beneath them and asked, "What is it you want me to do?"

Cassidy pointed upward with a grin. "Interrupt a party!"

Chancellor Praedor, observing that the quorum was in attendance, called the meeting to order. "We'll begin with a roll call," she announced, although only one member of the council was absent. "Where is Councilman Horn?"

"He did not present himself from his apartments this morning, and it's rumored he stayed abroad in his private residence," Councilman Wilman revealed.

The Chancellor raised an inquiring eyebrow. "You apparently watch his movements closely, don't you Councilman?" This brought laughter into the chamber.

Her quip drew his anger and Wilman spat. "He's a cur! A self-serving upstart with dangerous aspirations! Can his absence serve as evidence that he is unsuited for the position?" Arguments erupted both for and against the son of Jakata. Speaking over the ruckus, the portly councilman added, "Like his father before him, he views himself *above* the collective good of the Council. Mark my words, he'll try and claim the Chancellorship some day!" The shouts against were then more clearly heard over the shouts for Artema.

Praedor allowed her voice amplification device to squeal noisily throughout the chamber, then spoke once she had everyone's attention. "We have a quorum, so we can proceed. Note in the official attendance that Horn is not present for the proceedings."

The door at the far end of the chamber suddenly burst open, and a paige sprinted forward. He was caught by a large hand by one of the numerous armed guards lining the chamber exits. For each of the thirty in the room, another would be in the outside hall. After a brief exchange, the soldier took a dispatch and handed it to the bailiff. The two spoke quietly, then the missive was presented to the Praedor.

"From our communications ministry, Chancellor," the bailiff said as he handed over the tablet.

She read the lines carefully, blood immediately running cold from the report. "Ladies and Gentlemen of the Council, it appears that we are placing the Rotunda into lockdown. We'll continue our proceedings, but the main entrance will be barred for the duration, and we shall shelter in our apartments tonight."

Upon her words the soldiers moved to physically secure the room. She looked up to see more than one hundred staring sets of eyes, each waiting with anticipation. Praedor read the missive several times, both unbelieving and very much stunned by the contents. She was opening her mouth to inform those gathered when a commotion announced the arrival of Artema Horn. Beside him was Fatwana Nakala, the fugitive lead sister of the Winter Oracle.

"Stand aside," he barked at the soldier barring his way. "Lockdown or not, I will not be kept from my rightful seat in this chamber!"

Praedor waved him in and the guards stood down, locking the doors behind him. "Have a seat, Councilor. Your tardiness is the first blackspot on your young record, and will not be easily forgotten." Artema chuckled and waved a dismissive hand as he continued forward. "I said to have a seat, Councilor Horn. Yours is in the upper gallery due to your low seniority."

"And yours, Praedor, is in a prison cell," he replied with a sneer. To the gasps and complaints from his peers, he turned with an air of confidence.

"I will not spar words with you Horn, but harboring a fugitive is a crime and bringing said outlaw into the chamber is grounds for insolence."

"Before you charge me with insolence, perhaps you should execute your final act as Chancellor, that of reading evidence of your own treachery aloud so that we can judge your guilt."

She leaned over the railing and whispered to the bailiff. He nodded and signaled two soldiers to accompany as he approached Horn. She then accused Artema directly. "You are out of line, Councilor. You are new to the Council, so I'll have you escorted to your seat. If you refuse, I'll have you escorted to your apartments."

"Just read your news, Praedor," Artema growled. "I will not cow to corruption," he said. "because I am a bull of justice!" He spoke with such formidable authority that even the Chancellor flinched. "Read it so that we can proceed!"

"It seems," she said to the assembly, "there has been a chain of simultaneous bombings within our borders," she explained.

"Tell them," Artema roared, "what kind of devices were used!"

The others were piqued with curiosity by now, and many rallied behind his demand with shouts of "Tell us!"

"All four blasts," she admitted, "were of nuclear fission devices." Her eyes shot to Councilor Merek as she spoke, willing him to keep silent regarding his knowledge.

"And who claimed responsibility, Chancellor."

She fired back in anger, shouting, "The Humanitarian Freedom Society, of course!"

"Tell my esteemed colleagues how the Society came into possession of not just one, but four of those devices which you are solely responsible for their use?"

"Why don't you tell them yourself," she snapped, "since you are the leader of the Society!" The words had flown before she had chosen them, and shut her mouth immediately. She had yet to provide proof of his involvement and this would come across as an empty accusation.

Artema laughed. "Need I remind you that my father ordered the reset of Andalon? You told me yourself that those troops, now under your command, have failed to report in, and that you actually lost five nuclear devices." He stepped forward and raised his arm over the Council. "You said that four devices detonated, yet you told me that there were five in total. Where is the fifth weapon of mass destruction, Chancellor Praedor?"

"I am not under inquiry, Councilor, and you are out of order."

"Actually, I have the floor," he said with his usual smile. "I was late to the chamber due to difficulties procuring certain documents. He raised a packet of pages into the air. These bear your signature and changed the procurement of those devices ahead of the mission launch. You defied my father's orders for a full reset by sending inert bombs instead." He wheeled around to face her, sending a private wink as he did. "You interfered several days before my father's untimely death. Did you kill him as well?"

"A foolish notion, Councilor. I censure your time on the floor."

Artema refused to stand down. "You authorized inert devices, and that is not the crime. But somehow radioactive material found its way into the hands of the Society, and that was in turn used against the oracles. Fatwana Nakala possesses the answers we seek, and I demand she's given time to testify."

Praedor hissed her reply. "No one *demands* anything from the Astian Council!" She scanned the room, unable to ignore the shouts for the oracle to speak. Anger seethed inside, clouding her judgement and fogging her options. She locked eyes with Merek who shook his head slowly back and forth, willing her not to allow the testimony.

"I will award three minutes for a private testimony in my chamber."

"Private," said Artema, "will not do." He grandiosely waved a hand over the assemblage. "Not when they deserve to hear these words."

Chants when up immediately for a public audience. Praedor searched her gut for the correct action. Her instincts begged her to adjourn pending investigation, but she could not during a lockdown, they were not only trapped in the Rotunda, but locked in perpetual session until the emergency situation is lifted. Her eyes shot to Horn, smugly awaiting her decision. Whatever sly comment he mouthed was drowned by the increasingly hostile assembly.

I've listened to Fatwana Nakala speak many times, Praedor thought. *Never have I known her to conspire or lie. She is dutiful in her position, and has no information that can damn me.* When she finally spoke it was with resignation. "She has three minutes to testify so that we may continue with actual business."

Artema directed Fatwana to the speaker's pulpit in the center of the room. She took her position with dignity, but Praedor could sense terror lurking just below the surface of the woman's bearing. She drew her posture tall and her face took on regal determination. *Every time I've listened to her speak it has been dire news she utters,* the Chancellor lamented, suddenly feeling sorry for the lead sister on display. *At least I've nothing to fear from her.*

Horn began the charade. "Tell me about your trip to Andalon, Fatwana."

"I was summoned to speak here before this very Council. While I rode the train from Oslot, I was approached by a woman who claimed to be from the Society."

"What did she want?"

"For me to fulfill my brother's mission." The room erupted. Everyone on the Council knew of Samani Nakala's betrayal to the Oracles before his death.

"Did you tell anyone of this," Artema asked.

"No." Her answer was definitive.

"Why not?"

"Because my brother revealed himself in a Ka'Ash'mael. I learned he was alive and well in Andalon." The revelation shook the entire room. "I wanted to confirm this, and so I agreed to meet with the Society."

"What did they ask in return for this information?"

"They asked for me to give them a single prophecy."

"Is that the one your second in command, a certain Subba, gave to us after your disappearance?"

"Yes," she replied and then paused. "No, actually. There was confusion in the translation and so he brought you the misinterpretation."

"Tell the Council what he reported."

"Only the son of Esterling can slay him in time."

"What was the actual translation?"

"Only the son of Andalon can slay him in time."

Praedor interrupted. "That's impossible. Every child in Astia knows this history. David Andalon was sterile, unable to reproduce, and that was the only reason he was allowed to colonize Estowen's Landing."

"Yes," Fatwana agreed, "and the rest of the story was that Michael Esterling took pity on him when dealing out punishment for his crimes. He ordered the exile after feeling guilty for siring a child with his friend's wife."

"Exactly. What does all this have to do with Horn's insatiable desire to have you speak?"

"Andalon succeeded in his experiments. His wife truly delivered his child and not Esterling's. This prophecy cannot be wrong, and there are two descendants colliding at this very moment. The son of Esterling and the son of Andalon."

"What," Praedor asked, "does any of this have to do with Horn's claims?"

The lead sister of the Winter Oracle cocked her head as if listening to a distant voice. When she spoke, her voice held the same regality as before, but Praedor instantly recognized that her words were more deliberate. "The son of Andalon will stop the Destroyer. But the son of Esterling *is* the Destroyer. He will be born of water like his ancestor, while Andalon will be a mortal man. The difference in the prophecies suggest that the outcome is not predetermined when these two forces collide. A choice must be made that will decide the future of both continents."

"Again," Praedor pressed, "what does this have to do with your brother, or the treason alleged by Artema Horn?"

"I was kidnapped following the bombing at the train station, and smuggled to Andalon to meet with my brother. He shared with me the truth behind the plutonium his people used to arm the devices."

Artema asked, "What is the truth, Fatwana? Tell us now how the plutonium made it to the Society!"

"My brother carried it. He claimed that it was requisitioned by Councilor Merek more than twenty years ago, when he was a junior aide to then Councilwoman Praedor."

"I have that paperwork here," Artema proclaimed as he raised a bundle of papers into the air. "Either he acted alone or on your orders," he said to the Chancellor.

Praedor searched her memory. *I've never procured plutonium,* she mused. *I've never given the order either!* "That was twenty years ago. I don't recall how or why we would've needed plutonium in the first place, much less why it would surface now."

"My brother explained that as well," Fatwana said. "He stated that the leader of the Society gave it to him for safekeeping in Andalon, telling him he'd know when the time would come to use it, because he would also have the devices in his possession."

Merek stood and cleared his throat, suddenly aware the insinuations against his mentor. In that moment he made a choice. "I made that requisition based on her orders," he said. "I did not know her plans at the time. If she is the leader of the Society, I have never shared that knowledge!"

"This is preposterous," the Chancellor objected. "I want to see those signatures!" Artema handed her a copy. The document was authentic.

Horn proclaimed, "I levy a vote of no confidence against the Chancellor."

The room spun around Praedor; everything had fallen apart in a single session.

"I second that levy and ask Councilor Horn to give up the floor," Merek said.

Artema asked, "where did you say my seat was?" He pointed to the upper gallery. "Up there? No, I think that I'm more comfortable down front," he said with a cool smile. He slid in next to Wilman and winked at the Chancellor. The vote was called and tallied, and she was escorted unceremoniously from the Rotunda.

Artema Horn glanced up at the ceiling, watching closely for his next cue. A slight vibration caught his eye, as one of the fire mains strained against building pressure. He sprang to his feet, and shouted, "I call for an immediate vote for Chancellor!"

Councilor Wilman spun to his left, mouth agape and staring at the audacity of the junior politician. "Are you daft? No one will second that!"

Horn leaned in real and showed the senior official the object in his hand. It was a detonator. He whispered "The fifth bomb is actually planted in the councilor's district, in your parlor. Your son is still visiting with all your grandchildren, is he not? Second that call for me, will you?"

"I..." Wilman sputtered, "I second that call for a vote of Chancellor!"

"Thank you," he replied, slipping the device into his robes. "Now, nominate me."

"I nominate uh... Artema Horn fuh... for Chancellor!" That was right before the pipes burst above them, raining cold water on every statesman in the room.

As the other councilors leaped to their feet to escape the downpour, Artema grabbed ahold of Wilman's cloak and pulled him into his seat. "You will stay," he ordered.

Merek casually strolled toward the pair, moving against the stream of fleeing councilmen. "Well gentlemen, since the quorum was called, and the others have taken an unauthorized recess, why don't we take that vote now? Any other nominations," he asked, then made a show of waiting for a name. "No? Good. Let's get down to business. All in favor of Artema Horn," he said, "say 'Aye.'

Wilman couldn't believe his ears. "What does he have on you Merek?"

He didn't reply, just turned to Horn and asked, "Didn't you show him the detonator? Why isn't he voting?"

Wilman's eyes grew round with surprise. "You're in on this?"

Artema smiled. "You said yourself that I'll need a sponsor to help with my rise, let's just say I found one who works faster than you, and with less prodding if not more leverage. What's your vote?" He held up the detonator.

"Aye," he replied with a huff, turning on his heel and striding from the room.

Fatwana, who had been standing by with a look of confusion on her face asked, "What just happened?"

"Dear Sister," Samani Kernigan said from Merek's lips, "Artema Horn is now the Chancellor. And you will now forget that I've ever held control over your mind. The new Chancellor will reward you when he reestablishes the single oracle system. Congratulations, lead sister."

She stared back with confusion, "You two were working together as a team?" After her brother and Artema nodded, her eyes blinked shut and she collapsed into a chair.

Raising the pressure in the pipes was easy, and Johan had no difficulty in his task. He simply backed up the outflow while increasing the input.

"Good," Cassidy said, "now freeze the water above the main chamber."

That was something he had never tried, but picked it up rather easily. By slowing the movement of the particles, he was able to lower the temperature enough that the pipes did indeed burst. It was less work after that, as he kept a constant flow of water through the pipes and hoped it would be enough to flood the Rotunda.

Doors opened above them, and footsteps informed the trio that someone approached. They looked around for somewhere to hide, but ran instead for the doors on the opposite side of the gallery.

"Come quickly!" Cassidy held the passage open for the children, urging them through. "We can't leave the way we came," she said, "we'll have to exit another way!"

Johan jogged past and stole a glance into the woman's eyes. Their usual disinterest was gone, replaced by a bit of sadness. *Or guilt,* he thought. He recognized too late that they had been betrayed. As soon as he and Kali entered the next hall, the door slammed shut behind them. He tried the handle, but it was securely latched. He turned and banged until his hands hurt from the effort. Turning to Kali, he asked, "What do we do now?"

Kali watched as her friend tried the door. He beat upon it and shouted for Cassidy, but it was obvious they had been tricked into entering the main Rotunda. She looked around, trying to get bearings within the foreign architecture. Everything looked the same and there were no obvious landmarks to point their way. They were lost in the massive structure.

"What do we do now," Johan asked as he turned, fear having consumed his wits.

"We press on," she suggested. "There must be a way out." The pair rounded the first bend, cautiously peering around the corner and listening for sounds of soldiers. Hearing none, they darted down the righthand corridor with haste, holding their breath and bracing for trouble around every turn. Suddenly the maze of corridors made sense to Kali, and she pointed to a stairwell. "Up," she said.

"How do you know?"

"I can't explain," she said, "I just do. I was lost at first, but now I feel like I've been here before." She pointed once more to the stairwell. "We go up two flights and will emerge in an atrium. Just beyond that are the main doors and beyond that the city."

Johan closed his eyes and she watched as he felt for the water flooding above. When he finally opened them, he grinned broadly and said, "There's water raining from the ceiling up there! If there are any soldiers, I can fight them off!"

A voice in the back of Kali's mind whispered, *That's wonderful!*

"Come on," she said as she grabbed his hand. Together they hurried up the stairs, careful not to slip on the water cascading under their feet. When they reached the top, they found that the worst of the flooding was held back by a single door, with a strong current finding its way underneath.

Johan felt the pressure on the other side, pooling and waiting for the door to open so it could rush to the cistern beneath the building. He reached out carefully, holding the forceful current with his mind and willing it to remain where it stood. He grabbed the handle and pulled. What remained was a shimmering wall two hands high, wriggling like gelatin and holding fast. He pulled the heavy door shut behind them, denying the exit the water desired.

Kali abruptly froze in place and Johan slammed into her back, causing her to nearly topple over. "Wait," she said. "I hear voices." She spied two large doors on the far side of the atrium, manned by several soldiers whose full attention was focused through tiny windows into the adjacent room. Just beyond them was a wall of glass doors reaching high toward the ceiling above, a magnificent marvel that she wished she had time to view. "Keep quiet," she cautioned, "or they'll see us."

Abruptly the wooden doors burst open. Soldiers, mixed among elegantly robed men and women, rushed into the atrium. They were drenched from head to foot and the room they fled rained with a torrential downpour, harder even than in the atrium. Kali watched as several slipped and fell while the others nearly trampled them where they lay. A voice in her head commanded, *Hold now and allow this scenario to play out.* She tried to run but found her legs could no longer move.

Johan pulled on her arm, trying to drag her away but she resisted. "Come, Kali! We cannot stay." But it was too late. The soldiers had spotted the children and they formed a perimeter surrounding them.

"Don't move," one of them shouted.

"It's just a couple of children," another remarked. "They probably wandered in during the commotion."

The first man pointed at their coveralls. "They've got no business here. They're from sector twelve factories, see?" He stepped forward. "Present identification."

Kali was suddenly very worried. She reached out but could find no living creature or flora nearby to bond. It would be solely up to Johan to get them out of this mess. The voice whispered in her mind. *He must attack them now. They will kill you both if he does not kill them first.*

"Johan," she said through clenched teeth. "You must fight them. They'll kill us if you don't."

He stared back with wide eyes full of fear and hesitation. "I don't want to," he said. "It's not like they're Falconers! These are real people."

"You must," she urged him with a face full of terror and eyes that begged his protection.

He had never seen her this frightened or so vulnerable. Normally she remained calm no matter the situation, and had always led them out of danger in the past. The sight of her trembling before his eyes proved too much, and he jumped into action.

The water between them and the soldiers spun into a high wall that pushed the other men away. As it spun into a cyclone, shouts and cries rang out from the people adorned in robes. "The Destroyer," one of them shouted, "is here!"

One of the soldiers fired his weapon into the spinning maelstrom, randomly striking Kali in the stomach.

Johan watched the pain as it spread across her face, buckling her knees and forcing her eyes to close against pending death. He screamed rage into the storm, sending it wilder and faster as he lost control. The massive current drove into the soldiers, forcing water into their lungs and drowning each of them on dry land. Another shot rang out.

Johan felt the projectile strike his chest and dropped the wall of water, splashing it against the floor with an audible slap. As it fell, it revealed a man standing across the room with fiery red hair. He held a rifle in his hands, plucked from the hands of a dying soldier. He smiled smugly at the boy. Johan fell to his knees, hands dangling useless at his sides as he tried to breathe. His vision swam with bright lights as he crawled toward Kali. With a final gasp he collapsed beside the girl he loved.

Kali opened her eyes just in time to watch the bullet rip through Johan's heart. He fought against death to lay at her side. When the life left his body she rolled over, still clutching her bleeding belly as she felt for a trace of lingering lifeforce. It barely resonated against her own.

Now is the time, Kali. This is why you are in Astia, and you know what you must do.

She nodded silently, accepting that the voice spoke only truth. "I don't remember how," she whispered.

Yes you do. His lifeforce is scattered all around, feel it in the water as he bleeds out.

The pink water surrounding the children blended together what was lost from each. She felt with her mind, separating the traces of him and pouring it inside. Careful not to make the mistake she had done with Beth, she repaired the tissue of his heart and the cartilage and sinew that had been ripped apart to reach the beating muscle. His eyes blinked open and she collapsed once more.

Someone screamed and the men and women of the council turned. They were fawning over Artema, congratulating him on a perfect shot. His daring had accomplished what they had been too afraid to try, and put down the Destroyer with a single bullet. He turned toward the alarm and witnessed the boy rising to walk once more, the girl at his feet having restored his lifeforce so that he may continue fighting. His eyes glowed with a brilliant blue that swam like the ocean depths.

Councilman Merek whispered, "Rise the Kraken from the depths, dealing destruction and slaughter. Watch him destroy our legacy."

Another bystander added, "On land the monster roars and walks, death surrounds in light and shadow."

Someone else whispered, "The son of Esterling!"

The assemblage stepped backward, trembling with fear as the boy stared down Artema Horn. They murmured amongst themselves, marveling at Horn's bravery and whispering about his stand against the Destroyer. They gazed upon him with newfound awe, moving to safety and hoping he could repeat the miracle.

"He will not destroy our legacy," the once pirate king yelled, charging the boy just as the maelstrom kicked up around them.

He disappeared into the wall of water with a single shout, "I am Andalon!"

They waited patiently for the wall to fall, somehow believing in their newfound savior.

Kali watched the man with fiery hair wrestle against Johan in the eye of the storm. She lifted a weak hand to draw a blade from her belt and tried to crawl toward them. *I must help him,* she thought as she urged her body forward.

Stop! The command of the voice froze every muscle in her body. *Hand Artema Horn the knife.* She reached out a hand and placed the hilt in his. *Control your puppet,* the voice ordered. *Place his hands at his side. Good. Now lock them in place.* She collapsed from the effort, but her friend's body complied. Frozen and vulnerable.

The man with fiery hair lifted the blade and shoved the tip ever so gently into Johan's sternum, piercing his heart and stopping it forever. She lay there, slumped on the ground as torrent of water collapsed, unable to lift her body in her weakened state. She died with sadness in her breast, yearning to be free of the treachery of Samani Kernigan. In death she joined the boy who could have been her love, had not those who manipulated fate been so unkind.

Chapter Forty-Eight

King Marcus Esterling, High Emperor over the principalities of Eston, Norton, Logan, Weston, Middleton, and Eskera had lost every major city in his vast domain. Each savaged by the rampaging Skander Braston. Only Eston remained in his control, and it no longer resembled the bustling city from before the war.

The citizens hid in their homes, both from fear of pillaging invasion forces, and also their own ruler. Armed soldiers patrolled the streets, armed with steel and forcibly conscripting every one of fighting age. News had spread quickly of the king's massacre of the ten thousand in Unification Square, betraying the love each citizen had held in their hearts since the tragic passing of his mother. The young king did not care whether they loved him or not. He no longer needed their support.

The Rose Palace had become ghostly devoid of life, with guards pulled from their stations and moved to the front lines. There was no need for protection, not with vines overgrown as thickets throughout the structure. Wriggling with life, the vines stretched outward from the king's nest, filling every open space and spying upon the citizenry with open blooms as scarlet as his people's blood. Their color served as a constant reminder that death had fed the strange growth throughout the city.

The king's decline intensified following the disappearance of Kestrel, as he worked furiously day and night to find the wayward Falconer and Campton Shol. He sprawled across a dais in the throne room, casually popping black and white beads into his mouth and sucking on them like decadent candies. His eyes had grown permanently wide from the stimulating effects from the drug, and his pupils were so large that only a thin ring of brown revealed they held any color at all. His mind focused not on the window from which he stared without blinking, but instead scanned the streets and alleyways for the Eston Rookery.

That's where I'll find Shol, he had reasoned, *or Kestrel or both. I need final control over one more aspect of my kingdom if I'm to wrestle it away.* He finally found them, nestled far beneath the palace and indeed scheming his downfall.

The Astian overseer shouted at the Falconer, "What do you mean he tolerated the Autumn bead?"

"He didn't just tolerate it," the feathered specter had replied, "he worked it as well as if he had affinity. He swallowed four beads and commanded every vine in the city at once."

"He killed his own citizenry," Shol had gasped before collapsing into a chair. "He raised them?"

"More than ten thousand."

"No," the chancellor had said, "that isn't possible. What if he... No. He can't be..."

"Yes, Lord Shol," Marcus whispered out the window, "I am your Destroyer, and I shall begin with you." Saliva dripped from the corners of his mouth as he spoke, his glands working overtime to render the beads he held in his cheeks. "I'll finish with Skander and then I'll seek out your entire continent and ensure that nothing stands."

"We must unleash them," Kestrel suggested. "He'll have no power against fire."

"That's too risky," Shol argued, "Those we sent to The Cove never returned despite their abilities. We will need those for Braston."

Marcus was suddenly aware of the other lifeforms of whom they spoke. He left the two pathetic schemers and traveled through solid rock and crossed into a vast room. Laughter erupted from deep in his chest as he recognized the awesome potential of the power contained within. He rose from the dais, hovering in the air several hands above the floor, and made his way to a certain section of wall.

"You always appeared over here," he asked, "didn't you, Kestrel?" He cast out feelers of air with his mind, testing the seams and searching for a latch. When it opened into a passageway, he cackled with joy and proceeded inside.

He descended several hundred feet beneath the palace, followed by a slithering scratch against cobblestones. He emerged into a room full of slabs, raised tables that spread out as far as the eye could see. As he entered, overhead lights blinked on with his motion and shed their brilliance upon thousands of slumbering men, women, and children. Unimpressed and with drug fueled eyes fixated on the prize ahead, he ignored the sleeping forms and glided toward a door on the far wall. With a flick of his wrist it flew open, revealing a bigger chamber.

Inside were hundreds of Falconers, standing in rows like slumbering statues awaiting release from their masters. Each stood with eyes open and facing forward, staring but unseeing the world around them. He coiled in and out of their military-like formation, the scratching sound growing louder as he ran a sinister finger along each of their bodies. He chittered with glee at the sight, flinging spittle from his open mouth as he suckled the beads.

He paused at the end of the column, staring up at several large forms resting on roosts. Below the creatures stood ten odd looking Falconers, with crimson hoods adorned with orange and yellow feathers that matched their beasts.

"I know what you are," he said with satisfied laughter. "Mommy told me bedtime tales before she abandoned me to study under Matteas. And you," he said with satisfaction, "are a Phoenix."

The snakelike slithering was beneath his feet now and grew louder as tall vines filled the room. Everywhere the rose bushes blossomed, tangling the dormant Falconers and slowly writhing around their bodies. A slight humming made him turn. Ten large beasts growled before twenty fur-clad humanoids, each kneeling on the floor and swaying to the tempo of their magic. He could feel the sweet music then, a language of its own that spoke to the soul of the flora surrounding him.

"You'd like to take control of my roses," he remarked through the rounded pebbles in his mouth. "You'd use them against me, wouldn't you? But there's a reason Mommy chose them for her sigil," he warned. "The rose symbolizes love, something she desired from everyone around her, yet proved incapable of giving. And these roses are hers," he explained as he plucked a bud from its thorny stem. "She planted every single one, willing them to live while caring not what happened to her children. She was truly a bringer of life, my mother, but surely never capable of loving anything but her flowers."

He stepped toward the animals, slithering vines twisting their way alongside. "I got that from her, you know, apathy for human-kind. Surely, I won't pity your failure in your wasted attempts. I won't allow you to interfere with my destruction of everything Charles Esterling deemed dear. Watch as her symbol of self-love instead changes to glorify hatred and spite, for those are the only virtues I've ever known or will ever give."

The jaguars between him and the specters whined as the thorny vines crept toward them. The kneeling men swayed faster, trying to wrench away the bond between the foliage and Marcus. Pain throbbed within his temples as they found the connection he held. He reached into his pouch and pulled another white bead, placing it inside his cheek next to the others. He surged with power and the vines slid ahead, winding around both animal and man, up their bodies and around their throats.

"Die," he told the room. "Die and become mine to hate and despise. Die and become my children."

Campton Shol sat across from Kestrel, recapping their plan to wrestle control from the boy king. "We'll have to kill him in his chambers, I suppose. He's more powerful than I had ever imagined and he…" Kestrel's eyes were open but staring blankly forward as he did when communicating with the collective. Shol would have to wait until his mind switched back to the part he controlled.

A few seconds later, the empty eyes shot open and his friend's dry voice said, "Flee this place now! Go and never return. It is too late."

"Kestrel, I don't understand…"

The Falconer's eyes suddenly burst from the pressure within his skull as the son of Crestal Esterling crushed his mind with the power of the entire collective. His body slumped forward onto the table.

Lord Campton Shol fled.

Chapter Forty-Nine

Night fell softly upon Logan, sending the market goers scurrying to their homes. The darkness masked the dangers of the city like a veiled widow hiding her sorrows; in plain view but ignored by any who ventured a glance. Only the tavern district showed life, loudly proclaiming their sins to the waterfront while the pious rested their souls after praying to their gods. The only other movement through the city feared breaking the silence of the streets, and so they moved with stealth.

Sippen led Hester and the others to the place Caroline had identified as the Rookery. Krill ambled upon his pegged leg, bringing up the rear and carrying most of their gear. Everyone carried one of Yurik's grapeshot guns, even the northern queen who moved with confidence despite her uncomfortable breeches. She held her weapon the way Cedric had taught her, pointed to the sky so that she wouldn't shoot off any of her friends' heads.

The roost of the Falconers turned out to be well hidden in Logan, mostly underground and tucked under a curiously small building nestled between two shops. The door, much like in the other cities, was unadorned and easily missed even by the locals and neighboring business owners. Passersby never looked twice.

Getting in would prove a challenge, despite that no Falconers guarded the entrance. Cedric broke the silence with unnecessary volume that made Hester jump. "How we gettin' in thar?"

"For Cinder's sake," she snapped, "there's an 'are' in that sentence!"

"Yes, I know that there arrr," he replied with a stupid grin that made her want to lower her gun.

"Buh... be quiet, buh... both of you," Sippen cautioned. Pointing to the door he asked Caroline, "Cuh... can you uh... open that?"

"I will try," the girl promised, inching forward so she could get a better look. "There's no mechanism, so you're probably right that it's unlocked with a thread of air."

"Then go uh... ahead and puh... pick it," Sippen commanded, standing by with one of his grapeshot grenades at the ready. "Wuh... when the duh... door swings open," he directed the others, "buh... be ready with guh... guns in case wuh... one runs out."

"And don't shoot any of us, Hester," Cedric added.

"Oh, but wouldn't I enjoy that," she replied. *But I wouldn't,* she knew, *because these two idiots are all I have left to call family.* She removed one hand from the gun and briefly touched the hilt of the knife hidden inside her bodice. *That is,* she thought, *until Braen returns and finds his lover dead. Soon I will be there in his grief and he'll remember his love for me.*

"Okay," Caroline said, "I'm about to open it." Hester watched as Sippen readied a grenade, finger on the flint wheel and positioned so that he would not be seen by any Falconers inside. He nodded and the girl flipped the door open with a wave of her hand. She immediately leaped out of the way and shouted, "There's two!"

Without hesitation Sippen lit the fuse and counted in his head. Hester remembered that the magic number was three. If he held it too long the ceramic device would explode on his team instead. His hand arced around the doorframe and the sound of the device tumbling against stone caused Hester to want to peer inside, but she fought the urge and covered her ears like the others.

Even muffled, the explosion was deafening. The smell of sulfur and gunpowder drifted into the street, and Hester jumped at the concussion blowing through her hair. Groans from within let her know that the Falconers had at least been wounded and that emboldened the tiny assault force. They had committed to the attack and there was no turning back.

Cedric entered first, spinning into the room with muzzle forward. Another explosion rang out, this time less deafening than the first. A click of a second shell chambering informed the team that at least one of the Falconers had been put down. Sippen nodded and he and Hester entered as well, side by side with muzzles forward.

They found the peg-legged fool standing over the remaining specter, grinning down at the dying man. The sight within was grotesque, so the northern queen looked away. Even with eyes averted, she could not unsee the missing limbs and torn flesh. She stared instead at the darkened stone against the far wall made wet with their lifeforce.

A moment later Caroline entered. "There will be at least five more birdmen and two Jaguars."

Hester kept her eyes on the walls, seamless and without doorways. "Where? They aren't in here."

Caroline sent out tendrils of air that tested each panel and crevice until she called out, "Got it!" A hidden mechanism released in the wall and part of the floor lowered slowly to reveal stairs.

Two massive beasts sprang from the opening, snarling and baring teeth. They leaped simultaneously at the squad. Without thinking, Hester raised her weapon and pulled the trigger, sending one of them veering off course and crashing to the ground with a massive hole in its side. A shot to her right resounded as well, but Sippen's cat continued with course unabated, landing atop the little man in a lifeless heap of fur.

Cedric did not waste time and tossed a grenade into the dark stairwell, spinning around and ducking to the ground just as the landing beneath exploded. The tiny room amplified the sound of the blast, and Hester did not have time to cover her ears. They ran with muted echoes as she looked toward Sippen.

His mouth was moving, calling out orders that she could not understand as he struggled to get out from under the fallen beast. Slowly her hearing gathered focus and she understood his commands.

"Puh... put on gas masks!" He slipped from underneath the animal and scrambled to his feet, then added, "Toss in a cuh... carcass!"

She quickly pulled on her mask, taking notice of Cedric doing the same. To her left Caroline formed a bubble of air around her head, its shimmering border hovering just beyond her mouth. A thought suddenly popped into her head. "No!" She pointed at the girl. "If she can do that, so can they!"

But it was too late, Cedric had already tossed the carcass grenade down the stairwell. The choking gas bellowed up on the drafting breeze, filling both the upper and lower rooms. As Hester had feared, visibility in the tiny room quickly vanished, plunging them into a smokey darkness. Footsteps pounded as several figures stormed the room from below.

Hester caught the blur of feathers pass closely by and she fired her gun. Two more reports let her know that the others had done the same. She drew shells and fed them into the barrel, the audible clicks giving her comfort that she had reloaded successfully. All at once the weapon was ripped from her hands, hurtling across the room and disappearing into the billowing gas. Shouts from Sippen and Cedric announced that theirs had met the same fate.

Hester had lived her life trusting instincts, making decisions based less on right or wrong and more to do with her own survival. These same impulses screamed warning in this moment, and she screamed, "Duck!"

Three shots rang out just as she hit the floor. A strong blast from Caroline slammed the Falconers against the far wall and forced their aim high. Another gust pushed the smoke out the door, revealing that Sippen was spared as well. Cedric lay face down, pointed toward the door. He stirred. As she scrambled to her feet, Hester paused. The two specters, killed when they first entered, had already begun to reanimate.

Hester gripped the hilt of the Berserker Blade and ripped it free of her bodice, channeling the fury that flowed in her veins. She raged against the two Falconers on the floor, slashing and stabbing as she roared like a banshee set free on the tundra. In her tirade, she felt constricted by the strap on her satchel, stretched tight against her chest and preventing her from using full range of motion. With frustrated anger she tore it off and tossed it on the ground, straddling one of the specters and barely noticing the items that spilled out. She sliced and hacked at the men, not stopping until there was nothing left to reanimate.

Her fury seemed to confound the others, who stared with mixed awe and fear as she ensured the feathered specters were put down. Finished but not satisfied, she hastily scooped the spilled contents from the ground, shoving them into the satchel and replacing it over her head. Dripping with blood, she turned to Caroline and roared, "If you're going to do something girl, do it now!"

The Dreamer nodded and went to work, dueling the three Falconers with tinsel thin wisps of air that cracked the air like whips. Hester had to admit that the girl was amazing, quick and agile with precise strikes that made her foes appear clumsy in contrast. While she kept the three men busy, Hester sheathed her blade and drew one of Sippen's pistols from his belt, firing into one of the feathered hoods. The man fell immediately, dropping the grapeshot gun which she quickly scooped into her arms as she ran past.

The commotion behind her did not cease as she sprinted down the stairs into the actual Rookery. *How many did she say? Two Falconers and Jaguars each?* She no longer cared about the odds as she pushed forward. The next door was simple, with only a knob for access. It was unlocked and turned easily. She readied two grenades and rolled the flint against the striking stone, lighting them as she counted down.

Three. Braen's Hussy had better be here, she thought. *Two. I can't make it messy, or the others will know. One.* She pulled the door open and tossed in the round objects, slamming it shut and taking cover behind the wall. The two explosions were simultaneous and blew the door inward. She rounded the corner with her gun trained forward, ready for the nearest threat, and found that two Jaguars had received the direct impact from the shrapnel. Both lay bleeding on the ground.

She fanned the barrel left and then right, scanning the room for the remaining creatures. A flapping of wings stirred the air and she whirled to see two falcons speeding toward her. She pulled the trigger and dropped them both, leaving them writhing on the floor. Now she was certain the room was empty and proceeded with caution. She spied another door and hurried toward it, reaching her hand into the satchel but finding no more grenades. She had plenty of shells for the gun, however, and some curious round objects she did not have time to inspect. She drew out several shells and reloaded, holding one more at the ready.

She twisted the knob and pulled it open slowly, peering around the opening. *Surely the Falconers wait inside,* she thought. But the only life she found lay atop hundreds of stone slabs. *These are the ones they described,* she realized, *those who Skander seeks.* She fought down a sudden urge to kill them all while they slept, just to keep them from her husband's clutches. *No,* she reasoned, *I will kill only the one.*

The sounds of battle in the upper room had ceased. She was quickly running out of time and ran from table to table, searching the faces for that of Eusari. The tubes that ran from their bodies were translucent, flexible and graceful. These ran from the nose, the mouth, the skin, and the more sensitive areas, bringing fluids in and taking them out to some unknown location. When she finally spied the trollop who had stolen her Braen, she raced to the woman's side. She, like the others, slumbered soundly while the tubing transformed her lifeforce into those miraculous beads Delilah had described.

She stared at the naked body of Eusari, perfectly formed but hideously scarred from the tips of her fingers to several inches above her wrists. *What monstrosity could drive a woman to do that to her own body?* She flinched as she considered the scars marring her own body. With a choked sob she answered, *The same monstrosity who would do that to another living being.*

Eusari slept on her back, with rounded belly and swollen breasts exposed to the air. Hester placed a gentle hand atop her naval, feeling for movement of the child within. *Braen's child,* she thought, *his true legacy.* She placed her other hand on her own belly, feeling Skander's abomination growing within. *I'm not a fool,* she assured herself. *He will accept my child. Braen loves everyone, even Skander, despite the evil residing within. Of course he will raise his brother's child as his own.*

She drew the Berserker Blade from her bodice and held it over Eusari's breast with the tip slightly dimpling the flesh. She hesitated, suddenly aware that what she was about to do was murder. *I will do anything to survive this world,* she reminded herself, *just as I did when I learned of Skander's plans to kill Krist Braston. Survival is the key to living,* she thought. Hester raised her free hand above the one holding the knife and closed her eyes. *This will be easy,* she hoped, *all I have to do is press.*

Her thoughts quickly returned to Cedric, Sippen, and the girl, but especially of Cedric wounded and lying on the floor. His wounds had appeared superficial, so they would arrive any moment. She must make this death appear natural. She returned the blade to its sheath and placed a trembling hand over the woman's mouth and nose, clamping it tightly and denying her breath.

"We're actually very much alike," she whispered into the woman's ear, "made strong by the actions of the men who've scorned us."

She stared down at the child in Eusari's womb and thought, *No, that's not true at all, is it? We think that hatred strengthens our resolve, but it doesn't.* Her hand began to tremble as she realized, *a woman's strength is her ability to love, even as she is surrounded by the brash brutality of men.* Her hands were still red from the blood of the Falconers, and it reminded her of the anger that had flooded through her weapon.

Sober truth suddenly overcame the northern queen, and she finally understood her purpose. *Anyone, man or woman, can take life, but only a woman can gift life,* she realized. *That is our true strength, isn't it? Our power resides not in how we survive, but how we teach those around us to live. We are the balance of life.* She removed her hands from the mouth of Braen's true love, and placed them instead on the life growing inside of her own womb. *I have nothing to offer this child,* she realized, *neither as a mother nor as a teacher. All that I know is how to survive, not to live.* A sob rose in her throat and she backed away. *I don't even know how to love, but she does.*

"Thank you for not killing the vessel," a deep and emotionless voice resounded from across the room.

Her eyes shot toward the source and spied two Falconers walking casually toward her. "It would have been a shame to have lost the emotant within her womb. That one," the specter said, pointing at Eusari, "is as powerful as the child you will bear to us."

At first Hester didn't understand, but then realization took over. "That's why it was so easy to get inside," she said. "You knew that you would draw both of Braen's children together."

Both of the Falconers laughed, and Hester's skin crawled at the chilling sound. "Come now, you may drop the charade with us. We know you carry Skander's child and not Braen's."

"How do you know that?"

"Because" the voice rumbled, suddenly different in pitch than when he spoke before, "I am Marcus Esterling, King of Eston. Your husband and his brother are a keen interest of mine," he said.

"What is it you want? You have her so let me go." She retrieved the grapeshot gun from the floor and raised it.

"What I need is already foretold," the voice of Marcus replied, "and will have them eventually. What I want is control over all four children who challenge my rule."

"All four? There are only two..." but Hester trailed off, the suddenness of understanding sending shockwaves through her mind. "The Pescari woman and Esterling's bride," she realized. "You'll have all four elements at your disposal." She trained the gun at the chest of the taller specter, and stood defiantly. "I won't let you do that," she said.

"Come now, Lady Hester, you've never fought for anyone else but yourself. Why start now to pretend you care about Skander's child in your womb," he chuckled and then added, "much less all of Andalon?"

"The child is Braen's," she protested.

"Ah," he said with amusement, "the rumor spread by a desperate queen hellbent on keeping her throne. No, we know whose child that is, even if the world doesn't."

"I'll never allow the world to believe otherwise," she insisted, "no matter the cost."

"Oh, Queen Hester, the price is not yours to set. Would you die to keep that secret?" The eerie specter casually reached a hand into a pouch and drew two perfectly round beads as black as night. He tossed these into his mouth and swallowed.

Of course, she thought, *Delilah told me of these. Those beads are the source of their power.*

The Falconer raised his arm and the gun abruptly lurched forward, directly into his outstretched and waiting hand. He held it curiously, staring at the construction. While he was distracted, she felt around in her own satchel and found a handful of pearls, scooped up when she had gathered her satchel. She didn't bother to count as she shoved these into her own mouth, swallowing them dry and nearly choking as she did. The beast before her did not notice.

"I'm impressed," he said with a sincerity in his voice as he inspected the hilt. "I hope your husband brings more of these contraptions to Eston."

The world changed rapidly around Hester, tilting and listing as she felt her body become one with the air around her. Beyond and through the door she could see Sippen and Caroline running fast toward the room where she stood off with the Falconers. Krill limped slowly along after them, obviously injured. She had to hurry.

She focused on the air particles around her, then understood what she had to do. As a girl in Fjorik she had learned to spin wool into thread – the only pastime in which she was allowed to mingle with the other daughters of the nobles. She quickly realized that spinning air was no different, and she braided a tight thread just around the stock of the grapeshot gun.

The Falconer as Marcus Esterling was still admiring the instrument of war, and commented. "I had heard that the northern engineer was cunning, but this," he said as he peered into the barrel, "is magnificent."

With a tug of her finger the thread tightened, and the trigger pulled. The concussion of the blast rocked the room as the face of the Falconer exploded against the ceiling.

Sounds in the doorway announced that the others had arrived, and Hester watched with amazement as Caroline engaged the second specter. While they dueled, she knelt and retrieved the gun where it lay on the ground. She loaded another shell and trained it on the remaining foe. Without hesitation she dispatched him, as well.

"There she is," she directed Sippen and pointed toward Eusari. "Do what you need to do to wake her."

He wasted no time and he and the others went to work, examining the tubes and working out the safest way to rouse her sleeping form. While they fussed over Braen's true love, Hester stepped away to sulk in the corner of the room, with images of events yet to come flashing before her eyes. *These are possibilities,* she realized, *things that may occur if certain key choices are made.* Hester became one with the future in that moment, suddenly aware of what she must and must not do to interfere. She absently stroked the hilt of the Berserker Blade, tucked safely within her bodice, and finally decided to put others before herself. *I must make the correct choice when the time comes.*

Eusari fought against the confusion, straining her eyes to focus first on Sippen, then Krill. *Of course those fools would come,* she thought with warm appreciation, *they deserve all the love that Braen gave them.* The fact that Caroline had come did not surprise her either. Little could have kept the girl away from saving her captain, and Eusari smiled sleepily at the teen and nodded approval of her rescue. The sight of Hester confused her greatly.

The queen brooded in the corner of the Rookery. The first oddity Eusari noticed was the woman wore breeches. *Probably the first time in her life,* she realized. The woman held a rifle in her hands, which was surprising as well. *No, not a rifle. The barrel is bored larger and is much shorter.* Whatever the weapon was, Hester held it like she had taken part in the raid.

With a groan she allowed the boys to lift her from the table and she swung her feet onto the ground. Only then did she realize her state of undress, and shyly looked toward Caroline for help. The girl reached into a satchel and drew out a simple linen tunic and a pair of men's breeches.

"It's all I could find at the workshop," she explained, "big enough to cover your belly."

"I'm sure it will do fine until we find my leathers," Eusari said with a thankful smile, pulling them on. She noticed that both men had turned away, affording what little privacy they could under the circumstances.

Krill winced with pain as he turned, his back covered with blood. With concern for her friend, she asked, "Are you okay?"

"No, dearie," he said with a mournful face. "I was shot during the fight to save you. My wounds be nearly fatal, and can only be cured by the kiss of a maiden fair."

"Buh… Bullshit," Sippen declared. "You were shuh… shot in the ass and will be fuh… fine!"

Eusari managed a chuckle for her friends as she slipped the tunic over her head. She scanned the room, suddenly very aware that she had not been the only naked figure in the room. The vast hall contained several hundred men, women, and children of various ages.

As if reading her mind, Hester said, "Here it is." She gestured around the room at the sleeping forms.

Puzzled by the queen's meaning, Eusari asked, "Here what is?"

"Yours and Braen's army against Skander." Something obviously weighed heavy on the northern woman's mind as she spoke, and it found its way into her words as she added, "Together you two can conquer Eston and rule the two kingdoms as one. With a force like this you'll be unstoppable."

"Braen is dead, Hester. You know that as well as I."

Caroline shook her head. "No. He's somehow restored and on his way here."

Eusari suddenly felt woozy. "Here? How? When?" She looked to the girl for confirmation and she nodded with a smile.

Hester's words suddenly made sense and she looked at the sleeping forms, considering the possibilities. The myriad of slabs surely contained an army of emotants, but, unlike Hester, she could only see them as men, women, and children. She walked toward one of the tables and gazed upon an old lady with skin deeply etched with ancient lines and her hair greyer than the ocean under fog. What she noticed most was the lack of certain lines around the eyes and the mouth.

With a gasp she exclaimed, "These people have spent their entire lives in this room. They've never smiled nor frowned," she told the others. "They'll not remember love nor loss when they awaken, much less know if what we teach them is reality." She ran a finger along the woman's arm, stopping to squeeze a wrinkled hand. "If we turned them into our army then we're no better than Skander."

"Aye," a voice from the doorway gently agreed. "So we mustn't at any cost."

She recognized the soft rumble of his northern accent and turned with excitement, joy briefly overcoming the sadness she felt for the lives in the room. He had changed his appearance since the last time she had seen him, having shaved his beard and trimmed his flowing locks of hair, but she recognized him immediately. Standing in the doorway was the man she loved.

She immediately noticed the others in his party. Alec Pogue was there, and so was that odd girl Marita. As usual she was grinning at some private silliness that existed only in her own mind. She also recognized Cuyler, Sebastian and Amash. The others she did not know. Except for a shy face peering out from behind Braen's legs. *Charleigh,* she remembered, the sweet child from The Cove. *There's a story behind her appearance for sure.* She smiled warmly and the child waved.

"We won't make them our army, Hester." Braen never took his eyes from Eusari as he spoke to the queen in the corner of the room. "We've already done wrong by the children in our charge, and turning the tide of damage we've caused will be difficult." He was such a beautiful sight, standing in the doorway and speaking to the room and directly to her heart. "Difficult," he repeated, "but not impossible. We're disbanding the Dreamers and sending them off to safety. The rest of this war is no longer theirs. I agree that they should form an academy for future generations."

Cuyler, Caroline, and Sebastian each protested, but Eusari held up a hand for silence. "He's right," she said. "I want you to take them somewhere safe. Teach and train them to use their powers in constructive ways, and not only to fight. I don't want to lose them like we've lost all the others."

Caroline asked, "Where do we go?"

"We can take you to Eskera," Alec Pogue suggested. "Marita and I will pass through there on our way home."

The girl, upon hearing his words, spun on her heels. "You mean we won't be helping Braen fight?"

He shot a glance at Braen, briefly exchanging some dark knowledge of events to come, then said, "No, dearie. We need to return to Mattie and the girls."

"Please take Charleigh with you," Braen asked of his friend. She is in need of the stability you and Mattie alone can offer."

"Of course," the duke replied, smiling down at the child. "What's one more girl child in the household?"

Marita, upon hearing this, slapped her adopted father on the back and said, "At least you have me to pirate with!"

Braen turned to Eusari and opened his arms, saying, "Please forgive me, my love. I did not knowingly lie with her, and never would have intended to do so."

Eusari looked toward the northern queen, still slumped in the corner and staring off into nothingness. In a timid voice she asked, "Is that so, Hester?"

The woman did not turn when she dryly responded, "It is. I drugged and took advantage, so don't blame him for my deceit. It's not Braen's fault he sired this child upon me. He most likely doesn't even remember the act," she lied.

Eusari could no longer contain the excitement in her heart. She ran, wrapping him tightly and crying tears of joy into his chest. He held her close, arms reaching around hers to gently but firmly embrace his love.

In a soft voice he asked, "Eusari, why didn't you tell me about the baby?"

"How did you find out?" She looked at the Dreamers and Amash, then thought, *Of course, they would have told him.*

Braen followed her eyes and gently corrected her thoughts. "No, Eusari. They didn't tell me. I know because I've seen the future."

Her eyes shot back to meet his. "How," she asked, "did you see the future?"

"I don't know, exactly," he said, "but I know what I have to do if our son is to survive."

She recognized the sadness behind his eyes. "What *you* have to do? This isn't something you can do alone, Braen."

Sippen started to speak but Braston cut him off. "No. You've both preached to me many times about my bearing the load for everyone else. But my vision was clear, and I must do this alone, but I do need your help if I'm to succeed."

"Anything," she said. "What must I do?"

Hester answered before he could respond. "He lost his power when the Kraken revived him, and you must kill him and do it yourself if they're to be restored."

Braen nodded. "I don't know how she knows, but she's right. That's the only scenario that plays out well for Andalon." He pointed at the Dreamers. "They have greater work they must finish and so do you, separately. But I must go ahead alone and face my brother."

Yurik protested. "Nuh... not alone, Bruh... Braen."

"No, you won't join me, Sippen. You must go away with Eusari."

Tears filled Eusari's eyes as she gripped her lover tighter. "No," she said, "there must be another way. You saw it wrong and I won't do it."

"You must do it," he insisted. "Once my powers return, I can defeat Nevra and Shol both."

"I won't do it," she protested, "and I won't allow anyone else."

"There isn't anyone else, and, even if there was, it would still have to be you who does the deed." A single tear ran down her cheek as he added, "Both of the deeds. But we need to hurry, Skander is already on his way to Eston."

"Come on," she said. "It'll take a day or two for Cuyler and Caroline to do what is needed here, so the rest of us should load *She Wolf* and get going." Everyone in Braen's party stared back as if there were more grave news that no one wanted to tell. She asked, "What?"

Braen broke it gently. "*She Wolf* wasn't in the harbor, Eusari."

She choked back both anger and grief when she realized how deep Jacque's treachery ran. When she spoke it was with a chill calm to her voice. "Then we'll load whatever ship brought you."

"We have another problem," Amash said to the others, "that we must deal with before we go anywhere."

Eusari turned slowly and asked, "What problem is that, Amash?"

"Robert Esterling is dead, and so is his pregnant wife, although she's controlled by Lord Campton Shol."

"Bring me to his body and I'll revive both him and our hopes for the rebellion." She watched as the others once more exchanged glances. "What now?"

"We've rendered his body to the sea," replied Amash with regret in his voice.

"After burning it atop a Fjorik funeral pyre," added Braen.

"Where is his wife, Sarai? Does the baby still live within her womb?"

"Yes," Amash confirmed. "The baby still lives within my sister. She's currently chained in the brig of our ship."

"Then we have to keep her alive until she delivers," Eusari decided. "Keep her locked in the hold and pray Shol can't feel her presence when we near Eston. No more innocents need to die today, and his offspring deserves to live. Andalon deserves an Esterling on the throne."

The others exchanged more glances, this time focused on Amash.

Eusari rolled her eyes and sighed. "What else haven't you told me?"

Braen slapped Amash across the back and proclaimed, "Our bookish friend here is the *actual* heir of Charles Esterling."

"Now that," she said with an eyebrow raised, "I did not expect."

Braen scanned the room, narrowing his eyes. Noticing a missing member of their party he asked, "Where's Gelert?"

Eusari fell into his arms and wept.

Chapter Fifty

The moon hid from view. Tucked behind clouds and fed up with Andalon's chaos, she refused to shine light upon Eston, the city about to fall. Thousands of fires dotted the walls, lighting the night and flickering atop ramparts like fireflies dancing in the darkness. Some moved back and forth, patrolling the water side for signs of invasion and keeping watch while the city slept. Others shone on the fallen western bridge, rubble moved aside, beaming light on the channel reopened to shipping traffic. Despite its clearing, the approach was still impenetrable.

Malfeasance and the northern armada held fast, raising sails and waiting patiently for their king's next move. The madman stood alone on the forecastle; his dark face far more sinister after leaving Norton. A more terrifying visage no boy could ever imagine, the sight inducing fear unmatched by any bogeyman. Hair had fallen out in clumps and only a few strands clung to the areas above his ears. His sneer revealed brown teeth either rotting from his head or cracked in half, and his tongue bled as it rubbed his jagged jaw, exposed by receding gums.

"Cowards," Skander muttered. "They're all cowards hiding in their hole and hoping I'll pass them by," he said into the air beside him, "but I won't."

No sire, Artur answered, *you won't. You'll charge in and kill your entire force because you've lost your mind.*

"I have not! Mind your tongue or I'll rip it out," the king snapped. He paused, suddenly aware of oozing infection from his cheek. As it tickled the corner of his mouth, he licked his lips, wetting them and tasting the sweet decay of his body. "Their ships will have to exit one by one to face us, so we approach unchallenged. All we have to do is get over that wall."

Their guns will tear our ships apart before we're close enough for artillery. You've lost before the battle even began. Your Krakens have perished, sacrificed to take a city you didn't need. You're a failure, my liege.

"Silence!" He screamed at the shadows around him, focused intently on his mutinous first mate. "You underestimate my power, Artur!"

He fingered his ear, pulling away a clump of reddish-brown flesh that he flicked onto the deck. He turned to face a cadre of Saber Cats, and his sneer turned into a smile when he looked upon the ten perfectly carved faces awaiting his orders. Some still dripped from the ministrations of his blade.

"I need to get through those walls," he said as he pointed toward the city. "Ready your brothers and sisters for the onslaught." They nodded silently then closed their eyes to converse with the others. Each eyelid bore his sigil as they fluttered in time with their brief trance.

He returned his attention to the city just in time to view a signal flare fired into the air. *Curious,* he thought. *Who would they signal except a fleet?* He quickly scanned the massive lake surrounding his own. His ships were alone, unopposed. The attack sprang from thin air, the sound of roaring cannons announcing the enemy's whereabouts.

Cloaked in the harbor by Falconers, he had unknowingly sailed into range of their guns. The first shots tore his fleet like strewn matches, casting splinters into the neighboring vessels. The veil of deception did not linger long after the initial volley, as his white-clad children quickly unraveled the weave of air like a curtain ripped from its rod. Thankfully the armor lining many of the hulls of provided protection. He roared with anger and quickly ordered the counter attack, returning fire with superior guns. His anger turned to laughter as he cackled his delight with each direct hit.

In that moment of madness, Lake Norton became one with the northern king, thrashing about and carving the ships with pounding waves. Heavy warships were easily tossed hundreds of feet into the air. The scene exuded chaos, all except for the peaceful tranquility that surrounded his own vessels. These drifted with currents that aided the sighting of their guns, lining up shots that split hulls and ruptured powder magazines. The destruction and confused seas matched well the disrupted mind of Skander Braston.

Marcus Esterling stood atop the highest point of the western defenses, suckling the raw power of the beads nestled between cheek and gum. He ignored the dripping of drool down his chin, staining his regal robes with a mixture of black and white. The color of his eyes was gone, replaced by the empty void of oversized pupils. The whites had turned a solid grey.

The flashes from cannons strobed against his senses, altering the euphoric rush and granting him clarity of thought. He stared down at the pathways of future that no longer depended on chance. He deciphered these true lines of possibility and realized the sea battle would be over soon. His diversion had ended sooner than he'd hoped, but the real battle was about to begin.

He drew from his pouch an object of curiosity, taken from the strange Falconers with the red and orange plumed hoods. Other than color, it resembled the other beads, perfectly rounded and just as firm, but feeling different in his hand. The power within frightened the king and he yearned to taste the mystery of fire hidden within the bright redness. He carefully tucked it away with the others, caution of knowledge warning the mixture could end his life.

The soldiers on the wall were his to command, not by signal or military order, but through the connection he felt with each. *Clear the section above the rocks,* he sent through their bond. They complied and parted, just as he had seen in his vision of things to come. They moved to safety just as explosive rounds blew the section to rubble. *Return fire.* Six defensive batteries rang simultaneously, obliterating the ship with coordinated fire. Marcus laughed, spittle flying into the night.

Skander staggered from the blast, the ship directly to his starboard exploding into splinters and fire. He roared into the sky, pulling water from the lake high into the clouds above and whipping them into frenzied storm. They rained not water, but ice the size of cannonballs upon the city, followed by bolts of lightning. Soon random fires erupted throughout every sector, igniting everything that could burn.

Marcus let these distract him from the walls, as he snuffed each flame with pockets devoid of air. He had mostly succeeded when the sound of roaring water compelled him to turn once more. The contents of Lake Norton crashed against the ramparts, washing his army over the side and sweeping them into the streams and channels that were once city streets. He cursed as his footing slipped, sending him staggering and clutching his precious satchel as his momentum plunged him over the side.

Candlelight flickered as the wick neared the last of the wax, softly illuminating the people huddled around the tavern's hearth. No fire raged within – Samani Kernigan wouldn't allow it. He claimed that the extra light would draw soldiers when the looting began. It didn't matter which army won, he had warned, there would be no way to escape the violence unless Braen Braston fulfilled the prophecy.

Gus and his family had not protested, they were heartened by the sudden arrival of Society agents. "When the messages stopped," he explained, "I'd feared you been compromised. Or worse," he added, "had perished during the battle for The Cove."

"Yet here I am, walking and breathing and seeking out your help, old friend. Pearl has passed on and we," he indicated Delilah and Gretchen, "are all the only remaining members of our network except for you."

"So the Destroyer is coming? It's happening now?"

"Yes, my friend, the age of the Destroyer is upon us. We will witness the fulfillment of many prophecies tonight, and hopefully the dawn of a new age, one which cannot be foretold."

"What of our home? What about Astia? The Council will send another invasion force to cleanse Andalon, even if you prevail."

"I've already taken care of that. As of tonight Artema Horn leads the Council and the oracles are no more."

Gus marveled at the deeper meaning behind the words. "The Collective is broken? The people of Astia are finally free?"

"Their cages are not yet broken, especially those that exist in their minds. But yes, Artema will usher in the new system as agreed."

"You can trust him in this? His ambition is generally ruled by selfish arrogance."

Samani smiled reassuringly. "I have no doubt that he will adhere to the plan. His passion to do so will compel his actions no matter what temptation works against his allegiance to the new system."

"Then you've succeeded."

"Not yet," Kernigan warned. "There is still much to do here, and I will not return to Astia until I see it through. Foremost is the favor I must ask of you."

"Anything!"

Samani pointed to Gus' daughter, a young woman in her late teens slumbering peacefully on a pallet. "How faithful is Colette to our cause? Did you train her in the way of the bead?"

"She's never demonstrated sensitivity," the tavernkeeper lamented, "so I gave up that endeavor. But I taught her well the goals of the Society. She'll serve the rebellion however you need."

"The bead tells me that she lost a child recently. Has she run dry?"

Gus flinched. "No. She's been wet nursing for a merchant's wife in the upper sector. She's adequate supply."

"Good..." Samani trailed off, staring into the waning light of the candle. "She will be approached in the morning by a man, small in stature but large in fortitude. You will know him by his stutter. You must convince her to go with him, for a wet nurse will be needed before this night ends. She will journey far but will serve as eyes and ears for the Society, even if she has no power to control any of the beads."

"She is my daughter, Samani. Will I ever see her again?"

"Perhaps, in a decade or two, she may find her way back to Eston. Until then rest assured, that if she chooses to go, she will prove instrumental to the new system."

"So she does have a choice?"

Samani smiled. "Do any of us, really?" Loud noises outside caused both men to jump, and Kernigan and the two women stood. He pointed to the door. "You'd better place sandbags in front of that door as soon as we depart. The flooding will be awful."

Gretchen tricked the locking mechanism and the trio stepped outside. In the west the sky glowed orange, signifying the battle raged. "Come," Samani urged, pointing at the palace looming above. "Let's get to higher ground."

Skander surged with the wave as it crashed into the wall, sending shockwaves of delight through his quivering muscles. The rippling cascade washed thousands of soldiers into the streets below, creating currents of screams as they flooded through the city and toward the sewer system underneath. Somewhere in that torrent he knew he'd find the boy king of Eston.

The chill of the air intensified as the lake slowly refilled, most of the water already backwashing under the western bridge. This froze and slowly climbed the wall, building a gradual incline of jagged ice upon which his army would march. "Send the kill squads to find and put down the survivors," he ordered his men. "Leave no one alive in this city." He gave the signal and they charged, a second wave of evil pouring over the defenses and into the streets below.

The king of Fjorik wiped sweat from his face, now feverish despite the freezing temperatures under his gale force storm. His hand came away smeared with blood. He coughed violently then. Spitting darkness onto the deck of *Malfeasance* as he ran her against the ice.

"Come," he told the white robes gathered behind him. "Let us finish our work."

"You've lost your mind," one of them cried. "There'll be nothing to rule over when you're finished!"

Skander whirled, stepping forward and removing the hood of Stefan Nevra. His eyes followed the perfectly scored grooves that snaked over the man's skin, oozing pus and reeking of the infection within. He leaned in and breathed deeply to take in the aroma of fear. *This was the source of the voice,* he knew, *but I have many voices much more powerful than his.* He yanked hard against a chain affixed around the pitiful man's neck, dragging him forward as he stepped over the side and onto the ice.

His army was already hard at work when he topped the rampart, defiling bodies and dismembering the living they uncovered. He scanned the faces, looking for the boy king.

You won't have your fun, Skander, his father's voice scorned, *in your haste you washed him into the sewer.*

Arrows flew toward him, fired by a small group of Estonian archers gathered behind a thicket of rose bushes. His escort of Saber Cats threw up a current of air that cast the projectiles aside and he roared laughter at the futile attempt. They ran like cowards around the corner of a stone building and a kill squad chased after.

This battle is messy, his father's voice warned. *You've committed to a street by street incursion that will bog down your attack.*

"Shut up," he growled, causing Nevra to whimper. Skander gave the chain a hard yank and the pox-faced man stumbled, skinning his knees on the cobblestone street. "I must find Esterling and end this once and for all."

He rounded the corner, expecting to find a pile of slain archers, but instead found his own men lying dead in the thicket. *Father was right,* he realized, *this will take all night if not longer.*

Marcus Esterling watched the northern king's face closely, twisted in anger when he discovered the fallen squad. Having been washed far away by the flood waters, he now sat upon higher ground, a stairwell leading into the merchant quarter above. With eyes tightly closed and mouth hanging open, he watched through the roses as Skander approached the bodies. The blooms turned in unison as they focused on his enemy, but the crazed northerner was too consumed with rage to notice. Slowly the vines reached toward him, grasping at his ankles and those of a white robed old woman standing beside her king.

Skander leaned in close as he searched the bodies of his fallen troops. *There are no arrows, no felling wounds which I can see, only scratches from the thicket.* He stepped into the bushes and flipped one over with his boot, again failing to find any cause of death. He felt the reaching tendrils before he saw them. He sprang to safety just in time as several vines coiled where he had stood.

The Saber Cat standing to his left was not as lucky. The rose thicket reached out and pulled her inside the brambles. She kicked wildly as the branches wrapped around her throat and silenced her screams. The others in Skander's squad recoiled from fright, having never imagined such an enemy.

"Inform the others," Skander advised his children, "we fight against the entire city tonight, and our enemy hides in every shadow." He abruptly whirled on Nevra and yanked hard, with so much force that the skinny man fell to his knees. "Look at me," he commanded the voice made flesh.

Nevra refused, sniveling and scraping nails against the rough ground as he tried to scramble away. "Why won't you obey me," he cried to the ground, "when I need you most?" He placed both palms against the cobblestones as if pouring his entire lifeforce into the soil beneath.

Skander lifted the chain, raising the man's chin and forcing him to look upon superiority. "Open your eyes, voice. Open them and look upon your master."

He did, slowly, with tears streaming down his cheeks and with sobs choking his shallow breaths.

"You will raise these soldiers to once again follow my command. Raise them and bring them back into my fold."

Nevra nodded and complied, pouring lifeforce into the tangled bodies while Skander cut away the vines. The northern king paused, staring at the weapon in his hands. *This was hers,* he thought, *the axe she tried to use on me. It was meant to cut flesh, but now I use it as a tool to chop vines.* He ripped the rest away with his bare hands as the fallen soldiers stirred.

Across the city Marcus chittered with glee, watching the bodies rise from the bushes. His mouth, full of as many beads as he could cram, sprayed spittle as he proclaimed, "I did not expect you shared my power, Northman." He did not wipe the drool as he added, "Tonight shall be more fun than I had imagined." He stood, running up the stairwell to the top of the span, leaning far over the rail so that he could view the entire city from a single perch. With arms raised above his head he spun around, dancing in the night as the dead rose to join his ranks.

"Father," one of the Saber Cats urged, pointing to a low area in the street. Atop a sewer grate dozens of Estonian soldiers had piled, washed by the current and covered in muck by the floodwaters.

"Yes," Skander said of the dead. "We'll raise them as well."

"No, Father," his child insisted. "They rise already."

The king stared at the pile with anticipation, waiting and watching as their limbs animated. He raised his axe high and roared, charging the foe before they could regain their footing. His children followed, lashing and binding those who threatened their king and holding them for him to silence. As soon as they fell, they rose again.

"We must find his Jaguars," Nevra explained. "They do his bidding throughout the city as do the Falconers."

"Rein in the squads," he ordered his children. "We must organize the search." Movement caught the king's attention and he turned, just as several rose blossoms focused on his position. "Is this how you view me, king child? You hide like a coward and watch through the bushes?" His axe swung through the air, severing buds from stem. Turning, he roared at the risen dead and charged them once more.

Chapter Fifty-One

Braen awoke to the gentle rocking of nighttime waves. Eusari lay nestled in his arm, quite content to sleep off the incident in the Rookery. They had agreed to one more night together before he would journey to meet his fate. Her body pressed firmly against his, their child showing as a rounded bulge of her belly tucked sweetly between them. He looked longingly upon that growing life, regretting that he would never live to see their son grow into adolescence or beyond. But the rules of natural restoration were clear, and there was only one option with which he could defeat Skander and Nevra once and for all.

She's so beautiful, he thought, *inside and out.* That she had forgiven and embraced him without hesitation filled his heart with joy, erasing any doubts he previously held about her love. *I should have told her immediately that I lived, saving her the pain and suffering endured at the hands of the Falconers. She could have joined me in the Southern Continent, and would have.* But that was before he learned the truth the future held. Without his death, the world would descend into chaos. Both continents would face extinction, and all hope for the future of his children would end with his and Eusari's selfishness. *No,* he thought, *this must be done.*

He slid his arm from under her sleeping head. *Gods above,* he prayed, *instead of the heavenly banquet, couldn't you damn me to an eternity of this?* He stood for a moment, soaking in her naked beauty and knowing in his heart that this would be the last peaceful visage he would look upon. *This is truly the calm before the storm,* he thought. Without awakening his love, he dressed and slipped from the stateroom.

The city of Eston loomed up river, an imposing city despite the fallen western bridge. He had never seen neither the walls nor the bridges, and yearned to finally lay eyes on the structure that defeated both his father and Fjorik way of life. They were magnificent, nearly as much as the storm that raged over the city. Braen winced at the sight of his brother's sigil written with lightning against the clouds.

"Skuh... Skander already uh... attacked," Sippen said. "Thuh... battle is in the struh... streets."

Braen's eyes followed his friend's finger and focused on the hundreds of shattered Imperial ships littering the lake. Each told the tale of an epic sea battle lost, and warned of carnage yet to come. "How did he get beyond the walls?"

Sippen pointed to a dripping iceberg nestled against the westernmost ramparts, now crumbled. *Malfeasance* and the rest of Skander's armada ran aground just below the massive ice bridge. "He wuh... walked uh... over instead of thuh... through."

"The time has come. I must wake Eusari and get this part over with," he said to his friend.

"Uh... I'll miss you," Sippen stammered. "I uh... already went through hell when I luh... lost you last time."

Braen placed a brotherly hand on his friend's shoulder and smiled. "I'll miss you too, but I'll rest knowing you'll be watching over my boys."

"Buh... boys?"

Braston nodded. "Yes, two strapping lads." His face grew serious. "Promise you'll take them far away. Get them and Eusari to the mountains as far west as you can travel. Whatever happens, and whoever claims this throne, there will be jealousy over my boys and any ambitions they imagine. They'll be targets long after they're born, Sippen." He stood for a moment, watching the city over the rails, then solemnly departed to wake his love and beg death by her hand.

Eusari woke to a gentle kiss, not something she's used to, and pulled a knife from under her pillow.

"Careful," Braen said with a laugh, "I need you to kill me cleanly," he added.

Suddenly remembering where she was and what they had to do sobered her quickly. She dropped the knife like it was hot. "Don't remind me," she said, wrapping her arms and holding him tight.

"It must be done, and it must be now." He retrieved the blade and offered it. "Skander is in the city and the fight has begun. If I leave now, I can arrive in time."

Her eyes narrowed, "In time for what? To galivant off and sacrifice your life for all of us? That's such a Braen thing to do! I swear," she said, "you're the most selfish *selfless* person I know."

"Aye," he agreed, "it's my biggest fault." He kissed her gently then pulled away to gaze once more into her green eyes. "But I love you, and I want that baby to grow healthy and strong. I've seen the future," he reminded, "and if we don't do this then my children become the seeds to another period of Astian control. Either I regain my powers or it's all over for everyone on this continent."

Eusari wanted to argue. She yearned to turn the ship around and flee south, but she believed in him. The theory about regaining his powers made sense, despite that instincts stayed her hand the last time. "I just wish I didn't have to. You'll never be the same."

"No," he agreed, "but I'll always love you. At least you'll know that."

The ship suddenly lurched in the water as if it had struck a rock. Their eyes widened with alarm. They both leapt to their feet and she hurriedly pulled on her clothing while he darted out the door. A moment later she emerged topside, expecting to find a flurry of activity, but instead found a quiet mutiny.

Braen faced off against his friends. Each was geared for battle, armed to the gills with an assortment of Sippen's gadgets, swords, and cutlasses. Even the girl Marita stood topside, twirling her blades as if she led a parade.

The northerner roared, "What's this about?"

Cedric spoke first. "We won't let you do it, mate. We're with you till the end."

"Krill, I understand your loyalty, but you have a bigger mission. You need to look after the children." He turned to Horslei and Pogue. "You're my friends but I can't have you dying in this battle. It's certain death!"

"I'll protect them," said Marita as she tossed one of her swords in the air, catching it behind her back. "That's my job. I look after my dukey-daddy and his sea-sick friend." They all ignored her so she strode away to watch the city.

"I won't allow it," Braen said, "there will be hundreds of Falconer's as well as Skander and his goons."

"Well," offered Eusari hopefully as she buckled on her holster, reaching out to take a pistol from Sippen, "none of us takes orders from you."

"This is mutiny," Braen protested, "from my friends nonetheless!"

"It's not mutiny if you're not the captain," Eusari decided. "We're all going, whether you like it or not."

Braen felt the world spin around him. *She won't do it. She must but she won't.* "Eusari, the only way this works is if you flee west with the children. Take Hester and go. Get the boys to safety. I'm fine from here."

A voice from the lee deck turned every head. "No," Hester protested. She still wore the breeches and tunic from the Rookery raid, and wildly unkempt hair gave her an exhausted appearance. "We all have interest in this fight," she said, pointing to the city. "Skander has wronged all of us, not just you. Eusari and I deserve a chance to participate in his death."

"She's right," Eusari placed a hand on Braen's chest. "I once lived my life fueled by revenge against Skander, until you taught that love and compassion are more important than revenge. I lived with constant worry over death, both in wielding and avoiding it." She touched her round belly. "But you also taught me life brings the opposite of worry, both when sparing or creating a soul. You've taught all of us that life is love and death is hate." She hugged him close. "But now it's time to teach you a lesson, Braen."

Sippen stepped forward. "Suh... sometimes violence is nuh... necessary. That buh... berserker inside of you has puh... purpose."

"Sometimes," Eusari explained, "death is the protector of life. And it's time for Skander to die so the world can learn to love again, just as I have after losing everyone dear to me. But don't make me lose you a second time."

Braen paused, considering her words before turning to the naval officer standing nearby. "Captain Santos," he asked, "what's the name of this vessel?"

The man had been listening and watching with a silent tongue, no doubt amazed by the unwavering loyalty of Braen's friends. "She's called *Inspiration,*" the captain replied.

"I'm truly in your debt for delivering us to battle. I hope you don't mind if I ask one more thing from *Inspiration* and her crew."

"It's no longer my ship," he replied. "If this truly was a mutiny, then the crew has clearly chosen their captain and my allegiance is also sworn to you."

Braen pointed at Percy Roan and the steward Philip. "Take the civilians to Logan to await news of our success or failure." He glanced at the Pescari woman by the rail. "Take Flaya as well."

"I can do that," Santos vowed.

"No," the woman protested. "I am Pescari, warrior enough to be helpful." She touched her rounding belly. "My husband swore under Felicima we would help end this war, and I carry all that is left of him."

Braen nodded, unwilling or too tired to argue. He called for the Dreamer hiding behind a pair of barrels. "Sebastian, come out son, I need your help."

"I can't help you, Captain Braston. There's nothing I can do with my power that you can trust. I freeze up every time we're in a fight."

"Sebastian," the Northman said as he knelt in front of the Dreamer, "you don't lack courage, or you wouldn't be here. You freeze up because you're fighting a bigger fight, one to protect your friends. You've witnessed much more death than a young boy should, and you're too small to protect the rest of your family with only muscle. Don't you see? You freeze because you want to keep them safe."

"I do love all of you, Braen. But I don't understand how I can help."

"I need you to protect little Charleigh. Go with Captain Santos and bring her to Cuyler and Caroline and the others in Logan. Keep her safe until you either know of our fates or Alec comes to claim her as his daughter. Protect her like you wish you had done for Suzette."

The boy nodded.

"Also," Braston added, "help the captain sail fast like your lives depend on it, because they do. The battle ahead will require much from the lake and I want you clear of danger."

"I will," the boy promised.

Braen turned to the others. "We'll need to sail undercover into the heart of the city. Marita," he called, and the girl hurried over. "Do you remember when the Dreamers in The Cove turned invisible? Can you replicate that trick?"

The girl with the freckled face grinned and shot two thumbs in the air.

He turned to his loyal friend. "Sippen, get us alongside *Malfeasance*. We'll take her into the city."

The little man complied and within minutes they had boarded the flagship and searched it thoroughly. Their inspection turned up nothing, as they found her completely deserted. Braen returned topside with Alec and Marita and Eusari met them on the quarter-deck. "No sign of Nevra?"

"Only a dead rat, but he was there. I'm certain," he said as he stepped aboard. He signaled Sippen to continue onward and everything shimmered as Marita cloaked the ship in a veil of air.

The ship lurched beneath their feet as it pushed away from the iceberg, and Eusari stumbled into his arms. He took advantage of the moment and held her close.

She looked up with eyes that betrayed worry. "What if we can't find him?"

"He's with Skander, and we'll find them."

The entrance to the city was unguarded, and the walls above devoid of defenders. They sailed slowly down river, using the current instead of sails in case the unnatural wind betrayed their position. Slick walls loomed high above both banks of the river, channeling the current toward the center of Eston. The journey took far longer than Braen would have preferred, but soon they reached the harbor.

They found the expanse of piers abandoned, the Imperial ships having fully committed to the battle west of the city. They pulled in unopposed, tying off *Malfeasance* and stepping off into the night. Krill jogged past the others, a bundle of cloth in his arms.

Braen smiled when he recognized his banner and asked, "What will you do with that?"

"I'll hang it from atop the palace," the gunner said, "so Skander knows who the real Kraken be."

Amash approached with Sippen, and Braston held out a hand, waving them out of earshot of the others.

Horslei appeared worried by his friend's sudden secrecy. "What is it Braen?"

"Remember what I told you aboard *Inspiration*? You must kill me if Eusari won't, and do it in a way that she'll be forced to restore my body."

Amash protested, "I beg you. Don't force that upon me. The prophecy is wrong," he insisted, "and I won't kill my friend."

"You must," the northern captain pressed, "and I want you to do it with a clear conscience."

Amash shrugged at this, his conscience obviously working over-time. "I'll consider it," he said. "Braen, I need to retrieve my sister from the brig. Campton Shol or not, I don't want to leave her aboard the ship when you and your brother battle."

"Just ensure Marita keeps her bound." He waited until Horslei departed then turned to his engineer. "Sippen, after the battle is over, he will have to kill me a second time, or Skander if he wins. If he won't then you will."

"Never," the engineer vowed. "I wuh... won't duh... do it uh... either."

"If you don't, then I will finish the destruction my brother began. I've seen that as truth while deep under the lake." He looked around to ensure no one listened. "The Esterling child will also be born tonight. Regardless of how that happens, make sure Sarai is near Eusari. I've seen her future, and she's the mother of many, not just one. No matter what else happens to me, you must swear loyalty to her and those children over me." Eusari approached with Alec, Flaya, and Marita. Braen turned and acted as if their parlay was not filled with dark omens. With a smile he asked, "Are we ready?"

Hester emerged from below decks and pumped her grapeshot gun, chambering shot and causing everyone to turn her direction. "I need some of those grenades," she said casually, "and more rounds for this."

Braen raised an eyebrow and looked toward Sippen. The little man held up several satchels, handing one to each member of the tiny crew. "Nuh... now we're ready."

"Good," Braston said. "Stay together and don't get separated."

Chapter Fifty-Two

The hailstorm had softened into wet snow, highly unusual for the springtime temperatures and further proof that Skander Braston had breached the walls. The current of the tidal waters had tested the city infrastructure and proven the engineering of Charles Esterling. He had built Eston City to stand for ages. The last of the lake water snaked like a river through the sewers below.

As they approached the first overlook, Samani peered over the railing, surveying the damage and estimating the time remaining in his task. The scene below would have horrified any who had not been prepared for the night. Several Estonian soldiers washed with the current, and the occasional Falconer bobbed alongside. Everything searched for a way to return to Lake Norton.

"Watch," he told the others, pointing to several bodies caught up with flotsam. "The dead stir although I hear no song of the Jaguar. There are none nearby."

"The boy king then?" Delilah averted her eyes, adverse to the unnatural death. Gretchen stared with apathetic eyes.

"Yes, most certainly Marcus' doing."

"And you are certain he's consumed by the beads?"

"He's his father's son, after all, with a pension for addiction. When I witnessed his Ka'Ash'mael, I felt his drunken state. Most fear the oracle beads, aware of their killing qualities in high dosage. He lacked discernment for the pearls." He waved them to follow as he continued their climb. *Why must there be so many stairs? You were ever the showman, Charles.*

"No one has trained him," Gretchen agreed with her father. "He does not respect the bead as he should."

"That surmise is correct," Samani agreed. "He has too much of his mother in the form of ambitious pride. Campton Shol erred by not catering to that, choosing instead to control him through fear. Now the boy's petulance has accepted the bead as proof of his divinity, and he won't cease his tantrum until he rids the world of opposition." He added, "Or when the pearls rid the world of him."

Cedric Krull, better known to his friends as Gunnery Sergeant Krill, raced after the others with a shotgun cradled in his arm. His free hand stuffed the Kraken banner into his shirt and his satchel full of Sippen's goodies hung over his shoulder, slapping against his hip as he ran. Truth be told, Krill hadn't run since losing his leg in that *mishap* in Estowen's Landing. More realistically he hobbled around on his peg leg. The Cinder-cursed thing itched constantly, sort of like that time he caught scabies on the docks of Fjorik. But that is a story for a different time. On this night, he had a job to do.

The way out of the harbor was a steep staircase with many flights reaching upward. He marveled at the engineering of the raised city and the amount of stone required to elevate the burgs above the broad floodplain. *There must be a massive sewer structure underneath,* he considered as they climbed, *acting like a giant rain barrel and feeding the river underneath.* He'd try and remember to discuss the construction with Sippen after the battle.

He reached a hand to his face; aware the moon would remain hidden behind storm clouds throughout the night. He flipped his eyepatch over to night vision, or, as he liked to call it, *covering his bad eye.* He ambled passed Sippen and grabbed the overstuffed wadding, shaking it like a belly. "First Mate," he asked with a grin, "do I be lookin' fat in this outfit?"

Hester hissed, "Be quiet, moron!"

"Both of you," Braen cautioned, "need to shut the hells up."

"Now look what ya did, Hester. Ye got us both in trouble like that time in…" The rest was silenced by a cuff to the ear and a fierce look from Eusari. He shut up abruptly.

Krill shot a worried glance at the Esterling queen, half-dragged by Marita. *She's quite the brilliant lassie, underneath that troubled mind,* he considered of the Dreamer. *But this pregnant queen deserves a keen eye as we get closer. I don't like that Amash made us bring her along.* He moved into a better position, one that gave his good eye a better view in case of trouble.

They topped the staircase and emerged into a scene from the seven hells. Braen stepped into the street just as six city guardsmen leaped out. He swung his axe, ripping one down, and moved into position to face the others. One of Eusari's knives flew through the night, catching one in the throat and dropping him instantly. Marita took on the other four.

The girl glided past everyone on a cushion of air, dual blades spinning and slicing as she landed on nimble feet. She proved an expert swordsman, cutting all four down before Amash and Alec, both master bladesmen, could even draw their weapons. They exchanged a knowing look and kept them at the ready from that point on.

Krill offered encouragement. "Way to cut 'em to ribbons, dearie! Ya flew in thar like a flittin' fairy, ya did!"

She gave him a wink and whispered, "You can say the other word if you want, we be piratin' tonight!"

"Aye," he replied, "that we arrr…"

Three more soldiers advanced from starboard, the side closest to Hester. She whirled and pulled the trigger, sending one flying backward. The other two were dropped by Flaya's rapid succession of arrows.

Braen smiled his approval. "Let's move," he commanded. "We need to get off the main streets."

Sippen pointed to the palace, looming not far, but seeming an eternity away given their need for stealth. "Ah... are thuh... those people?"

Krill strained his good eye and could barely make out three figures in the moonlight. They peered over the side into the slum district below. He raised his spyglass and focused, abruptly turning to the others with a toothy grin. "It be Kernigan!"

"Figures," grumbled Eusari. "I can't help but believe that man's behind all we've been through."

"I stuh... still trust him," Sippen disagreed. "He muh... means well."

"Well, I don't." Braen spat on the cobblestones.

Lightning struck in rapid succession in direction of the Span. They were close to the battle. Eusari pointed to the flames rising from rooftops. "That's Skander!"

"Aye," Braen agreed. "We're close. Let's move in."

Marita hollered, "Wait!" They all turned and saw that she stared at the Esterling queen. "She wants to say something."

"I don't want to hear it," Braen said and turned to leave.

"Braston," the cautious voice of Alec gave the big man pause. "We need to trust Marita. She's had a better plan than we for the past few weeks. Why don't you hear Shol out, and, if you don't like it, we can gag her right up."

Braen nodded his approval and Marita lifted the gag. The voice that rumbled from the queen's lips was not Campton Shol. "It's not too late to work together, you and I, Braston," the voice suggested.

Amash perked at the change and demanded, "Where is Shol?"

"You're guess is as good as mine," the voice chuckled, drooling froth on the queen's chin. "He fled as soon as he witnessed my true power. It's a shame, really, but I must say I've been very much looking forward to our meeting. Thank you for bringing the queen so close to my control. I've felt her sailing closer these past few days, and this child in her womb threatens my claim to the throne." He pointed at each of the pregnant women. "Thank you for drawing each of them nearer."

Everyone exchanged glances, suddenly realizing the power of Marcus Esterling. Amash spoke with authority, emboldened by the way his sister's body had been used. "It's you then, fighting against Skander? You control the Falconers as well?"

"Come visit me in the temple, Horslei, so that I may deliver you to the gods. But first, a demonstration of my power to encourage you along."

A single shot ran out from behind and the group wheeled. Down the lane a lone rifleman wearing Skander's colors shouldered a rifle and jogged down the lane. Hester screamed. Krill, who had been standing closest to the queen, took most of the blood splatter, saving Hester from the worst of the overspray. He wiped his good eye clear and saw that Sarai bore a single wound to her temple. She lay crumpled in a heap on the snowy cobblestones.

Eusari sprang into action, bent over the queen and feeling for any lifeforce remaining. "There's not enough to save," she reported, "not with how the Jaguars restored her last time. The child though," she leaned close and placed two scarred hands on Sarai's pregnant belly, "lives for now."

"Huh... how fuh... far along is she?" Sippen knelt beside the fallen woman.

"I don't know," Eusari said, feeling with her mind.

"Six or seven months," Amash said with sadness, sorry to see his sister's lifeless frame, despite that he had accepted her death days before.

"Marita," Sippen called the girl over, "I'll need your huh... help when I bruh... bring the baby out."

"Wait!" Braen couldn't believe what he was witnessing. "You'll deliver the child here?"

"We huh... have no chuh... choice. He'll duh... die in the womb if we duh... don't."

Krill felt movement behind him and turned to see two dozen rose blossoms move in unison, as if laughing at their plight. "He be

watchin' us wit the flowers, mates. Best hurry so we kin move along."
He handed Sippen his knife, figuring it to be sharper than his.

The others looked away, taking up a perimeter of defense while also avoiding witnessing the gruesome birth. Braen helped Krill cut the blossoms from the vine, hacking with his axe and showing a bit more anger than the gunnery sergeant felt necessary. Marita, however, stared with wide-eyed fascination as Sippen carefully extracted the child. As soon as the infant felt the cold, he tried to cry, underdeveloped lungs fighting to breathe on their own.

"Cuh... careful now, Marita. You huh... have to be gentle with him. Just a little to stuh... start him off."

"I don't know if I can," she said with hesitation.

"You can do it, dearie," her father urged. "Just a trickle like Sippen said."

Krill sneaked a peak just as the tiniest trickle of air reached into the child's nose and traveled down to feed his lungs.

"Guh... good, Sippen said. Kuh... keep it going until he bruh... breathes on his own." Eusari handed the engineer a piece of cloth to swaddle the boy against the chill. He placed the child gently into Marita's hands and smiled. "Kuh... keep him suh... safe. He'll be our king one day."

Krill watched Amash closely as his friend spoke to the girl, watching for signs of betrayal. Any flicker of dissention would have raised alarm in the pirate, whose only interest was shared with Braen who, so far, wanted the child to live.

"Let's move," Braston commanded. "We're running out of time!"

Skander Braston paced the streets, frustrated and exhausted from constant harrowing by Esterling's troops. Their guerrilla tactics, although cowardly and sporadic, had proven quite deadly. Although his kill squads had displayed effectiveness in the other cities, the sheer size of Eston forced him to abandon the strategy. Once reunited, however, his forces faced a bitter reality. They had been cut by half within the first few hours. Despondent, he took census of his children, their numbers just as dwindled and pathetic as his marauders.

The storm above intensified with Skander's anger. Snow fell in wet clumps, piling in the streets despite the warm temperature of the ground. The clouds above dropped fierce lightning bolts into the city, exploding trees and setting fires to stables and homes. Occasionally a family would flee their home for safer ground, only to become unwilling members of Esterling's army.

He screamed at Nevra, the voice made flesh, kneeling over several fallen Snow Cats. "Why can't you revive them faster?" A squad of archers rounded the corner, and he left the voice to his work. He pointed out advancing ranged troops, and his riflemen brought them down with a single volley. Turning, he watched his children rise. The archers behind regained their footing.

A blast of air caught him by surprise as one of the Saber Cats, a young boy of nine summers, let loose an attack. Slender tendrils sought out Skander's neck while the others worked quickly to bind him. After one of the riflemen strode forward and put him down, Nevra went back to work. "The enemy revived him first," the pox-faced man grumbled, recovering the boy once more.

Skander rubbed his throat and panned the skyline, now glowing against the fires raging through the city. He spied a single silhouette perched atop the Temple of the Gods. "Come," he ordered, "we must push toward that church."

You'll never make it, his father's voice echoed in the night. *His army is hidden all along that avenue, ready to pick away your most loyal of warriors.*

Skander replied with a sharp tug of Nevra's leash, willing himself to remain silent. *He's dead,* he reminded himself.

Yes, Skander. I'm very much dead. Denied the heavenly feast by your insolence, and so I linger.

He directed what was left of his army forward, choosing a broad parkway lined with shops and the wealth laden homes of the merchant class. Normally he would have ordered the sacking of these manors, reaping the wealth for Fjorik. Instead he summoned six thunderbolts in rapid succession, igniting the roofs like matches in a row. The sudden eruption sent a dozen or more infantry scurrying from cover, easily picked off by his riflemen.

You push too deep, his father warned, *over committed, and outflanked for sure. This will be the end of my lineage.*

"No!" Skander screamed. "I did my job, he cried into the night. I sired a whelp that will lead Fjorik when I'm gone!"

You mean the child Hester bears in the name of your brother? No, he'll be raised by another, and taught the ways of the cattle our people harvest.

The trees on their left suddenly sprang to life, ripping free their roots and ambling forward. Flashes lit the streets and explosive lightning split their trunks. Skander urged his men further. Step by step they moved, inching forward until they neared the arching ramp of the Span's approach.

The heavy flapping of wings signaled the arrival of large birds of prey and Skander raised an ear to the sound. *Ah,* he reasoned, *the Falconers finally show their force.* But when his eyes focused, they found condors unlike any he had ever seen. Fiery red and orange plumes announced the arrival of six Phoenixes, the mystical birds of flame.

"Shoot them down," he roared to his riflemen. "Take the air from their wings," he pleaded with the Saber Cats. Before any could respond, the flames lit the night. His front line broke, consumed by the fire that seemed to cling to their skin as they ran. A few succeeded in plunging their bodies into drifts, rolling and dousing the flames in the snow. The others were less lucky, and leapt from the high walls into the Logan river below. One by one those tiny plunging lights winked out.

The Saber Cats succeeded in bringing down two birds by stealing the air under their wings. These plummeted to the street below, slapping hard like wet meat on a butcher's block. Rifles retorted, silencing the pain-filled squawks. While Skander's troops reloaded to face the remaining four, a second wave of heat erupted, this time blocked by shields of wind as his children pushed the flames safely aside.

These aren't so troublesome, the northern king realized, emboldened by his sudden success. A second volley was fired, and the great birds retreated as another of their brethren plummeted to the snowy stones below. Each fallen Phoenix burst into a fiery pyre with their passing.

Shrieks from the rear guard caused Skander to turn, just in time to witness a massive entanglement spring to life. The roses quickly enveloped much of his army. *It was a feint,* he realized, *to sacrifice the Phoenixes.*

Are you so ignorant? Or merely blind? His father commanded. *Watch closely.*

The northern king felt fear in that moment, fear unlike any he had experienced since – *no,* he refused to remember that moment. He raised his mother's axe and held it aloft against the firelight. It reflected his terror and, beyond that, the rising visage of three reincarnations joining the sky on thunderous wings.

You destroyed that girl's innocence, the voice of his mother insisted, booming from the steel. *You forced her to watch as you desecrated her mother's womb before defiling her own. I'm ashamed of you, Skander, abashed to call you my son.*

"What you did was worse, Mother!" He gripped the weapon, staring into the reflected eyes of her ghostly image. "You tore our family apart," he screamed. "You deserved death!"

Braen may have interfered, stealing my right as your mother to serve you justice, but I live on in the feast. I am seated at the table among your ancestors, a privilege neither you nor your father will ever know. Cowards both. She comes for you, Bleyda.

"No," Skander begged, "do not call me that!" He whirled around, intent on taking his anger out on Nevra. He found the pox-faced man struggling to breathe against the tangled vines, now encircling his throat, clawing at them with eyes as large as the full moon lingering above the storm. He brought the axe down hard, severing the hold and giving the man air to inhale. With a tug he dragged the voice made flesh from the battlefield, fleeing into the shadows of a nearby building.

Just as I said, his mother's voice echoed in his mind, *you are Bleyda, a coward wearing a man's facade.*

Marcus watched as the remnants of Skander's army fled the city, running toward their boats with intent to escape north. *I should kill them all,* he thought, *but I will let them live to tell the tale of their king's defeat.* Raising his hands once more, the fallen returned to his service. He could feel the red bead of fire pulsing in the palm of his hand, yearning to taste the power.

Chapter Fifty-Three

Braen led the others deep into the city, snaking their path to avoid patrols and the tangling vines belonging to Marcus Esterling. They were only accosted a few more times, twice by roving bands of city guardsmen and once by an errant Fjorik kill squad. These dispatched easily, and the snow proved a tougher opponent as it piled higher. More lightning strikes exploded just ahead, shaking the rooftops of the surrounding buildings.

They emerged into a meeting square, not the famed Unification Square, but a smaller area used for lesser events. Braen froze in his tracks and the others nearly collided with his abruptness. Eusari crept forward, placing a hand on his arm to steady his nerves while Hester approached on his left. Each focused on Skander with private thoughts fueling their next moves.

His army had dwindled much since the Battle of Middleton, with only a hundred or so men at his back. Of them, many were emotants, clad in thick white furs that resembled the saber cats of the north. These hid their faces under heavy hoods, but Skander's mark was written with blood on their faces.

Braen stepped forward but Sippen pulled him back. He pointed to the sky as large birds descended onto the battlefield. The captain exchanged a glance with Alec Pogue, both of them having experienced these beasts in The Cove.

"What in the name of Cinder are those?" Hester had noticed the creatures as well, and instinctually grabbed Braen's other arm for a sense of safety. He yanked it away and moved closer to Eusari.

"I believe they're the mythical Phoenix," Braston explained. "We encountered them before, and narrowly escaped."

"They breathe fire," Marita chimed in, excited to get another view of the birds.

"Huh... How narrow? I nuh... need to know how to fuh... fight them."

"You don't," Alec replied. "Not unless you aim to die. When those things are around, you run."

The creatures abruptly attacked. The Saber Cats brought down two and the line of riflemen brought down a third. Another volley later and the remaining birds fled.

"That doesn't look so difficult," Amash observed.

"No," Braen pointed. "They're a diversion. Look to the rear-guard!" A massive entanglement of rose thickets swallowed up half the remaining army. Almost immediately the dying beasts burst into flames. As those extinguished, the ashes stirred, and freshly reanimated Phoenixes rose into the air. Skander's army broke, fleeing the way they'd come. Even the Saber Cats abandoned their father.

The younger Braston fled as well, pulling a robed figure by a chain. They raced across the square toward a row of larger buildings, disappearing into the shadows. Braen ran after him, charging out into the snow-covered field.

Eusari called out, "Braen!"

To his right more than fifty of Skander's army rose to their feet, turning to pursue him across the field. The Phoenixes, fully engulfed in flame, dove upon him as well.

"Guh... Go!" Sippen told Eusari. He reached into his satchel and drew out a grenade, lighting the fuse and pitching it into the onslaught. "Go after him!"

She did not hesitate, and sprinted after her love. Hester followed. The others leaped into action. Amash and Alec's swords slashed and cut as they fought off the advance, and Marita, with the Esterling heir in her arms, did her best to form a shield to keep the enemy away from the newborn. She shouted for the Pescari woman to take the baby, but Flaya was too busy flinging arrows to hear the call.

Eusari and Hester broke into a sprint, hurrying to keep pace with Braen. He was focused, driven by the awareness of Skander nearby, and no longer heeded the dangers lurking all around.

"Slow down," she urged. "Hester can't keep up."

He only glanced over his shoulder for a moment, before resuming the pace. "She's not in danger yet."

"How do you know this? How are you so suddenly aware of the future and what must happen," she pleaded as they ran, "yet you keep us in the dark?"

"I can't tell you everything, Eusari. I saw so much underneath that lake, things to do with our child's future that you'd alter given the chance."

She grabbed his arm and swung him around. His eyes, as blue as the sea, reflected the sorrow residing in his heart. "Don't you see? This is the Braen who I despise. The arrogant fool who makes decisions for everyone he loves. That is the root of your failures, your constant desire to keep everyone safe!"

"Eusari," he said with sadness in his voice. "That Braen is dead, don't you see? I have a second chance to right some wrongs, but my time here is brief. I will most certainly die tonight, for good this time, and you mustn't revive me a third time."

"And what? I should simply trust you because you love me, and have sired a child in my womb? You're not a god, Braen. You don't know everything." She placed her hands against her belly and pleaded, "this child…"

"This boy," he said, placing on hand atop hers. "He's a boy."

She softened, feeling the anger rush out at the simple knowledge. "This boy," she continued, "needs his father. He must learn things from you I cannot teach."

"He'll have men in his life for that," Braen vowed, "Sippen and Krill will always be at your side."

"Sippen and Krill," she laughed, thinking of the things those men could teach, "are not you. He needs his father."

"He'll have me," he said, placing his palm against her heart, "because I reside in here. You'll pass on everything I wish him to know about life." He abruptly drew himself to full height, as a hunting dog would sniff the air for quarry. He turned toward a brewery across the street. "This way," he urged. "Hurry!"

Eusari glanced at Hester, panting and out of breath. "Can you make it further?"

The woman nodded, barely able to speak, and with wet eyes from hearing their conversation. "He speaks only of your child and nothing of mine."

Eusari grabbed her hand and smiled tenderly. "He means both. Come, we're almost there. We'll go slower than he so you can catch your air."

Hester nodded her thanks.

Ahead, Braen had drawn his axe and kicked open the door. Stepping cautiously inside, he looked both left and right before engaging further.

He is about to berserk, she realized. *Barreling like a bull to protect the world, all the while losing more of himself.* And then a thought crept across her knowing. *What if he is correct, and loses himself completely to anger? Killing his brother could cause that, and he would indeed become a pawn of evil.*

She and Hester followed, stepping cautiously inside. Eusari drew her pistol and Hester held her shotgun like she had been born with the weapon in her hands. The northern woman approached a corner, peering around a stack of barrels with muzzle downward, turning and fanning any danger that may lurk. The haughty queen had somehow transformed into a stealthy soldier, Eusari realized, and suddenly admired her confidence with the weapon. *In another world, I could like her,* Eusari realized. *We're so alike in ways I never imagined.*

Braen stood just around the next corner, looming over two huddled forms. Hester let out a roar and rushed forward, no longer cautious but filled with rage. Eusari instantly understood why. Skander Braston lay at Braen's feet, unseeing and muttering madness aloud. Next to him was Lord Stefan Nevra, iron collar locked around his throat with a chain pulled tight in Skander's hand. His eyes pleaded for rescue from behind the pox-scarred face, now carved with bloody lines of indiscriminate insanity.

Hester raised the barrel of her gun, intent to send her husband to the hells he deserved, but Braen swatted the muzzle aside, sending her shot into the wall instead. She wheeled with fierce anger that lusted for revenge.

"Why did you take that from me?" She pointed toward Eusari. "Would you rather that she be the one to exact revenge? Stealing the only hope I have for revenge over his crimes?"

Eusari felt something she never expected. Her own need for vengeance had passed. She looked upon the pitiful face of the monster who defiled her, who tortured and murdered her mother before stealing away her innocence. *No*, she realized, *he's no longer a monster.* She gazed upon him with awareness, suddenly understanding why Braen had never wished him dead. The child lurking within had won over the man who had never fully controlled his emotions. She listened to his mutterings.

Eusari could barely look upon the wretched man propped up against the wall. His skin had festered, decayed from the evil residing within. He clutched an axe to his chest as a child would cling to a toy, terrified and seeking comfort in the dark. He never focused his eyes on any of the newcomers, but somehow sensed Braen's arrival. His gums bled and his teeth dangled in his mouth as he asked, "Brother, is that you?"

Braen knelt beside him, placing a loving hand on his brother's shoulder. "I'm here, Skander. Tell me what happened."

"She struck me again," he said, "because I argued against her. I have bruises, and my ribs hurt so badly."

Braen asked tenderly, "Why did you feel the need to argue?"

"She told father that I had stolen his knife, but I didn't. She stole it and hid it so that I would receive his wrath. She was afraid that I would tell him, Braen, and wanted to get even with me, her son."

"What did she fear you would tell father?"

"I saw her and a soldier," Skander sobbed as he relived the memory, "making love in the stables."

"The same as before?"

"No, a different man this time. She saw me, but I wasn't going to tell father, not after the whipping she gave me last time. She stole his knife and hid it in my room, then wasn't satisfied when he only lectured me against stealing. As soon as he'd left, she struck me, not letting me off the bed."

He's pitiful, Eusari realized, *a product of hatred and traumas way different than mine. He never knew a mother's love, and that's why he stole mine away.*

Hester stood dumbfounded next to Eusari. "Did this really happen, Braen? Did your mother beat you as boys?"

"Aye," Braen confirmed. "Any time she feared she'd be caught in her own treachery, she beat us to regain control."

Hester's eyes were wide with understanding. "How did she really die? I was told there was an accident, but I never truly knew the story."

"We'd only just returned from Brentway, and she laid with one of her many lovers. He bragged about what Skander had done to..." he glanced at Eusari, searching her face for signs of whether he should continue. She nodded for him to proceed. "What he had done to Eusari and her mother," he finished. "The soldier had taken a turn and bragged that Skander was finally a man."

"What did she do," Eusari asked quietly. "How did she respond?"

"She killed the man in her own bed. She detested the forcible taking of women, apparently having the same done to her when she was young. She hacked him to pieces and made quite the commotion. Skander heard and came running to her defense, believing our mother in trouble. She turned on him in her berserker rage and swung her axe…" He placed his hand against the one Skander held. "This one. He fought her off, but she disarmed him, beating him with the pommel and breaking his ribs. I came along and found her with blade high over her head. I drew my knife, her own father's Berserker Blade, and stabbed her through as she swung downward."

"That's awful," Hester whispered. "I never knew."

"No one did. We kept that secret within the family, both her infidelities and the rage we endured."

"And Krist never stopped her?"

"He loved her very much, and believed she could change. All Father ever wanted was peace. He was a strong ruler, a wise king, but ignorant in many things. The first of which was the raids on Loganshire, believing those were the only option to feed his people. The second was in the belief that she could be both wife to him and mother to his boys. But she couldn't or wouldn't change her nature."

Eusari stepped forward, placing a tender hand on Braen's shoulder. "It isn't nature that defines us," she said. "It is the love that we receive as children. You turned out different than your brother. Tell us how."

"I was more closely bonded with my father early on. I was eldest, and spent all of my time with him. Skander never figured out how to get close with him, and instead chased after mother's love like a moth to flame. He was burned each time, and never learned to love himself. He learned only to demand love without giving."

Hester said the words that made Braen flinch. "He has to die. You know that as well as we."

"He's already dead, Hester. Don't you see? Killing him won't cure the hurt he's done to anyone. It will only prove what he believes to be true, that he's unworthy of love. No," he said, "he'll have a chance to attend the heavenly feast, but it won't be him we kill."

Nevra's eyes grew wide with fear as he heard Braen's words. He stammered, "I no longer control him! He wrestled free of my bond! Killing me will do nothing for you!"

Eusari knelt beside the pox-faced man, gazing with pity into his rat-like eyes. "Killing you is a mercy, Nevra, one that will end abominations across this continent." She pointed outside. "How many of his troops do you hold?"

"None, please believe me! I only hold The Cove! Marcus Esterling has bonded nearly this entire city!"

Braen nodded to Eusari then laid down next to his brother with his back to the wall, strong arms holding the king of Fjorik like a weeping child. "Skander," he said, "can you still hear me?"

"I hear so many voices," the northern king said with tears streaming down. "I hear the infant the loudest. Is that me, Braen?"

"Yes, she left you to cry in your crib every night, brother."

"She spurned my love, but you didn't."

"No, I didn't."

"You came every night and held me, rocked me to sleep and told me stories. I remember that brother."

"Focus on those memories."

"Am I about to die?"

"Yes, Skander, it is time."

"Please tell me another story." He clutched his mother's axe to his chest as he whimpered and cried into Braen's shoulder.

Eusari drew her blade but waited, respecting what Braen must do. "This is a story about the bravest of heroes, born in Fjorik to a king and his wife," he recited. "They loved their son very much, even though he had treated people very badly." He nodded to her through tears of his own and she plunged the knife, deep into Nevra's sternum and piercing his heart. "His brother loved him most of all."

Braen felt Skander shudder with his final breath. "You should both wait outside while I do the rest. I must ensure that Esterling cannot raise either of them."

Eusari did not hesitate. She wiped the tears from her eyes and rushed from the room. Hester lingered.

"Go," he said. "You don't need to watch."

"Why didn't you tell me about your mother? Did you not trust me?"

"Hester, I loved you, but that was a family matter."

"That was when I chose him, did you know that?"

He looked up from his dark work. "When?"

"When you withdrew from me, hidden within that brooding place of your heart where you blame yourself for the problems of the world. I was jealous, worried that you no longer loved me, and I chose him to hedge my bets for the future."

"Hedge your bets? I don't understand," Braen said.

"I could no longer trust you to take care of me. Fjorik was cruel, but worse so for a woman. I feared that you were too weak to sit upon the throne, and I had no idea the weakness resided in him."

"That was fear, Hester. I wasn't responsible for your fear and I won't accept that accountability now." She turned to leave. "Wait," he said.

She whirled around. "What? Are you not finished breaking my heart?"

"Eusari won't do it, and neither will Amash or Sippen. I need to ask one more thing of you. My final act in Andalon will be to beg a favor from the woman I wasted my lifetime loving."

"What," she asked, "can I provide that your abundance of friends cannot?"

"I need you to kill me, so that I may defeat Marcus Esterling."

Eusari stood in the doorway, watching helplessly as Alec and the others fought off Esterling's forces. *I feel so free,* she thought, with a tinge of guilt for thinking of herself while the others battled. *I've hated Skander for so long, blamed him for all of my pain and suffering, when really, it was pity for him I should have felt. I am now, and have always been, so much stronger than he.* She no longer felt weakness from the fateful day in Brentway, it had been replaced with power and control, those simple words once lost to her, but now strengthened with confidence and love. *Thanks to Braen,* she thought, *for teaching me those virtues were always within my heart.*

The retort of the shotgun made her jump. The sound distinctly came from behind in the room she had just left. Her legs moved like she had never pushed them before, racing toward the catastrophe she would surely find. When she arrived, she fell to her knees and wept. Hester had collapsed, gun lying on the ground as she pounded the ground with grief.

"Why?" Eusari screamed for her to answer. "Why did you do it?"

"He made me," Hester sobbed. "He told me it was the only way! He promised you would bring him back!"

His blue eyes stared unseeing, but aware of so much more than she. "Do it," he commanded, "so that Franque will live out his own fate."

"Franque?" She marveled at the name, the life Braen had stolen on that night in Brentway. "Why Franque and not Braen?"

"Because the circle of life must continue," he said with lips tinged with blood, "and I have wrongs that I must right with my passing."

"No," she argued. "You're fine, you won't die! I won't raise you!"

"You must," he begged. "Or everything was in vain."

She wiped away a tear, choking back a sob. "Because you saw it at the bottom of the lake? Because you know the future?"

"Yes." He coughed, a puddle of blood suddenly beside him. "Raise them with love, Eusari. Teach them to trust and love the way you've learned. Instruct them how to lead others with compassion and sincerity. Be the mother to all."

Eusari shook her head, trying to clear the confusion from his words. "I only carry one child, Braen. What do you mean by *them*?"

The light left him, evaporated with his final breath.

Chapter Fifty-Four

Marita held the tiny baby in her arms, suddenly unsure how to fight without a blade in each hand. She stood helplessly by, maintaining a shield to stave off the magic of the Saber Cats and flapping Phoenixes. She yearned to join Alec and Amash dancing through the enemy ranks. They sent many a man down the river, necessary so they wouldn't rise again. Krill and Sippen had rifles raised, doing their best to help prevent the onslaught.

Robert's heir squirmed in her arms, so wrinkled and new, *kind of disgusting,* she realized, *and boring as hell.* She decided in that moment she wouldn't have children when she grew up. *Unless they're Sebastian's,* she thought. *I could tolerate his.*

She scanned the horizon for new dangers, expecting reinforcements would arrive soon. So far none had. She stole a glance toward the brewery where Braen and Eusari had run. *They'd better hurry,* she scolded.

Movement atop the palace caught Sippen's eye and he raised a spyglass. "I see Suh... Samani again." He pointed. "I nuh... need to talk to him."

Krill suddenly became very serious, dropping his pirate act which disappointed Marita, she liked it when he cursed and said "arr." He whirled around to warn his friend. "Don't do it, Sippen. You heard Braen, he's behind all of this for sure!"

"I need to guh... go," he insisted.

Krill felt at the padding in his shirt and suddenly grinned up a hairbrained idea of his own. "I'll go with ya," he said, "I've got a job ta do myself."

"You guys go on," Marita urged. "I'll cover you." The pair darted off toward the palace as a veil of air settled over them. They disappeared to all but Marita.

Alec, Flaya, and Amash finished off the remaining soldiers and moved beside Marita. Beyond the shield the Saber Cats paced and the Phoenixes beat massive wings. Each waited with eerie patience.

Her father asked, "Where'd the others go, dearie?"

"They had something to do at the Palace."

"And you let them go?"

"They're pirates and had to parlay with someone. And that's part of their code."

The two men exchanged a look and shrugged. Amash whispered but she heard him say, "What in Cinder's name is she talking about?"

"I've no bloomin' idea sometimes," Alec replied. "Come on, let's check on the others before reinforcements arrive."

The group hurried to the brewery, arriving just as Eusari and Braen emerged. Marita could clearly see that Braston had changed. She hugged Eusari with her free hand, fighting tears that yearned to fall for the woman.

In a whisper she asked, "Are you okay?" Eusari shook her head. She wasn't. Marita could tell in a way that only women can that the woman would never be the same again. The men, of course, were oblivious to the change.

Braen spoke with determination in his voice. "You three take the child into the brewery. There's a room in which you can hold out, easily defensible if Marita puts up a shield. Go now," he ordered. "Hester is there already." He and Eusari made their way hand in hand toward the waiting Saber Cats, strolling away from the brewery without waiting for a response from the others.

Amash turned to Alec, his face changing as if suddenly aware of his mission. "Sorry mate," he said to Alec. "You'll have to watch over the child, I've got a promise to keep." He jogged toward the pile of fallen soldiers, drew out a rifle, then headed off to the temple.

"By Cinder's Crack," Alec cursed.

Marita thrust the wriggling baby into Alec's arms. "Nope," she said. "I'll make a shield, but I ain't stayin' behind with the women and children."

"You will do as he commanded, dearie," her father warned, "because he's your captain."

"Then I just mutinied," she replied, "and you can hang me later. But you boys already had fun killing soldiers and now it's your turn to babysit." She looked over her shoulder and gave him a grin and a thumbs up, just to let him know everything would be okay.

Alec tried to hand the child to Flaya, but she darted after the girl.

Sippen Yurik approached the throne room, careful not to make a sound. Each step threatened echo, and he could not afford to announce his arrival. The building was completely empty, with the many occupants either in hiding from fear or fighting in the streets below. The eeriness of the void clung to his soul, but fate had chosen him to end this war.

The grapeshot gun hung heavy in his hand, not for the weight, for he had balanced the construction perfectly. No, the weapon carried a substantial burden that comes with all instruments of war, the discernment over action. The human element decides the difference between justified and unholy killing, and that mechanism, although greatly flawed, is the only power mortal man retains against evil. He swallowed hard and took another step, his task loomed ahead.

Krill tapped his shoulder, pointing to a staircase leading upward and giving his friend a quick salute as if to say, "I'll catch up with you later." Sippen nodded and trudged onward.

The throne room waited, only a dozen or more steps until he entered. He paused when he saw two singed bodies just inside the entrance, guards who had stayed behind only to meet a mysterious death. *There's more to Samani than we know,* the engineer knew, *and I must decide if he's friend or foe.* Another thought caused the shotgun to weigh even heavier. *And I must kill him if he's not our friend.*

The agent from Astia stood at a large window, gazing at the churchyard below. Delilah and Gretchen stood nearby. Without turning he greeted the engineer. "Hello, Sippen." Kernigan gripped his head as if massive pain coursed his temples.

"Heh... hello, Samani," he replied. "Uh... Are you fuh... feeling okay?"

"I'll be fine, our northern friend just accomplished the first of his many tasks. He removed both Nevra and Skander from their shared collective, along with the multitude they controlled." He pointed to the temple below. "His final act is about to begin."

"I huh... have questions for you, Suh... Samani."

"I somehow knew that you'd seek me out, I'm sure that enormous mind holds many questions I must answer."

"Shuh... should I kuh... kill you, Samani?" Out of the corner of his eye Gretchen stirred slightly, steadying her feet for action if needed. He remembered the bodies in the entrance. One mystery solved.

"Is that what you feel you must do? Must you kill me to fulfill the prophecy?"

"I'm nuh... no Destroyer. It isn't muh... me."

"No, it isn't you." Samani turned from the window and met the little man with honest eyes that betrayed his sadness. "The Destroyer isn't even a man."

"Thuh... then it's Eusari?"

Samani chuckled, not with sarcasm, but true merriment at the thought. "Oh, but I wish she were. She is truly a fine conveyor of death, but no. She's acquired much control over her emotions in this past year, and she's no longer interested in destruction." He took a sip from his goblet and added, "Besides, she has a much bigger role to play in Andalon, especially since she's the mother of its future."

"Then huh... who is the duh... Destroyer, Samani?" Sippen raised the muzzle of the weapon, holding it in line with the Astian man's chest. *He's stalling,* the engineer thought. From his peripheral vision he watched Kernigan's entourage. Neither Gretchen nor Delilah had made a move to stop him, and both now seemed content to listen to the men talk.

"To understand the identity of the Destroyer, I must share with you, as the most intelligent man in Andalon, the entire prophecy." Samani cleared his throat and spoke the words as an orator reciting a poem.

"From the corners of Andalon children awaken,
Remembering not their past nor the powers that slumber,
The pain of their suffering increases with numbers.
Come, witness the birth of their salvation!

Rise the Kraken from the depths,
Dealing destruction and slaughter.
Watch him destroy our legacy.
On land the monster roars and walks.

Death surrounds in light and shadow,
Destroy the seed before it roots.
All forces of nature have awakened,
Chaos sown without distinction.

No longer controlled by boundaries,
Siblings consume each other.
Emotions of water but born of land,
Lord of beast and friend of man.

Pain and suffering early known,
Raised a King without a crown.
Life of Misery, Death not binding."

Yurik fought the urge to lower the rifle, despite that it had begun to shake in his hands. "It's a riddle," he said.

"Yes, and one taken to be literal translation by the Astian Council." Samani frowned and added, "Wrongly, I must point out, but recently used much to our advantage."

Sippen's mind worked fast, dissecting the words and deciphering their double meanings. "People are born with only basic functions of their brain," he pointed out. "Their mind grows as they mature, gaining years so to speak."

"Aye," Samani agreed. "Increasing in numbers."

"But along with maturity and intellect comes emotion, the bringer of pain as we accumulate experiences." Sippen lowered the rifle and stood across from Samani. "Their salvation is the ability to dominate their emotion with logic and reasoning instead."

"A daunting task for sure, but certainly the ultimate sign of humanity."

Sippen thought hard on the second stanza. *Everyone assumed the Kraken was Braen,* he thought. *But that isn't so. He controls the beast but isn't the beast himself.*

Kernigan guessed at the man's thoughts. "You are pondering your friend's role?"

"Yes," Sippen replied, "the Kraken lines could be a warning, an indicator of what and when the fulfillment will occur."

"Only it isn't." Samani leaned forward with a smile, "Think, Sippen. When were Braen's powers strongest? When were anyone's at their fullest, for that matter?"

"When they were fueled by their deepest loves and fears. When they put others before themselves."

"If you cut off a Kraken's tentacle what happens?"

"It grows back."

"And if you cut off its head?"

"Same thing. It regenerates." Realization shook Sippen to his core, causing him to raise his head with eyes wide of understanding. "Their traumas and experiences fueled their strongest emotions, but the death and destruction followed their selfish anger. It means that when they relive their pain and suffering, they spread it to others, feeding the monster. Selfishness is the Kraken that lurks within and threatens chaos."

Samani beamed like a proud schoolteacher before his favorite pupil. "And the rest?"

"Love and jealousy are siblings, made of the same substance if they were flesh. They struggle constantly against one another until logic and reason is lost."

"Go on."

"Instinct guides beasts but logic and emotion rules human nature. Instinct is firm and solidly formed like the land, but emotion and logic are fluid, moving back and forth like water."

"Very good. Now the final part."

"Each man and woman are the king over their intellect and emotion. They wear no crown, but are supreme rulers over their choices both instinctual and logical."

"By all means, please continue."

"If they do not learn to control their base instincts and illogical emotions, then they pass their traumas to the next generation and the cycle continues."

"Yes. It continues without abatement forever." Samani gently asked the final question, "Sippen Yurik, who is the true Destroyer that our subconscious minds have warned against since the dawning of our latent abilities?"

"The Destroyer is selfishness."

"Well done," Samani praised, "and I'd like to point out that you never stuttered, not even once."

"Thuh... thank you," Sippen smiled but then abruptly frowned. "Wuh.. what about the part that uh... Amash told us, that only the son of Esterling can sluh... slay him in time?"

"Hogwash, I assure you. That was foretold but unrelated to the prophecy. Kestrel himself foretold the event on the night he transcended. But a young initiate hid much of the transcription of the actual Ka'Ash'mael."

"You?"

"Yes. I alone knew that little shit Marcus faked his own prophecy, thus sending the Astian Council into their tireless crusade to keep an Esterling on the throne." He grinned and added, "Even if that ruler wasn't even a true Esterling."

"And so Amash…"

"Oh, he's the true son of Charles Esterling but has nothing to do with the Destroyer."

"But he's about to do something rash."

"Define rash," Samani commanded.

"Braen ordered Amash to kill him if he survives the battle."

"That's the most foolish thing I've ever heard, especially when Braen finally has a chance to live out his days with Eusari." He stared out the window as the battle raged below. "You must hurry, but one more thing before you go."

"Wuh… what is it?"

"You must keep all the children safe, each of them is important. Evil lurks in this continent, men like Campton Shol may re-emerge and try to harm the children of Andalon. Has Robert's heir been born?"

"Yuh… yes, an hour uh… ago."

"Soon the others will follow, and you will do more than deliver them." Samani turned to face him once more. "You'll find a wetnurse in the lower quarter at a tavern called the *Prancing Puck*. I've already made arrangements for her to accompany you and the others to the mountains out west."

The engineer nodded as Samani once again faced the window. "Thuh… thank you, fruh… friend."

"No trouble at all, my friend. I will miss you the most when I return to Astia, I'll always lament that I never beat you at cards."

"Nuh… no one ever does," Yurik replied. He ran to save his friend.

After the little man had departed, Samani turned to Delilah. "It hurt to lie to him, almost as much as it did to send those children to their deaths."

"At least The Council will no longer interfere with Andalon," she reassured.

"No, not for a great while, I'm sure. But until then, their control is lifted and emotants are free to walk the continent unmolested, just as Dr. Andalon was promised by his friend Michael Esterling."

"You're still troubled, my love?"

"Yes. I hate cracking eggs when I make omelets, and I broke quite a few in the past month."

"Your sister?"

His eyes darkened as he thought about Nevra and the others he'd controlled over the years. "Among others."

Chapter Fifty-Five

Braen stood hand in hand with Eusari, facing the temple and staring down the emotants trapped by Marita's shield. The snowstorm had ceased the moment Skander died, and the looming battlefield glistened under the full glow of moonlight. The packed snow reminded him of the meadows in Fjorik, unmarred by footsteps and tempting him to rest and reminisce. The sight would have been peaceful, had it not stood between them and unnatural life.

Marita jogged up with both swords drawn, followed by Flaya with her bow held at the ready. Eusari cautioned them both, "Go back to the others and get away," she said. Take the heir from this place and head west."

Neither moved. Marita spoke with her usual defiance. "I already mutinied, captains. I'm a rogue pirate now, and I'll do as I please. Besides," she added while pointing to the horde, "you need the help."

"I agree," Flaya added with her thick Pescari accent. "Let Alec Pogue babysit the infant. It's his turn." This made both Braen and Eusari raise amused eyebrows.

"Before we do this," Eusari asked, "should you test your powers?"

"I have them," Braen replied. "I knew the moment I awakened. I feel... different, yet somehow the same. You did a fine job putting me together."

"I'd rather not think about that," she replied. Turning to Marita she asked, "According to Alec, you always have the best plans. What do you suggest?"

"Finally!" The girl beamed at the praise. "Someone recognizes my brilliance!"

"Well," Braen asked, "What do you propose, Marita?"

"I've no idea whatsoever. I'm just kind of winging it like you guys always do. Guess you rubbed off on me." She shot him a smile and a thumbs up.

Braen laughed aloud at the girl, letting honest merriment flow as he stepped forward. He reached out with his mind, feeling for the snow littering the city, and drawing from its wetness. It melted away immediately, leaving the streets as dry as if they'd baked under the summer sun. He felt the power course through his body, holding more energy than he had ever dared before. Next to him, Eusari knelt and touched the cobblestone street. He watched as it vibrated slowly beneath her scarred hands, building power as she awaited his signal.

"Marita," the captain ordered, "drop the shield."

The Saber Cats attacked at once, pouncing on their abrupt freedom. Strands of air whipped around as Marita parried each one with a tendril of her own. She made a show of yawning for the adults.

Flaya fired several arrows toward the Phoenixes, now screeching toward them with smoke billowing from its beak. Each projectile traveled true, but the wooden objects exploded into flames as they neared the bird's fiery corona. She succeeded however, in turning the beast's attention toward her, allowing the others to react.

Eusari poured energy into the cobblestones, exploding them upward with massive force. These pummeled their wings as bones crackled from the impact, sending the great birds spiraling to the ground. The street cracked underneath, swallowing them whole as the sand beneath the stones flowed like water to fill the void.

Braen waited for the animals to crawl free from their prisons, driving their beaks upward and gasping for air. He casually approached the protruding bills, kneeling and leaning over. The water flowed from his mouth, drowning the mythical raptors with the cooling waters that had once been snow.

As he stood, he watched Marita dance among the Saber Cats. Her choreographed balance of air and steel glided in and out of their formation, dealing death with grace and precision. She used her powers to open angles of attack as she flowed under and through their defenses. He did not interfere. After she had finished, he nodded his approval and stepped forward, signaling for Eusari and Flaya to do the same.

Ahead stood the place of worship, standing tall but dwarfed by the looming palace overhead. Movement atop the highest point of the city pulled their eyes upward, just as cloth unfurled from above. Braen saw Krill standing atop the highest point and the black banner waving in the wind, giving life to a giant Kraken smashing ships in its tentacles. The man waved and then spun around, bent over, pulled down his britches, and mooned everyone watching the scene. Sippen had been correct, his wounds were actually quite minor.

Braen led the women across the open square, leading them to the steps of the temple. Between them and the heavy wooden doors stood an army of Falconers and Snow Cats. Among them he picked out twenty or so Jaguars. Just beyond those he spied a different kind of Falconer, adorned in bright feathers the color of fire. *These must be bonded with the Phoenixes,* he reasoned. Behind the emotants, and marching across the span, were rows upon rows of soldiers, comprised of men, women, and children who had once been citizenry.

"Promise," Braen begged from his love, "that you'll never forget me."

Without waiting for her reply he let loose, pouring moisture into the air, forming and gathering clouds into a massive thunderhead. Feeling depleted, he drew upon the water beneath the city, finding it flowing through the sewers and in the Logan River under The Span. He fed this into the storm as well, until lightning cracked and lit up the night.

Several bolts slithered across the clouds, striking many places at once. Down the way, a barn bust into flames as horses whinnied and cried, kicking free of their stalls. These fled into the night, spooked and searching for safety from the storm. Another massive strike exploded atop the church, cracking the beams and toppling the entire steeple. As if answering a simple knock upon his door, Marcus Esterling stepped out into the night.

The boy responded with a display of his own, as the gathered emotants swirled the air to suck the fueling winds from the storm, creating a massive downdraft that pushed Braen and his tiny gathering backward. Marita reacted just in time, creating a shield that deflected most but not all of the gust to either side.

Eusari looked up, suddenly realizing the futility of their fight. "There's really no way to beat him, Braen. How did you see this end? How will you kill him?"

"I don't," he replied with a mournful tone. He pointed toward thousands of soldiers suddenly charging their way.

Eusari let his words pass through her body as she begged the gods for a future safe for her child. *But not just my child,* she realized. *The Esterling heir will need me as well.* Eusari, the woman pirate was gone in that moment, replaced by a stronger identity. The child within her womb stirred, sending surges of love that fueled her compassion for the entire world. Abruptly, she understood the powerful emotion overrode her ability to destroy. *This child is special,* she realized, *with power that, if wielded, would far surpass my own.*

"Braen," she protested, "When I used my powers before, it was in anger, or with vengeance. I can't use it to destroy. It will affect our child!"

He took her in his arms, holding her close and whispered, "Every time before, what were you thinking about?"

"The first time, in Diaph," she recalled, "I feared for the safety of you and our teams. I thought only to help them to safety."

"And you felled the gate atop an entire regiment, giving your friends a path to life. And the second time, in Pirate's Cove?"

"I feared for the troops I had landed, realizing I had trapped them against the beachhead with no escape."

"And again, you toppled the wall to give friends a path to life. What about in Middleton? After my death, what did you do?"

"I swallowed the enemy with the sand itself."

"Why, Eusari?"

"To cover our escape to *She Wolf.*"

"Once again," he revealed, "to lead your loved ones to safety. Don't you see? Your powers are not destructive, they are a mother's instinct. You possess the compassion that Skander's and my mother lacked. Where she used violence to punish and lies to manipulate, she acted selfishly. That's the opposite of a mother, Eusari. A true mother is the most powerful force in the universe, wielding power that is unstoppable while others are in danger. Use it, mother of my child, use that power now."

The enemy soldiers were nearly upon them, only a dozen or so strides away as they charged. She knelt, placed both hands against the ground, and channeled the power within. She poured control over life, once stolen but now restored. She added friendship, loyalty to others she had never dreamed possible. Forgiveness flowed, both for Skander for the pain he caused, but also toward Braen as she finally understood his motivation. Compassion and love followed, fueling a drive to live always for others, both those dependent upon her, and also those she'll never meet. It all bubbled forth as she channeled, shaking the ground and granting her complete control over the earth below.

Eusari channeled the power of motherhood into the stone, focused on the feet of their attackers. It cracked and fissured, splitting and falling away into the massive sewer below. One by one the resurrected horde of Marcus Esterling tumbled, ending their unnatural life when confronted with true power, that of selfless giving. Slumped and exhausted, Eusari smiled weakly toward Braen.

"That was amazing," Marita exclaimed. She knelt beside the woman captain and hugged her tight, whispering into her ear.

"You're gonna be a wonderful mother," she promised. "I know, because I've had two of them."

Braen smiled down on Eusari, proud that she was finally ready to face life without him. He stepped to the edge and stirred the waters below. *I must do the opposite of her, if I am to succeed. There is time for love and time for violence,* and he reasoned this was a time for anger. This time he understood that vengeance would consume him, the vision beneath the lake had been clear and there was no avoiding his fate.

He poured hatred into the swirling current, aimed at the entire continent of Astia for their meddling. He added resentment for the freedoms stolen from the emotants farmed for their abilities, used without their permission by those respecting power and dominion over life and liberty. The pain of desperation crept into his rage, anguish for injustice he was too weak to prevent from consuming his thoughts.

His selfish anger exploded upward, washed over the side, and he directed those emotions toward the scores of emotants, taken by Marcus and used as shadows to this wicked self-interest. He roared as they washed toward the span, rinsed clean of their unnatural life. He formed a bridge across the divide, water frozen by an urge to destroy the boy standing alone on the steps of the church. He drew his axe and charged, his berserker blood pumping fury to his muscles and fueling a desire to destroy.

Braen felt his humanity weaken as he charged, emotion taking over and no longer clinging to the morality that once anchored him in life. He was dead, after all, his lifeforce lost twice from the world and put together by the woman he loved. *She knew me best,* he thought as he lost touch with the man inside, clinging instead to the beast driven by hate. *She was bound to fail in the restoration, limited by her misunderstanding of the tenuous hold I maintained over anger.* But that was the way it had to be; he knew because he saw both their futures beneath the lake.

Marcus twirled the red bead between his fingers, daring himself to add it to the bulging collection between his cheek and gum. *Do I really dare?* The woman had opened up the ground, devouring his army, and the man had washed his emotants into the Logan. He raised his eyes to watch the charging Northman, fierce and full of rage.

The power of the bead tickled his hand. *Surely it won't hurt me,* he wondered, *I handled the others so well.* He yearned to taste the flavor, to suckle upon its power, and wield fire like the Phoenixes lurking inside the church. *I'm so powerful with the other colors. I no longer need an army, for I am one upon myself.*

The crazed berserker was close, feet pounding on the cobblestone and breath panting in Marcus' ears. The king waved his fingers and swatted the creature aside, sending him sliding into a thicket. He curled his fingers, tightly closing them upon his palm. The thorny branches wrapped around the man and pulled him deep inside the bush, piercing his skin and scratching deep as it choked out his life. His blood fed the leaves and Marcus licked his lips across the metallic taste in his mouth as Braen Braston struggled.

Marita was the next to charge, gliding on her pocket of air and racing after Braen. She watched as a single gust tossed him aside, flinging him into the roses. She increased her speed, sprinting with the wind she created. She watched the boy closely for any sign, hell-bent on avoiding the trick that had fooled the captain. He watched her as well, curiously, with amusement in his colorless eyes.

Eusari cried out from behind, warning her of... of something she couldn't make out. She looked around as she ran. *What did she say?*

Hands reached over the edge, pulling reanimated soldiers over the steep ledge leading to the Logan River. Here and there she witnessed Falconers crawling over a mound of climbing flesh, resembling ants piled on a mound. Captain Thorinson shouted again, pointing to the temple rooftop. Marita scanned, settling her eyes on gunmen with rifles trained. She tried something new.

She leapt, just as the horde reached her feet, casting a fine net of air, so delicate and tightly woven, the storm caught and swept her higher. She glided upward, watching as the men trained their muzzles. *Twenty men,* she counted. One, *the shield protecting Alec and the infant.* Two, *the air she fed into the child's developing lungs.* Three, *the chute that bore her aloft.* She held too many bindings.

Closing her eyes she felt rather then watched the tendrils as they formed, each tighter and more compact than she had ever attempted. While hands grabbed for her legs she soared, placing herself in line with the gunman searching for Braen. *See me,* she begged. *Look at the flying girl!*

Her ears rang with pressure as she pushed her limits farther than any Dreamer ever dared, never having attempted such tight weaves in tiny places. Her eyes throbbed as if they would explode from her skull. *That would be a sight to see,* she giggled at her play on words, and swung higher on the winds that fed the storm. *I need to distract them,* she realized, *something to draw their fire.* She sheathed her blades and lifted both hands toward them, sending her favorite gesture. They only briefly glanced and then covered Braen's struggling form as he fought against the thicket.

King Marcus stood on the steps, staring at Braen and willing the vines to squeeze his life. When he looked from the northern captain, the riflemen followed his gaze toward Eusari. She had made it across the bridge, and was holding ground against the encroaching army. She fought with a flurry of knife moves, bobbing and weaving and sending cobblestones flying at her foes. Just past her, atop Braen's ice bridge, rode Flaya, fast and nimble, bareback atop one of the escaped horses. She leaned under the neck of her steed, sending arrows to aid Eusari as she rushed to assist Braen.

Marita's heart thumped with worry as the rooftop riflemen trained their weapons on the Pescari woman, and she realized they followed the king's gaze wherever he turned. *They're fully under his control,* she realized. *I don't want their attention, I want his!*

She shouted from above, drifting lazily as she passed the gunmen. "King Marcus!" He ignored her call. "King Marcus," she screamed loudly, voice carried by the storm, "You ain't the real king!" His head cocked to the side. Emboldened, she added, "Your mother was a horrible queen!" He returned his attention to Braen.

"Queen Crestal was a dirty tavern turner!" He froze. "Her cootchie smells like a Fjorik fish market!" She thought for a moment, then added, "Crestal was so ugly, King Charles cheated on her!" Marcus glanced and the rifles trained, then he returned his attention to Flaya. "Charles *loved* making a baby with Abraham Horslei's wife!"

The rifles and Marcus swung immediately in her direction, ready to deal death to the girl floating on the storm. With the slightest pull of the trigger, all twenty rifles rang into the night. The explosion was deafening as each wadded and twisted braid of air securely blocked each muzzle. *Twenty-three connections,* she beamed with pride. The gasses expanded behind each trapped ball, building back pressure in every weapon. The massive blasts blew into the face of each rifleman, killing definitively and rendering them unable to rise again.

Once again controlling the winds Marita wheeled around, diving swiftly against the king. He countered with a crosswind that veered her slightly off course, just enough that she crashed into the side of the temple. She tumbled to the ground and landed in a heap, unmoving and unconscious.

Flaya watched the girl tumble to the cobblestones, turning the head of the crazed king as he laughed at her plight. His focus turned, an opportunity opened. As the horse raced toward the steps, she loosed three arrows. The boy, sensing danger, turned but not in time. Each arrow took him in the belly, knocking him backward. As quickly as he fell, so did she, caught from behind as Falconers emerged from below. The tendrils of air pulled her from the horse, holding her suspended in the air before the fallen king.

She watched as he stood, clawing for something on the ground. All around him were dozens of tiny black and white beads, spilled from his satchel and rolling down the steps toward the street. He grabbed several, shoving them into his mouth before approaching Flaya. He drew his knife and approached, barely noticing the arrows protruding from his belly.

"I'll cut that baby from your womb, Pescari whore."

She turned her head, looking toward Eusari and praying to Felicima she would help. The woman had just cut Braston free of the vines, and they were running as fast as they could toward her. The color red caught her eye. On the ground, among the white and black beads, rolled a single stone, perfectly smooth and the color of Taros' fire. The child in her womb rolled, drawn to the power held in that single pearl, and she wondered, *Is this the child of my shappan or not?*

Eusari cut Braen free but he swung wildly, gnashing his teeth and biting as he untangled from the vines. "Braen," she pleaded as he nearly struck her as well, "it's me! But he was too far gone, deep in the berserker state and unable to recognize his love. Once she had him freed, he shoved her aside, sprinting toward Marcus with his axe held high. She chased after, reaching for his mind and trying to wrestle control. His madness had broken their bond.

The army overtook them before reaching the steps. Braen was a blur beside her, swinging wildly and cutting through soldiers to reach Esterling. His wild attack sprayed blood without reason, nearly hitting her once or twice in his rage. She reached out once more, sensing a sliver of connection and speaking reason. *Settle down,* she begged.

He wheeled around, lunging at Eusari and screamed, "Get out of my head!"

Her lover was gone, lost in hatred and full of lust for dealing death. She staggered backward, tripping over a loose stone and landing on her back.

The king was nearly to Flaya, knife held over the Pescari infant in her womb. He foamed and frothed as he sucked on several beads at once, the black of his eyes larger than the color and nearly filling the whites. Braen's axe flew, striking him in the chest, but not piercing his heart. Marcus staggered backward, dropping his own blade but recovering his balance.

The ground rumbled and thousands of wisps of air shot out at once, lashing onto Braston's arms and legs and suspending him in the air next to Flaya. Eusari turned, suddenly afraid of what she'd find. The yard around the temple was filled with Snow Cats, Falconers, Jaguars, and Phoenixes, having scaled the massive stone walls and fully under Esterling's power.

Something in the bushes stirred, and Marita was hoisted as well. They spread her just as Braen and Flaya, arms and legs extended and stretching outward. Eusari was the next to rise, displayed like the others and held for the king's pleasure. He scrambled to his feet, pulling the axe from his chest and tossing it aside, flesh and sinew mending where it had been cut. He retrieved his blade and casually returned to Flaya.

The temple doors blew open and seven flapping Phoenixes emerged, hovering behind their sovereign. Their eyes glowed with fire, with smoke billowing from their nostrils and flame building within. Eusari would like to remember this night as her turning away from the heat, but truth be told she shied away with fear.

She watched as a single Falconer strode forward, untangling the knots that bound the pitiful heroes, dropping them to the ground, and causing the king to turn. With confusion in his voice, Marcus Esterling asked, "Who controls you?"

Before she could answer, Braen had his axe, maniacally hacking and chopping the giant birds atop the steps. Marita, still dazed, nearly fell to a wild swing as a Phoenix fell. Eusari sprinted toward her, pushing the girl away and taking the brunt of the blow. She rolled, looking up with both terror and pity for her lover.

Braen turned toward Eusari, gone from this world as well as her mind. His eyes were as blue as the sea, devoid of white and unseeing of his love. All he could see was more blood to spill. Fully consumed by his berserker lust, he raised the axe high and prepared to strike. A single shot rang out. Eusari turned toward the sniper who had fired the weapon.

Amash turned away from the choice he had made, laying his rifle on the ground as he wept for his lost friend. Eusari slowly turned back toward Braen, now frozen in time as a trail of blood leaked from his forehead. The axe toppled onto the cobblestone street, discarded as Braen's empty husk lying atop cold stones. The nearest Phoenix rendered his body to ashes while Marcus Esterling roared with laughter.

Eusari yearned to shed tears for her love, sick with loss but only feeling amazement as Ashima, the sister of Samani, approached the king from behind. Her hood was gone, revealing a smooth face and head without a single strand of hair. Even her eyelashes had been shed long before. She smiled as she drew one of Sippen's hand cannons, pulled the trigger, and sent a hot ball of lead into the cold heart of Marcus Esterling. He collapsed on the steps of the temple, staring up at the Falconer looming above.

"But you are mine," Marcus pleaded. "I control you."

"No," Samani Kernigan spoke through the pale lips of his dead sister. Eusari gasped as she recognized the voice, bile rising in her throat as she realized the control he held over his sister's form. She reeled as he continued, "you have no power over anything. You are a slave to the bead. You wield power you have no right to draw without consent of the people over whom you've claimed dominion."

"But I'm... son of..."

"No," Ashima's mouth whispered as the boy king breathed his last, "you are not the son of Esterling. You're a craven bastard."

Samani's voice explained, "And I have released the children of Andalon from their bondage."

Ashima beckoned to the Pescari woman. "You are Flaya," the voice of Kernigan called, "and the child within your womb is the child of the shappan?"

She shook her head, honestly unsure. "The night I conceived there was another, an Andalonian guard. I know not who the father is."

"Trouble yourself no longer," Samani's voice promised, "for I have seen your child's future. She is as true as the bravest of the Pescari. Now come," he beckoned again, "and aid me in cleansing this city."

"What do you ask of me?"

"Look around," he commanded, gesturing as Esterling's entire army collapsed one by one onto the cobblestones. The empty husks of Phoenixes, Snow Cats, and Falconers lay discarded, their bond extinguished from the Collective. "Commit all remains to Felicima, so that no one will ever be tempted to draw upon their power again."

Flaya begged, "What do I do after?"

"The choice," Samani Kernigan promised, "is yours to make." The husk of Ashima Nakala, no longer animated, folded into a heap of feathered robes.

Flaya plucked a single bead from the steps and placed it in her mouth. At first nothing happened, but then her eyes burned like embers. Tendrils of fire leapt from her fingers and whirled tightly around the king's body as she obeyed the command of Kernigan.

Chapter Fifty-Six

The sun rose over a crippled Eston, defeated and no longer the center of Andalon culture. Though the walls held, safety was far from certain for the lives once thriving under Esterling rule. The people who cowered in their homes would eventually venture forth, but chose instead to remain indoors for the time being. Amash hoped they would take plenty of time to mourn the tens of thousands who had fallen during the night.

Eusari approached the man who would become their king. He sat upon the temple steps, defeated and with a weary head resting in his hands. *Please go away,* he pleaded silently. *I'm not in the mood.* She settled beside him and spoke softly.

"You did what he asked. No one blames you," she promised.

"I do."

"Don't."

"What if he could have been saved?"

"He couldn't have been. I know because I tried. We would've had to kill him again, just to try and restore him once more. From what I can tell," she said, "we would have lost more of him each time."

"I just wish it hadn't been me who did it." He flinched at his own words. *I swear it wasn't me who pulled the trigger. I held my finger there, but the act... I don't remember actually pulling it.*

"No," she agreed, "I suppose that's true. But you did it in time."

In time. The phrase echoed in his mind. He reached below beside his feet and retrieved a small chest, simply adorned and very plain. He held it out to Eusari. "We gathered most of his ashes, figured you'd decide best how to lay him to rest."

She took it and stared down. "Where'd you find the box?"

He pointed over his shoulder at the temple. "Funny thing, that. Those crazy priests of Lady Crestal's had several of these laying around, that one held some of those white beads."

"What did you do with those?"

He paused. *What did we do? Last night was such a blur I truly can't recall.* After a moment's consideration he replied, "We disposed of them." Amash changed the subject, still overcome by guilt and shame for killing their friend. He lifted his eyes, taking in the scene around him. "I know what you guys desire of me, but I can't do that either. I've no army to hold the empire, and not much in the way of advisors. Logan is the strongest city now. The empire is fractured."

"Yes," she smiled, "and that's a good thing. It will be best if you leave it as city states for now, while you get Eston on its feet."

"Will you help? With you and Sippen around I'd feel more confident."

"No, Amash. I promised Braen I'd take the children far away. But Santos is returning with the Dreamers. Cuyler and Caroline will build their school here instead of Eskera. Just promise you won't continue to use them as a fighting force once your army is restored."

"I won't." Thinking of Marita and the death he and Alec had exposed her to he said, "They've already experienced too much violence." He paused, then added, "Will you take away the Esterling heir as well?"

"Yes, him too." She narrowed her eyes. "Is that a problem? Do you see him as a threat?"

"No. I see him as a way out of this public life eventually."

"I don't understand."

"In eighteen summers he'll be of age, and as far as I'm concerned, he's the legitimate heir. Return with him then and I'll abdicate." Voices approaching the steps caused them both to turn. Sippen escorted a young woman, dressed simply and wearing a pretty smile. Amash asked Eusari, "What do you reckon is this?"

"I'm not sure," she admitted. "Sippen? Who's your friend?"

"Thuh... this is Collette. She's ruh... recently lost her child and is wuh... willing to wuh... wetnurse the child."

"Well," Eusari whispered to Amash. "Now that's *very* handy." To Sippen she said, "Take her to the Brewery. That's where you'll find..." She paused.

Amash spoke up. "Robert," he said. "His name's Robert." He turned to Eusari and explained. "Sarai told me that was to be his name if he turned out a boy. He was to be Crestal if he were a girl."

"Was that before?"

"Yes," his sad eyes focused on the stairs. "I was the first she told as soon as she knew. That was right before the celebration ceremony in Eskera when the Jaguars took her over."

"Take her to meet Robert," she said to Sippen with a warm smile for the girl. "Poor fella's probably hungry." She watched the pair leave then suggested. "Philip is returning with Santos. He seems a handy person to keep at your side."

"I will, and I'm considering letting Percy assist as well."

"Wasn't he part of the corruption in Weston?"

"Yes, but I believe he was truly changed by Eachann's attack on the Pescari. He seems eager to right wrongs and," he said with a grin, "he has connections with the bankers. We should be able to get started rebuilding right away. He said that he and Eachann had frozen several accounts that belonged to Nevra. I should be able to absorb those into the coffers."

"Such an accountant," Eusari laughed, "you turned out to be."

"There's nothing wrong with that." They sat in silence for a moment, until he noticed Flaya sitting in the shade across the way. He pointed her out. "She's a tough girl. Will you take her to her people at Lake Weston?"

"No. She told me earlier that she wants to come with me. Braen said before the battle that he saw me raising all the children, and she feels inclined to believe I will need help raising the child of Taros as well."

"Will you?"

"Me? Allow another woman near when her child is the same age as the two I'm raising?" She laughed. "You're damn right I will. I need the help and they'll need the friendship. Sippen and Krill will take us west to the mountains."

This surprised Amash. "I figured you'd hunt down Devil Jacque and reclaim *She Wolf.*"

"No, the sea's no place to raise children. I'll go west as Braen suggested. You'll grant us a homestead, won't you?"

"Of course," he promised, "after I secure some sort of hold over the city states. Right now I'm king of nearly nothing." He trailed off, staring at something approaching.

She followed his eyes, suddenly frowning and suspecting trouble. "What?"

"It's *her.* She approaches."

"Her?" He turned and saw Hester making her way to the steps. "Oh yeah, *her.*"

"Eusari!" The northern queen had assumed some, but not all of her regal air.

"Yes, Hester?"

"When do we leave? I'm eager to get on our way."

"What do you mean *we*? You can go wherever you want whenever you please. My son won't make a claim on your precious Fjorik, and you're welcome to charter a vessel north as soon as merchants return."

"I'm not returning to Fjorik," Hester replied with stinging arrogance. "I'm going wherever you decide. You and Flaya can't raise these boys by yourself, and I'm not..." Her voice choked a little as she spoke. "I'm not *up* to parenting without help. That new wetnurse will serve fine as a nursemaid as the children get older."

"Absolutely not!" Eusari stood, fingering the knives hidden within her leathers. She stormed down the steps, backing Hester away. "I've had my fill of carting you around, you... you *over-pampered* princess!"

"I'm a queen," Hester demanded, but kept backing away.

"I don't care if you're Cinder himself! You're a coddled prima donna who needs her ass kicked! I'll skin your hide if you come anywhere close to me or my boys. I'll ship you to Fjorik in a box if I have to! A *pine* box, to be exact! I don't care if that's beneath your *dignity*!" She continued to pursue Hester down the steps and across the field, finally saying her piece and giving the woman her dues.

Amash laughed, his first honest laugh in weeks since learning his lineage. He spied Alec Pogue approaching, his adopted daughter in tow. Horslei greeted them both with a weak smile. "My friend," he said.

Alec nodded and took the seat Eusari had held moments before. With exhaustion creeping into his voice he asked, "So, you're to be crowned the King of Eston."

"I don't want it," Amash insisted.

"Aye, I'm sure that's true, as true as I didn't want to become the Archduke of Cargia. But here we are," he lamented, "two doomed souls destined for a life of servitude and leadership."

"Where did we go wrong, Alec? Neither of us wanted this," he gestured around at the city, "any of it."

"I think it was when that cursed northerner Braen Braston entered our lives," Alec replied. "He ripped everyone from their comfort zone and tossed them into a sea of friendship, guaranteed never to remain the same after allowing him into their lives."

"Friendship does that," Amash agreed.

"Aye, it does. Marita says that Santos will return this evening. In the morning he promised he'll take us and Charleigh home to Cargia. We must return to Mattie and the girls, but I don't want you to feel that you're alone here in Eston. I'm willing to lend aid whenever needed. Consider me more than your friend and see me now as your ally."

Amash smiled and rose to grasp his hand. "Alec," he asked, "Back in The Cove, when Nevra took over. I almost died on that pier. Why did you take so much care to nurse me back to health?"

"I was certain that you'd perished. Your wound was as fatal as any I'd ever seen. But, by the time I found you, the worst was past, and I couldn't let Andalon or myself lose such a good and learned man as you."

Uncertainty washed over Horslei, or Esterling, whoever he really was. His mind returned to the night before, when he held the rifle in his hands and fought against pulling the trigger. In a shaky voice he asked, "You don't think Nevra…"

"Gods no! You were alive when I found you. Nevra ordered you kept alive for your name, but never visited or showed interest in you. If you're worried if he had control over your mind, forget it. I know he did nothing of the sort. No, friend, the only odd thing I saw was the way Samani Kernigan lingered before escaping on *Ice Prince*. Sippen had to practically drag him aboard." He shook his head and added, "No, I think you were simply lucky. The gods above destined that you'd guide Andalon into a new age."

"Thanks, Alec." Amash turned to Marita. "You take care of your father," he commanded. "Keep him safe."

"Oh," said Marita, "I have to. I'm a pirate and keeping your captain alive is part of the code!"

Chapter Fifty-Seven

Eusari held her round and swollen stomach as the wagon train moved northwest along the Misting River. The body of water, more narrow and less full farther north, flowed within narrow banks and foamed white against the many jagged rocks. Beyond the foothills loomed mountains taller than any she had ever set eyes upon. Another contraction warned that her miserable caravan wouldn't make it to the river's source.

A glance toward Flaya confirmed her fear, as the woman flinched against pains. "You're tough," Eusari told the woman resting in the wagon beside her.

"I don't know that expression," the Pescari girl responded. "My Andalonian is poor. Does it mean that my skin is not supple?"

"Actually, over the past few months you've done quite well with our language." Holding the edge of the wagon Eusari made her way closer. "It means that you are very brave," she said. She placed a hand on Flaya's belly and felt the muscle constrict. "How far apart are they?"

"It is nearly time," was the reply.

"Can you make it a few more hours," she asked? "I want to make it into the trees."

"I can try."

Eusari peered into the next wagon in the train. Hester had demanded privacy during the entire journey, but that was fine since no one wanted to travel with her anyway. The former queen was near term as well. She called out to Sippen who rode on the buckboard next to Krill. "Let's push for that tree line and set up camp," she shouted.

The engineer responded with a thumbs up before placing a finger over his mouth as if saying to hush. He quickly pointed at baby Robert who apparently slept in his arms.

She mouthed apologies and leaned back to rest. Her own contractions began not long after.

The clearing proved a perfect place to stop, with plenty of cold mountain springs and many surrounding trees to protect them from the elements. The spot would make a wonderful settlement, should they decide to finally stake claims, especially since Amash had promised them homestead rights wherever they decided to call home.

Sippen worked fast to set up camp. "Suh... Sebastian," he said, "Uh... I've guh... got to fetch wuh... water and boil it clean. Yuh... you help Krill muh... make shelter."

"Aye, Mr. Yurik!"

The one-eyed man growled, "Over here, boy! We need to slacken these sails and cast them over the lassies."

The boy scratched his head with confusion. "We're not at sea, Sergeant."

Eusari suddenly lost her patience and shouted, "He means the tarps!" Then to Krill she added, "For gods sakes speak Andalonian today!" She paused to breathe between contractions, "At least be normal until after the babies are born so I won't be forced to cut off your ear and gouge your good eyeball. Do you hear me, Cedric?"

Sippen laughed aloud at that. Once she had learned the man's given name, she had ceased to call him, "Krill."

The pirate looked left and then right before grinning and replying, "Aye, but me parts be safe. Thar be no one here by that name, Captain."

She groaned with frustration and said, "Just put the tarps over the wagons, Sebastian."

Sippen patted the boy on the shoulder then went down to the stream to gather water.

The first woman to birth that night was Hester. She quickly delivered a tiny baby boy with a big voice. He screamed as soon as Sippen cleared his nose and mouth. "Heh... He looks just like his duh... daddy," he said. "Huh... here, he said, holding the baby toward the mother.

"I don't want to hold him," she replied. "Take him away so I can rest."

"Buh... but he's hungry," he protested.

"Give him to the wet nurse." Hester's eyes had turned red with either sadness or anger, and she turned away to avoid his judgment.

Screams from the other wagon sent the tiny man scurrying across camp. He found Collette near the campfire breastfeeding Robert. He handed over the newborn. "Heh... He's hungry," he said.

The young woman cradled him with her free arm and unlaced her tunic. The ravenous little boy immediately latched on and went to work filling his belly. "Aren't you just a tiny little piece of adorable," she cooed at the infant.

Sippen didn't wait around. Another scream let him know that Eusari had joined Flaya in labor. He checked them both and found Flaya further along. He felt the position of the head and found it breached.

"I huh... have to tuh... turn the body," he told her. She nodded and closed her eyes as he pulled her onto her knees. "Puh... place your head on the blankets, he commanded. "Duh... don't puh... push. No muh... matter what." He positioned his hands and felt the baby retract from the birthing canal. He gently turned the infant as it found its natural position.

He helped her onto her back and marveled at how quickly the child crowned. "Uh... almost here," he said. "Tuh... take a breath and puh... push." The baby girl entered the world in the way of the Pescari, wearing her people's future on her worried face.

"She's beautiful," Eusari commented from nearby.

Flaya smiled back, "Thank you. Yours will be as well."

"He's coming, Sippen." Eusari leaned back and lifted her sheet. Sure enough the head was visible. A few pushes later and Sippen Yurik held the second of Braen Braston's sons. Despite being younger by a few minutes, the boy was a giant among babies. The engineer quickly estimated that he weighed nearly eleven pounds.

"Wuh... what is his nuh... name?" He handed him over to a smiling Eusari.

She smiled when she answered, "Franque."

A tear formed in the tiny man's eye as he asked, "Tuh... bring suh... circle the life that Braen took?"

"Yes. To bring everything full circle, just as Braen promised."

"Sippen!" The shout came from outside.

He hurried, racing to the other wagon where Krill and Sebastian stood staring inside. He pushed past and froze. Hester laid motionless among the blood-soaked blankets; her wrists bled dry. Nearby lay the knife that Braen had carried on the back of his belt every day until the moment he had died in Middleton. There was nothing Yurik could do but turn away.

He walked over to Collette, still nursing the babies. "Luh... let me have the newborn," he said. Seeing the look on his face she nodded and allowed him to pull the suckling baby from her breast. He returned to Eusari's wagon and entered, placing the tiny infant in her arms.

When she tried to protest, he held up a finger and said, "This is Krist Braston, son of Braen. If we truly want to close the circle then these two are twin brothers, born minutes apart." He pointed at little Franque. "Everyone here will swear that this first born is the heir to Fjorik, if and when they decide to retake their home."

Eusari stared back with shock. "You didn't stutter."

"Because I confidently spoke the truth, and, if I didn't, I spoke the truth we all will tell."

Epilogue

The council had gathered to hear the new Chancellor's address. His first order had been to purge the chamber of corruption, and never before had so many council members been removed. Fear no longer controlled Astia. The old system had been swapped with new blood from new families, each as ambitious as the next. The noise in the chamber echoed through the halls and grew louder when the attendants opened the heavy steel doors for their supreme leader.

Artema strolled casually into the great hall, soaking in the discord that reminded him of his pirating days. *Politics is no different than privateering,* he thought. *The goal of each is to line your own pockets while putting on a convincing show.* His greatest roles had been played and the end goal was finally in his grasp. His father and brother were gone, he was chancellor in his own right, and the young council would look to him for guidance. His new role was no different than the one he played in Pirate's Cove.

The stage was starkly absent of adornment, something that failed to sit well in the new ruler. *I will have to bring some of my charm to his continent,* he mused. He smiled when he imagined a Kraken banner hanging from the wall behind him. *No,* he corrected himself, *a dragon is better suited.* He approached the amplification podium and waited for all gathered to quiet down. They did so immediately.

All eyes were on Artema Horn, just as he preferred. He was, after all, the greatest showman the world had ever seen. His warm smile reassured the assembled that all was well, or rather would be now that he was in charge.

"Esteemed council," he began, "we no longer have anything to fear. The Destroyer is gone, dead from this world. The wicked people such as my misled brother and Chancellor Praedor are no longer threats to our way of life – replaced instead by you and me. As your chancellor I entrust you with the future of Astia, and charge you to lead with benevolence and always in the best interest of our citizens."

He held his smile as he gently flicked a lock of fiery red hair from his eyes, then continued. "My father had ordered Andalon reset, the experiment presumed lost and to be replaced by overseers loyal to our collective instead of individual ambition. I hereby announce that goal has been achieved despite the attempts of Praedor to interfere. We will no longer harvest the essential beads. Our technological advances no longer require their assistance. The children of Andalon no longer threaten our society or way of life."

He stood basking in the wild applause for some time, waving to his supporters and accepting their approval. When he felt that he must leave them wanting more he turned, strolling from the stage with the confidence of a king. For he was now, just as before, a pirate king.

He reached his chambers, pausing once more at the door and thinking of the residents whom he had replaced. Praedor had stripped it of his father's adornments, but that was no matter. He had a few of his own that he would bring in. He pushed open the door.

The room was as bland as the previous occupant had left it. The small chair in front of the leather lounger remained, but he would have it hauled away first thing. He did not need parlor tricks to gain the upper hand over his political rivals. As he entered a voice welcomed him eagerly.

"You've done well, Artema. I'm very proud."

The chancellor felt something shift at the sound of the voice, suddenly in his mind instead of his ears. His shoulders slumped with all confidence deflated, and he chose the awkward chair to sit and honor the supreme ruler. "Thank you," he said, careful to keep his eyes on the floor.

"I must say," Samani continued, "that you were my greatest accomplishment. I not only recreated your arrogance, but also your irritating charm." He toasted his pet with a bottle, embossed upon the side with a seven, a five, and a four. He poured some into a glass, took a sip, and nodded approvingly of the rich flavors. "I must also say," he remarked, "this is quite a fine vintage and I'm a bit sad to drink the last. I regret Andalon has no more to offer."

Cast of Characters
(Alphabetically)

ANDALON

<u>The Cove</u>

BRAEN BRASTON: Winter emotant. Pirate Captain of Ice Prince and Malfeasance. Eldest son of Krist Braston and exiled heir to Fjorik.

ADAMAS CREECH: Pirate Captain of Vigilance. Political opposition to both Braen Braston and Stefan Nevra.

ADOLPHUS DOMINIQUE: Pirate Captain of Aggressor. A slaver known for kidnapping families and selling them on the southern continent.

MATTHIEU DOMINIQUE: Deceased. Son of Adolphus Dominique.

GELERT: A wolf. Emotionally bonded and connected to Eusari Thorinson.

ARTEMA HORN: Pirate Captain of Wench's Daughter. Former pirate ping of The Cove. Whereabouts unknown.

AMASH HORSLEI: Son of Abraham Horslei and brother to Sarai. Left Weston University to live a pirating life to spite his father. Classically trained swordsman.

DEVIL JACQUE: Quartermaster of She Wolf.

CEDRIC "KRILL" KRULL: One-eyed Gunnery Sergeant of Ice Prince and Malfeasance. Childhood friend fiercely loyal to Braen Braston. Uncanny ability to estimate range.

PETER LONGSHANKS: First Mate of She Wolf. Personal confidant and friend to Eusari Thorinson.

LORD STEFAN NEVRA: Former Duke of the Southern Continent and pirate king. Imprisoned for the crime of slavery.

ALEC POGUE: Pirate Captain of Desperation and Captain of the Guard for The Cove.

ALEXA POGUE: Fifteen-year-old daughter of Alec Pogue.

MATTIE POGUE: Wife of Alec Pogue.

LIZA POGUE: Seventeen-year-old daughter of Alec Pogue

SA'MOND: Deceased. Former First Mate of She Wolf and best friend of Eusari Thorinson. Eunuched by unknown means in the southern continent.

CHARLEIGH STATION: Survivor of the Day of the Kraken and daughter of Ralphe Station, merchant in The Cove and ardent supporter of Braen Braston.

EUSARI THORINSON: Autumn emotant. Captain of She Wolf. Originally from Loganshire, was kidnapped and sold to pirates at thirteen years old. Won her freedom through mutiny. Lover of Braen Braston. Bonded with Gelert the wolf.

TURAT: Deceased agent of Stefan Nevra. Slaver and conspirator of Adolphus Dominique.

SIPPEN YURIK: Engineer and Weaponsmith of Ice Prince and Malfeasance. Best friend of Braen Braston. Stutters when anxious.

<u>Dreamers</u>

ADAIRIA: Autumn emotant with affinity for air.

BEARNARD: Autumn emotant with affinity for air.

BETH: Deceased. Autumn emotant with affinity for air. Bonded with Akili. Eldest Dreamer.

CAROLINE: Autumn emotant with affinity for air. Favorite of Eusari Thorinson

CUYLER: Autumn emotant with affinity for air. Eldest Dreamer following the death of Beth.

GALAYN: Autumn emotant with affinity for air.

HALLBERA: Autumn emotant with affinity for air.

JASPER: Autumn emotant with affinity for air.

JOHAN: Winter emotant with affinity for water. Friend of Kali.

KALI: Spring emotant with affinity for earth. Friend of Johan.

KADLIN: Autumn emotant with affinity for air.

LEANA: Autumn emotant with affinity for air.

MAGNUS: Autumn emotant with affinity for air.

MARITA: Autumn emotant with affinity for air. Adopted daughter of Duke Alec Pogue.

NATHAIRA: Autumn emotant with affinity for air.

NEILL: Autumn emotant with affinity for air.

OLIFUR: Autumn emotant with affinity for air.

SEBASTIAN: Autumn emotant with affinity for air. Traumatized by the death of his friend, the Dreamer Suzette.

<u>Esterling Empire</u>

ARNE: An eagle. Emotionally bonded to Robert Esterling.

LORD CAMPTON SHOL: Sensitive to Autumn Oracle beads. Astian agent and overseer of Andalon. Chancellor to the Eston Empire and secret head of the Falconers.

MATTEAS BROHN: Captain General of the Eston Army. Mentor and secret father to Marcus Esterling.

CHARLES ESTERLING: Deceased. Former king of Eston. Unified the kingdoms under the Esterling Empire and drove the Pescari across the Misting River.

CRESTEL ESTERLING: Deceased. Former Queen Regent of Eston.

ROBERT ESTERLING: Autumn emotant. Eldest son of Crestal Esterling. Fathered by General Maximus Reeves. Assumed the title of King of Eston in opposition to his brother.

MARCUS ESTERLING: Second son of Crestal Esterling. Fathered by Captain General Matteas Brohn. Recognized by the council as King of Eston.

KESTREL: Lead Falconer. Childhood friend of Campton Shol.

MERRIMAC LOURDES: Deceased. Retired General of the Eston Army and Governor of Eskera. Renowned for defeating and driving the Pescari across the Misting River alongside Charles Esterling. Mentor of Maximus Reeves.

MAXIMUS REEVES: Deceased. Former General of Robert Esterling's army. Former protégé and aide-de-camp to General Macmillan Lourdes. Secret father to Robert Esterling.

CAPTAIN SANTOS: Imperial Navy Captain of *Inspiration.*

FREDERIQUE TITUS: General of Robert Esterling's army. Former Aide-de-camp to General Maximus Reeves.

<u>Fjorik</u>

ARTUR: First Mate under Skander Braston.

KRIST BRASTON: Deceased. Formerly king of Fjorik and father of Braen and Skander.

SKANDER BRASTON: King of Fjorik. Second son to Krist Braston and husband of Hester.

HESTER: Queen of Fjorik and wife of Skander Braston. Former lover of Braen Braston.

<u>Outlaws of the Diaph Forest</u>

MARQUE GARRETT: Right hand man to Shon Wembley.

SHON WEMBLEY: Former Loganshire constable. Leader of the Outlaw band living in the Diaph Forest.

<u>Pescari</u>

CORNIN: Deceased. Former shappan after killing the father of Taros in the right of Shapalote.

DASKA: Deceased. Elder of the Pescari. Fears Taros from ancient prophesies.

FELICIMA: Goddess of the Pescari. Rises in the east and settles each night west of the Caldera of Cinder.

FLAYA: Granddaughter of Daska. Wife of the Pescari Shappan Taros

LYNETTE: Deceased. Mother of Taros.

TAROS: Summer emotant. Shappan leader of the unified Pescari clans.

TEOT: Uncle of Taros.

<u>Southern Continent</u>

CHARRO VALENCIA: Duke of Cargia.

<u>Weston</u>

CASSUS EACHANN: Leader of the Humanitarian Party. Governor of Weston.

ABRAM HORSLEI: Deceased. Father of Amash and Sarai. Former governor of Weston.

SARAI HORSLEI: Wife of Robert Esterling. Assumed the unrecognized title of Queen of Eston.

PERCY ROAN: Accountant. Clerk and notary to Cassus Eachann.

<u>Loganshire</u>

BERT: Member of the Harbor Sharks, a street gang in Loganshire.

KARLA: Leader of the Harbor Sharks, a street gang in Loganshire.

MATT: Leader of the Wolf Pack, a street gang in Loganshire. Afraid of dogs and insects.

ASTIA

<u>Astian Council</u>

SIMCOR BRALOG: A member of the Astian Army.

BACHIR DILEK: A member of the Astian Army.

CHANCELLOR JAKATA: Deceased. Former chancellor over the Astian Council.

COUNCILOR MATHEIU MEREK: A member of the Astian Council. Former intern to Praedor.

COUNCILOR PRAEDOR: A member of the Astian Council.

COUNCILOR WILMAN: A member of the Astian Council.

<u>Humanitarian Freedom Society</u>

CASSIDY: Society agent in Astia.

DELILAH: Society agent in Fjorik.

THE DRAGON: Society agent in Astia.

GRETCHEN: Society agent in Fjorik. Daughter of Delilah and Samani Kernigan.

SAMANI KERNIGAN (Formerly Samani Nakala): Society agent in The Cove. Was a member of Artema Horn's Inner Sanctum. Advisor to Braen Braston.

MADELYN: Society agent in Diaph, protégé to Perlana. Now aiding Shon Wembley.

PERLANA (PEARL): Deceased. Society agent in Diaph.

<u>Winter Oracle</u>

ASHIMA NAKALA: Deceased and Restored as Falconer. A member of the Winter Oracle who perished revealing a prophecy that powers awakened in Andalon. Younger sister of Samani Kernigan.

FATWANA NAKALA: Lead sister of the Winter Oracle. Elder sister of Samani Kernigan.

SUBBA: Assistant to Fatwana Nakala, lead sister of the Winter Oracle.